Little Victories

Nathaniel M. Cerf

Last Chance Press
Chicago

To my mother, Loy Cerf, who taught me a deeper understanding of psychology and how it applies to real people in the real world.

To my father, Art Cerf, who taught me to stand up and fight for the defenseless.

&

To all of the mental health workers out there who really understand psychology and how it applies to their patients and continue the fight to help them.

Chapter 1

New Hire

"You cunt," spit the office manager at the recent college graduate. "I can't believe you let that slut use my pencil."

Before the young woman could reply, the child psychologist butted in. "Are you gonna let that bitch talk to you that way? I'd bitch-slap that ho if I were you."

Angela was convinced her interview was going well. The crude language of her inquisitors didn't faze her in the slightest, and she suppressed a smile, reprimanding them both as part of the role-playing exercise. "That type of language is inappropriate, and I am taking away points from both of you."

"What?! That skinny skank started it," yelled Donna, the office manager, pointing at Beverly, the child psychologist.

"Who you callin' a skank, Miss IsuckBobbyRayWilliston'scockeverydayatlunch?"

Beverly and Donna squared off for a mock fight.

The sight of the matronly, black 50-year-old office manager dressed in a suit and pearls and the scrawny, turtleneck-wearing, white 30-something psychologist having a fake, limp-wristed sissy fight sent Angela into a fit of laughter.

"Enough," stammered Angela, trying to catch her breath. "I'm sending you both to time out."

Donna and Beverly started laughing, too. This was their favorite part of every interview with candidates for the job of behavior specialist at Average City Mental Health Center. Could the candidate handle the language and aggression? Could they be rattled? Could they stay focused and remember the proper steps in handling an escalation between two students? Would they piss their pants due to the intensity of the interview and role play, remain calm or laugh their asses off?

The two professionals felt Angela answered all these questions to their satisfaction.

For Angela, this was by far the craziest interview she ever experienced. Who on earth heard of mental health professionals being so much fun and … well … mental?

Settle down, Angela thought to herself, *they haven't hired me to be the assistant to this deranged elementary school therapist, yet.*

"I'm sorry I started laughing," she apologized.

Beverly smiled. "That's quite alright. It's important to know you have a sense of humor. This is a tough job, and if you can't laugh at its intrinsic lunacy, you'll never make it."

"Do the kids really talk like that and fight over pencils?" Angela inquired, trying to help get the interview back on track.

"You better believe it," Donna explained. "I've worked in this office since I was your age and have heard every derogatory word for genitals, race, gender, sex acts and just about everything else that can offend someone.

"Plus, and I hope you have a strong stomach, I've seen every bodily fluid squirting, dripping, running, oozing and smearing in this office."

"Every?"

"Every," reiterated the veteran. "That doesn't bother you does it? Because if you take this job, you'll be dealing with it five days a week."

Donna hated sugar coating jobs so that applicants would take them. She'd been around long enough to see scores of nice, clean middle-class people take a low-paying mental health job to make their mark on improving society only to see that same person quit in a matter of weeks or months because of the chaos, frustration and filth. Kids can be dirty and messy to begin with; severely emotionally disturbed kids tend to magnify that by a factor of 10. It wasn't that Donna wasn't a nice, clean middle-class person herself; she just didn't see the point in wasting the time of everyone involved if she could describe the negative side of the job in graphic detail and make sure the applicant knew exactly what they were getting into.

Angela cringed a little at the bodily fluids. Images of little kids with diarrhea and early pubescents in a rage smearing semen or menstrual blood on her flashed through her mind. She knew, at least in theory, exactly what she was getting into but was hoping for the best.

Seeing Angela wince, Beverly decided to step in to keep from losing the only applicant for the job they had seen in a month's time. Unlike Donna, Beverly was desperate for help and willing to risk a potential drop out at this point. "Well, the words, yes. You'll hear those every day. The fluids, not every day. And even then, the school janitors are kind enough to clean up for us."

2

"I can take whatever they can dish out," Angela said, regrouping her moxie.

Cool, Beverly thought, *the kid is willing to take risks in her comfort zone. Let's see how she handles a hot-button issue.* "What do you think about giving kids psychological medication?"

"I'm not a trained nurse; it's illegal for me to administer medications," Angela said, avoiding a possible trick legal question and a greater debate in the psychological community.

What type of answer is that? Beverly thought, already certain Angela knew about the legal issues and wanting to know more about her professional opinions. Beverly carefully rephrased her question, "No. Do you think it is ethical, or better yet, good practice to treat young patients with meds?"

Without knowing Beverly and Donna's position on the issue, Angela wasn't sure how to honestly and tactfully answer. She had studied the research proving the validity of using medications to suppress symptoms of psychological disorders, but she knew the meds could rarely "cure" a problem, only mask its symptoms. She was anti-meds because she had witnessed her own mother overcome great psychological distress with talk-based therapy and not a single pill. More than 90% of the profession seemed to think meds were the way to go, but she was a hold out to an older era. She felt she needed this job too much too much to give the wrong answer to her interviewers, but she didn't know what they wanted to hear. She viewed this job as her springboard into graduate school. She stalled in an effort to tip her interviewers' hands. The younger woman bit her lip and hesitated.

These two poker players aren't giving away anything, she thought.

"I think we, as a profession, overmedicate our patients – most especially children," Angela explained. "Studies often show Attention Deficit Disorder and Ritalin are way too overdiagnosed and prescribed."

God damn, she is sly, Beverly thought. *That answer was an easy out.*

"Angela," the therapist applied more pressure, "While most of the children in this program do have legitimate attention issues, the issues that cause those issues are much worse. I'm talkin' the heavy-duty stuff."

Spotlight properly readjusted, the interviewee sighed with the realization that there were no shadows left in which to hide. "I don't think medication is necessary to treat psychological disorders. The

3

medicines, while great at reducing a patient's symptoms, don't cure the actual problem. I think that cognitive-behavioral modification is usually the best method to help someone overcome a psychological disorder. If patients don't confront their problems and learn how to properly cope, they will never heal."

Christ, Kid, it's not that big of a deal, Beverly—of a more practical school of thought that found great success pairing talk therapy with enough medication to take the edge off a patient's psychological distress—said to herself. *I couldn't make it through the day without a pill or three. If these kids weren't on meds, we'd be lucky if we could maintain damage control.*

Donna refrained from shaking her head and taunting: "Just you wait."

Beverly picked up the conversation with only a hint of sarcasm. "I hope you won't think any less of us, but all of our clients are on at least one medication, usually two or three, sometimes more."

Arr. I should have lied, Angela thought.

Beverly continued: "But we do try to get as much talk therapy in as possible. We have two group sessions every day, and we try to see each child privately for therapy two or three times a week."

"That's good," Angela said, hoping to regain footing she thought she lost. "As long as they are getting to talk."

The two colleagues turned to one another and shared wry smiles. While they agreed with the general principle of Angela's ideals, the kid had never been in the trenches. She looked as if she had never seen how badly damaged some people's psyches could be and how a little chemical relief could ease the daily demons while allowing the patient to address the issues.

Nonetheless, Angela was the first *qualified* person to apply in six months. The program had a reputation for grinding up behavior specialists of which Angela was blissfully unaware.

And the two mental health workers were completely unaware of the true acuity of Angela's skills in psychoanalysis and her ability to work with people in crisis. They weren't skills learned at school. They were learned from experience at home: talking her mother down out of panic attacks, dealing with her mother's germ phobia and obsessive cleaning and acting as a secondary therapist trying to help put together the pieces her mother's violent past. Still inexperienced in the realms of professional psychology, Angela was years ahead of her peers at school in applying the principles of the science to real life. Yet to divulge such

4

experience in an interview for a job of this nature would guarantee not being hired. So Angela didn't give away any information they didn't request, affecting a plucky, can-do spirit that she knew would win over the crowd.

Ignorant of all this, Beverly and Donna silently weighed the pros and cons of hiring the young woman. At first, each gave Angela a 50-50 chance of seeing out the school year. The trim and pretty young Hispanic woman looked like the perfect "girl-next-door" type from the Big City. She earned her bachelor's degree in psychology at Average State University in town last spring and made it clear this was a stepping stone to grad school. Her sharp brown eyes were full of stars. Her ideals were, no doubt, further out of reach.

Regardless of her wholesome innocence, the two professionals liked Angela from the get go. She was bright, thought and reacted quickly under pressure and her heritage would bring some much needed diversity to the program. But as their seesawing mental calculations continued, they remembered the seemingly countless number of others who cracked under the pressure and brutality of the children in the program. Donna calculated the final odds in her head and gave Angela three months to snap. Beverly was more optimistic: six months.

There was another calculation Donna was reluctant to admit she was making. She was becoming more than somewhat worried about Beverly's mental health. The therapist had been alone with those beastly kids for too long. Donna was privately worried her friend was dangerously approaching the breaking point.

Of course, there was a chance Beverly and Angela would persevere. She knew what a tough bird Beverly was and Angela already proved herself more knowledgeable than many people who had attempted the behavior specialist's post.

Beverly looked at Angela then Donna and shrugged her shoulders as if to say, "Why not?"

Donna began addressing Angela with the preamble to the job offer.

"Although you haven't any previous experience working with severely emotionally disturbed children, you have passed your background check and impressed me, for the most part, with your answers in the first half of the interview. You obviously didn't sleep through your psych classes and handled the role playing well, even if you did laugh.

"Yet, before we offer you the position, I think it's only fair to have

5

Bev give you a good rundown about how the program works and what you'll be expected to do."

Beverly took over. "You're going to start off at a bit of a disadvantage. We are already a month into the school year. The classroom daytreatment program team is pretty tight and in a set routine. The kids, some new and some program lifers, know everyone else's limits and will probably target you simultaneously to find yours."

"Excuse me," Angela interrupted, "but what and where is the program?"

"Oh, sorry," Bev backtracked. "We are a program of up to 12 emotionally disturbed children at Average City Elementary School. Our goal is to provide psychological therapy in an academic setting, allowing the kids to attend a traditional public school. And, in all honesty, we are the last stop before these kids are institutionalized at the state children's mental hospital."

Angela interrupted with another question. "Why are these kids in this program? Are they strictly emotionally disturbed or are they also mentally disabled?"

"They are strictly E.D. Few, if any, show signs of retardation or brain damage."

Although she would never admit it out loud, this was a relief for Angela. She had nothing against the mentally disabled, but she had a very difficult time working with them. Emotionally disturbed kids were "normal" kids with severe psychological problems that made them disruptive to "normal" classes. However, no matter how twisted their logic could become, their brains were fully functional and she could always find ways to reason and communicate with them. This was not always the case with her and the mentally disabled. Furthermore, a classroom of emotionally disturbed kids could and would make life unbearable for the comparatively defenseless mentally disabled kids.

Beverly continued. "Our kids all have Posttraumatic Stress Disorder from some kind of severe abuse. Their stories are all unique. Some have been neglected and are all but feral. Others have been raped. Some were beaten beyond recognition. Some even witnessed murders.

"How the PTSD manifests itself is different with every child, as are the triggers that escalate their behavior. Most have other disorders from depression on down the line."

These facts about the kids didn't surprise Angela. She had known many victims of abuse throughout her 22 years, and, while still empathetic, she was already pretty unflappable when it came to hearing their stories. Given what she knew her mother had been through, her bar for suffering was set pretty high.

Beverly continued describing the program situation. "However, it's not all miserable. These kids are so strong and resilient. They are survivors. I've worked with some for five years and have seen amazing strides in their growth and development."

Angela asked about the one thing that was still gnawing at her. "Donna, you told me that you had seen and heard everything from these children. What can I expect from them physically?"

"I don't interact with them physically, so I'll defer to Bev."

"You should expect everything," Beverly explained. "These kids will lash out as they try to cope. We are very protective of our personal boundaries, but they will violate these boundaries almost every day. Mostly, it is hitting and a little hair pulling. They occasionally spit. We also have some sexually aggressive children who will, every now and again, grab at your breasts and more rarely your groin. It normally isn't a problem, but it does happen. Keep in mind, we also will teach you how to avoid and prevent most of the physical assaults."

Angela fell back on her bravado instead of showing that she found the prospect of 10-year-olds touching her breasts more than a bit nauseating. "Ha. I survived a few frat parties without being felt up once; I think I can handle a group of eight-year-olds."

"Don't be so sure," Bev warned. "These kids are very unpredictable."

"Are these kids in safe places, away from their abusers?" Angela asked.

Beverly looked at Donna, and both women slowly shook their heads. With a low hint of sadness in her voice Donna explained, "We usually send the children back to the very people who abuse them."

This bothered Angela. In her undergraduate studies she learned it was extremely difficult for anyone, especially children, to recuperate while living in the same situation that caused the problem.

The reason she didn't apply for this job before the school year started was because she didn't want to fix children all day only to have them broken again at night. She really wanted to work with adults who were already in a safe place, but those jobs were difficult to find and get in Average Little City. What overpowered her concern about working with difficult-to-help kids was a combination of being fed up with working in retail and realizing the need to get back into the field if she wanted to attend graduate school.

"Can't we report the abusers and get the kids into foster care or a group home?" Angela pushed.

"We must," Beverly said. "It's the law, but it also is difficult to get anyone to act on those reports. Removing a child from an abusive home is a difficult task to accomplish. Please remember, though, these kids are very strong, and their progress is clearly noticeable—even if they are stuck in a bad situation."

Angela silently vowed to do her best to get her students out of any dangerous situation. Out loud, she changed the topic. "What are my duties?"

Donna read from a form: "You are to aid in the therapeutic treatment of the children under the psychotherapist's care. You will safely assist in physical restraints and interventions, for which we will send you to training. You will complete all assigned reports and paperwork in a timely manner. And you will attend our weekly training meetings and case discussions."

Beverly smiled. "i.e. You're the hired muscle."

"It sounds good so far," Angela said, smiling back. "I don't want to sound greedy or disrespectful, but no one has mentioned anything about compensation."

"This position pays $22,000 a year," Donna said. "It's not a lot, so we try to make up for it with our benefits package. We offer comprehensive medical and dental insurance. We also offer a 401(k) retirement plan."

"Sounds good enough to me," Angela said.

"Alright," Donna continued. "There is only one thing left to do. We need you to talk with the program's director, Richard. Normally, he'd sit in on your interview, but he had too many meetings today. He should be back in his office by now. Let's go see."

The three stood and left the small meeting room. At the end of the small beige hall, Richard's open door was decorated with client-made art. Donna led the way in and introduced everyone.

Richard was a wan-looking, middle-aged man with wavy blond hair and a sad smile. He rose from the towering stacks of paper on his desk and shook Angela's hand.

"Well, you must have impressed Donna and Beverly if you made it this far," Richard stated. "And if they like you, you're okay in my book."

"Thank you, sir," Angela demurred.

"Just call me Richard. Have these two emphasized the stress, responsibility and challenges of this job?"

"Yes."

"And you still want it?"

"I sure do."

Richard extended his hand again. "Great. You start Monday in room 36 of Average Elementary at 8 a.m. Donna, sign her up for next month's MANDT physical restraint seminar. Also get her signed up for CPR, First Aid training and a TB test. Until then, Angela, you pretty much can't touch the kids. But I'm sure Bev can find other ways to keep you busy."

Richard patted a mountain of papers on his desk to emphasize what he implied. Beverly gulped hard and took the subtle, yet strong, hint from her boss. She was more than six months behind on her filing. That alone was enough to get her fired—if they weren't so understaffed. What Richard didn't know was that the problem was far worse than filing. Beverly hadn't even kept up on her notes and reports. That was grounds for immediate dismissal, regardless of staffing shortages.

"Any other questions?" Richard asked.

"A million, but I think they'll be answered when I meet the children and start working with them."

Richard sadly smiled again and thought, *She's got a great attitude; she might last until Christmas.*

Chapter 2

Sallie
(Monday Morning)

"Not now, Dad. I'm late for work," Billie anxiously pleaded as she quickly exited the bedroom of her trailer home.

Wayne, her father, followed wearing only a T-shirt. His erection led the way, as he casually pursued her into the kitchen.

"C'mon, Honey. Just a morning quickie."

Billie poured a bowl of cereal and set it down for her 4-year-old daughter sitting at the kitchen counter. The little girl tried not to look as her grandfather pulled her mom close from behind.

"No, Dad. I'm running late for work, and if I lose this job we won't eat."

Billie grabbed her purse and keys and headed for the door. Wayne followed.

"You know you want to. You're dyin' for it. C'mon, real quick."

Billie dodged his grasping hand and slammed the screen door shut behind her. "Make sure Sallie gets to school on time. This is already her second one; I don't want to have to move her again."

Sallie watched her mom walk out of sight. Wayne closed the door and sheepishly grinned at Sallie.

Sallie closed her eyes and, without moving a muscle, escaped the only way she knew how.

If she focused hard enough, she could completely disengage her mind from her body. It wasn't an out-of-body experience. It was a common coping mechanism called dissociation that she learned around the time she developed conscious thought. It was a great way to insulate herself when people were being mean, arguing or yelling. Regardless of pain or noise, she was oblivious to the outside world.

She loved to focus on the things that made her happy. Animals always made her happy. She thought about them a lot. There were ponies and zebras and koalas and puppies. Once she wound up her brain on a subject, she could absorb herself in a state of dissociation for minutes, hours, even days. Whenever it was safe to come back out of hiding, she would. But sometimes it was just easier to stay safe and happy.

Today was going to be a bad one, so she concentrated on her favorite subject. And the faster and harder she thought about it, the easier it was to ignore the rest of the world.

Puppies have to be the greatest animals on earth, she thought. *They're always happy, and nobody ever would hurt a puppy. Puppies just like lovies. And they give lovies, too. I wish I had a puppy. I hope Mom gets me one. What would it be like? She would be so soft and cuddly; she would fetch Frisbees and lick my hands. She'd have spots, and I'd name her Dot. She would always be happy to see me and wag her cute little tail every time I came home from school. When we're done playing fetch we could go for long walks. Maybe runaway someday. And at night when it's scary and dark, Dot could crawl in bed with me and protect me from the monsters in the closet.*

Wouldn't it be so nice?

The only thing better than having a puppy would be being a puppy. Imagine how nice that would be. Running and chasing and playing... .

Chapter 3

Honeymoon
(The same time Monday morning less than a mile away)

Angela looked at herself in the mirror. Her yellow, floral-print sundress complimented her brown skin nicely. She had spent a long time figuring out what would be most appropriate to wear on her first day. A dress would be more formal for the adults she worked with, but the pattern would be more playful and less intimidating for the kids. The skirt came down to mid-calf and had enough material to allow her to run after the kids if need be.

She smiled and cocked her thin left eyebrow. It didn't hurt that the dress also demurely accentuated her slender waistline and gentle curves—just in case there were any attractive young men who also worked at the school.

Her drive to work was a short one.

Average Elementary was a one-story building that sprawled over a large green acreage of soccer fields, a baseball diamond and two playgrounds. Surrounding it was a quiet middle-class neighborhood.

The morning bell hadn't yet rung, and several hundred little kids were outside playing. As she walked in through the main door, Angela wondered which ones were hers. Her pulse quickened. She couldn't wait to meet them.

Inside, Angela went straight to the main office and greeted the secretary: "Hi, I'm Angela Marengo, the new behavior specialist with Average City Mental Health Center. I was told I needed to check in."

The secretary looked her over from head to toe. "Those are the rules these days," she said. "You don't look like a terrorist; lemme get you an employee security badge."

"Well, I've made it my policy to leave my jihad at home before starting a new job," Angela quipped.

The secretary spit out a raspberry laugh as she retrieved a badge and lanyard under the counter.

"Sign for it here." She opened a three-ring binder. "I'm Doris, by the way."

As Angela shook the woman's hand, a man's voice called out from

13

behind Doris. "What's this about a jihad?"

A bald, roly-poly man in his sixties stepped out of his office.

"Mr. Franklin, this is Angela Marengo, the new B.S. ... uh ... behavior specialist for room 36," introduced Doris. "Angela, this is our principal, Mr. Franklin."

The new hire let the B.S. line slide. *So that's what they think of the psych program.*

Angela just smiled and shook Mr. Franklin's hand. "Good to meet you, sir."

"It's good to meet you, Angela. We've been anxious for you to start."

"I hope I live up to your expectations."

"You'll do fine, I'm sure," he said. *Christ, you showed up. Any live body we can stick in that hell hole is an improvement.* "Well, school's about to start, you probably better get to your class. Would you like me to walk you down there?"

"No, thanks. Just point the way; I'm sure I'll find it."

"Room 36 is down at the end of the hall on the right-hand side."

Angela thanked them, and they all bid a cordial good-bye. The walk was fairly long, and Angela took the time to appreciate her surroundings. She got a kick out of all the decorated doorways and the hand-colored name tags on lockers. It brought back many fun memories of her days as an elementary school student.

The door to room 36 was closed. Behind it came a crash and shout.

Angela hesitated, inhaled, exhaled and entered.

A big table was overturned, crayons were scattered on the floor and Bev, the therapist with whom Angela interviewed, was wrapped around a struggling 11-year-old boy.

Bev was leading the boy to one of two large wooden boxes: "Kevin, that was not okay. You have to go to timeout."

When the boy spotted Angela, his muscles went slack and he became passive.

Bev looked up and stared. "You're wearing that?"

Confused, Angela coiled the I.D. lanyard around her finger. "Uhh, well, they told me I need to at the front desk."

"Wait a sec," Bev said, and spoke to Kevin. "Just go sit in time out for a minute and then you can meet the new behavior specialist."

"Okay," he agreed, still scrutinizing Angela.

"I'm sorry, Angela," Beverly apologized. "I didn't mean the I.D. badge—although the kids might try to choke you with it. I meant the dress. Perhaps I didn't warn you more clearly last week. Most of the kids in the program are boys, and they will look and reach up or down your dress at the first opportunity they get. Some already have sex offender records with the police."

Angela worried. "Should I go home and change?"

Bev thought it over for a moment before replying. "Nah. You'll probably be okay today. That skirt is fairly long. Just be on your guard."

Beverly turned her attention to timeout. "Okay, Kevin. If you are ready to clean up this mess, you can come out and go back to class."

The sandy haired boy agreed, righted the table and picked up the wax rainbow strewn across the flat, coarse, ugly green carpeting.

Bev and Angela followed Kevin through a pass-through door in the wall that led to room 38. The morning bell still hadn't rung, and it surprised Angela to see all 11 students in class. The children were either playing with Legos or coloring at three large circular work tables. All of the students noticed her instantly, but half ignored her while the others studied her skeptically. Contrary to the image she got during her interview, most of the kids looked relatively clean and well dressed.

Also in the room were three women who made their way over to greet Angela.

The first to introduce herself was Ronnie, a big-haired blonde with a dry, weathered face behind a set of large brown-celluloid framed glasses. Angela tried to gauge the woman's age. Dressed in an old jean jacket and new Land's End jeans, Ronnie could be an aging biker or grandma—maybe both. Regardless, she had a warm inviting smile and a firm handshake.

Next was a brunette in her mid-30s wearing an old sweat suit. Her name was Carla. She was friendly but seemed a little distant to Angela.

Both women were teacher's aides.

The teacher, Mrs. Regina, was a slight black woman in her mid- to late 60s. Her curly grey hair was closely cropped. She looked frail dressed in blue jeans and a sweatshirt. She smiled and offered her hand to Angela out of professional courtesy, but she was only covering her disapproving gut reaction to the bright-eyed young woman entering her classroom.

God, Mrs. Regina thought, *this girl won't last a week. After 35 years of teaching, you'd think I could get a team that would last out the year—my last year, at that. Well, good luck B.S. 66. Bev, start looking for B.S. 67.*

All three women warned Angela about wearing a dress as the bell rang, and the adults promised to catch up later. Bev took Angela back into room 36 and closed the door behind them.

"Okay, kiddo. We've only got 15 minutes before the first group so let me give you a quick tour," Bev said. "How about we start with the padded cells? I mean timeout booths."

"Sure."

They walked over to the two wooden structures that stood next to each other.

Bev explained, "The timeout booths are what wig-out everyone the most. Each is 10-feet tall and 7-feet wide. Inside they are lined with 4-inch thick, canvas-covered pads that cover the floor, walls and ceiling. And yes, the kids will bounce off the walls. Go ahead and step inside."

Angela did. The cushioned floor was firm but gave a little under each foot. She reached out to touch a yin-and-yang symbol drawn with a black ballpoint pen on the maroon canvas.

"I wouldn't touch anything in there if I didn't have to," Beverly cautioned. "Now hang tight, I'm gonna close the door so you can get the full effect."

The door slammed closed. Angela refrained from touching anything and calmly waited for whatever was supposed to happen next. A light and fan protected by a metal cage turned on above her. The fan vented the slightly musty funk of the chamber. Light also came in through a small 8" X 8", steel-wire reinforced window.

Beverly continued to talk, her voice only slightly muted by the padding and vent fan. "Can you hear me?"

Angela said yes, and then Bev continued, "Good. Never believe the kids if they say they can't hear you in there. When they say they can't hear you, they either don't want to listen to you or are plotting an escape by getting the door opened a little. When they are calm, ready to talk and ready to come out, they can hear you just fine."

Bev opened the door. "Did it scare you to be trapped in there?"

"No, I was fine."

"Huh. Well, these damn booths scare me senseless. We only use them as a last line of defense. My goal is to give a child every chance possible to avoid being put in there."

"Why shouldn't I touch anything inside the booths?"

"Because those surfaces have been repeatedly covered in urine, spit, blood, semen and fecal matter."

Angela cringed and felt like taking another shower. "Don't you ever clean them out?"

"With the exception of spit, we are legally mandated to have the booth steam cleaned after each messy incident, and we do. Regardless, they still gross me out.

"Now take a closer look at the outside of the booth."

Angela paid particular attention to the door. Connected to it was a metal bar with a D-shaped handle. The bar was on an axis that could swing up or down. On the other side of the door frame was an upside-down cradle for the bar to help keep the door shut. "Why is the latch for the door upside down?"

"That's the way it is supposed to be," Beverly explained. "It is illegal to lock up the kids and leave them unattended. If you want a child locked in there, you must hold the bar yourself. Furthermore, if you have a heart attack, collapse and die, the child won't be forever trapped. Gravity will release the bar."

Angela nodded her head in understanding. "That makes sense."

"Good. There's one last detail about timeout that you need to remember. After every timeout, you must fill out a form documenting every 30-second interval of the event. Both of our desks have plenty of these forms in them."

Bev led Angela to her new desk and had her open the bottom file drawer, which was filled with dozens of file folders containing a multitude of forms.

"Hide your purse in there," Bev warned. "Anything left in the open is fair game for being stolen or destroyed when a kid escalates."

"Escalates?"

"Throws a temper tantrum. Goes ballistic. Spazzes out."

"Got it."

"Good. Now open that little wooden cabinet behind your desk."

In it, Angela was surprised to find a small 13" TV and two VCRs recording. The muted TV showed everything going on in the other room.

"Channel One is the other room," Bev explained. "We're Channel Two. There is a camera in each of our rooms running at all times when the kids are here. It is as much for our protection as it is for theirs'. Plus, it gives us an instant replay to find out what really happened when we, for example, miss what started a fight. It also gives us a chance to review our own performance. I hope you aren't too camera shy."

Angela shook her head. Bev handed her a pen and a clipboard with

17

a blank sheet of paper. "Good. Now it's time for group. Why don't you keep a bead count for me?"

"What are the beads for?"

"Our token economy. I'll have the kids explain it to you."

Before Angela could ask another question, Beverly was at the side door calling for the members of "Big Kids' Group."

The kids raced to be first in line. Everyone was wiggling to look around Bev to catch a glimpse of Angela.

"Okay. Everyone get your rugs and form a circle in the middle of the room. Someone get the special guest rug for Angela."

Six bodies burst into the room, running to a shelf in the back under the windows. Kevin got there first, followed by an athletic blond boy. The two grabbed their rugs and had a brief tug of war with the guest rug. The blond won. Kevin was frustrated but followed close behind the blond. They set down their rugs with Angela's between them.

A skinny black boy got his rug and Bev's. Two more boys wasted no time getting into the circle. Only a tall, skinny red-haired girl lagged behind.

"C'mon, Violet," Bev gently urged. "Get your carpet and sit down with us."

"Ooookay," she groaned. But she didn't speed up; she just kept touching the rugs piled on the shelf. She examined each rug's name tag, as if she were a scientist studying microbes under a microscope.

"Today, Violet," Bev more forcefully pushed. "You want to meet the new behavioral specialist don't you?"

"But I can't read my tag," she whined.

"Violet, you can read. Besides, you've been using the same orange rug for the past two years. If you hurry, I'll give you a blue bead."

Violet heaved a deep sigh and contorted her face into the sourest pout Angela had ever seen. The tall girl reluctantly dragged her carpet to the circle.

"Good," Bev said with a smile for the group. "Everyone earned a blue bead for following directions. Lashaun and Charlie get brown beads for being extra helpful."

Angela scribbled furiously.

Beverly began the opening introduction. "I know you are all dying to meet our new behavioral specialist, and here she is. Everybody say hello to Angela."

Angela looked up from her writing and gave the group a little wave and said hello. The group responded in kind before Bev continued:

"Why don't you guys use your great communication skills and introduce yourselves. Tell her who you are, how old you are and a little something about what you like."

"Hi, I'm Charlie," swooned the blonde boy to Angela's left. "I'm 12, and I really like your dress. It's very pretty."

Charlie was the only kid in the room to have hit puberty. He had gone girl crazy about two months previously and had become a shameless flirt.

"Thank you, Charlie," Angela replied. "Do you like anything else, aside from my dress?"

"You have pretty eyes."

The other kids groaned. Angela laughed, "I mean hobbies or sports."

"I love football."

"Are you gonna be a famous football player when you grow up?"

"Yeah."

"What position do you play?"

"Anything that gets the ball."

"Great," Angela encouraged.

Then Bev took over briefly to keep the introductions moving. "Good job, Charlie. You get a turquoise bead for sharing."

Angela looked at the boy to Charlie's left. "And who might you be?"

"I'm Jefferson," said the spiky brown-haired boy. He looked cheery and accommodating but wasn't flirtatious.

"And how old are you?"

"Nine-and-a-half," he said. Jefferson looked at Charlie and then at Angela. "And I like football, too."

Jefferson didn't like football or Charlie for that matter. Charlie was the oldest, most outgoing and seemingly organized. Most of the boys took their cues from him. Besides, Charlie could easily beat you bloody, and it was a helluva lot better to have him on your side … or at least have him think you were on his.

Bev knew this and awarded him a sharing bead any way. There was nothing to be gained by putting him on the spot for no reason, especially while everyone was testing out Angela.

"And you?" Angela asked of the next boy.

"Franz," replied the child with some reserve. He seemed to want to hide within his filthy white T-shirt and beige shorts. He could deal with people in most any situation, but he harbored a deep fear of most everyone—especially new adults. His big-green eyes observed Angela's every move.

"How old are you?"

"10-and-a-half."

"How do you like being so old?"

He really wasn't certain what Angela was asking, so he looked over at Charlie for any possible guidance. "Uh. I like football, too."

Charlie gave a mocking laugh, and Bev shushed him.

Franz was decidedly spacey and disengaged. Angela wasn't exactly sure what was going on, so she gently pushed him a little. "That's great, but you didn't answer my question."

Franz seemed to zone out and suddenly snapped together and asked, "What was the question?"

Charlie laughed but the other younger kids looked nervous. It was never a good sign if someone started losing their grip.

"How does it feel to be 10-and-a-half?"

He shrugged his shoulders. "Iduhno."

"You don't know?! Oh no. You're not dead or something are you?"

He smiled a little, "Maybe."

"Maybe?! Maybe?! Do I have to come over there and tickle you to find out for certain?" Angela acted as she was going to stand up.

Franz flashed a buck-toothed grin. "No, no. I'm alive."

"Then how do you feel?"

"Fine, I guess."

"Oh good. You had me worried you were dead for a minute."

"You're kinda weird, ya know."

Angela winked at him. "Duh."

Everyone laughed except Violet who continued to scowl. She hated not having the spotlight. At least her sour expression kept drawing glances from Angela.

Beverly awarded more beads.

The next boy in line addressed Angela. "You don't talk like most grownups. I thought only kids talked that way."

"I don't feel like a grown up," Angela returned.

"You look like one," the boy responded, looking at Angela quizzically.

"Ah, but looks can be deceiving," Angela challenged, hoping to test this kid and all the kids in group. She wanted to see who was the smartest, most logical, most silly, etc. This boy seemed to be the smart one. "I never did catch your name."

20

"I'm Lashaun."

In addition to being the smart one, he was the most-well laundered. He also was the only black kid in the program, which Angela thought must have been a little lonely for him. She decided to play with him a little more. "Let me guess. You're 43."

"Nooo. I'm only 10-and-a-half."

"And you're gonna be a famous football star, too?"

Lashaun looked at Charlie and then Angela. "No, I prefer to read, especially the Harry Potter books."

"Nerd," muttered Charlie in retaliation for Lashaun breaking the pecking order and not agreeing football was king.

Before Bev could reprimand Charlie, Lashaun whined to her, "Did you hear what Charlie called me?"

"Yes," Bev acknowledged. "Charlie, I'm taking away one of your beads. That was very inappropriate.

"However, Lashaun you need to keep learning to ignore Charlie when he sets you up to make you angry."

"Okay."

Charlie wasted no time giving Lashaun a chance to practice: "Suck up."

Lashaun clenched his jaw and said nothing while expectantly looking at Bev.

"Very good, Lashaun," Bev complimented. "You get two beads for ignoring that set up. Charlie, you lose another one."

"What?!" Charlie said with an exacerbated whine. "I didn't do anything."

Lashaun stuck out his tongue at Charlie when he thought Beverly wasn't looking.

Charlie pointed and started making noise.

Bev straightened out the squabble. "Lashaun, now you lose a bead for sticking out your tongue at Charlie. But Charlie, you need to learn to ignore Lashaun's setups, too."

Lashaun wasn't about to give Charlie a chance for more beads. But Charlie felt vindicated because Lashaun had lost one.

The therapist kept the ball rolling before more trouble started. "Hi, I'm Beverly, but most people call me Bev. I'm 37, and I love making arts-and-crafts projects."

She gave Violet a head nod, prompting her to take her turn.

The girl was slow to erase her frightful scowl and start talking. She wanted attention, positive or negative, at all cost, and it was her goal to draw out her time as long as possible.

She spoke slowly at first. "I'm Violet, an' I'm 10."

"That's great," Angela encouraged. "What do you like?"

Violet decided to take a new tactic in holding the group focus, switching gears from turtle to manic. "Welllll, I like bugs. Bugs are really cool. They're also called insects. All bugs have six legs. Spiders have eight, but they aren't bugs, they're arch...arac...a"

"Arachnids?" Angela offered.

Violet smiled. "Yah, arachnids. They eat bugs, but they aren't bugs. So I don't like them." She took a deep breath. "Insects are so neat because they have six legs. Some have wings. Some don't. Some fly. Some can't. Some that have wings prefer to walk." Violet took another deep breath for effect. "Didya ever notice how some bugs have soft bodies and others are crunchy? I think..."

"Shut up already, Violet," Franz groaned. "Nobody cares about your stupid bugs."

Violet's scowl returned. "Bev."

"You have to ignore his setups, too," Bev explained. "Now, Franz. That was completely uncalled for. I'm taking away two beads."

Bev knew she had to keep group moving. "Why don't you reintroduce yourself, Kevin?"

Kevin gave a nonflirtatious, boy-next-door smile and was about to speak when Violet started talking again. "Wait. I'm not done, yet."

"I'm sorry Violet, but it's time to move on and give Kevin a chance to talk," Bev explained.

"One more thing? Please."

"Okay."

"Do you like bugs, Angela?"

"I suppose I like them more than spiders."

"Well maybe we could talk about bugs sometime."

"That sounds lovely," Angela agreed, hiding all trace of the sarcasm she felt.

Bev gave Kevin a bead for being patient. Violet scowled, even though she got a bead for sharing.

When Kevin got his chance to talk, he was more terse and competitive than the others.

"I'm Kevin. I'm 11, and I like football more than Charlie."

The classroom power struggle was becoming clear to Angela. "It doesn't matter who likes it more," Angela explained. "Do you enjoy playing it?"

"Yah."

"Then that's all that matters. What do you like playing most?"

"Wide receiver."

"You must be pretty fast."

"Yep."

The boy looked so scrawny and underfed, Angela wasn't convinced but she didn't contest his statement.

Charlie couldn't help himself. "Nuh-uh. I can beat you."

Bev intervened, "What did I say about setting people up?"

"I was just telling the truth," Charlie insisted.

Bev let it slide and changed the subject. "Okay Angela, now it's your turn to tell us a little about yourself."

"Well, I'm 22. I have a cat named Fur-nando. I graduated from Average State University this past spring. My favorite hobby used to be going to debate tournaments, where I could win prizes for arguing with people. That was a lot of fun, but now I'm looking for a new hobby. What else would you like to know?"

"Are you married?" asked Charlie.

"No."

"Do you have a boyfriend?" he pressed.

"No."

"Would you like one?"

"No thank you," she replied with a smile.

"Rats."

"Anybody else have any questions?" Angela probed.

"Where are you from?" Jefferson asked.

"I've lived here for the past 4-and-a-half years, but I'm originally from the Big City."

"Where are you from?" Violet repeated.

Angela gently reiterated her answer. "The Big City."

"Yah, but your skin is brown, not like most people in Average City."

"Lashaun's skin is brown," Angela countered.

"Yah, but he's from here," Violet said, growing frustrated with her inability to communicate her meaning.

"I'm still from the Big City," Angela said, aware of what Violet was getting at and toying with her just a little more to see if the girl could pick up Angela was trying to explain. The growing scowl convinced the behavior specialist to move on. "Buuuuut, my dad's side of the family came to the United States from Puerto Rico after the

Spanish-American War. My mother's side of the family came to the United States from Mexico about 30 years later. Do you know where those places are?"

Everyone shook their heads. Angela looked around the room and found a globe sitting on the window sill. She got it and showed the kids Average Little City, Big City, Puerto Rico and Mexico.

When Angela finished, Bev started to wind down group. "We're just about out of time. Angela, do you have any questions for the group?"

She nodded and showed everyone her scrambled notes. "Can anybody explain what these beads mean?"

Lashaun, Kevin and Charlie's hands shot into the air.

Bev picked them in turns.

"We get beads for talking in group."

"Actually, anytime we're in this room."

"What are they for?" Angela probed further.

"We collect them to buy stuff in store."

"What's store?"

"It's these toys on the shelves by Bev's desk."

"How much are the beads worth?"

"25 cents."

"No, that just the turquoise beads. The rest are 10 cents."

"How do you get a turquoise bead?"

"By sharing your emotions."

"What do the other colors stand for?"

"Red is for sharing."

"No, blue is for sharing; red is for courage."

"Uh-uh. Green is for sharing and blue is for courtesy."

Clearly the kids didn't know what was what. Bev assured Angela she'd get her a bead key to define colors and actions.

Angela asked the group, "When do I give you your beads?"

"Oh no," Beverly interrupted. "We just add up the tallies at the end of group and read off the value total for the end of the session. Store is at the end of the week, and you'll just keep a running count at your desk."

Angela knew this wasn't the proper way to run a token economy, and she figured that she'd address it later. For now, she had to add up the totals. Bev doled out another handful of beads for such a productive group session and dismissed the kids.

After the children were out of the room, Angela took a deep breath.

"I think that went pretty well."

"Yep. Ready for the next group?"

"Sure, why not?"

Angela flipped the paper on her clipboard over, and the little kids' group was ushered into the room.

A new fight ensued over the carpets. This time a spiky black-haired boy with a scar on his chin won the honor of sitting on Angela's left side. His best friend (and top nemesis), a sunken-faced runt who probably suffered fetal alcohol syndrome took her right. Both beamed at her in hopes of winning her initial affection.

This group was smaller with only five children. To the left of the scarred boy was another seemingly nice boy, with big angelic blue-green eyes. The other two children were the group's live wires, sitting on either side of Bev. To Bev's right was a wild-eyed boy who could not stop moving. The trunk of his body weaved spastically. His hands constantly combed through his rug. He made indistinguishable loud, soft and guttural noises. He was a violently shaken bottle of champagne about to blow its cork.

On Bev's left was an extremely small blonde girl in pigtails. She was perfectly well behaved—for a cocker spaniel. She sat like a dog at attention, thumping its happy tail and panting, its tongue lolling out the side of its mouth. Angela thought this little girl was the most adorable kid she'd ever seen, but she couldn't fathom how the girl could be old enough to be in first grade, or even kindergarten.

Beverly started the group by awarding beads and using a similar introduction to Angela as she had in big kids' group. But before she went further, she wanted to get the puppy next to her to act like a little girl.

"Sallie, please stop pretending you are a puppy," Bev requested. "Let's show our new behavior specialist what an amazing little girl you are."

Sallie cocked her head as a dog would and studied Bev's face.

"I'll give you a bead for following directions."

"Woof." Sallie gleefully barked and sat Indian style on her rug. Her tongue still peaked out between her little pink lips on the side she thought was hidden from Bev.

Bev still saw the tongue, but this was more cooperation than she was used to, so she awarded the bead. "Lionel, why don't you start us off?"

The soft-featured boy harrumphed and glowered, but the scarred

25

boy was radiant and quickly took center stage. "Hi. My name is Lionel. I'm seven. And my favorite thing is my little sister."

"That's awfully sweet," said Angela. "What's her name? How old is she?"

"Her name's Persephone, and she's four, but we all call her Sephie."

"What do you like to do together?"

"We like to play together in the front yard, and I keep her from hurting herself and running into the street."

"Wow. You sound like a great protective big brother," Angela exclaimed with praise that made Lionel blush and swivel his trunk in proud delight.

Bev prompted the boy with big-eyes and mussed up brown hair on Lionel's left.

"I'm Ted, and I'm eight. I love my Daddy," the boy lied in a lispy, 3-year-old's voice. Ted really did want to love his father and be loved by him, but given the man's violence and hatred, Ted only felt terror and hatred. He envied Lionel's ability to love, and even more greatly envied that Lionel was indeed loved by anyone.

"What's your daddy do?" Angela inquired.

"I don't know," Ted said. He meant it.

"What do you guys like to do?"

Ted shrugged his shoulders and continued to smile angelically at Angela. Behind his veiling expression, his mind raced. *My favorite thing to do is stay away from him. Stop asking so many questions. You didn't ask Lionel all these stupid questions when he got lovey-dovey about his stupid sister.*

"That's okay," Angela gave the silent boy an out. "You don't have to tell me, if you don't want."

He shrugged again, and she moved on to the nearly feral boy next to Bev.

"What's your name?"

The boy gave a startled response, as if awakened from a nightmare. His brown eyes were big and wild and locked on to hers. He spoke with a rasp: "Fred-dy."

"That's not true," Bev corrected. "Your name is Sammy."

Sammy kept looking at Angela with the same jarring crazed look of Charles Manson.

"How old are you, Sammy?" Angela calmly continued.

"Fred-dy is go-ing to get you," said Sammy, accentuating every

26

syllable.

"You're six, Sammy," Bev said.

Sammy was the only child Bev couldn't figure out. The token economy never worked with him, and regular talking—not even talk therapy, just talking—would usually put him off into his own psychotic little world. Furthermore, she never came close to understanding Freddy.

"Who's Freddy?" Angela asked.

Bev was impressed Angela was not afraid of the boy and trying to tackle the question of the century head on. Of course, she also braced for Sammy's inevitable psychotic episode that resulted whenever anyone questioned him about Freddy.

Sammy gave a remarkably demonic smile for a small child and responded by raising his long crooked fingers like Nosferatu, the silent movie vampire. "Freddy's going to kill you. Chop-chop."

His finger motions gave it away to Angela, who, unlike Bev, had seen her share of horror movies. "Do you mean Freddy Kruger? The pizza-faced bad guy with the bladed hands in the movies?"

Sammy was amazed that Angela knew who he was talking about and for a brief moment became a little boy again remaining silent, giving only a solemn head nod.

God damn! Bev thought. *How the hell did she figure that out, on her first day no less? You go, girl! But what the hell does this Freddy stuff mean?*

"Sammy," Angela explained. "Freddy's not real. He's just a fake monster on TV."

The little boy's eyes glazed over. He shook his head no, and the delirious expression crept back over his lips. "He's right behind you!" Sammy shouted in his normal voice.

Angela coolly looked behind her and saw nothing closely resembling Freddy. "I don't see anything, Sammy."

"He's over there!" Sammy pointed to the top of a timeout booth.

By now the other children were totally silent and motionless. They weren't afraid of Sammy's imaginary Freddy. They were afraid Sammy was two steps away from going berserk. That was a real threat to all of them.

Well, actually, the sunken-faced boy was both horrified by Sammy and his demon-haunted world. He clung reflexively to Angela's arm and trembled.

Angela extricated her arm from the boy's grip and reassuringly rubbed his boney back. She could feel vertebrae and ribs under his worn-flannel shirt. Even she had to admit it was a little disconcerting watching a 6-year-old loose his mind. "It's okay. There is no Freddy," she warmly explained to Sammy and the group. "He doesn't exist."

Sammy got more excited. He began laughing maniacally, pointing out more Freddy sightings.

Bev braced herself for the worst. If she didn't take control, group would melt down.

Sammy's voice got high and raspy again. "I am Fred-dy."

Bev knew through two years of working with Sammy and Freddy that the only thing that would calm him down was to take all attention off of him. Don't look at him or talk to him. And for the love of God, don't reach out to touch or comfort him.

"So, Sallie," Bev said. "Will you tell Angela a little something about yourself?"

Angela got the unspoken clue and diverted all obvious attention away from Sammy.

Sallie resumed her puppy act, nodding her panting head.

Great. The perfect storm, Bev sarcastically thought. Sallie the Puppy was a defensive reaction to any and all threats—most notably Sammy at the moment. However, Sallie the Puppy usually set off Sammy's defenses. The two were ticking time bombs.

"And how old are you, Sallie?" Angela asked.

"Woof, woof, woof, woof."

What an ingenious girl with a powerful imagination, Angela thought. "Four?"

Sallie nodded.

"Please don't encourage her," Bev warned, as she tried to think of a plan of action in case she had to safely restrain two small psychotic kids at once.

Angela tried to engage Sallie with a conversational question. "What's your favorite type of dog?"

Sallie the Puppy pantomimed a breed of dog, but Angela couldn't figure out which.

"If you can't use your human voice, I'll have to move on to the boy next to me."

Sallie looked at her and thought, *Okay. I'm not talking today.*

Angela waited for a reasonable amount of time and began talking with the soft-featured boy.

"Wow. You have been so patient. I'm going to give you a bead,"

Angela declared, taking her first stab at the bead thing. "Actually, I'm going to give you all a bead for being so patient. And then I'm going to give this gentleman next to me an extra bead because he hasn't even gotten a chance to talk yet."

The sad-faced boy smiled a smile full of holes and incoming teeth, and Angela continued the inquisition. "Okay. What's your name?"

"I'm Edward."

"Does anyone call you Ed or Eddie?"

"No."

"How old are you, Edward?"

"Six," he said as he held up six fingers to emphasis the point.

"And what do you do for fun?"

"I watch cartoons."

"Cool. Who's your favorite?"

"SpongeBob SquarePants."

"And what do you like about it?"

"He farts."

The other two "angelic" boys laughed and traded favorite fart jokes from the show.

Bev had a much easier time settling them down.

Angela in turn gave the same bio-spiel she had given the older kids and opened the floor for questions.

Sammy and Sallie had settled down and were equally impressed by the description of Fur-nando, Angela's cat. Pets were always big winners in daytreatment discussions.

Yet it was Lionel who was bravest to ask the first question: "Are you a mommy?"

Angela blushed a little. It was an innocent question, which she perceived as oddly sexual. *I can't imagine being married, let alone a mother yet.*

"No. I'm not a mommy," she replied.

"You have to be," said Edward.

"Mommy!" said Sammy, as if claiming her for his own in a remarkably babyish voice.

"Nope," Angela playfully shook her head.

"You're just teasing," said Ted. "Of course you're a mommy."

"No, guys. I promise; I'm telling you the truth. You're the only kids I have. I'm not even married."

"You don't have to be married to have kids," Lionel defensively asserted.

Angela regretted her last statement immediately, as she realized many of these kids probably didn't have traditional nuclear families.

"You are right," she apologized. "But I still don't have any kids."

The children stared at her as if she were the most abnormal human being alive. *All grownups are mommies or daddies. What's wrong with you?* Was the collective thought.

Bev decided to help bail Angela out. "Not all adults have children. It is normal for some people to decide not to have kids."

The group watched Bev in astonishment as they tried to soak in the concept.

"Mommy?" Sammy asked Angela softly.

Angela shook her head and shrugged her shoulders.

Deep in thought, Lionel scrunched up his face and inquired, "Don't you like kids?"

He sounded hurt.

"I love kids," Angela explained. "I'm just waiting until I fall in love with the right man before I decide to have any kids of my own."

While Lionel thought about that, Ted walked over and gave Angela the sweetest and most awkward hug she'd ever gotten. It was a hug that was strictly for show and empty of emotion. She felt a little violated.

"That's okay," he said in his eerie lisping baby voice.

While Angela was trying to figure out what the hug was for, Bev intervened, questioning Ted. "Did you ask for a sidehug?"

He shook his head, still standing next to Angela.

"What must you always do before you hug someone?"

"Ask permission," Ted replied, and then asked Angela, "Can I have a sidehug?"

"What's a sidehug?"

Bev explained, "For everyone's safety, we only allow sidehugs where you put your arms around each other's shoulders and have side-to-side contact—no front-to-front contact."

"Ah-ha," Angela acknowledged. "Okay, I guess."

Ted gave her another creepy hug. It wasn't sexually suggestive, but Ted was clearly putting on a show, angling for something yet undefined and masking his true thoughts, motivations and emotions with syrupy-sweet false sentiment. She agreed to the hug on the principle that she didn't want the kids to think she was either afraid or repulsed by them. Now she was questioning whether she was setting appropriate boundaries.

The insecure little Edward took his cue from Ted and asked for a hug. Angela consented, and he hugged her arm again. Unlike Ted, Edward felt vulnerable, no longer trembling but still seeking security. Both children clung to her for too long, and Bev had to ask them to let go.

Lionel reserved judgment on Angela, as did Sammy. Sallie just wanted to be a puppy.

Bev wrapped up the remainder of the group session by distributing a few last beads. Angela gave the final tallies, and then the kids returned to the next room.

Once the kids were gone and the adjoining door closed, the two women were free to talk openly.

"Well, Angela, what do you think?"

"I think that went pretty well. They all seem like good kids."

"You might change your mind by the end of the week, but deep down they are good. They just need a lot of help dealing with their issues. Do you have any questions?"

"Tons. I'd like to know more about each child's history and diagnosis. I'm also confused about the beads. What do they each stand for? None of the kids seems to know for certain what each bead represents."

"Of course they know what they mean," Beverly scoffed. "I'll just get you a chart defining each color."

"Thanks," Angela said. "I'd also like to know why we don't give each child an actual bead the second they earn it. All of my textbooks insisted this was important for instant gratification."

Bev smiled. "That's because your textbooks didn't work in the real world. You saw how quickly the conversation moved and how fast we needed to react to them. Hand distributing the beads takes too long. It's tough enough to write them all down. Plus the kids will lose them or fight over them or steal them, which sets up all kinds of unnecessary problems."

The therapist retrieved a recipe box from her desk and gave it to Angela. "This is our official bead bank. From now on, you're our head teller. Inside you will find a card with each child's name and bead count. After group, add the new bead tally to each card. This way, on Friday when we hold store, we'll know precisely how much each student has."

"Okay," the behavioral specialist said, taking the box.

A little while later, as she finished adding up all the beads, there was a knock on the door. Ronnie stuck her head in the room. "Hey,

Angela, you wanna join us for morning recess?"

Angela turned to Bev for permission.

"Go ahead. Afterward, I'll show you how to write up the group notes."

"Thanks."

Ronnie opened the door all the way to let Angela into her classroom.

Mrs. Regina was lining up the students. Any break in silence or intrusion of someone's personal space sent a kid in line back to his or her desk to start over again. The process seemed to last an eternity because a classroom of kids with attention deficit disorder tends to not excel at silence and stillness.

Finally Ronnie and Carla shepherded the class into the hall and out into the schoolyard. The children ran like 11 bolts of lightning the second their sneakers hit the pavement outside the school's double doors. Time outside meant little oppression, and it would be much more difficult for a teacher to see you do all of the things you shouldn't.

Carla and Ronnie began tutoring Angela on how to spot and stop the kids doing the things they shouldn't.

"All we can really do is damage control," Ronnie stated.

"Yeah," Carla added. "Make sure no one fights and make sure none of our kids perps on some kid from outside our class. The last thing we need is for one of our kids to molest someone."

"Also," Ronnie whispered, "make sure our kids don't swear in front of the regular kids. There is nothing that will piss off a teacher more than when one of our kids calls one of their kids a mother fucker. We'll hear about it from the teachers and principal for a month."

Angela asked, "Can we play with our kids?"

The two weary women exchanged wary glances.

"I don't see why not," Ronnie answered, then asked, "But why would you want to?"

It was clear by her intonation that she didn't think Angela would somehow perpetrate some sex offense on one of the kids. Given how filthy and depraved their students could be, she was genuinely curious why anyone would want to spend any extra time with them.

"'Cause it'd be fun. I could get to know them better, build their trust in me."

"Makes sense, I guess," Ronnie said with a shrug.

While getting to know Ronnie and Carla, Angela was startled when

Carla suddenly ran toward the playground without a word.

In the gravel pit, near the high bars where girls were showing off their penny twirls, Sammy was throwing handfuls of pebbles at some second graders.

The kids stared at him as if he was the traveling freak show come to town.

The more they stared, the more he threw gravel and shouted, "Bitchell! You Bitchells!"

Carla swooped in and wrapped Sammy up in a restraint with the same speed and dexterity of spider biting and cocooning a fly in its web. She apologized to the kids and led Sammy to the door and ultimately timeout.

No regular teachers were close enough to overhear the boy cuss.

"What was he shouting?" Angela asked Ronnie.

"Bitchell. Aside from rhyming with Mitchell, I have no idea what it means," she explained. "He's been saying it since he started coming here. None of us knows what it specifically means."

"Has anyone asked him?"

"Sure, but he's usually too amped up to explain it. And when he's calm, no one wants to risk bringing it up because they don't want to set him off, again."

Carla rejoined them, having left Sammy with Bev in time out and some therapeutic intervention.

Sallie bounded up the three women on all fours with a large stick in her mouth. She wanted Angela to play fetch.

Angela knew that Sallie's pretending to be a dog was a coping mechanism for repressing an issue about which Angela had yet to learn. And though Angela knew she shouldn't encourage the behavior, she knew that she wouldn't break it today, either. Aaand because Sallie was such a cute and creative kid…Aaand it was recess after all…

…Angela took the stick.

Sallie barked and panted.

"Okay now, Sallie—the cute little puppy. If I play with you, I want you to promise me not to carry the stick in your mouth. Carry it in your hands, and pretend it's in your mouth."

Sallie enthusiastically barked twice and nodded her head. Angela threw the stick. Sallie chased after it on all fours.

"Uh. Angela," said Carla. "Ya know we really try to discourage that sorta thing."

"I know, I know. It's just that it's recess and playtime. And I figured it wouldn't really hurt to let her have some fun."

"Okay," Carla said with a tone of warning. "But I won't be responsible for anything that happens from it."

"Fair enough."

Sallie trotted back on two feet, her hands holding the stick as close to her mouth as she could. They kept up the game for several minutes, and even Carla smiled and thought the two were cute together.

"Okay, little puppy, my arm is getting kinda tired," Angela said. "Why don't we take a break?"

Sallie dropped the stick and gave Angela a big hug from the front.

"Whoa, whoa," Angela said. "Aren't you supposed to ask first?"

Sallie let go and looked at Angela pleadingly. Sallie was so happy to play with someone who understood her, or at least so she thought. This was the first time anyone had played with her in a long time. She wondered what she could do to make Angela feel as happy as she felt.

"Okay. You can give me a side hug," Angela said.

The only way Sallie knew how to make anyone happy was the way she made her grandfather happy.

Angela was surprise when the tiny girl shimmied up her leg and trunk, locking her little legs around Angela's hips. Angela was mortified when a giggling Sallie gleefully began humping her groin as fast and hard as she could.

Angela froze and could only stutter. *Oh my God!* She thought. *I'm being raped by a four-year-old girl!*

The terrible stuttering from Angela caught Carla and Ronnie's attention and the two jumped to action—prying Sallie off of Angela. They harshly scolded the confused little girl who only was trying to do Angela a favor and make her happy.

Sallie began to cry and pee. As the urine began to flow, she shrieked until it stopped darkening her pants.

The recess bell rang.

All four stared at one another in stunned inaction. Ronnie came to her senses first and took charge.

"Angela, you take Sallie inside and get her cleaned up. Carla and I will get the other kids inside."

The program's kids were already lining up and threatening to riot. Carla and Ronnie got them under control and moving.

Angela knelt in front of the sobbing Sallie, whose wet eyelashes formed star points. "Are you okay?"

Sallie nodded.

34

"Good. I'm okay, too." Angela soothed. "Let's go inside."

Sallie reached one hand up for Angela to hold. Angela took her tiny hand, and they slowly walked inside and went to the little girls' room.

In the bathroom, Angela opened a stall door that didn't lock. "Do you want any help?"

Sallie shook her head no, so Angela closed the magnetically sealing door to give the girl some privacy.

Ronnie entered the bathroom carrying a plastic grocery bag. "Here are some clean clothes her mother left in case of an emergency."

Angela passed them under the stall door. She began to apologize to Ronnie for freezing and panicking earlier when Sallie shrieked again—this time while peeling off her soaked panties.

Ronnie popped open the door and rushed into the stall.

"Oh my, God," she muttered low under her breath.

Sallie sat on a closed toilet lid, naked from the waist down—trembling in pain and fear. Sores speckled her angry red groin that had been rubbed raw. She wasn't bleeding, but even without penetration, it was obvious what happened.

Sallie raced to put on her clean, dry panties. She didn't care if anyone saw her naked. She cared that Ronnie and Angela looked at her with such horror and pity. Even though she was only four, she knew that if they did something to try and "help" her, it would only lead to her being hurt worse.

Ronnie gently lifted Sallie's face and caressed a trail of tears away with her thick, knotted old thumb and stroked the girl's hair to try to calm her. "Honey, are you okay? Is there anything I can do for you?"

No, Sallie thought. *Leave me alone.*

Sallie remained silent and shook her head no. She pulled up her new pants, and raced past both women to go back to class.

"Angela, you call the authorities. I'll clean up in here."

Angela was gone in a flash.

Ronnie inspected Sallie's old clothes for blood or semen. Seeing none, she put the damp clothes in the grocery bag and tied it shut. The whole therapeutic team knew Sallie was being molested because of her sexualized behavior, but this incident confirmed their worst fears.

Discoveries such as this one were about the only thing Ronnie truly hated about her job. She was a tough-old bird who had seen and dealt with it all before, but, if only briefly, it reopened old scars on her psyche from when her father molested her and when several dates raped her during her teenage years.

35

A single tear rolled down her leathery right cheek. She sniffed and wiped it away with the back of her hand. The tear wasn't for herself but for Sallie. For the misery she knew the girl was going through, and for the misery she knew lay ahead of the child—even with an intervention from the police today.

Yet it was these same incidents and old memories that fueled her passion to protect and help heal these kids as best she could. It was her ardent belief that her past experiences, awful though they were, had one benefit and that was how they allowed her to ease the recovery of others—assistance she had never received when she needed it most.

When Angela ran into room 36, she told Bev what had just happened. Bev told her to call 9-1-1.

It was the first time she'd ever called 9-1-1 and was a little bit nervous. She remained calm on the phone and clearly identified herself and her location.

"What is your emergency?" the dispassionate voice of the operator asked.

"A little girl at my school has been raped."

"Is she being raped right now?"

"No."

"Is the rapist on the premises?"

"No."

"Does she need immediate medical attention?"

"I don't know."

"Is she bleeding uncontrollably? Does she have any breaks or sprains?"

"No."

"Then, ma'am, we can't help you."

"What?!" Angela practically shouted. "She's been raped. She's four. Her vulva's been rubbed raw. She needs a policeman to arrest the man who did this and permanently remove her from her home."

"I'm sorry, ma'am; we don't do that."

"Of course you do. This is 9-1-1, isn't it?!"

"Yes, ma'am. But this type of case isn't in our jurisdiction. You need to speak with someone at the Department of Child Welfare. Would you like me to give you their number?"

Angela was so astonished and appalled, she was speechless. She couldn't believe her ears. A little girl had been raped and 9-1-1 was refusing to help. *This is bullshit.*

36

The operator interrupted her train of thought: "Ma'am? Are you still there?"

"Uh, yeah."

"Here's that number, ma'am."

Angela wrote down the number on a scrap of paper and hung up without another word.

"What happened?" Bev asked.

"Nothing. She told me to call the Department of Child Welfare."

"That's nonsense. This is a police matter. Call the real cops. 9-1-1 is only a dispatching service." Bev had played this game before, but she was pretty certain they had more than enough evidence to warrant real police intervention.

Angela looked up the regular police number.

The dispatch sergeant made it painfully clear that he empathized but it wasn't the police department's territory. DCW would make their lives miserable if the police got involved this early. It was strictly DCW's turf.

Angela politely said good bye and slammed the phone down on the cradle. "This is unconscionable," she spit. "Protect and Serve, my ass!"

"Shhh." Beverly put her fingers to her lips. "Remember, we're still in an elementary school."

"But, but, but ..."

"Call DCW."

Angela stabbed the numbers with her finger. When she was finally directed to a case worker, she spoke with an icy determination. She was surprised to learn that the caseworker was familiar with Sallie's case.

"Yeah," agreed the caseworker. "We have a file about a foot thick on Sallie and her grandfather."

"You do, and you haven't removed her from her home?!"

"Well, it's not that easy."

"Sure it is. Granddads aren't supposed to rape their 4-year-old granddaughters. The kid needs a safe place to live."

"Listen, are you trying to tell me how to do my job?"

Angela eased off the gas. She didn't want to lose Sallie her chance for safety.

"No. I'm sorry. I just saw some graphic, brutal evidence of this recent rape, and I want my student to be safe. That's all."

The caseworker calmed down, too.

"I understand," she said. "I'll be by to investigate it today."

"Thank you," Angela said and hung up. She turned to Bev and

fumed, "I can't believe how impossible it is to get any help for a little girl who's been raped."

"I can," Bev countered softly.

"Isn't the law designed to protect the young and innocent?"

"No. The laws have been written to protect parental rights in this state. You have to do something overtly egregious to lose your custody of a child."

"Worse than rape?"

"It's more complicated than that," Bev explained. "Sallie is in her mother's custody. Her mother didn't abuse her, her grandfather did. Sallie won't talk to anyone with normal conversation, let alone admit that her grandfather molests her. Her grandfather usually cleans her up so we have no DNA evidence, and he hasn't hurt her bad enough to put her in the hospital. We know he's raping her. DCW knows he's raping her. But no one will speak on record that they've witnessed the actual rape, and there is no physical evidence linking the grandfather to the rape. No judge can legally remove Sallie to a safe place because you and I are mental health professionals and say she must be removed."

Reality slapped Angela hard upside the face. All she could say was: "That's not fair."

"Don't tell me you believed it was ever otherwise," Beverly said.

Angela hated it when other people said stuff like that. *No shit. But it doesn't mean it shouldn't be, and it doesn't mean you have to roll over and take it.*

"There has to be something more we can do. Can't we get our state lawmakers to change the law?"

"Sure, I encourage it. Get everyone you know to write and demand it. But you aren't going to change anything overnight—if at all."

"Why not? Aren't they supposed to represent the people and the demand of the people? Even if most people won't acknowledge how prevalent abuse is in our society, I can't imagine many people being okay with kiddy rapers."

Beverly laughed cynically. "My God, you are precious, Angela. Naïve but precious."

"What do you mean?"

"Of course the public would be outraged about what's happening to Sallie or any of our kids. But they don't know about them, and we aren't allowed to talk about specific cases because that would break our confidentiality laws. However, they've been led to believe that the necessary laws and funding are in place to take care of the problem.

"Without pointing fingers, the political powers in our state think it is imperative to cut taxes at all possible cost, especially for their wealthy campaign contributors. In an effort to reduce government spending, they cut the programs that have no corporate benefit. Spending on programs that benefit society but not the pocketbooks of the wealthy or private companies is either eliminated or reduced to bare-bones minimums. Hence, we have a desperately underfunded DCW and foster-care system along with underfunded group homes and mental health programs like ours. And despite the gross underfunding, they outsource group homes and mental-health programs to companies that ultimately charge them much more than it would cost the state with a well-organized and run bureaucracy. It's about greasing palms, not about helping people."

"Yeah," Angela conceded, "but the public demands that we take care of defenseless abused kids."

"Of course. That's why these politicians haven't cut these programs and services entirely. They feed the public a few bones to keep them quiet and turn around and cleave the budget of some group such as DCW and blame it on underperformance. A logical public agrees because we all hate to see wasted tax dollars—it's just that the public isn't told the reason DCW is underperforming is because its budgets have been hamstringed for decades."

Angela fired off another volley. "Okay, but certainly the public would be outraged to know no one is doing more about a cute, little 4-year-old girl being raped in their community."

"Again, you're absolutely right. The public would rightfully lynch the guy today if they found out. However, we still can't tell them because of the confidentiality thing. AND, whenever good-hearted citizens do learn of such events and go crusading for tighter child abuse laws, these same tax-fearing politicians know that tighter laws mean more programs, regulations and employees, which in turn raise taxes—usually for their biggest campaign contributors.

"Don't get me wrong, rich people don't want kids getting raped. It's just not usually something they put on the front burner or think they should have to pay to fix.

"So even if most Americans would gladly pay an extra $10 to $20 bucks a year to guarantee the proper mental health services for those in need, the anti-tax politicians come at the problem sideways.

"They'll shoot down good anti-child abuse laws and programs by playing on most parents' deepest fears. 'Don't let some liberal wack-

39

job shrink pass this law. If you do, they'll outlaw spanking next and take away your babies. They'll make it so that if you send your kids to bed without dinner, they'll throw you in jail for neglect'

"Of course the public will hate the proposed law that wouldn't actually get them in trouble for sending their kids to bed without dinner but would make it legal to remove a child such as Sallie under these circumstances, placing her in a safe situation with psychological help.

"And even if I've overdramatized the anti-tax people, that really is the cut-and-dry situation at the heart of the issue. It's all about money and short-term bottom lines. The long-term advancement of American civilization, fairness and justice has got nothing to do with it."

Angela's heart sank, as she sat at her desk, head in hand. "Bev, that is the most depressing thing I've heard in years. So it's hopeless then? There's nothing we can do?"

"Slow down there, Little Miss Bipolar. I admit the situation is bleak, but it's not hopeless. Until the politicians cut us off, we have a very important job to do. First and foremost, we teach these kids how to cope with their problems and make their own lives better. Our second responsibility is to document every awful thing that happens to these kids and to hound the establishment until it is forced to take action in the best interests of these children. Do you think you are up to that?"

The fire returned to Angela's eyes. "Where do I start?"

Bev was impressed by Angela's determination. There was a fierce, combative side to the rookie she hadn't seen in the interview. *Maybe she'll last longer than we thought.*

"Let's start with the documentation. While it is still fresh in your mind, I want you to fill out our incident report. Then we'll tackle the group notes."

Although Angela hated tedious bureaucracy, the knowledge that these forms were part of a broader fight to help these kids made it more endurable. The whole process lasted until the children's lunch break at 11:30. The only events that transpired in their room were a therapy session with Franz in which Angela was not allowed to participate and a visitation by the school district nurse who came to deliver a hefty load of meds for the students.

As 11:30 approached, Ronnie peeked inside the room and asked for a hand with lunch duty. Bev gave the green light and went to take her own lunch break. Angela hoped lunch would end less tragically than recess.

The same tedious line-up process used for recess was used for the lunch dismissal. Again the kids joined the line, only to act out and sit back down. Again, Violet created the most difficulty. The only difference between now and recess was that the kids were really hungry. Their fuses were shorter. More trips back to their desks and back into line.

Clinically, the classroom staff was providing immediate, appropriate rewards and punishment as consequences for the children's behavior. Nonetheless, it seemed to Angela that the students were having an impossible time learning and accepting these conditions. She knew the problem stemmed from the children's psychological disorders, but she also knew it was September and that most kids would have had this routine down four weeks ago. On days such as this, the adults, and some of the better-behaved kids, felt like they were beating their heads against the wall with this necessary, yet painfully slow, routine.

After eight full minutes, the line was quiet enough – barely – to proceed down the hall and into the cafeteria.

The cafeteria was a veritable zoo. The noise and constant activity, while normal for most children, brought about sensory overload for several of the hypervigilant abuse victims with Angela, Ronnie and Carla. (Mrs. Regina took the time for her own lunch.)

Sammy was especially agitated. Angela observed his eyes darting around the room and the wild look of Freddy possess his face. Despite the storm brewing in Sammy's mind, Angela was more worried about missing the DCW agent who might be wandering about the school looking for Sallie and missing her in row after row of long tables and benches seating about 300 ravenous grade-schoolers.

So, as the line crept toward the ladies dishing out trays of warm food, Angela kept watch on the cafeteria doors.

"Plotting your escape?" quipped Carla.

Angela smiled: "No, just waiting for DCW. I don't want to miss them."

"I wouldn't count on the cavalry anytime soon."

"You heard what happened to Sallie, didn't you?" Angela whispered.

"Yeah, but I wouldn't count on seeing anyone from DCW until around 3:30—if at all."

Angela acknowledged Carla's prediction but didn't believe it. Carla didn't see what she saw earlier. She hadn't heard Angela's impassioned plea to DCW to help a raped 4-year-old. They'd be here any minute; Angela was certain.

Checking back on the progress of the lunch line, Angela was surprised by how politely the children got their meals, some making appropriate conversation with the lunch staff. She also thought it was rather fortuitous that they got the table closest to the door. It wouldn't take much effort to spot the DCW worker.

"Wow, this is great they saved us the table closest to the door," she proclaimed to Carla. "How'd we luck out?"

"Luck had nothing to do with it," Carla explained. "In case we need to restrain and remove a kid, we'll do less damage this close to the exit."

"Oh." Angela shrugged and decided to switch gears and get to know the students better.

As she observed the kids eat, she became appalled by their table manners. Their gaping mouths were full of food lolling from cheek to cheek. She fought her gag reflex as the kids talked to each other spraying a sea of saliva and partially chewed food.

Sammy, Sallie and Violet ate with their hands, and the other kids could barely manage to use forks or spoons as more than shovels. With the exception of Violet, none of the kids could get their food in their mouths fast enough.

Angela was glad she didn't bring her brown-bag lunch and was amazed that Carla and Ronnie were eating their lunches oblivious to the culinary carnage.

Lashaun was the only child who ate with his mouth closed and properly used his utensils. Angela decided to focus on him until the others were done eating.

"So, Lashaun, what else do you like reading?"

He eyed her suspiciously, as did the other kids. Adults told them what to do or moderated disputes. They didn't talk to you for conversation's sake. What did the new lady want?

"I don't know. All sorts of things I guess," he replied with a nonchalant shrug.

"You guess?" Angela playfully prodded. "What are you reading at home?"

Lashaun looked up and down the table. If he answered in detail, the other kids would call him a nerd. If he tried to blow her off, his cool stock might go up with the other boys. After this morning's group he needed some cool stock to keep from getting beat up. "Just some magazine."

Lashaun looked away and tried to look intent on eating his lunch. He hoped that maybe she'd just go away. Charlie gave him a nod and began discussing football with Kevin.

"Cool. What magazine?"

Man, Lashaun thought, *and Bev used to think I was obsessive. This new B.S. doesn't give up.*

Charlie and Kevin turned to watch him respond. In hope that he wouldn't be overheard, Lashaun mumbled, "National Geographic World."

Charlie overheard and mocked him anyway. "Ha-ha. Nerdboy reads National Geographic World."

Kevin laughed.

"That's not okay," Ronnie said.

"Yeah," Angela added. "Let's take away a bead from each of them."

"What?!" blurted the two boys in unison. "That's not fair."

Angela ignored them. "Thanks for sharing with me, Lashaun, and ignoring them. I'm giving you two beads."

"Charlie," Angela continued. "You shouldn't laugh. That's a good magazine—lots of bugs and animals eating animals."

Animals eating animals had some street cred. "Cool," he replied.

"Bugs? Did you say bugs?" Violet beamed. "I told you how much I love bugs, didn't I?"

"Yes."

"Maybe we could catch some together after lunch."

"Maybe," Angela tentatively agreed. Violet continued to babble incessantly about bugs.

Carla tapped Angela on the shoulder. "We don't use beads in our room or at lunch."

"Oh?"

"We use a play-money system," Carla said, pulling a wad of fake dollar bills from the front, muff-style pocket of her sweatshirt.

"HA. HA," Charlie chided. "You can't take away my be-eads."

"No, but I will take away $2," Angela coolly fired back. "One for mocking Lashaun, and one for mocking me."

The other boys tried not to laugh. Just because Charlie was top dog didn't mean they didn't enjoy seeing him taken down a peg. They just didn't laugh too loud because he'd sock 'em one when the adults weren't looking.

43

Angela looked at the other end of the table and saw Sammy playing with his food, stirring it with his hand. The room was loud with the whole school eating lunch and talking. Sammy was full and growing scared as his senses overloaded. The glint of Freddy was returning to his eyes.

Shit, Angela thought. She didn't know what to do but saw things getting ugly real fast.

"Uh, Sammy. Sammy, don't do that."

Intuitively, Ronnie and Carla looked over.

Sammy ignored Angela's request and stirred faster, slopping food onto the table.

Carla was stern: "Sammy. Are you done eating?"

The little boy's head snapped up to look at her. The beast temporarily left his eyes through his gapping mouth. He nodded.

"Good. Now go put away your tray and wash your hands."

Sammy obeyed silently.

"Who else is done?" Ronnie asked.

Everybody shouted, raised a hand or wiggled to indicate they too had finished. Ronnie excused them individually to avoid food fights at the trash can.

Once all the kids returned, Ronnie stood up and went to the exit. Carla called out the names of the best behaved to form a line and subsequently go out to recess.

Angela helped shepherd the kids outside where they each took off like planes set at full-throttle. The teacher's aides took their usual lookout post.

Angela wasn't surprised that Sallie was keeping her distance. She was playing near, but not with, Sammy in the gravel. Angela decided to give Sallie a little space at first. Besides, it didn't take long for Violet to come bounding up with a new pet.

"Look what I found, Angela! Look what I found!"

A large daddy longlegs was thrust in Angela's face. Angela flinched backward and made the internationally understood big-spider-in-my-face sound effect: "Blahuhh!"

Violet thrust the spider back in Angela's face. "What? It's just a little ol' spider."

"Violet!" reprimanded Ronnie. "That's not okay."

Once Angela had sufficiently recovered she explained, "Violet, that's a very nice spider. It just isn't very nice to surprise someone by throwing a spider in their face."

Violet cupped her hands around the harmless 8-legged creature and protested, "I didn't throw it in your face."

"You know what she means," Carla said.

Violet's monster pout enveloped her face. "Can I keep it?"

"You know we don't let you keep bugs in class," Ronnie said.

"What if I just keep it in my pocket?"

"He'll get squished," Angela said.

"No he won't. I'm not that fat."

Angela almost tripped over her tongue trying to extinguish Violet's image concerns. "I never said you were fat. In fact, I think you are way too skinny."

"You think I'm too fat. How else could I squish this beautiful, pretty, wonderful spider in my pocket?" Violet scowled at Angela.

"That poor daddy longlegs would get squished by you simply running around and playing. It has nothing to do with how fat you are."

"HA! You said it. You think I'm fat."

"You know that's not what I meant," Angela said as she tried to keep her frustration in check as Violet toyed with her. "I don't think you are fat."

"Nuh-uh. You said it."

Ronnie could see Angela was running into trouble and gave her an out. "Come on, Violet. Let's go put Mr. Spider back where you got him."

Violet's lip protruded even farther, but she followed Ronnie to the high grasses along the playground fence line.

"I never said she was fat," Angela told Carla. "I never meant to imply it. The poor girl is practically anorexic."

"I think she is anorexic," Carla replied. "She never eats much at lunch. But don't worry about what you said. She's just messin' with you."

Angela shook her head, upset that a child had played her so easily on the first day. "I'll try not to let it happen again."

"Don't sweat it," Carla encouraged. "That type of stuff happens to each of us every day."

Angela felt a little better and asked, "Mind if I play with Sallie and Sammy."

"Knock yourself out."

Angela made her way over to the gravel pit and sat between the two most outwardly disturbed children in the program. She regretted wearing her dress, as the pebbles dug into her knees. She folded the hem several times to act as a pad protecting her knees from the rocks.

Sammy and Sallie played contentedly but separately. Sammy was spitting on each individual stone—sticking some in his pockets. Sallie was happy to build up little hills and smash them back down.

"How are you feeling?" Angela asked the little girl.

Sallie paused to scrutinize Angela and then continued working on her piles.

Angela shrugged her shoulders and pushed a small scoop of pebbles to Sallie. Sallie stared silently at the pile and then at the rookie behavior specialist. She accepted the little stones, putting them into her growing mound. Angela shoveled another pile to Sallie. She accepted, again. They kept up the wordless routine.

Sammy casually observed this little scene as he spit on his rocks. Deeming Angela safe enough to tentatively trust, he took a handful of pebbles from his pocket, spit on them, chose one and handed it to her.

"Pitty," he said in a babyish voice.

Fighting her mild revulsion, she smiled and took the stone. "It is pretty, Sammy."

The boy was right; when the dust was washed away the pebble glistened black and emerald green. Of course knowing it was washed in a gob of saliva that still dripped from it distracted from some of the beauty.

Angela handed the little rock back.

Sammy shook his head no and pointed at Angela.

"A special gift for me?"

Sammy nodded.

Without a hint of sarcasm, Angela sounded enthusiastic and playfully royal. "Thank you, kind sir. It's too much. You shouldn't have."

Sammy beamed and began spitting on more rocks for Angela. She really wished he wouldn't, but she didn't want to break their first fragile bond.

A gaggle of second-graders playing tag broke the peace in the gravel pit. As the mainstream kids ran around them, pebbles kicked up from their shoes and sprayed Sammy. Freddy was back. Sammy pocketed his pebbles and began spitting at the nearest second-graders.

Angela tried to politely dissuade him from spitting, but the situation already was out of her control. She looked pleadingly to Carla for help, but Carla was watching students elsewhere. Angela didn't think it would be polite to yell for backup. She didn't know what to do, especially because she wasn't trained to physically restrain children.

The second-graders began teasing and taunting Sammy. Instinct took over, and Angela scolded the students and told them to leave.

As the group began to disperse, backup arrived in the form of a second-grade teacher. "This type of behavior is reprehensible and intolerable!" the middle-aged educator shrilled and pointedly peered at Angela's I.D. "Miss Marengo, I don't know what they are teaching in college these days, but you must remove this child from the playground and escort him to the principal's office."

"I'm terribly sorry," Angela stammered and blushed. "This is my first day, and we're with the daytreatment program…"

"BITCHELL!" Sammy exclaimed in defense of Angela.

"Uhhhh," Angela was mortified.

The teacher was stupefied into silence verging on rage.

"Bitchell!" Sammy shouted again followed by his maniacal laughter.

The cavalry arrived, and Carla wrapped up Sammy with a spider restraint and whisked him off to time out.

Ronnie tried to help Angela explain the situation and the condition of the students. Nothing would appease the teacher.

"I don't care what's wrong with these children. These incidents won't be tolerated on the playground. If it happens again, I'm telling the principal and making sure your students never interact with the rest of the school population."

The teacher stormed off, ignoring further apologies and explanations from Ronnie and Angela. The two women looked at each other, neither knowing what to say.

When Ronnie saw that the teacher was out of earshot she muttered, "Bitchell."

Angela clenched her teeth to keep from laughing too loud.

The recess bell rang, and the daytreatment kids lined up quickly. With little fuss, Ronnie and Angela herded the kids back into class.

Beverly returned from lunch, and Angela gave her a detailed account of the children's lunch and recess.

"I wouldn't worry too much about the teacher," Bev explained. "If it's who I think it is, her name is Prudence Bobtail. She's actually pretty nice, but she really hates having this program at this school. I don't think she has quite accepted that the world is not as perfect as TV sitcoms portrayed it in the 1960s and '70s."

"Yeah," Angela insisted, "but she was really angry and threatened to segregate our students from the rest of the school. How will our kids get used to normal kids and situations if they aren't ever allowed to see or interact with them?"

"Don't get yourself too worked up," Bev soothed. "Unless the principal says something to us, we're okay.

"I'm more worried about Violet," Bev continued. "She has never mentioned any body-image issues to me before. She's screwed up enough as it is; anorexia is the last thing she needs. I'll be sure to see her, Sallie and Sammy this afternoon. In the meantime, you'd better take a lunch break."

Angela didn't need to be told twice. After such a chaotic morning, she was starving. She retrieved her brown-bag lunch and headed to the teachers' lounge.

She was a little embarrassed to admit it, but the prospect of eating in the teachers' lounge was exciting. She barely considered herself an adult, remembering from her own school days that the teachers' lounge was this great secret, forbidden inner sanctum.

Discovering that the teachers' lounge was merely an extension of the office with four beige walls, a shabby couch, some tables and plastic chairs, a fridge, a phone and a coffee machine was a major let down. No secret handshake even.

Angela set her lunch on one of the tables in the empty lounge before making a brief visit to the adjoining bathroom.

While washing her hands Angela laughed and said to herself, "Well, half-way through the day."

She looked herself over in the bathroom's full-length mirror and was upset to see her favorite sundress caked in pebble dust from the knees to the hem. Her shins were in the same condition, except she could discern the imprint of every individual piece of gravel that touched her legs.

Brushing and beating the fabric of her dress did little to remove the determined dust. Brushing off her legs only seemed to grind in the pale grit.

After several minutes she gave up on the dress and washed her lower legs with a wet paper towel. One final look in the mirror and she knew she looked like somebody's poor relation.

Emerging from the bathroom, Angela spied a slender, 30-year-old woman who had long, curly red hair peeking inside her lunch bag. "What are you doing with my lunch?"

The woman inhaled sharply, caught in the act. She nervously

scissored her long fingers, which she positioned in front of her like a praying mantis.

"Ohhhh, we were just checking to see if anyone had brought some fine, tender chocolaty morsels to share and snack upon," the woman explained in character with a comical air of sophistication.

Angela was game and replied, "No, did you bring me any?"

"Don't be silly. You are but the rookie, and I am the tenured marm."

Okay, Angela thought. *To hell with the students, this chick takes the cake on the weird factor around here. At least she's kinda fun.*

"I'm Angela Marengo, children's behavioral specialist," the rookie introduced herself. "And who might you be?"

The woman scissored her right mantis hand as she examined Angela's outstretched paw. After a second's pause, she delicately shook hands. "I am Rachel O'Malley, and I, too, specialize in childish behavior."

"So I noticed."

"You disapprove?"

"Tut-tut, dahling," Angela said affecting a sophisticated character of her own. "You dar'st not think it in the least."

"Oh, good," said Rachel, coming out of character and plopping down on the couch. "So how are the little monsters down in room 36."

Angela sat next to her but became defensive. "They're not monsters."

"It's okay to speak freely in the teachers' lounge, Honey. I'm about ready to strangle some of the little shits in my room. It's only natural."

"I still don't think I'd call 'em monsters."

"You will one day."

The principal strode into the room oblivious to the women's conversation. "Miss Marengo, I just got off the phone with Mrs. Bobtail. She told me the most terrible story. Is it true?"

"Maybe. What did she say?"

"She said one of your students spit at her students and that he called her a bitch," Mr. Franklin said, whispering the B-word.

"That's mostly true, sir. The boy did spit at her students, but he actually called her a bitchell."

"What's that?" he asked.

"We don't know either, but we doubt it's a good thing. We took him straight to the timeout booth and apologized profusely to Mrs. Bobtail. I promise I'll do my best not to let it happen again."

49

"Good," he said. "I know it's only your first day, but we do not tolerate that type of behavior on the playground. Our children should be sheltered from that behavior and language."

So should mine, Angela thought but did not say. She couldn't figure out why everyone kept telling her this stuff. *No shit.* It's the type of behavior they hired her to help eliminate.

Instead of making a fuss, Angela respectfully said, "Yes, sir."

Rachel tried her hardest not to laugh at the scene Mr. Franklin described.

Satisfied, the principal sauntered back to his office.

"Not little monsters, eh?" Rachel gently nudged her elbow into Angela's ribs.

"Well, they're dealing with a lot of issues," Angela remained politically correct. She was pretty sure Rachel was okay, but she wanted to play it safe.

"I know," Rachel said with honest candor. "But there's nothing wrong with blowing off a little steam with friends on a frustrating day."

"Monsters they are then," Angela toasted the air with her bottled water.

Rachel smiled slyly. "Then I suppose you will tell me what a bitchell is?"

"I would if I could. But frankly this kid seems to have everyone mystified as to its actual meaning. I just assume he means bitch."

The tone bells rang.

"They're playing my song," Rachel sighed. "But stop by my room as soon as you learn what a bitchell is. I'm dying to find out."

O'Malley was gone in a trice, leaving Angela to finish her lunch in peace.

Rested and restored, Angela headed back to class.

She could hear the buzz of noise from her classroom from halfway down the hall with the door to Room 36 shut. Chaos seemed to be in store.

She was neither afraid nor concerned. Standing outside the door to her room, she felt recharged and ready for action. She entered.

Inside, Bev and Mrs. Regina had their hands full with Sammy. Therapy hadn't gone well.

Mrs. Regina was carrying Sammy's feet and Bev had him under the arms. Sammy was trying to spit on both of them.

"Can I help?" Angela asked, rushing to the rescue.

50

"Yeah, open the door to timeout," Mrs. Regina said.

"Which one?"

"Always closest and emptiest," Bev grunted, cocking her head just in time for a goober from Sammy to fly past her ear.

Angela ran to the timeout nearest and opened it wide.

The women shuffled over quickly and gently lay Sammy on the padded floor, then they ran out and Angela started closing the door.

She was too slow and gentle, and Sammy bolted half-way out before Bev—facing a barrage of spit and bitchells—caught him and redeposited him back on the floor of timeout. Again Bev ran out, but this time Mrs. Regina demonstrated just how quickly and forcefully the padded door needed to be shut. Sammy slammed against it just as she clasped the latch closed. She held the latch until Bev took control of it.

"Gotta be quick," Mrs. Regina said between gasps for breath. She headed back to class before fully getting her wind back.

Sammy spat on the window and repeatedly charged the door, as if a six-year-old had the power of Superman to bust through the foam, wood and steel.

"Out!" he shouted before each slam into the door.

"When you are sitting quietly against the back wall, I'll let you out," Bev soothed.

"Now!" Slam!

"Just as soon as you are sitting quietly against the back wall," Bev calmly repeated.

Angela sardonically inquired, "How'd therapy go?"

"Great," Bev sighed. "Sallie didn't say a word. She would only color in a coloring book using every marker until each page she colored turned black. Aside from it being a fitting metaphor for her life, the session was a bust."

Sammy kept ramming against the door. Then, within a split second, his rage turned to fear. "Freddy! He's gonna git me!" Sammy hollered, his horrified brown eyes pleading out the window. "He's in here. Lemme out! Lemme out!"

Angela stepped closer to the window and only saw Sammy.

Sammy scraped his fingernails against the canvas of the pad, as if to dig his way through the door.

"Sammy," Bev said patiently. "As soon as you sit quietly against the back wall, I can let you out."

Angela put her face to the wire-reinforced glass of the window.

Sammy jumped at the window and roared. His eyes were wild, as if possessed by a demon.

The boy cackled at the sight of Angela jumping backward in fright at his surprise attack.

"Freddy's gonna git you," he menacingly taunted as he flexed his fingers like blades.

Bev laughed at Angela. That had to be about one of the oldest tricks in Sammy's book.

Realizing she'd been tricked by the boy, Angela gave Beverly a sheepish grin. Sammy just began head-butting the door.

"Shouldn't we stop him? Isn't he going to hurt himself?" Angela asked Bev.

"I'm not going in there after Mr. Kruger," Bev explained. "He'll stop when it hurts, or when he gets too tired."

"Is there anything I can do to help?"

"Nope. But you can get started reading all of the kids' case files. There's a key ring in the left-hand drawer of my desk. It has keys that'll open the small therapy room next to us and the file cabinets.

"I'll probably be in here for the rest of the school day if you need me. Sammy will probably keep this up for another half an hour. In the meantime, you get to know these kids as best you can on paper."

Angela got the keys and did as she was told.

The therapy room was a mess. Toys, games and puzzles were scattered all over the floor and furniture. The furniture included a ratty looking couch, a kid-size table-and-chair set and two metal double-decker file cabinets. The walls had built-in shelves, and the thin carpeting was threadbare. There were no windows, but the fluorescent overhead lights were bright, as was the 1970s lime-green paint on the walls. Angela reasoned that the room had been primarily used for storage until the program was started.

The mess was almost enough for Angela to kick into obsessive-compulsive cleaning mode, but that would take too long and she had lots of files to read. She satisfied herself with clearing a path to the file cabinets and clearing off a seat on the couch.

In addition to the clutter, Angela was surprised by how large the children's files were, especially given how young they were.

Sallie, 4, had a bulging 8-inch-thick file. Sammy, 6, had one 8-inch file and another 4-inch file. Charlie, 12, had 3 8-inch files.

Each file folder was made of stiff, brown cardboard about twice as thick as a manila file folder. Its spine was folded like the bellows of an accordion. This allowed it to expand. Between the covers there were two dividing tabs as thick as the covers, at the top of each side of which were two folding metal prongs to attach 2-hole-punched documents.

When Angela opened a folder, the first section was the basic information about the child obtained during the mental health center's intake session. Opposite it were all of the pieces of emergency contact information. She turned the tab to see the insurance billing information on the left side. On the right side were copies of group notes. Turn that tab and there were the private therapy notes. Inside the back cover were examples of the child's art work and writings.

To expedite the process of reading the 11 case files, Angela scanned the intake info, quickly read the group notes—stopping to read the interesting nuggets such as the time Charlie discussed drug use in his family, which got Kevin to discussing how his mom smoked something that made her angry and violent. Bev noted that Lashaun didn't say a word, even though his mother was a recovering crack addict.

Angela was a little disturbed to see how many previous behavioral specialists had signed off on the notes in the past year. She wondered if the women that held this job before her were wimps or if the kids were only taking it easy on her today. She acknowledged it had been a really rough day, but she had expected rough.

Next, Angela took her time reading the therapy notes. She was impressed to see that Bev had such a good read on the kids—the causes and effects of their problems. Angela excelled at the analytical part of the business. She had a rougher childhood than she ever let on, and it taught her a thing or two about reading people. In college, she was mortified at how poorly many of her professors and some of the theorists in the science seemed to understand human behavior. She was glad to see that Bev was the type of therapist who saw things the way she did.

Finally, the artwork helped to provide a little more personality to the kids. The children's rage, depression and sexuality leapt off the pages. So many were still young enough not to have learned to mask their drawings. There were very few rainbows, puppies and sunny scenes. Well, Sallie drew puppies, but by the time she was done all of the colors bled into a full page of black.

The only real artistic deviation was Lionel. He occasionally drew animals taking care of one another. Angela assumed they were mother animals taking care of baby animals until she read a caption Bev had written under one. "Brother blue jay feeding baby sister blue jay."

Very telling, Angela thought. *Lionel must be the care taker in his family—a pretty heavy role for a 7-year-old.*

All of the children suffered PTSD from past and/or on-going abuse. The PTSD manifested itself in a multitude of subdiagnosies: Attention Deficit Disorder, depression, bipolar disorder, obsessive compulsive disorder and several others.

The children's bodies could be mined for all the pharmaceutical chemicals that were pumped through their veins to keep them functioning on a somewhat even keel: Ritalin, Adderall, Prozac, Risperdal, Seroquel and Paxil to name a few.

Angela thought it was appalling that these kids were on so many medications. However, she kept in mind that if they were this amped up on their meds, seeing them off their meds might be scary.

However, the meat of the files was more fascinating than anything Angela had previously studied. Each child had a life so tragic that the ancient Greek poet Sophocles could have stolen material from them. *Oedipus, step aside.* She put together summaries about the kids in her head.

Jefferson: Overall a good kid until the age of 5 when he witnessed his mother stab his father to death for reasons unknown. She then stabbed Jefferson in the stomach and left him for dead in a ditch by the highway. By miracle or cruel twist of fate he was rescued by a passing motorist.

His mother went to prison, and he went to live with his paternal grandparents—until he started drowning their cats in the toilet bowl. He bounced around loveless and unwanted through half a dozen foster homes where he developed a reputation as a young fire bug. After setting his last foster home on fire, he went to the state mental hospital for two years. It was the best thing that ever happened to him. He now lives in a group home and has been fairly stable. Nonetheless, he's having a difficult time coping with his mother's recent release from prison and her efforts – albeit futile – to regain custody.

Ted: His mother beat, starved and neglected him and his little sister for years—usually while telling them she was the only person on earth that loved them. Conflicted, Ted loves and hates his mother with all his heart. Ted's father was detached and enigmatic in the case file. What's known is that Mom abandoned them to live in another state. In an act of reprisal for the abandonment, his father strangled his toddler sister. His dad went to jail for a short while but the case against him was thrown out on a technicality. He subsequently retained custody of Ted because he showed no malice toward the boy. Ted lives in absolute terror of his father, yet has no choice but to live with him.

In the meantime, Ted is actively seeking love from any source under any conditions. Unfortunately, all he knows and understands is aggression, violence and power. He attacks other students and staff with no conscious thought. He hasn't hit puberty, but he has already begun grooming younger boys for sexual perpetration. He also gladly accepts the sexual advances of the older boys. Anything for love. When staff intervene or grooming fails, Ted goes into a violent rage. Staff must always be on guard. Essentially, Ted is on the fast track to be coming a sociopath. Given the maliciousness of his attacks, often using stolen knives, scissors or blunt objects, it would not surprise the treatment team if he became a serial killer.

Of course, not everyone's case was so bleak.

Lashaun's mother was suffering PTSD and became a drug addict. Now, after years of therapy, she's sober and coping with her past. She has a steady job. She and Lashaun have undergone extensive family therapy, and he is about to begin the process of entering the mainstream school program.

Other kids lived in circumstances that seemed neither hideous nor good. Charlie's mother says his father abandoned him, even though he gets occasional visitation rights. Evidence in the file seems to indicate that this same woman is rather delusional and domineering over Charlie and his two siblings. Regardless of the problems at home, Charlie seems to have learned how to effectively cope with most of his troubles. He no longer fights as often as he used to, although he does try to mentally establish control over the other kids in the program. His behavior is improving, and he is scheduled to begin mainstreaming after Lashaun settles into the mainstream program.

The only thing Angela found confusing about the files was the way they were updated. Some kids had group notes and therapy notes right up through last week. Others had been missing going back to the past school year.

There were no explanations for the missing notes, such as a stay at the state mental hospital. Angela wondered if Bev misplaced the notes or if the kids just weren't getting any therapy. She made a mental note to ask Bev about it.

Time seemed to fly, as Angela read the case files. Before she knew it, the 3:30 bell had rung and every student in the building was clanging through his or her locker, packing up for the exodus home.

By the time Angela returned the files to their rightful cabinets, her class had been dismissed. Mrs. Regina, Bev, Carla and Ronnie were slouching with exhaustion in small chairs around a circular work table in the classroom.

"Welcome to the meeting of the minds," Bev greeted.

Angela took a chair.

Mrs. Regina sat up and explained what they were doing. "Every day after school we review each student's day and make plans for how to handle them tomorrow."

"So what's the plan for Sammy," Angela sarcastically inquired.

"Straight jacket."

"Duct tape."

"A leash."

"Cattle prod."

Angela laughed, "Not that any of you have given it any thought."

"I know we're not supposed to have favorites or least favorites," said Ronnie, "but my God that kid is a nightmare."

"Yeah, too bad he's no longer confined to Elm Street," Carla quipped.

Everyone chuckled, but Mrs. Regina quickly reigned in the group: "Okay, okay. The key, so far, has been patience and remembering to give him his space.

"If we're all agreed that he's awful, why don't we just have him transferred?" Angela asked.

"Where to?" Carla bluntly asked.

"We're the last stop in our district before a child gets sent to the state mental hospital," Bev explained. "There's no relief; we're the last line of defense. The hospital doesn't want him, and he doesn't qualify for a forced admin."

"How on earth does that kid not qualify?" Angela asked incredulously.

"Two words," Mrs. Regina said. "Budget cuts."

She gave Angela another lecture about the frustrating politics behind children's mental health similar to the one Bev gave earlier.

Bev elaborated on the specifics of Sammy's case. "The only way for Sammy to go to the state mental hospital is A.) for his mother to give up custody to the state, which will eventually determine he's unfit for foster care or group homes, B.) for him to prove that he is a serious physical threat to the community—i.e. shoot up a school yard full of kids, or C.) prove he is a threat to himself. Threats or requests for suicide don't usually count, either. He's gotta have a plan and make a legitimate attempt."

"Oh my God," Angela said as she absorbed the difficulty of actually getting the child the help he really needed.

"Of course," Ronnie added, "The state could find reasonable cause to terminate his mother's custody because of abuse or neglect."

"Yeah, right," Carla bitterly scoffed.

"The state hasn't been convinced by the sheer tonnage of evidence we've amassed so far," said Bev, explaining Carla's reaction.

"What about Sallie?" Angela inquired. "What did DCW say about her this afternoon while I was reading the files?"

The four women were silent and nervously looked at each other before Mrs. Regina spoke. "They didn't come."

"And you sent her home?!"

"Had to. It's illegal to keep her here," the veteran teacher solemnly declared.

"Given the circumstances, isn't it illegal to send her home?" Angela pushed.

"No," returned Mrs. Regina. "Immoral, yes. However, if we keep her from her family without evidence she's been raped and without police permission, it might be considered kidnapping. And kidnapping is a federal crime for which we'd all go to prison for a very long time."

Angela was boiling with anger and frustration. "But the police won't give us permission because they won't investigate, and they won't act until DCW investigates. And DCW couldn't get around to investigating because they've got their heads up their asses. So we're forced to send a victim back to her abuser?"

Chipper with irony, Ronnie added, "And if the authorities found out we sent a 4-year-old girl back to her rapist, we'd all go to jail."

"I feel pretty safe then," Angela blustered. "The authorities would actually have to do their jobs. At least for tonight we can all rest peacefully."

Mrs. Regina lowered her brow and leveled a piercing, brown-eyed gaze at Angela. "We can rest peacefully every night."

Angela felt a chill as cold, wicked reality set in.

"Welcome to the Catch-22 of our work," Bev said, before voicing a controversial but fair point of contention among the staff. "Yet, I feel I should point out one other fact. I'm not disagreeing with anyone here. You all know I fight against DCW with the best of them, but you also know they do the best they can with how little they've got. They only have about 25% of the staff they need for a city and county of this size."

"Yeah," Carla contested, "but that quarter ain't worth a dime, if you know what I'm sayin'."

"Well," Bev countered, "paying just a couple bucks above minimum wage has a tendency to scare off the most qualified social workers to bigger cities or private companies in bigger cities. So I suggest we move ahead with our meeting; there's little else we can accomplish by complaining right now."

They knew Bev was right, but it felt good to vent some of their anger and frustration.

The meeting lasted another 20 minutes. Angela enjoyed the mixed perspective about what was expected of the children. Their academic goals were as varied as the kids were, and Bev gave the classroom team tips about how to better adapt to and control the kids' behaviors.

After the meeting, Carla and Ronnie tidied the classroom and went home. Mrs. Regina prepared her next day's lesson plans and went home.

Bev and Angela were on the clock until five, so they quickly cleaned their room freeing them to relax and discuss the case files— also giving Bev more time to work on the day's therapy notes.

"You survived you're first day. What do you think?"

"Overall it was pretty good. It's harder than I thought it would be on some levels and easier on others. The kids are cool. Some are totally F.I.T.H., but I think I'm gonna work well with them."

"What's Fith?" Bev inquired.

Angela laughed. "That's my family's technical diagnosis for anyone with severe issues: Fucked In The Head."

"I like it. F.I.T.H," Bev repeated. "What didn't you like?"

"The legal stuff." Angela shook her head. "Poor Sallie; I can't believe we had to send her home. I can't believe DCW didn't come."

"Poor all of them," Bev sympathized. "What did you think about the files?"

"They're amazing—11 Russian epics. I can't get over how some of these kids have two or three file folders and what they're filled with."

"Do you have any questions about the kids?"

"Not really. I'm still trying to absorb everything I learned today. It's like an entire semester crammed into six hours."

Bev chuckled. "It's crazy, but it'll get easier, I promise. How about the files and their actual organization?"

"That was pretty straightforward," Angela said. "However, it seemed as if many of the files were missing a lot of notes."

"Not to fear," Bev said. "That's your assignment for tomorrow"

The psychologist pulled about a 100 copies of notes from the bottom drawer of her desk. "Tomorrow afternoon you can lock yourself in the therapy room with these and file away. Lucky you."

The remainder of their conversation was light. Angela finally had time to organize her desk and was dismissed a little early.

On the drive home, her brain was awhirl with the euphoria of having completed her first day. Yet as she pulled into the parking lot of her apartment complex, exhaustion swept over her. She could hardly believe all that had happened in one day—a roller coaster of action and emotion.

Before she could even think about dinner, she crashed on the couch for a well-earned nap.

Chapter 4

Lionel
(That Evening)

"Damn, this is some good shit, Cletus," Lionel's mother said as she took a second drag off the joint before passing it on to her common-law husband.

"Dude," he giggled deeply. Cletus had already smoked a phat one with the dealer before Beulah got home. He took a hit and passed it back.

Beulah took another lungful. She watched Lionel and his sister, Persephone, play with stuffed animals on the floor of their relatively barren living room. "You know what would be really fuckin' funny?" she asked Cletus.

Grinning from the buzz, he only shook his head no.

"Let's let the kids try it," Beulah suggested.

"Awesome," he agreed.

"Lionel," Beulah called. "Come over here."

Eager to please, and seeing his parents in such a good mood, the boy took his little yellow stuffed rabbit and quickly went to his mother.

She lifted him up and set him on her large lap. "Man, you're gettin' to be so big. You wanna try this like a big boy?"

Lionel loved being a big brother and being considered a big kid. He couldn't wait to be a grownup. He wasn't about to pass up an opportunity to do grownup stuff like smoking when offered. "Sure, Mommy," the seven-year-old said, eagerly taking the joint. He held it carefully between his fingers, pantomiming the way his parents held it. They laughed. He did, too, not knowing that he was the joke.

When he inhaled, he began coughing uncontrollably. Beulah grabbed the joint from his hand before he could drop it. Lionel's parents couldn't stop laughing.

Lionel's feelings were hurt because now he knew his parents had set him up and were laughing at him.

"Maybe you're still too young for this," Beulah said.

Defiantly, in an effort to prove his big-kid status, Lionel demanded another hit. Not even his parents could get away with setting him up, especially implying that he was a little kid. In many ways, he was the only adult in the house, and he hated being treated like he wasn't one. Without him, Persephone would almost never eat breakfast or dinner or get a bath. His parents would never wake up in time to get him to school or go to work. And if he wasn't around, who would take care of his mother when she started crying.

Beulah gave him the joint, and he sucked down a breath. It burned, but he held it for a second before coughing. Again, his parents laughed. Nonetheless, Lionel was convinced he proved his point. He could smoke like a grownup.

Finished coughing, he wiped away the tears caused by the smoke and hopped off Beulah's lap.

He was surprised at how light-headed he felt when his feet hit the floor. Beulah and Cletus laughed more when he stumbled back to the living room.

Beulah finished off the joint. "Ya know what I really want right now?" she asked Cletus.

"Uh, Cheetos."

"No, dip shit. I dunno why, but I really wanna screw."

"The kids are still up."

"Well, let's put them in the basement. Then we can do whatever we want."

Persephone and Lionel overheard their conversation only understanding the concept of basement. Their eyes widened into saucers. They hated the basement. It was very dark, very scary, very cold and very empty except for the water heater, furnace, spiders and monsters.

"Basement," commanded Cletus.

"No," Lionel pleaded. "We'll be quiet in our room. I promise."

"Nope," he replied. "Early bedtime in the basement."

"Please," begged Persephone.

"Basement. Now!" shouted Beulah. "You heard your father."

The children knew it would be useless to argue further. It would only lead to a beating, then the basement. Each child picked up a stuffed animal and trudged to the ominous basement door. Cletus herded them on to the rickety old wooden steps and locked the door closed behind them.

Lionel tried the light switch in vain. The bulb burned out more than a year ago.

The kids trembled and waited for their eyes to adjust to the near

62

total darkness. A single small window let in a little light from the street, but it was only enough to make out basic shapes in the unfurnished basement.

Lionel took Persephone's hand.

"C'mon, we'll be safe if we can get to the bed," he said.

The bed was a moldy, stained old mattress under the little window. It smelled funky and served as a home to more bugs than the kids would be comfortable knowing.

Together the siblings created a fantasy that the mattress was an island of safety from the monsters in the basement. The monsters were real. The children heard them. They saw them, especially when their parents shared their drugs—not that the kids even knew they were doing drugs. After all, they learned to say no at school.

In addition to their unspoken arrangement with the monsters, Lionel always felt a little safer at the mattress because he had hidden an old steak knife under one corner. It wasn't much protection, but it was better than nothing.

But for the time being, there was a huge, black territory to navigate before arriving safely at the island.

One step down into the abyss, the creaking old wooden stairs cautioned them to go no farther. Another step, another sound.

What was that?

Their hearts beat like the wings of a humming bird.

The longer we stay here, the easier it'll be for the monsters to find us, Lionel thought.

Step. Creak.

Their hands sweat. Their pulse thudded in their ears.

Step. Creak. Step. Creak. Step. Creak. Step. Creak. Step. Creak. Cement floor.

The monsters aren't deaf, Lionel thought.

"Run, Sephie!" he commanded with a whisper.

"I can't see!" she returned with a panicked whisper.

"Keep holding my hand!"

Lionel charged for the faint light of the window and the mattress below it. Persephone slowed him down, but she'd be eaten if he let go. He ran with one hand feeling the darkness in front of him, the other tightly gripped his sister's hand.

Almost there.

He could see the mattress but not whatever sent him tumbling face first onto the floor.

What was that?! He felt no pain. His system blazed on adrenalin. Persephone shrieked.

Where's Sissy?! He panicked.

Lionel was a fighter and would not abandon Persephone no matter how terrified he was.

He managed to stand and slowly walk into the blackness, hoping his hands would touch Persephone before some hairy, flesh-eating beast. *Was that something licking its chops?*

Contact. Shriek.

"Sephie, It's me," the boy whispered. He grabbed her hand, and they jumped onto the mattress. Lionel scrambled to the corner hiding the knife.

Safe.

Sort of. Both children hoped and prayed the monsters still respected the island sanctuary. The monsters had their chance to eat them.

As Lionel's adrenalin began to subside, his chin felt wet and his lip tingled, tasting salty.

His mind was racing. *I hope the monsters can't smell blood. Sharks can. Some fish can live out of water. Some sharks probably can, too. They're just big fish, right? Shit.*

Lionel scanned the void hoping to spot an impending attack. His right hand clenched the knife. His left wiped away the blood. Persephone leaned against him, trembling.

"Go to sleep, Sephie. You're safe now," he lied.

She almost believed him. Then they heard the banging upstairs. Their mom made awful, muffled moans that got worse as the banging sped up.

"Are the monsters killing Mommy?" Persephone asked softly between her tears.

"I don't know," Lionel replied.

Lionel didn't know what to do. He loved his mom very much and thought he could save her. He had a knife. The only thing that stood in his way was the locked door. He knew he couldn't get through it; he tried before. If he tried again, the monsters would surely eat Persephone if he wasn't there to protect her.

He tried very hard not to cry when the banging and moaning came to a frenzied conclusion.

Persephone cried, "Mommy's dead."

The two children hugged and clung to each other. This had to be the end.

They gave up all hope when the banging started again.

"The monsters must be killing Daddy now," Lionel said.

They knew if their parents couldn't survive the monsters, they didn't stand a chance. A grim acceptance fell over them.

They were startled when they heard their Mom moaning again. They were instantly gladdened she was alive but inconsolable she was being tortured again.

Beulah was tortured one more time before Persephone finally fell asleep.

Lionel guarded their island until dawn broke and exhaustion conquered his will.

It was a short hour and a half before he had to be at school.

Chapter 5

Honeymoon's Over
(Tuesday)

Angela felt completely recharged after 10 hours of heavy slumber. She moved with purpose through her morning routine and was ready for action and dressed for it too: sports bra under a T-shirt tucked into blue jeans—and not the cutesy hip-hugger variety.

At school, Bev approved of the wardrobe change.

Yet, Angela was almost disappointed when the big kids' group didn't act out.

Little kids' group was disturbingly short on kids.

"Where are Sallie and Lionel?" Angela asked a question open to anyone, as she lined up the kids at the connecting door.

Edward shrugged his tiny shoulders, Sammy spastically looked side-to-side and Ted babyishly lisped he didn't know.

Carla provided the only known details. "We don't know where Sallie's at, but we got a hold of Lionel's mom. She said they got a late start on the day and that she'd bring Lionel to school. They ought to be here any minute."

Angela let the kids into the room, and they got their rugs without a fight.

Bev had no sooner started group, when Lionel stormed in from the hallway door. He hadn't bothered to hang up his jean jacket or his backpack. In his haste, his shoulder accidently slammed into the door jamb.

"Fuckin' door," he grunted angrily. He unshouldered his backpack and slammed it into the steel door jamb as an act of vengeance.

Lionel didn't look at anyone in group; he headed straight for the connecting door.

"Don't you talk like that in school," commanded a woman's voice from the hallway.

The angry boy opened and slammed the connecting door shut behind him.

His mother stepped into the daytreatment room. She was built like an assembly line worker who made Ford big rigs. On top of her formidable size, she was obviously mad, and her scowl didn't make her look any less intimidating.

"Hi, Beulah," said Bev with a welcoming smile, as she stood to greet Lionel's mother. "How are you?"

"I'm fine, but that boy's got a real attitude problem this morning."

"Do you know what started it?"

"Nah, I just couldn't wake him up an' get him movin'. He's been a real pain, an' now I'm late for work."

Lionel was escorted by Ronnie straight to time out. His eyes were bloodshot. His hair was disheveled. His clothes were the same as the day before, and he was so furious that the veins in his little neck were bulging.

"Buster," his mother called out. "You better be nice in school, or you're gonna be in a lotta trouble when you get home."

Lionel huffed through flared nostrils, entered time out and Ronnie closed the door behind him.

"Bev," his mother commanded. "You let me know if he don't act right."

"I promise I'll let you know if anything bad happens," Bev convincingly lied, looking Beulah right in the eye. It wasn't her policy to lie to parents, but when the parents were threatening to beat their kids or at least threatening to threaten to beat their kids, she offered what protection she could.

"Okay," Beulah acquiesced and left.

"You take care, and have a good day," Bev called after her.

When Bev closed the hallway door, Lionel began beating and kicking the walls of the booth. He swore up a blue streak. He wasn't trying to escape; he was venting his rage. Ronnie patiently sat in a chair next to the time out door, holding the latch.

As they had no place else to go, Bev recommenced the group by awarding a ton of beads for good behavior. Angela soaked in the events transpiring, learning from her co-workers.

Once Lionel burned off his initial rage, he became upset that no one was paying him any attention and that no one else seemed to be as miserable as he. To make up for that, it was time to sow a little anarchy in group. He approached the wire-reinforced window of time out and studied the boys. The 7-year-old reasoned that Ted was too mature to set up easily from time out and set his sights on his little, weak-minded buddy, Edward.

"Edward!" Lionel enthusiastically shouted from the time out

window. "Go crazy. Run around. I'll be your best friend."

Ronnie told Lionel to be quiet or else he'd have to stay in time out for a full half-hour.

The threat had little effect on the angry boy who kept pushing Edward's buttons.

Several thoughts raced through Edward's brain. He liked Lionel's idea on several levels. He had to admit, running around, making noise and going crazy was just plain fun. But he also suspected Bev wouldn't approve of having such a good time right now. However, on the other hand, Edward considered Lionel his best friend and wanted to stay his best friend. His conflicted mind raced as he pondered what to do, leaning more and more toward following Lionel's advice. He began rocking from knee to knee on his carpet.

"Don't do it," Angela warned, not knowing what else to say.

"Do it! Do it, my friend," begged Lionel.

As the tension grew, Bev was calm and had the perfect counter offer. "I'll give you lots of beads for ignoring Lionel's set ups."

Edward's rocking paused for a moment, so Bev kept talking. "Just think of all the cool stuff you can buy this week in store if you earn enough beads."

Edward's eyes widened and he maintained self-control.

"That's one bead," Bev smiled.

"Who wants stupid old beads? Have some fun!" Lionel commanded.

Bev didn't give Edward a chance to misbehave before awarding him two more beads. She gave all three boys a bead.

The money was starting to add up. Three greedy sets of eyes focused solely and expectantly on Bev who kept rewarding their good behavior for ignoring Lionel. Lionel's assault on Edward faded, but Lionel was still pissed—more pissed because his initial plan failed. Nevertheless, he had an ace up his sleeve, guaranteed chaos, and now was the time to play it.

"Sammy! I seeeee Fred-dy."

"Where?!" Sammy's defenses were on high alert. His head swiveled back and forth in search of Freddy.

"Freddy doesn't exist," Bev tried to explain.

"He's right behind you!" Lionel shouted, laughing after Sammy jumped up and shrieked.

Bev had no magic cure to keep Sammy under control. Once Freddy was involved, she knew group was shot. She dismissed Ted and

Edward with a lot more beads.

"I see Freddy," Lionel continued taunting. "He's gonna get you."

A wild-eyed Sammy morphed into Freddy.

"There is no Freddy," Bev reiterated, preparing for a restraint.

"Uh-huh," Sammy now taunted, slipping into character.

Lionel had a satisfied glow about him as he peered into the room from time out. Total disruption. He watched Sammy with mild curiosity. As with all the grownups, Sammy was a total mystery to him.

"Sammy, we're the only ones here," Angela said, still pursuing the problem from the Freddy angle. She stood to block one of his escape routes out of the room.

"Angela, don't mention the F-word. It only heightens his paranoia," Bev explained, before turning to Sammy. "Would you like to color? I have some new crayons."

Sammy shook his head wildly and giggled maniacally.

"I haven't colored in forever," Angela continued the train of distraction. "Let's draw a picture together."

Sammy ignored Angela, lowered his head and charged Bev.

"Bitchell!" he yelled as he slammed his hard noggin into Bev's waist. The blow knocked the wind out of her a bit, but she managed to wrap him up in a restraint and guide him into timeout. Spit and curses flew in every direction.

Angela raced to open and close the timeout door as quickly as she had learned the day before.

"You get this one," Bev declared, pulling up a chair for Angela to sit on. "Ronnie, I'll take Lionel. You can go back to class."

Ronnie gave out a little cheer, as Bev took over guard duty. "Have fun, ladies," Ronnie teased as she left.

Sammy spazzed for another three full minutes before finally calming down enough to sit quietly against the back wall and eventually earn his release.

Lionel was burned out and in a good psychological state to start talking by the time Bev got to him.

Angela tried to listen to their therapy session but only caught snippets over Sammy's initial carrying on before his release. After Sammy was out of time out, Angela picked up something about no sleep and a rather sweet apology to Bev. Bev eventually left Lionel in time out with the door wide open.

"Won't he escape?" Angela asked.

"Nah," Bev whispered. "Poor guy is sound asleep."

"Shouldn't we wake him and send him back to class?"

"The old adage about sleeping dogs applies to E.D. kids." Bev explained. "If we wake him up, he'll only have another sleep-deprived episode. In this program, we get to make exceptions to the rules all of the time."

"Cool. So what did he tell you in time out?" Angela inquired. "Why is he having such a bad morning?"

"Lionel's a tough nut to crack. He's very secretive and protective of his family."

"Why?"

"He's dealt with the system before. He doesn't want to get his parents in trouble, and he doesn't want to be removed from the home. He's taking care of his mom and sister. All that he told me was that he got in trouble and didn't get much sleep. I wasn't about to argue and told him to take a nap."

There was a knock on the hallway door, through which a fat, gray-haired woman in her fifties entered without permission.

"Hi," she said. "Is there a Sallie here?"

Angela approached her with an extended hand and was cordially confrontational, "Who are you?"

"Oh, I'm sorry. I'm Janice with the Department of Child Welfare. Someone here called to make a report about Sallie."

As Angela shook her hand, she silently reminded herself to remain civil. "That was me, but I'm afraid Sallie isn't here today."

"Where is she?"

"We don't know. We called her home, but no one answered," Angela explained.

"Who's in charge here?" Janice asked, oddly aloof toward Angela.

"I am," Bev said from behind her desk. "But Angela's the one you want to talk to. She was the one Sallie perped on and witnessed the evidence that someone perped on Sallie. She's the one who called you."

Janice looked irritated. "Well, I better go."

"Wait," Angela said. "Didn't you see Sallie last night when you removed her from her home?"

"Why don't you guys take this in the hall," Bev said, cocking her head toward Lionel still asleep in time out.

Without another word both women entered the hall, closing the daytreatment room door behind them.

"We didn't remove her from her home," Janice said.

"Didn't you at least talk to her?"

71

"No. Now I must be going."

"Wait." Angela urged. "Why not? I called in the morning. You should have had plenty of time. Didn't they tell you what I said in my report?"

Angela hushed her voice to a nearly inaudible tone and added, "She was raped."

"I know what you reported," Janice explained. "But we couldn't get to it yesterday. All we had time for was to notify the family that a report had been made concerning their daughter."

"You did what?!" Angela couldn't contain her whisper, and teachers began closing their doors down the hallway.

"It's the law," Janice casually shrugged. "But don't worry; we didn't reveal that you made the call. That was completely confidential."

"No wonder Sallie's not here," Angela said between clenched teeth. "Who else would have called in that report? Couldn't you at least have waited until you talked with her before alerting her family? Who knows what her grandfather will do to keep her quiet or keep from getting caught."

Janice hated these situations. She hated these self-righteous moralists who tell her how to do her job. They made her want to scream. *I don't see them finding a place for the kid to live. I don't see them running a pen dry filling out all of the paperwork. They're only paying me $3 an hour more than minimum wage, without overtime. What do they expect?*

Janice tried to keep her cool. "Don't worry. We've got a file this thick on Sallie. We're doing the best we can, building the best case we can."

"You've known about this all along?" Angela was stunned. She could almost accept DCW's incompetence but not their duplicity.

"Did you save any evidence?" Janice inquired.

"Evidence?"

"Did you save her panties? Did you take any photographic evidence?"

"No," Angela stuttered. "I'm not gonna take any pictures of naked children. That's sick."

"Well, we can't convince a judge to remove a child from her home without evidence," Janice explained, exasperated. "Do you still have her panties, so we can test them for semen?"

"No, we sent them home with her. We didn't see any blood or semen, and they were soaked with urine."

72

Now it was Janice who felt as if she were dealing with a moron. "Christ, no wonder we can't get anywhere on this case."

She tried to lay a guilt trip, but Angela—stung though she felt—would have none of it. Her righteous indignation blended with her high school and college state champion debate team skills, and she quickly put the heat back on Janice.

"Listen," Angela pointed a finger in Janice's face. "If you did your job and showed up yesterday, you could've taken all the pictures you wanted and kept her underwear."

Without another word, Janice stormed out of the building.

Angela returned to her room. She had trouble wrapping her mind around the saga of Sallie and the DCW agent.

"How'd it go?" Bev asked, knowing full well that half the school just heard how well it didn't go. Although she had heard the entire conversation through the door, part of the trick to surviving this job was to give your teammates a chance to decompress.

Angela blew off plenty of steam but in hushed tones to let Lionel sleep.

"You know you probably made an enemy for life with that woman," Bev told Angela. "We can't afford to go angering too many more of those people. We're supposed to be on the same side. If we make them too mad, they'll do even less to help us."

Beverly's words weren't a reprimand or warning. She simply stated a fact.

Angela sighed and got her paperwork started.

The rest of the morning went very smoothly. Lionel slept so soundly that it took no small amount of effort to wake him for lunch.

Lunch went well, too. Bev had an early afternoon meeting to attend and left Angela to support the classroom staff. When Angela returned from her own lunch break, she saw that the lunchtime calm had not lasted.

Lionel was back in time out sleeping. Violet had been carried into time out because of her constant opposition to doing her school work. She scowled from the time out window, as Carla guarded its door.

"Anything I can do to help?" Angela asked.

Carla chewed the inside of her cheek. "Not really."

Violet began talking to Angela. She pleaded her innocence and pleaded for release.

Carla interrupted before the rookie attempted to say anything. "Just ignore her. The only thing she wants right now is attention, but she

73

can't have any until she sits quietly against the back wall and starts following directions."

Angela nodded and went to her desk and began organizing the notes she had to file.

Violet pouted and defiantly stood watch through the time out window. She wasn't particularly interested in the goings on of the room; she was merely displaying her sheer force of will in refusing to follow directions. When her legs could no longer support her, she sat with her back against the wall. With any other student, that wouldn't take much longer than five minutes. Violet once lasted an entire school day.

Carla and Angela were startled when the connecting door to the room was kicked open.

"Bitchell!"

"Which one's open?" Mrs. Regina shouted, struggling to motor forward with a squirming Sammy in a full restraint.

"Bitchell!"

"Neither," Carla stated.

Mrs. Regina grunted then commanded Angela, "Get me two chairs."

"Let me go, Fuckin' Bitchell!"

Angela raced over to the arts-and-crafts table and grabbed two chairs.

Sammy craned his head around to the left and spit a big gob of saliva into Mrs. Regina's face. Sammy cackled with glee.

Mrs. Regina made a guttural sound of absolute disgust. As she tried to wipe her face on her shoulder, Sammy spit in her hair. Sammy spit on everything within a 270 degree radius. He was a torrent of spit and bitchells.

"Where do you want these chairs?"

Christ, doesn't this new kid know anything, Mrs. Regina thought as she struggled mightily with the boy. "One right in front of the other facing the same direction."

Mrs. Regina positioned Sammy in the lead chair. He spat on Angela's T-shirt, baptizing her in the children's mental health tradition. She stepped back out of range. Mrs. Regina took the back seat, and she did all of this without letting Sammy out of the restraint.

Angela marveled at the older woman's skills.

Sammy was in a fury that would not subside. Mrs. Regina tried to sooth him, but every time she spoke, he tried to spit on her.

A sailor would have blushed at the six-year-old's language.

Pretending to do paperwork, Angela absorbed the scene and tried to learn as much as she could about Sammy through his "escalation."

The escalation carried on for 15 minutes of shouting and screaming, then his soliloquy of swearing switched gears to a new commanding shout: "Kill me! Kill me! Kill me, you stupid Bitchell!"

Mrs. Regina remained firmly in the restraint but didn't say a word. She had given up on trying to communicate with the boy. Angela looked up from her papers.

"Kill me," the boy shouted again.

Again no response from the elders in the room.

"I want to die! Let me die! Kill me!"

Angela couldn't remain silent. Instinct, background and training kicked into gear. "Why do you want to die, Sammy?"

"Kill me," he implored her.

Angela left her desk and squatted in front of Sammy. He spit on her thigh. She wiped it off, took a step back and squatted again. "Why do you want to die, Sammy?"

Mrs. Regina followed Angela's lead, tenderly encouraging, "Answer Angela's question, child."

"Kill me!"

Sammy's eyes were wide and wild, but in addition to those usual traits, Angela saw for the first time a profound emotional pain. Huge tears welled up but would not flow from the boy's eyes.

Sammy arched a luggie on her. Angela wondered how he hadn't dehydrated by now, but he continued shouting, "I said kill me, Bitchell!"

"Mrs. Regina, come quick!" Ronnie shouted from next door.

"Can't!" she shouted back.

"NOW!"

A table flipped over next door, and Kevin and Charlie could be heard brawling.

"Angela," Mrs. Regina commanded. "Take over with Sammy's restraint. Carla, clear the time out booths."

Carla did as she was told.

Angela hesitated. "It's illegal for me to restrain him. I'm not trained. I'll be fired."

"It's illegal for you to let those boys kill each other. Now get over here."

Mrs. Regina stood and Angela slid under her arms between her and

75

Sammy.

"Pass your right arm under his and take his left wrist," Mrs. Regina instructed. "Do the same with your left. Good. Don't hold too tight or let go."

Mrs. Regina took off to the classroom with Carla.

Sammy and Angela sat down, and Sammy resumed screaming and spitting—sometimes hitting Angela in the face and hair.

There was nothing she could do about it, no matter how much it made her skin crawl.

"KILL ME! I want to DIE!"

"I won't kill you, Sammy. I'd miss you too much." Angela knew about talking down suicidal people from a few lessons in suicide intervention at school, but, dripping in spit, she was not sure she'd actually miss him at that moment.

Sammy began pounding his head against her upper sternum. It hurt like a sonofabitchell and began knocking the wind out of her.

"Kill me!"

"No. I'd miss you. You're (head pound) such (head pound) a (head pound) sweet (head pound) boy."

Angela gasped for air. She squeezed Sammy as close to her as the chairs allowed. The surprise move momentarily prevented him from slamming her. She rested her cheek against his spiky head, hoped he didn't have lice and rocked with his every motion.

The near mother-son intimacy only freaked Sammy out more. "Kill Me!" "Bitchell!" "Kill Me!"

Angela held on for dear life and wished she could kill him. Instead, she whispered into his ear all the reasons she wouldn't kill him. He was so smart, so nice. He had beautiful brown eyes. He found her such pretty rocks.

Mrs. Regina and Carla watched in silence, as they guarded the timeout booths. All of their doubts about the new girl vanished as the feral beast in her arms began to transform into a whimpering, vulnerable little boy whose tears cut tracks into the gravel dust on his cheeks.

Sammy settled down but wouldn't tell Angela why he wanted to die. He did promise her that he wouldn't kill himself that night.

The little boy was silent and still for several more minutes in her arms.

Angela eventually asked, "If I let you go, can I trust you?"

He nodded.

She let go.

He didn't move.

Angela asked, "Would you like to color with me before going back to class?"

Sammy nodded and wiped away his tears.

Angela got a bucket of crayons and some paper from a shelf by the windows. She and Sammy sat across the table from each other. Sammy didn't say a word. He was physically and emotionally drained. He drew some stick figures using only one of hundreds of crayons. Angela drew him a rudimentary picture of her cat. He didn't ask her about Furnando, but he did accept the picture before going back to class.

A wave of euphoria flooded Angela's system. She wanted to dance around the room after Sammy left. *I just talked down my first suicide. I did it! I did it with the most fucked-up kid in the program at that! Woo hoo! I always wondered if I could. I can!*

Regardless of what she thought and felt, Angela kept a level-headed countenance, not wanting to showboat in front of Mrs. Regina whom she was convinced thought she was in incompetent idiot. "Are you sure I won't get in trouble for restraining Sammy?"

"Well, if they fire you for that, I'll walk out with you in protest," Mrs. Regina said with an approving wink. "That was very good work."

"Thank you," she said. "I'm sorry I wasn't more helpful earlier."

"No, you did fine. You kept your cool under intense pressure, and you're the only person who has successfully talked Sammy down without timeout."

Angela allowed herself a blushing smile at the compliments.

"Now, I have one more favor to ask of you," Mrs. Regina said. "Will you watch this door? I'm covered head to toe in Sammy spit, and I need a shower before his I.E.P. meeting after school."

"Sure, but what's an I.E.P meeting?" inquired Angela, taking the door's latch handle.

"An individual education plan. I'll tell you about it later. In the meantime, Kevin isn't allowed out until after recess."

"Sure thing," said Angela, suddenly remembering how much she wanted a shower.

Bev returned a little while later and covered timeout so Angela could at least wash her face in the teacher's lounge bathroom. When she got back, she described the whole event for Bev.

Bev struck Angela as being remarkably nonplused and distant. Angela switched the topic to the I.E.P.

Bev remained uncharacteristically emotionally hollow when she explained, "An individual education plan is usually a yearly meeting between the teacher, therapist and family discussing the child's accomplishments of the past year while looking to set new goals for the coming year."

"Makes sense," Angela said. "Can I sit in on this one?"

"Normally, I'd expect you to participate. This time I need you to babysit Sammy. You gonna be up for it?"

Angela sighed. "Yeah. At least there'll be plenty of people around to help in case he *escalates*."

Bev didn't smile or react to the irony of Angela's understatement, which also seemed odd to the new hire. She was perplexed by the way it seemed someone had flipped some kind of emotional switch in Bev. She wondered what triggered it, but didn't dwell on it as she needed to fill out reams of paperwork in conjunction with her Sammy experience.

Without a knock, the door to Virginia van Hess' office flung open.

Virginia, the director of DCW, was not startled. She coolly looked up from her decade-old keyboard. Her brown eyes showed no negative emotion, just the studied concern of an unflappable professional social worker. After 15 years in this business, she could mask most any emotion necessary. She had a talented poker player's grace with affect. Despite her outward demeanor, a shot of adrenaline hit her system.

Janice stood huffing in the open door jamb. Her sagging jowls were flush. A diaper bag-size purse was strapped diagonally across her lumpy bosom.

"I quit!" declared the caseworker.

"Janice, you know how short staffed we are," Virginia stated matter-of-factly. Everybody knew. She appealed to most people with this statement in an effort to squeeze a little more out of them—co-workers, other county services, hospitals and government officials time and again. It was not as if they really needed to be told. Any idiot could see her department was in dire need of at least six more full-time social workers—and that was the minimum she really needed just to make the department work. You could at least double that number to guarantee it worked reasonably well.

Worse, she already had an open position that was not yet filled because she hadn't gotten the results of the sex-offender tests administered to the last round of applicants.

"Two weeks!" Janice conceded. "I can't take all the nagging,

78

fighting and crap any longer."

Virginia wasn't going to get on her knees and beg Janice to stay. Janice wasn't much of a social worker, and Virginia saw this breakdown coming weeks ago. She managed to burn through about a dozen caseworkers a year. When they reached this stage, they were done. In fact, they were usually more trouble than they were worth.

"What happened?" was all she inquired.

Janice shut the door and paced the cramped office.

"Well, it wasn't one thing," Janice growled, winding up for her tirade. "But what pushed me over the top was this new B.S. over at Average Elementary...

As Janice raged, Virginia reflected, *that is the toughest program with the toughest kids in the district. They've vanquished their share of us over the years. Of course, they've vanquished their share of their own, too.*

"... She thinks she's so smart," Janice continued, breaking Virginia's train of thought. "Got all the answers. Tell me how to do my job. Blame me for getting a little girl raped ..."

Virginia interrupted, "She what?!"

Virginia could acknowledge her organization's shortcomings, but she fiercely defended her employees.

Janice bit her lip and faced Virginia. Her voice grew meek as she tried to dance around the claim she made which she knew was over exaggerated.

"What little girl?" Virginia patiently demanded.

"Sallie."

Everyone at DCW knew the Average Elementary caseload on a first name basis. They had the worst known case histories for their age group in the county. They also represented the largest liability for the county.

"Tell me the whole story," Virginia insisted.

"Well, yesterday this new B.S., Angela, called," Janice explained. Everyone and DCW loved to call behavior specialists by the initials. Professional rivalry? Perhaps, but behavior specialists often gave them a very difficult time and expected results yesterday. They seemed to have little concept of the law or reality. "She reported Sallie had been perped on again by Wayne. I didn't have time yesterday to interview the child, but I did call the family like I am supposed to. Then today I can't find the family, so I went to the school to find the girl. She wasn't there, and this Angela rips me a new rear end."

79

Virginia searched Janice's face. "What time was the report called in yesterday?"

"Ummm. 10:30ish a.m.," she reluctantly replied.

Virginia sighed and brushed her hand over her eyes. "You should have been there. We've been following this case for four years and need every shred of evidence and testimony we can get in order to get Sallie removed from that house."

"I'm sorry," Janice said with genuine regret.

"Why didn't you go?"

"I was busy. You know how far behind I am in my reports and filing. I was really getting a lot accomplished."

Virginia remained calm, but her frustration was clear. "Janice, you know rape cases take priority over paperwork."

Virginia felt a little bad for Janice. No, the woman wasn't much of a social worker, but her heart was in the right place. After a mid-life crisis, Janice decided to dedicate her life to humanity. She went back to school, earned her associate's degree in social work and got a job with DCW. Unfortunately, Janice learned too late that social work wasn't all sunshine and lollipops, as the career brochures can sometimes make it appear—finding good but needy families nice housing, removing abused kids from bad homes and feeding starving families.

In reality, a lot of poor families were lucky to live in hovels. Starving kids and adults were lucky to get one meal a day. And the abused kids, well they were screwed from the start—especially when the state mandates that every effort must be made to keep families together. And while it is a good policy in many—most—situations, it's the worst policy where sex abuse, violence, drug use and neglect are concerned.

The real trouble with losing Janice, Virginia knew, was that Janice was a born secretary. She wrote the best reports in the office. She understood the filing systems and functions better than most anyone. She had a knack for following protocol and procedures. Virginia really wished she could keep Virginia solely as an office manager, but there was absolutely no room for such a move in her budget.

Virginia continued her questioning: "What's your next step to find Sallie?"

"I don't know. I could go back to her house, again."

"If Wayne didn't answer the door earlier, I doubt he'll answer it now," Virginia explained. "Try Sallie's mom at her work. She's bound to be there. She needs the money too much, and she can't dodge you as easily."

Virginia wished she, herself, could go. She missed working cases. She knew by heart the 50 worst cases her department worked. She'd take them all, if it meant giving up the unenviable title of director. As distasteful as most people who quit found the job, she loved being a caseworker. She knew all the rules and ropes—how to get things done. Back when she started her career, she was tireless. The boss always asked her to train the newbies. But after a few years, the department had weeded through dozens of other social workers. Virginia's boss retired five years into Virginia's career. Virginia being resourceful, reliable and the most senior employee on staff was asked by the state to become the new director of her city's office. She didn't want to, but she couldn't responsibly say that she knew anyone in her department who would do better than herself. Besides, she wanted to double her salary to a director's $50,000 in order to better afford to start a family.

Now, 10 years since that fateful promotion, the weary director sighed.

Janice thought it was aimed at her and almost tripped over herself to follow up on Virginia's plan for finding Sallie's mom. "I'm on my way to her workplace now."

Virginia momentarily checked her retreat. "You still gonna quit?"

Janice hung her head and softly said yes. "I'm really sorry."

The director smiled weakly. "I understand."

She really did. Nonetheless, the stress of having to fill another position looped another rubber band around her heart—pushing her blood pressure up another 10 points.

"Do you want me to report back to you when I get back?" Janice asked, as she opened the door to leave.

"No, I'll be at an I.E.P. at Average Elementary this afternoon."

The yellow short-bus finally pulled up.

"Thank God," muttered Carla.

Mrs. Regina's famous discipline crumbled at day's end when she lined up the students. No one was sent back to their seat for nattering or squirreliness. She didn't care. No one wanted the yelling, screaming, combative beasts any longer.

It had easily been the worst day of the semester. Everyone was breaking down and fighting. Nothing got accomplished...and oh, the spit. Sammy must have been a fountain at Versailles in a former life.

"Sammy, don't get on the bus," Bev said, after entering the

classroom. "Your mom is coming for your I.E.P. She'll take you home."

Christ, the I.E.P., Mrs. Regina thought. *Won't this day ever end?*

Angela's heart stopped. She quickly learned the hard way that the moments of triumph don't last long in daytreatment. Sammy had more escalations, as did the other students. At least Sammy didn't threaten suicide, again.

Bev's announcement about the I.E.P. disturbed Sammy the most. His eyes widened with fear, and he gasped as the words left her lips. He didn't become Freddy. Instead his little body emitted an electrical charge of terror different than any other previous terror-based emotion Angela or any of the classroom staff had experienced.

Upon witnessing the change in Sammy, a fresh wave of adrenaline restarted Angela's heart. *Not again. No more spit. Don't we get time to rest? God, I want a hot shower. I need a hot shower.* Without a word, Angela clenched her jaw and braced for the worst.

While the other children walked out of the room and onto the bus, Sammy tried to climb inside a small cabinet next to Mrs. Regina's desk.

"What are you doing, Sammy?" Angela gently asked the trembling boy. "Come out of there, your mother will be here any minute."

Bev whispered into Angela's ear, "Why do you think he's trying to hide?"

Sammy moaned, grunted and squeaked in desperation, as he realized he couldn't shrink small enough to fit in the cabinet. He ran to the teacher's coat closet. It was forbidden for any child to enter that closet, and the penalty for doing so was usually the most stringent. Students almost never attempted to gain entry, even when raging. Sammy threw caution to the wind and dove in. He curled into a ball on his knees, his back against the closet wall. Then he began covering himself with all of the supplies and junk on the floor of the closet. He began closing the door to the closet when Bev stuck her foot in the door's path.

The door popped backward out of Sammy's hand when it hit her foot.

"What are you doin' down there, Mister Sammy," Bev playfully asked, her arms akimbo, head cocked, brow knit in maternal concern. With a child in crisis, she seemed like her normal self to Angela, who was still a little worried about her emotional downturn earlier in the afternoon.

Sammy said nothing and scrambled out of his nest to try closing the door, again.

Bev blocked his access to the door by kneeling before him in the door jamb.

"It's gonna be okay, Sammy," she explained. "This is going to be a good meeting. You won't get in trouble. You can even play with Angela while Mrs. Regina and I talk with your mom."

Sammy reared back as deeply into the closet as he could.

"You'll have fun," she said turning to Angela who was out of Sammy's line of sight, just beyond the pass-through door. "Won't you guys have fun, Angela?"

Angela grimaced but sounded chipper in response, "You betcha."

The behavior specialist peered over Bev's shoulder to discover Sammy trying to hide in a nest of winter boots, sweaters and school supplies. Her despair at having to wait another hour or two for her shower vanished as the sight of the poor, terrified little boy tugged at her heart strings.

"Yeah, Bev, I think Sammy and I are gonna have so much fun, the grownups are gonna wanna quit their meeting and join us. I've got crayons, puzzles, Play Doh. Heck, I might not wanna go home."

Sammy could not be distracted from his task.

A short, obese woman strode into the room while Bev and Angela watched Sammy with deep concern. She wore coke-bottle glasses, the lenses yellowed by the oil from her skin and dusted by crushed eye crusties. Her hair was helmet-like, matted and short. The woman's flesh looked equally in need of washing, but she didn't smell particularly foul. She wore a clean T-shirt with a gargantuan Winnie the Pooh face on it. Her huge purse had a dozen different Pooh character keychains of various sizes latched to the strap ring. Attached to the keychains were a zillion keys for which she couldn't have had any possible use.

To a stranger, her facial expressions, mannerisms and childish comportment could make her appear to be mentally disabled, but in reality she was very intelligent and exceedingly manipulative.

Bev was the first to see her enter and greeted her from the floor.

"Hi, Lulu," Bev turned to the frightened child. "Sammy, come on out. You're mom's here."

Angela looked over at the woman and caught her breath. A bolt of fear spiked down her spine. Her psychological fight-or-flight response kicked in.

La Bruja! A younger, whiter La Bruja, she thought. It was as if a ghost, or more accurately, a demon from her distant past reincarnated before her eyes.

Reading beyond Lulu's kid-friendly camouflage of cartoon buffoonery, Angela was mesmerized by the brown saucers scrutinizing her through the coke bottles. Angela saw through a mask she knew few others could see beyond. Yet, from under Lulu's veil of innocence, Angela recognized a roiling soul full of hatred and fury.

Suddenly, everything about Sammy made sense to her.

Angela didn't just see the monster who terrified Sammy into the state he was in. Angela already was intimately acquainted with an uncommonly vicious victim-turned-victimizer character similar to Lulu from her own childhood.

Angela's reaction to her fight-or-flight instinct was to fight.

An empowered adult now, flight never had a chance in Angela's soul. Her initial childhood fear of La Bruja vanished, and rekindled her burning desire to put an end to the suffering imposed by the La Brujas of the world. In fact, it was that desire that drove her to study and pursue psychology as a profession.

All of this flashed through Angel's mind in a split second.

Despite the churning emotions within her, Angela maintained an outer calm. Unafraid, she shook Lulu's hand and welcomed Lulu into the classroom. She wondered what Lulu read into her.

Lulu merely gave Angela a limp handshake and held eye contact until more women, different social workers, walked into the room. It was a subtle attempt at intimidation, but Angela never broke her gaze or welcoming countenance.

As coldly and accurately as Angela read bitter cruelty in Lulu's eyes, there was far more to Lulu than the pure evil in her treatment of Sammy. As her son's casefile already filled one-and-a-half large file folders, her's could fill a filing cabinet.

She, too, was a sterling example of the system's failure to protect the innocent. The motherless child of a child-molesting father, Lulu was beaten, neglected and raped for years. Sometimes her uncle and family friends joined in on the abuse. Eventually rescued by social services, she was given over to foster families and institutions that didn't treat her much better.

Unloved, grossly undereducated and virtually unemployable, the system finally put her to out pasture when she gave birth to Sammy.

Deemed a mentally-disabled single mother with little hope for sustainable employment, Lulu was given a free apartment, free food, free health care, free child services and more with nothing expected of her. As necessary and useful as those services are for many Americans, it was a miserably depressing situation for Lulu.

To escape and strive for more would mean the immediate dissolution of those services so crucial to her survival. Until she got an education and a job to support herself and Sammy with a livable income, Lulu would desperately need those services. Yet something as simple as a part-time, minimum-wage job at Big Box Store to occupy her time could take it all away from her.

The situation was genuinely hopeless and absolutely insane.

Yet, despite all of the personal misery and suffering Lulu had survived, it did not justify and excuse her intolerable perpetuation of the cycle of violence against her own son—the physical and psychological outlet for her powerful rage over every hideous thing done to her.

The women who entered the room were a fraction of her network of social service contacts. Lulu stoically turned to face them. To the various social workers there on her or Sammy's behalf, Lulu was the textbook personification of the woman they all hoped to save from a cruel, merciless world. Unfortunately, they were 20 years too late, and she had grown into a monster they never dreamed existed.

Bev introduced Angela to the women she later described as Lulu's entourage, ostensibly there in Sammy's best interest: Sammy's DCW social worker, Twyla; the DCW director, Virginia; Sammy's Average Mental Health Center social worker; Sammy's court appointed guardian ad litem; and Lulu's Battered Women's services coordinator.

Angela received them all warmly, still thinking they were on Sammy's (and subsequently her) side. They enthusiastically welcomed her into the fold of children's mental health services.

Then the DCW case worker approached Sammy in the closet. "What are you doing in there, silly? C'mon out an' say hi, and give your mom a big ol' hug."

Sammy would rather have hugged an electric fence during a rainstorm. He shook his head violently.

Bev shot Angela a nervous glance, and Angela rolled her eyes in disbelief as the case worker seemed poised to touch off another outburst and deluge of spit.

Virginia, who was extremely familiar with Sammy's case and the recipient of a gob or two of Sammy's saliva, witnessed the exchange between Bev and Angela. *Jesus,* she thought. *The kid's hiding in the closet. Who knows what these women had just gone through to get him this calm? Is Twyla setting him up to explode?*

"C'mon, Sammy. Give Mummy a big, ol' hug," Twyla continued.

"Shut up!" was all Bev and Angela wanted to scream at the woman.

Virginia wished she had the power of telepathy to warn Twyla, *"Don't push it."*

Lulu masked her thoughts with a flat affect. *I don't want that semen demon to touch me.*

The other women tittered innocently thinking that the cute 6-year-old's stage fright was caused by the age-old, boy-girl cootie social conflict.

Sammy's brain whirled in calculations geared to maximize his odds for survival. *If I hug Mom, I'll get less of a beating for making her look good in public. But will that make her less mad for me touching her?*

He was beyond crying in frustration. He completely disengaged his consciousness and emerged from his nest like a zombie to lifelessly hug the monster who damned by him giving him life.

The entourage smiled and cooed as they watched Sammy hug Lulu.

Angela watched Lulu instead and marveled at the momentary look of utter revulsion that flooded Lulu's face when her son made physical contact. She further marveled at how quickly Lulu recomposed herself as the ill-fated, sympathetic single mom.

No one saw the reaction but Angela.

Anxious to get the meeting over with, Mrs. Regina entered the room with an armload of copies and files. She ushered everyone to the big table in the room.

Bev dismissed Angela to babysit Sammy.

Angela quickly whispered in her ear, "Don't forget to tell them about the suicide threat."

"I got it covered. Don't worry."

Unfamiliar with I.E.P.s, Angela hoped this meeting would result in Sammy being removed from his home. After all, he threatened suicide, she made the proper reports and DCW was present along with a court appointed guardian. She assumed the day would end well for Sammy, not that she'd mention a word of it to him. She didn't want to handle any more weird behavior.

Angela led Sammy next door, leaving the pass-through door open for better eavesdropping.

During the next two hours, Sammy never spoke a word. Angela

tried to get him to talk about anything, but it was useless. They played with blocks, Matchbox cars, Play Doh and crayons. The time crept slowly for both of them. And maddeningly for both of them, they could barely make out what was being said in the other room.

What little they did hear was high praise for Lulu. Her strength, courage, love, tenderness, dedication, all for that deeply disturbed little boy. She simply sat there looking lost and pathetic, pretending to be confused by the intricacies of Sammy's I.E.P. That's what it took to keep the money and services flowing—to keep living. She defended her eligibility for such services with the skill of a consummate trial lawyer.

And while the women next door sang Lulu's praises, not one person mentioned doing anything to enhance Sammy's well-being.

Sammy didn't expect any help. He knew better. Everyone was supposed to be helping him, but no one did. Then again, your mother is supposed to love you.

Angela, on the other hand, was appalled. She wondered how all of these educated women could be so taken by the charade. Even if everything about the persona Lulu presented to the entourage was true, didn't the fact Sammy had shown virtually no progress in two years in the program, stand for anything? Didn't the fact his file was filled with reports of abuse by this woman have any bearing? Didn't the fact that those reports were still being made prove she wasn't changing her act? Why didn't they acknowledge Lulu's abuse of Sammy? Why did they remain duplicitous? Didn't they realize they were here for the kids, not to be cheerleaders for the abusers? Angela's mind raced.

Sammy absorbed himself in the construction of a Lego tower. Angela watched him thoughtfully. Sammy's Lego building was the most normal behavior she had ever witnessed in him. Reconsidering his plight, she silently forgave him for spitting all over her. She silently apologized for wishing she could kill him when he was raging earlier in the day. Too many others seemed to be in line to abuse him, while the line to save him was empty.

Remembering the spit, the head butting and the bitchells, Angela realized those were the ugly parts of this job she knew she had to accept. After witnessing the duplicity of the bureaucracy in Sammy's abuse, she knew that was the part of the job she would not accept. Taking a deep breath, she mentally moved to take her place at the head of the empty line to save Sammy.

Chapter 6

Beverly
(Tuesday Night)

Beverly sat on her sofa in the living room with the lights out. Her mind raced with ideas for group, individual therapy sessions, classroom interventions, breakthroughs in understanding the motivations of her students, their parents and her coworkers. She was having a blast riding a manic high. It sure beat the wave of depression that hit her earlier in the day before Sammy's I.E.P.

Bev had stopped taking her meds for her bipolar disorder against her therapist's recommendation shortly after Angela was hired. Bev wanted to be at the top of her game helping to train Angela. She also wanted to harness her manic energy to help get caught up on paperwork.

Regardless of Bev's perceived advantages to going off the meds, there were downsides to riding the highs and lows—48 hours of sleepless, mealless activity and flooding dark memories and flashes of suicidal ideation. The pills helped neutralize her emotions and keep her out of trouble, running on an even keel. Other pills took the edge off her anxieties tied to her diagnosis of posttraumatic stress disorder from childhood abuse.

Off the meds, it was quite possible to be "normal" for days, weeks or months at a time. But the highs and the depressions often still get as much time on the court.

The downside of the meds, Bev thought, was the way they made her feel like someone else. There was that low-grade mental fog, a lack of sex drive and constant hunger. She hated the artificial mellow that seemed to keep her from feeling like her normal self—the normal self that wasn't obsessing over her anxieties and dark memories.

Tuesday evening's racing thoughts felt good. They helped her decompress as she rehashed the day and the dramas at work. The only time the racing thoughts felt bad was when they turned introspective and negative. So far her racing thoughts seemed only to help resolve in her head the various problems at work.

Feeling freed of the medication's foggy grip, Bev was euphoric. It was good to be back in the saddle. *What the Hell does that shrink I go to know. I'm a goddamn shrink; I know when I'm ready to get off the meds.*

Fuck. I can't believe how fat those damn things made me. I was hungry all the time and couldn't stop stuffing my face.

Bev got up and found her way to the spare bedroom where she kept an elliptical trainer. She stripped off her clothes and mounted the machine naked. She pumped the machine with her arms and legs as fast a she could.

She watched a full-length mirror in front of the trainer, hoping to see her nonexistent body fat melt away. She hadn't eaten anything since breakfast, nor had she drunk anything but coffee.

"C'mon, Bitch," she locked eyes with herself, sweat forming on her brow. "Work off all that flab. Look at yourself; you're so disgusting. So fat. Pump faster, Bitch. You'll be dead at 40, you're so huge—not that you've done anything deserving of such a long life. Look at those stupid kids you can't help. Pump, pump! Sammy. Now there's the most fucked up kid in the world, and you can't do something as simple as getting him out of that monstrous woman's home. You're worthless. Faster, Bitch! No wonder your fucking husband left you—said he couldn't take your roller coaster mood swings anymore, your 'obsessions.' Whatever. Bastard. Christ, look at your big ass. Move it!"

Bev kept pushing herself on the trainer at her peak speed. Her soaked hair clung to her face. She didn't remove the strands stuck in her eyes. She didn't blink or lose contact with the mirror. Her pores rained freely, forming a small puddle at the base of the machine.

Hunger, dehydration and exhaustion were taking their toll on what little grip on reality she clung to. That's when a posttraumatic stress-induced flashback hit her like an armor-plated Hum-Vee.

Her eyes no longer focused on the mirror, just a distant place in time. She furiously worked the machine while crying and begging, "Don't touch me there, Daddy. Stop it. Stop licking me there. Please! Take it out; take it out. It hurts; it hurts; it hurts; it hurts. Please."

Beverly passed out mid-stride. The momentum of the elliptical trainer threw her body against the control console, severely bruising her ribs just below her breasts.

The pain woke her up, but she was too disoriented to regain her balance and fight gravity. As she continued to fall, she bruised her shoulder, slamming into the left ski-pole-like grip of the machine. She blacked out again when her head smacked the floor.

Chapter 7

Little Victories
(Wednesday)

Bev looked like death warmed over when Angela arrived at school the next morning. Bev's hair was a wreck. She had dark bags under her eyes. Her skin was ashen. She appeared to be wearing only pajamas and slippers. She had a foot-tall insulated coffee mug looming over several stacks of papers and files upon which she was furiously scribbling.

"You okay, Bev?"

"Oh, hi." The mildly surprised therapist greeted her warmly, looking up from the stack of notes she was writing. "What are you doing here so early?"

"I hope you don't mind. I thought if I got here a half hour early, maybe we could talk about yesterday's I.E.P. I just wanted to know what happened. We left so quickly afterward. I promise I won't mark it on my time card."

"Is it 7:30 already? Dear Lord," Bev said absently. "By all means mark it."

Bev had been in the school since 1 a.m. After she regained consciousness, she drank a glass of water, brewed a pot of coffee, put on her pajamas and decided to assuage her guilt by coming into work for an hour or two to get her reports up to date and burn off some of her frenetic energy. She thought it was 5 a.m. when Angela arrived.

"Bev, you are a mess. Are you sure you're okay?"

"I'm fine," she lied. Her ribs throbbed. Breathing hurt. Talking was almost unbearable. "I got up early, and thought I could get a few reports written, go home, shower and return before anyone was the wiser."

"If you want to go, I can wait to talk until after group. It's not that big of a deal."

"Don't be silly," Bev said. "What do you want to know?"

"What did you talk about? What did you decide?"

Bev groaned a little from the pain in her shoulder and ribs. "Well, to be honest, mostly we just talked about what a wonderful humanitarian Lulu is. Otherwise, our game plan for Sammy is to keep pluggin' away."

"That's it?"

"Lulu is gonna get some more free how-to-be-a-better-parent classes."

"Was that their response to Sammy wanting to kill himself?"

"We didn't talk about that. It really wasn't the time or place."

Angela's eyes bugged out.

Bev interjected, "To quote the Wicked Witch of the West: 'These things must be handled delicately.'

"Certainly, we want DCW and the rest of Lulu's precious entourage to know how vile she is. But if we drop a bomb in their laps in front of Lulu, they instantly run to her defense and insist that we are picking on a poor, defenseless, retarded single mother. She has them eating out of the palm of her hand."

Angela's hackles were up. "They'd defend her? Haven't they read the file of all the abuse complaints against her?"

"Maybe some of them have, but state law says to always give the benefit of the doubt to the parent. And you know poor Lulu is trying her hardest to be a good mom," Bev sarcastically added.

Angela sputtered invective.

"Hold on there," Bev interrupted. "I have never seen a woman as emotionally charged as I have seen in you these past two days. Are you normally like this, or is it just P.M.S.?"

Angela hated that question. It wasn't the first time she'd been asked it, and it only made her angrier. She didn't have P.M.S., and she despised how people blamed her logic-driven sense of righteous indignation on her period. It was as dumb as blaming it on a need to get laid. What could be more illogical? Why shouldn't you be mad as hell for allowing a suicidal 6-year-old to be forced to live with his abusive mother? Why shouldn't you be fighting mad about a raped 4-year-old being forced to return to her incestuous grandfather? Starting her period or getting laid wouldn't make her feel any better about being practically duplicitous in the abuse of children.

Instead of mounting yet another soapbox and telling Bev what she thought about the question, she deemed it wiser to hold her tongue. "No. That has nothing to do with it."

"I still think I'm gonna dread your cycle," Bev tried to joke. She was exhausted and sore. She'd have said anything to keep Angela from going on another tirade.

Angela heaved an exasperated sigh. "I just never imagined so many atrocities happen in the open and go seemingly ignored by the very people who are supposed to put a stop to them."

Bev yawned and regretted it the second her chest began to expand. "Kid, I'm afraid you're gonna have to get used to it. You are rarely going to succeed in saving or fixing some kid's life in one fell swoop. You have got to do it in baby steps."

Angela listened closely, and Bev continued. "It's like your debate tournaments. You never won just by opening your mouth. You took your time and picked apart your opponent's argument until there was nothing left to it. You delivered a crushing parting shot, and then the judges had no choice but to give you the trophy.

"It's the same at this job. You're building a legal case in which the state's various rules and options must be thoroughly pursued until the state has no choice but to remove the child. With these kids' treatment and with the state's legal system, you can't expect the big win with every phone call. You must be satisfied with the little victories because they'll ultimately lead to the big win."

Angela nodded as she processed all that Bev explained.

Bev stood, collecting her purse and coffee mug. "If you'll excuse me, I'll be back as fast as I can. If I'm not back in time, start group without me."

"Are you sure I can do that?"

"No problem. You can do anything you put your mind to. Just keep the conversation light and fluffy and hand out lots of beads."

"Okay," Angela hesitantly agreed. "Thanks for the pep talk."

Angela admitted to herself that Bev made a lot of sense. While getting the room ready, she hoped the day would go more smoothly than the previous one. Another day with wild banshees could turn her into a lunatic.

Before long, the arriving buses were viewed through the classroom window. Soon all of the students were present and accounted for next door...except for Sallie.

Mrs. Regina stuck her head through the open dividing door. "Would you please call Sallie's house?"

"Sure thing," Angela said, heading for the phone. After dialing Sallie's house, a phone company message explained that the line had been disconnected.

She reported this to Mrs. Regina who told her to call DCW to let them know. She did and then lined up the Big Kids' Group.

Ronnie gave her a wink. "Let me know if you need any help."

Angela graciously smiled and nodded.

Charlie, Kevin, Franz, Violet, Lashaun and Jefferson lined up at the door without a fuss. They got their carpets without bickering and seemed to be running on low energy.

Mrs. Regina later explained to Angela how frantic, miserable days usually burn out the kids worse than the adults—leading to unusually tranquil mornings after.

Following Bev's instructions, Angela heaped on the praise.

"Okay. Who wants to start?" she asked after passing out a round of imaginary beads.

"What do you want us to talk about?" Lashaun asked.

"Hmmm," Angela bit her lip, stumped on the first question. After the previous day's chaos, she didn't actually expect group to make it this far, especially without Bev.

All six kids laughed when they knew she was unprepared.

Angela's mind raced: *I can't discuss anything therapeutic without Bev. Man, I wish she was here.*

She fired from the hip. "What did you do after school yesterday?"

Charlie rolled his eyes. *How boring could she get?* he wondered.

"Lashaun, why don't you start?"

Even Lashaun looked bored. Nonetheless, to avoid Charlie's wrath, he still had to be careful about his response. That left one subject upon which they could universally agree.

"I watched 'SpongeBob SquarePants.'"

This caught the other boys' attention and respect, and the next 20 minutes were a barely controllable period in which every potty joke on the show was told…twice.

Charlie: "Which one did you see?"

Kevin: "Was it the farting one?"

Jefferson: "I love that one."

Lashaun: "Me, too."

Franz: "I love the bubbles every time he farts."

Hahahahahahaha

"Or the time that…or when…oh, oh and then there's the…"

Little did Angela know, Bev put a moratorium on SpongeBob discussion at the start of the school year, after all 5 boys began running around the room—each with a hand under an armpit making noxious sounds.

94

Violet scowled and kept remarking at how uncouth the boys were, but, in truth, she wished she could join them. Unsure how, she sulked in rebellious contempt.

Angela tried many times to rein in the conversation, but, as a rookie behavior specialist, she had temporarily forgotten the magical power of the beads' positive reinforcement. By the time she did remember, she only had enough time to settle them down for class.

Bev returned, clean but haggard, while the older kids filed out of the room. "How'd it go, Angela?"

She groaned. "I learned more about SpongeBob SquarePants than I ever dreamed possible."

"Boys," Bev reproached. "What did I say about discussing SpongeBob in class?"

The group collectively gave a sheepish smile and quickly crossed the threshold into the safety of the classroom.

Beverly managed to muster enough energy to cast a disapproving gaze mixed with a slow, shamey-shamey head shake. But that was all 24 hours without food and sleep would allow.

Having heard some of the farting noises through the patrician, the little kids group was eager to line up. They behaved beautifully, while getting their rugs.

Bev could barely drink enough coffee to stay upright, which concerned Angela, who ran the group.

Lacking a better idea, Angela again asked how the group members' nights went. Bev's presence kept the group in check, and they talked about playing with friends, siblings and pets. Appropriate T.V. conversation.

It was a silent Sammy's candor that provided interesting material to work with and brought Bev back on high alert.

When asked what he did, Sammy smiled and replied in his choppy, babyish manner. "I run 'way."

"You ran away?" Angela repeated.

"I run 'way."

"Sammy," Bev began, "Why did you run away? Where did you go?"

"Freddy," Sammy explained in a low voice, raising his fingers as if they were blades.

"Freddy isn't real," Lionel said, half convinced—both a little afraid and tired of Sammy's Freddy obsession.

Bev didn't want to linger on the subject of Freddy. It was enough to know that Freddy was the boy's manifestation of fear. Talking about Freddy would be counterproductive when she urgently needed other details.

"Where did you go?" Bev pressed on.

"The Cowboy."

"You met a cowboy?" Bev asked, confused.

Sammy shook his head, no.

"What did you see?" Bev continued, hoping to put the child's description into context.

"Daddies."

"Were the daddies with their little boys?"

"No. Just daddies." Sammy, as many of the children did, assumed that all grown men were daddies and all grown women were mommies. Angela, a childless adult, still confused most of the children by not conforming to their world view. Many thought she secretly had several kids she wasn't telling them about.

Bev knit her eyebrows and looked at Angela.

Angela had a glimmer of an idea. "Did you see any signs you could read?"

Sammy nodded and smiled, as everyone seemed fascinated by his adventure.

"What did they say?"

"Bud. Miller."

"The Cowboy Bar?" Angela inquired. "Is that where you went?"

Vigorous nodding. "That's what I said, 'The Cowboy.' "

"That's four miles from your house," Bev declared with astonishment. "How did you get there?"

"Run. Walk."

"What happened after you got to The Cowboy Bar?" Angela asked.

This was Sammy's favorite part of the whole adventure. He answered with great wide-eyed enthusiasm. "Police car. Policeman take me home."

"Were you scared?" Angela asked.

"No," Sammy said before listing every benefit of the ride—from the front seat! "Bang-bang. Sirens. Lights. Radio. Computer."

Sammy was still in awe. Lionel and Edward were jealous. Ted was too, but he refused to show it.

Bev decided to teach a lesson from Sammy's experience to keep the other boys from running away. "Sammy, that's very good that you got a policeman to take you home," Bev started. "But you shouldn't run away from home. We've talked about this before. Do you remember why it isn't good to run away?"

He didn't remember; anything beat staying home with his mother in a rage against him. He impishly, and uncontrollably, shook his head. Acting silly was another of his defense mechanisms when he felt insecure and needed a distraction from the problems (mental or physical) he was actively avoiding.

"Edward. Do you remember?" Bev asked, engaging the rest of the group.

"'Cause you'll get in trouble?" Edward guessed. Angela gave him a bead for trying.

Lionel's hand shot up.

Bev answered Edward before calling on Lionel. "Yes. You might get in trouble, but there's another reason to be careful."

Ted now had his hand up, but Bev chose Lionel who was using his right hand to brace his left arm held high aloft.

"Because you gotta beware of Stranger Danger," Lionel explained.

"Very good. You get a bead, too." Bev congratulated. "Ted, why should we beware of Stranger Danger?"

" 'Cause Stranger Danger might try to hurt you?"

"That's a bead for you, Ted," Bev rewarded. "Who should we go outside with, Sammy?"

Sammy was already lost in LaLa Land, still shaking his head. Remembering the fastest way to calm him down was to actively ignore his self-soothing behaviors and take the attention off him, she passed the question on to Edward. "Who is it safe to go outside with?"

"Ummm. My parents?"

"Very good. That's another bead for you. Who else, Lionel?"

"Teachers."

"Excellent. Bead. Who else, Ted?"

"My grandparents."

"Yes. Bead. Other relatives such as aunts, uncles or other adults your parents say it's okay to be with."

The phone rang, and Angela answered it while Bev wrapped up group. "Hello, Average Elementary Daytreatment."

There was a hesitation on the other end of the phone. "Uh, is this Angela?"

"Yes. Who's this?"

"Uh, it's Janice at DCW."

Angela stiffened her spine and remained polite, as she braced for another unpleasant encounter: "How can I help you?"

"I've got some bad news to report."

Angela's heart sank. "What's that?"

"I just learned that Sallie's family moved to another state."

"How's that possible in just two days?"

"Apparently, her grandfather has a house there, and they dropped everything when they knew we were intensifying our investigation."

"That's awful," Angela said, disgusted at how easily Sallie's grandfather managed to escape. "Is there anything we can do?"

Janice paused and almost choked on her suddenly very meek voice. "I'm really sorry. I should have talked to Sallie when I had the chance."

Janice's remorse was bottomless. She managed to hold back her tears as she explained, "We are going to forward all of our files to the other state's DCW and police. This case won't be dropped. If you can send your files to her new school that would be a huge help."

"I don't know what our waivers and restrictions say, but we'll do all that we can," Angela assured.

Janice gave Angela Sallie's new school's phone number, and they hung up. It would be the last time Angela would hear from Janice who was still determined to quit her job with DCW.

Angela related the call to Bev, who was too exhausted to be surprised by anything.

Beverly shook her head but tried to look on the bright side. "You see. Little victories."

"I don't follow," Angela questioned, feeling defeated.

"You had two of them. First, a DCW agent actually apologized to you. A rare event. Second, because of your aggressive pursuit of Sallie's defense, there will be more movement to further Sallie's case than there has been in months. What's more, DCW is doing everything it can to keep the other state's DCW on top of the situation. With any luck, they'll catch her grandfather before long.

"Well, I guess when you look at it that way, it was a *little* victory," Angela hesitantly agreed.

"You bet it was," Bev encouraged. "Did you talk to Janice about Sammy?"

"Shoot!" Angela said, remembering not to swear in an elementary school. "No. It slipped my mind. I'll call back after recess."

"Okay. Ask for Twyla, that's Sammy's case worker."

"Will do," she acknowledged, turning to head out for recess.

Bev stopped her. "Listen, I think I'm gonna call in sick to the office. I feel awful."

Angela faced her again. "No offense, but you look horrible. Are you going to be all right getting home?"

"Yeah. I think I'll be okay once I get some sleep and some food in me." And meds, she mentally added, as she watched her hands tremble. "Just remember to do all of your paperwork and help out next door."

"You got it," Angela affirmed before offering, "If you need anything, don't hesitate to call me. I can bring you some cold medicine or OJ from the store after work."

Bev nodded, and the women said their good-byes before Angela joined the class lining up for recess.

Outside, Angela told Carla and Ronnie about Sallie. Both were upset, but they'd seen this type of thing before.

Angela was hoping to spend the next 15 minutes of recess commiserating with her colleagues when Sammy warily ambled to her.

Without a word, he slipped his warm little hand into hers and gave her arm a gentle tug.

The young woman wasn't in a mood to play, but she realized this was perhaps the first time Sammy had ever reached out to anyone for anything. It was certainly the first time Carla and Ronnie had seen such behavior from him and quickly shooed Angela off to play with the boy.

"Where are we going, Sammy?"

"Swings."

Sammy hopped onto an open swing and asked, "Push?"

Angela gave him a few delicate pushes. His legs hanged limply below him.

"Higher?" he requested.

"You gotta pump your legs, and you'll go higher," Angela told him. "Push?"

Angela pushed, and Sammy began a discombobulated attempt at pumping. Realizing this also might have been his first time on the swings, Angela tried to help him. "Watch the other kids, Sammy. See how they pump their legs and swing?"

Sammy watched and began to get the hang of propelling himself. "Higher?" he asked again.

Angela pushed him, again.

Smiling and pumping he said, "Higher."

He giggled, and she pushed him a little harder.

Soon Sammy's joy and the exercise Angela was getting combined to make her feel better about the morning.

"Higher!" the boy shouted with glee.

Getting carried away in the fun they were sharing, Angela overdid the next push. Sammy squealed with delight at the rush of speed but shrieked when the swing's chains went slack—his back parallel to the ground. Panic flooded both their hearts as Sammy began to free fall. The chains snapped taut, and Sammy held on. When he realized he wasn't in danger, he cackled with euphoria.

"Harder! Harder! Harder!"

Recovering her composure, Angela kept pushing hard, but not hard enough to make the chains go slack again.

Sammy couldn't have been happier.

The two could have kept swinging until lunchtime, but the recess bell rang.

Sammy wasn't ready to pack it in, so Angela began to try to coax him back to class. "C'mon, Sammy. Time to go inside."

The little boy kept pumping, even though Angela had stopped pushing. "Nuh-uh."

"C'mon, Buddy. We gotta go."

Giggles and pumping.

"Don't make me stop you," Angela playfully warned.

Sammy pumped harder.

"Alright. It's time for this little airplane to land on its Navy aircraft carrier," she warned.

When Sammy reached the peak of his backswing, Angela grabbed the sides of Sammy's swing seat in mid-flight and gently brought him down to a stop.

Sammy hopped off the swing onto the playground gravel. "Fun!"

"I had a great time, too," she said, stroking his upper back and guiding him toward the line back inside.

"Push me again at lunch?"

"What's the magic word?"

"Pleeeeze?"

"Absolutely."

Sammy tightly held Angela's hand all the way back to the classroom. And as they walked, Angela basked in the warm sun and the trust of this little boy who only yesterday had been spitting on her.

She beamed radiantly.

Little victories.

Chapter 8

Staff Development Meetings
(Friday)

"Whew," Angela sighed as she walked back into the daytreatment room. "All the kids are loaded on the bus and on their way home for the weekend."

"T.G.I.F!" Bev exclaimed. "So how do you feel, having survived your first full week as a mental health professional?"

Angela kicked back in her desk chair. "Excited and exhausted."

"I don't blame you; it's exhausting work."

Bev had greatly improved since her mid-week breakdown. She had slept, eaten and gone back on her meds. She seemed her same old self to Angela on Thursday and this day. Angela's concerns about Bev's stability on Wednesday had dissipated.

"Well," Angela stated. "I think I'll wrap up all of today's assorted notes and filings and go home, if you don't mind."

"As a matter of fact, I do mind."

Angela straightened up in her chair and looked concerned. "I haven't screwed up anything too badly yet, have I?"

Bev laughed. "Hardly. It's just that every week I'm supposed to give you a performance review. It's harmless, I promise."

Angela relaxed, but only a little. "I suppose we could do that first."

"Official though it may be," Bev explained, "There's no rule that says we have to have said meeting here. I propose The Nook And Cranny."

The Nook, as it was called by the regulars, was a downtown bar for professionals. It was quiet, featured the work of local artists on its walls and was known for wines and appetizers.

"I'd love to, but I don't have any money."

"Not to worry," Bev stated. "I'm the one calling the meeting and picking the bar; it'll be my treat. Now hurry up and finish your bureaucratic nonsense."

Within 45 minutes the therapy team was getting comfortably settled at The Nook.

"What's your poison?" Bev asked Angela.

"I don't know. What are you having?"

Bev turned to the waitress and ordered the house white zinfandel, and Angela followed suit. The rookie then asked her boss how she had performed for the week.

"You're doing fine. Personally, I can't wait for you to be certified for physical restraints. Otherwise, keep pluggin'."

"There's got to be more to it than that." Angela said. "I really feel like I don't know what I'm doing half the time. I feel confident in reading and analyzing the kids, but I don't know what to do with that information."

"Angela, you do have an amazing gift for analysis. You just need experience working with the kids. Never hesitate to call their bluffs. What you really need to do is get faster at rewarding and deducting beads—and announcing the reasons for doing it. It's a lot to juggle, but you also need to catch kids on set ups. When Charlie sets up Kevin and Kevin escalates, you need to be sure to punish Charlie as much as Kevin. Most important, you need to reward positive behavior as much as humanly possible.

"But you're doing amazingly well for your first week. Decoding Freddy and Sammy-speak was more than any of us have been able to do since he started with our program two years ago. More incredibly, you're getting Sammy to reach out for human contact. We've still got a long way to go, but this is one helluva start."

"Thank you," Angela said.

"Do you have any other questions or concerns before our wine arrives and we get to party?" Bev inquired.

"Yesterday's meeting at headquarters has me concerned. Are we really on the verge of losing our jobs to state budget cuts like Richard said?"

Bev rolled her eyes, not at Angela, but at Richard.

"I've been working here for what seems like an eternity, and every week Richard tells us we are standing at the brink of oblivion. First of all, it *is* possible for a lot of us to lose our jobs, but it's also illegal for the state to kill children's mental health entirely. Richard means well by keeping us informed, but the budgeting process doesn't even start for another 6 months. There's little to do or worry about in the time being. Try not to let the doom and gloomers bring you down."

"So then, what was the point of that whole meeting?"

"There really wasn't a point," Bev told her. "It's just some regulation that we all must meet once a week. Ninety percent of what's said at our weeklies could be summed up in a two paragraph memo. The other 10 percent is a lame case review.

"Once a month, one of the district's seven school daytreatment programs must present a case with which they are having difficulty. Once you go to a few of these you'll quickly divine the quacks from the mental health professionals with any skill. The quacks have absolutely no understanding of human nature and psychology, even though they have probably read five times more information about the science. They can ace tests and impress certification boards, but they can't apply a single scientific concept to reality, or they constantly apply the wrong ones. The ones who understand what they're doing rarely have this problem and further ensure their reputations by selecting cases they have well in hand, minimizing their exposure and maximizing professional compliments.

"If you haven't already figured it out, we fit in the latter category."

"How many other groups do?" Angela queried.

"One full team, and about three behavior specialists or therapists paired with an idiot. Luckily, they're more experienced—keeping the programs running and the idiots out of too much trouble."

"That sounds kinda scary."

"It's horrifying," Bev affirmed.

Two large glasses of wine arrived.

"This meeting is adjourned." Bev declared, clinking Angela's glass. "Since you didn't run away screaming this week, it appears we'll be working together for some time. I think it's about time we really get to know each other."

Angela demurred and sipped her wine. "There really isn't much to know."

Bev looked at her suspiciously. "You don't have to play coy with me. No one comes straight out of college and talks down a suicidal six-year-old and battles DCW to a draw. You can't learn either skill in a textbook. In fact, I just got done bitching about how at least half the trained therapists in the company can't do that. What's your story? If you don't mind me asking."

Angela smiled slyly from under her veil of the girl-next-door.

"Uh-huh," Bev confirmed her thoughts aloud before sipping her wine. "I think there's an interesting story that's dying to come out. Let's hear it, if it's not too painful."

The young woman knew how to sell a story and took a slug of wine for dramatic effect and confidently leaned over her glass. "It's not too painful. I tamed my demons years ago, but this really isn't a story I want getting around. Can I trust you to keep it a secret?"

Bev answered with sincerity. "Absolutely."

"Fighting DCW was the easy part. Long before I became a debate team champion, my father taught me how to stand up and fight for my rights and the rights of others. Whether it was taking on the catty in-crowd girls in junior high or outright bullies in elementary school or whatever, I've always confronted people for myself and my friends. I was certainly not about to let DCW get away with not helping these kids. Nor am I about to tolerate any abuse from the parents or other perpetrators."

"That's pretty clear," Bev said. "Go on."

"The rest you will never believe. No one, aside from my mom, ever does."

"Why does she believe you?"

"She has the same skills I have. She trained me."

"I've seen you in action, so I have to believe you. What I want to know is, how the hell can anyone teach that to a child? I mean no offense, but at 22, you're hardly a wizened matron or grisled veteran of the field."

"Do you really want to know the details?"

"Oh yeah."

"It might cost you another glass of wine? This could take a little while. Despite several attempts, I've never been able to successfully describe it to anyone. It might sound rather unbelievable at times, but I swear I'm not making any of it up."

"Do your damnedest, girl. I can buy you all the wine it takes to get this story."

"Okay." Angela got comfortable, turning her chair to the wall and leaning back—keeping a casual eye on her surroundings, as she began her story for Bev. "The only real way to explain it is that I grew up in the eye of a hurricane. Despite what I'm about to explain, I really had a great childhood. My parents love me very much. They love each other, too. I was pretty much given anything I could ever really want, plus I was never hit or molested. My parents watched me, my sister and brother closely, were involved with our education and all that jazz. We always had a good home in a good neighborhood. We never lacked for food or clothes."

"So far," Bev interrupted, "This isn't how the story usually goes for those with great insight."

"I know," Angela said. "But to truly understand my abilities and where they came from, you have to know the whole story. What I just explained is all true, and it's a big part of the puzzle. In my family, it is all the outside world ever saw of us. Yet, what is also true is that my mother suffered PTSD. She was molested by her father. Yet to make the matter especially confusing, he was the good guy and her protector. I don't mean in a Stockholm Syndrome sense; her mother was blackest evil personified. Imagine Lulu on steroids. Her mother beat her, starved her, molested her, beat her siblings and beat her some more— sometimes knocking her out for days at a time. Sometimes, my mother would be locked in the attic for days at a time. As bad as my grandfather sounds, he was all that stood between my mother and death.

"By the time I came along, my grandfather was dead, and my mother had buried all of her abusive memories pretty deep inside. My father never knew anything about her abused past when he married her.

"They lived in loving peace and harmony, and my father never saw my grandmother as anything more than an overbearing pain in the ass. He never would have guessed a brutal abuser."

"Okay," Bev interjected, hoping to move the story along. "But I still don't see any connections yet."

"Hang in there; I'm getting to them," Angela explained before continuing. "As a very little girl, I adored my grandmother. But as I got older and began questioning more, my relationship with her changed. While she never hit or molested me, she started to belittle me and degrade me. What started with calling me stupid evolved to death threats by the time I was in the fourth or fifth grade. She lived to control everyone around her and ruin any enjoyment you could find in life. She'd break up family plans, whine, complain, carry on and belabor how the world hated her. Worst of all was the way she'd get inside your mind and play on your insecurities, fears and loves.

"When I was only four, I once stopped her from beating my mother bloody. By the time my little sister was four, grandma began turning against her, too. I was eight and often ran interference, protecting Marixa, my sister. She doesn't remember any of the bad parts about grandma, which is good on many levels, and my brother, Hector, was too little to remember grandma at all.

"My father was in the dark about most of this until I was about 10, when he overheard my grandmother riding me pretty hard one night.

105

He kicked her out of the house and never let her back in.

"From then on, he joined my mother and me in hating her. Between the three of us, we would only refer to her as La Bruja, or the 'old witch' in Spanish.

"La Bruja died when I was 12. I was truly happy she was dead and happy she could never harm us again…or so I thought."

Angela paused for a drink, Bev commented, "God. She sounds awful, but I don't understand how this made you Super Shrink."

The rookie behavior specialist smiled. "I told you this was a long story. Without knowing all of this, the rest of this madness won't make any sense."

"Okay. Carry on."

Angela sipped again and continued. "As you can imagine, very little made sense to me growing up. Tired of living in fear and doubt, I always turned to my mother for explanations about why grandma was so mean or lied or didn't make sense. Although my mom never went to college or studied psychology, she researched it on her own. That and more than 30-something years of abuse taught her a lot, and she explained to me the best she could about why grandma was so F.I.T.H.

"One of my earliest memories about these discussions happened when I was five or six, sitting on the kitchen floor as my mom washed the dinner plates. I remember that my question stopped her mid-rinse, and she joined me on the floor to tell me that grandma loved me very much, but that she was very sick in her brain—not cold or flu sick but a special brain sick—and that she really loved me very much and didn't mean any awful things she might say or do. That was good enough for me at the time, and I never took my grandmother's threats or mean words as seriously as I later learned they were meant. Obviously, she was sick.

"Of course, that didn't mean I didn't learn to hate her, but at least I began to understand her.

"As I got older, I asked more questions and my mother gave me more detailed answers.

"Then, several months after La Bruja died, I hit the misery sweepstakes. A death in the family is bad. Then we moved to a new city, which also turned out to suck. Then I dove headlong into puberty, which sucks for everyone. And then mom had a cataclysmic nervous breakdown. It all happened within six months.

"Mom's breakdown was the worst of it. It wasn't a little crying and time for self-discovery. Safe from her parents for the first time in her whole life, those deeply repressed memories came flooding back all at once—demanding to be dealt with.

"Mom went the obsessive-compulsive route, disinfecting the house constantly. She saw germs and blood everywhere, all the time. She hid under tables, chain smoking, trying to hide from the personal demons that were always attacking. She barely left the house for an entire year. The overall breakdown lasted about five years.

"She refused to go on meds, but she did go to some intensive therapy for that entire time. When she wasn't in therapy, she had me.

"It was never a role she intentionally put me into. I wanted to be her secondary therapist, to both help her and myself. I was scared to death about what was going on. This was so much more dramatic and severe than La Bruja. Mom was never violent or abusive to anyone but herself, but not knowing what was making her crazy was making me crazy. I had to be able to calm her down and get her through the afternoon until Dad got home. I also did as much as I could to help Marixa and Hector.

"Yet, there was far more to it than survival or desperation. I found what was going on to be really fascinating. Learning what made Mom tick amazed me. All of the causes and effects of the abuse. The motivations of her parents and what made them tick. It was like an epic novel that you couldn't put down, and a new chapter seemed to reveal more amazing details every day. My mom never skimped on the foundations of the story. She might not describe the graphic particulars, but I was told that graphic particulars did happen. She explained all of the psychological theories and details her therapist told her.

"I was completely hooked and loved learning more and more. As she got better, we got into greater and greater detail about what happened in her family to make it so fucked up. We traced the abuse back for generations, making the most of often seemingly benign family stories that were passed on to her."

Angela paused to take a drink, as Bev marveled and absorbed the story. Clearly, she understood and believed her. It was an incredible story made more so by being true. *Who can make up a story like that?*

"It's beginning to come together for me," Bev said, still soaking in the narrative. *What were the odds*, she wondered, *of someone having all of the experience and knowledge derived from surviving child abuse without physically experiencing the actual abuse? Phenomenal. It's like she said, the eye of a hurricane. Everything is safe and serene in the eye, but everything outside that perfectly safe bubble is so harsh and dangerous. No wonder no one ever believes her.* "That explains how you understand abuse through your mother, but how do you read it and understand it and deal with it so readily in our kids?"

"That's the part that was most painful for me."

"You've already told me far more than I expected. You don't have to go there if you don't want," Bev insisted, afraid she had tripped the wrong wire.

"Nah. Like I said, I've already come to terms with my own demons. I don't mind, and I wouldn't have told you any of this if I wasn't ready to tell you the whole story."

"All right then. I just don't want to pressure you, Angela."

"Not at all," she said, taking another sip from a fresh glass of wine. "Somewhere in late middle school or early high school, I began noticing similarities between my mom's psychology and the mental processes of the kids around me—the way they reacted to certain events or what they said and did. Eventually, I noticed smaller details—facial expressions, nervous habits, clothes, actions, mannerisms, reactions, defense mechanisms, choice of boyfriends, regular friends. What roles did those people fill in their lives?

"I scrutinized everything about everyone to try to understand them better, to see what made them tick. I'd bring my observations home and go over them with my mom. She owed her survival to reading other people, and she happily helped me better learn about other people.

"Our conversations gradually got more philosophical and analytical. We'd spend hours trying to understand what made people act the way they do and what factors in their lives influenced every minute aspect of their personality. Theories constantly evolved, as more details about people we observed developed. Bad theories got thrown out, and better ones grew in their place. There were no absolute rights or wrongs, but every theory we made about someone would be winnowed down to the most realistic possibility. Some of these profiles took minutes to construct. Other theories, primarily the ones behind La Bruja and my mother's other relatives, took years to properly develop. We still have a few open cases, as it were."

"Alright," Bev said. "I believe you, but I also don't. How the hell do you go about proving your so-called theories to be correct? And who the hell has time to collect that type of information without becoming some psycho stalker?"

Angela was used to losing people by this point in time. Credibility was tough to come by for this part of the explanation, but all she could do was tell the truth and explain as best she knew how. "It's difficult to prove our theories. I already said there are few absolutes. With my mother's family, it's like being a police detective. You start with a dead body or a crime that you know in fact did happen and work your way backward. We sought out all the info we could and deduced what we could about the person involved, and we threw zillions of theories at it until one would stick. If nothing sticks you move on until you turn over a new clue.

"Proving our theories about my classmates was easy. First of all, I'm hypervigilant. I see and at least temporarily follow everything going on around me, whether it's in my peripheral or right in front of me. Why do you think my back is to the wall, right now? I've been following what's generally going on around us while talking—scoping the personalities around us, kinda like listening to a radio somewhere in the background. Secondly, most of the people I went to school with were remarkably open, as most people in high school are desperate to be understood by anybody. I asked dozens of questions, both direct and indirect, about my classmates' lives, and they'd answer very candidly. Most people are pretty open about discussing far more than you'd think. It was pretty easy to prove or disprove my theories."

Bev was skeptical, but what Angela explained made sense. As a professional psychologist, she was well away of how open young adults were these days about very personal information. One need only scan the pages of social media to see proof of that. Even Angela was openly chattering away about some very personal details of her life, wanting to be understood.

"So how was this painful?" Bev asked. "I would think that the power to read your classmates and play upon that analysis could have made you queen of your school."

"I suppose it could have, but my ability to read people...to, as my mom and I would say, 'get it' or understand the people at their deepest levels...was depressing as hell," Angela explained. "I had no control over my own abilities. I couldn't turn off the part of my brain that was working in high gear analyzing everyone I came into contact with. I read depression, abuse and misery in far more faces than I would have ever reasonably guessed possible. I once read the statistic that 1 in 4 women will report being raped or sexually abused in her lifetime. I could see, by the time I was 16, that statistic was grossly undercalculated. I wouldn't be surprised if it was 3 in 4 or higher. I have never been able to read boys as well, but I can still read them

109

better than many, and they don't have it much easier. They suffer less sex abuse, but they have enough other problems that can make their lives miserable.

"I was suicidal at the end of my junior year in high school because I couldn't stop reading and analyzing everything and everyone. And little that I observed was happy. I was growing to understand that the world was nothing but a violent, miserable place from which there was no refuge.

"I eventually burned myself out. It taught me to shut down my racing brain. These days I like to say that my radar is always up, but it's rarely *dialed in* anywhere outside of work.

"By senior year, my mom had come out of therapy better than she had been in years. I wrestled my own demons pretty hard through senior year and came out swinging. Life began to look a lot better once I learned to disengage my brain a bit.

"And that's basically about all there is for the short version. Some things were probably better than they sound, and other things might have been a little worse, but all-in-all, that's it."

"Wow," Bev said for a lack of words. "That's quite a story. You've clearly thought this out pretty well. How long were you in therapy to get that all straight?"

"I've always been pretty good at self-analysis," Angela said. "That doesn't mean it is very easy. I found wrestling with my demons pretty grueling and that all fit in with my massive junior year depression. But tough as it is, I know it's necessary, so I face it head on every time I recognize a problem."

"Well, I think I'm beginning to see why you weren't into meds. Neither you nor your mother ever used them, right?" Bev prodded.

"Yep. I figured if we could make it without meds, everybody can. Plus, I'd be afraid of the medicine dulling or interfering with my thought processes—keeping me from working out difficult issues."

"Just remember those same meds keep a lot of people from going totally ape shit or blowing their brains out, too."

"I think I'm beginning to see that now."

"So how was college for you? Where do you stand now, psychologically?" Bev asked, genuinely needing to know from a work perspective and for the safety of the kids.

"College was the best time of my life. Far from home, I had no parents to worry about, no crazy people to deal with and no real responsibility. It was as if I had died and gone to heaven. These days,

I'm doing better than ever. I'm a strong survivor with my past behind me and a whole future of possibilities ahead of me. Although I'm still close to my parents, I love this little city. I'm standing on top of the world, now that I have a real careerlike job."

"That's good," said Bev, encouraged by Angela's self-report. "I just wouldn't count on ever being able to retire, working for $22,000 a year."

Angela laughed. "I was thinking I'd use this experience to get into grad. school for my Psy. D."

"That's probably a good plan. I think those doctorates in psychology are probably the way to go, too. Unlike a traditional doctorate in psychology, you'll be able to prescribe some limited medications. With the shortage in traditional psychiatrists who have to study for 14 years, I think someone with a Psy. D. will be in high demand."

"I hope so," said Angela. There was a temporary lull in the conversation, and both women sipped from their still full second rounds. "Well, what's your story? As our kids would no doubt say, I showed you mine, now show me yours."

Angela laughed at her own joke, not realizing she was pushing Bev across a threshold her boss was not yet ready discuss with anyone. Bev had yet to deal with her demons as Angela had. Bev just treated the symptoms of her psychological issues with moxie or meds. She wasn't ready for therapy.

It's not that Angela didn't already have a pretty good idea about Bev's background. Bev's anorexic physique, eagerness to appease authority figures around her—regardless of her own professional opinions—, reluctance to confront anyone directly and Wednesday's breakdown were all telltale signs of past sex abuse to Angela. Where Angela blundered into the conversation was not realizing that just because Bev was a trained and talented child psychologist it didn't mean she had already dealt with her issues.

As was her nature, Bev's first defense to Angela's question was her moxie, mocking Angela's initial reluctance when Bev had first questioned Angela's past. "There really isn't that much to know. I just got skills, is all."

"C'mon, Boss. You didn't buy that from me," Angela said playfully, not realizing that Bev wasn't playing. "You read people too well, too. I think there's a little abuse in your past."

Unwittingly, Angela had tripped the panic wire.

"I was never abused!" Bev exclaimed, angry about the insinuation. She felt both hurt and under attack. Her gut response was to attack the misperceived attack on her. "I can't believe you'd even think such a thing! My father was a good man."

"I never said he wasn't. I'm sorry. I didn't mean to upset you," Angela apologized profusely. This was far from being the first time she had inadvertently lanced someone's raw psychological nerve endings. The only remedy was to back-peddle as fast as humanly possible. She meant no harm by her questioning, and thought it was appropriate given the cozy discussion they had just had about her dark past. Some innocent, sisterly bonding. But now she was fully aware Bev was nowhere near ready to go there on this subject.

"You think you're so smart with your profiling," Bev continued. "Well, believe you me, you got it wrong this time!"

"You're right. I told you before there were no absolutes, and that I'm frequently wrong."

"Well, don't you go trying to find out what's right, either." Bev commanded, cooling down a little. "It's none of your Goddamn business."

"You're absolutely right," Angela agreed. But Bev had already given away far more details than she suspected. Angela had never mentioned Bev's father, but Bev had just unwittingly given him away. When Angela told Bev she agreed Bev's past was none of her business, she was kicking herself inside.

Of course it's my business, Angela's mind raced. *I work with you in a high-pressure environment. I need to know how you're going to act and react. I've got to get in your head as well as every other staff member and student's head to maximize my ability to help everybody in the room.*

Christ. I know better than to tell people I can read them in the first place. Too many freak out. I can't help reading people; it's impossible for me not to. But, I've got no business opening my Goddamn mouth about it. That's what I've got no business doing!

"I'm sorry," Angela repeated, very remorseful for inadvertently pushing Bev too far. Angela was scared, too. She'd only had this job for a week, and she didn't want to lose it by freaking out the boss this early.

Bev read the fear in Angela's face and calmed down. It didn't take a second for Bev to process how she overreacted in light of Angela's confession about her own past struggles with abuse, even if it was abuse once removed.

"I'm sorry I flew off the handle, Angela."

"No, I should never have said what I said. I'm sorry."

"No, it was a fair question, given how I grilled you. And while I've never been abused, it is fair to tell you that I'm on medicine for depression and obsessive-compulsive disorder. You should know that regardless, in case there's a medical emergency at work. I just don't talk about it, and I definitely don't want you telling anyone else about it."

"You got it, and I'm still sorry."

"How about we talk about something else?" Bev proposed, trying to clear the air. "How about men? That ought to be light and fluffy. You got any?"

"No. Boys don't like me. I like them; don't get me wrong. They just don't like me," Angela explained.

"You're kidding," Bev pushed, trying to totally erase the past minute or two from the evening. "You're cute; you're smart. They should be beating a path to your doorstep."

"I agree, but they don't. And the ones that are interested are all nutcases."

"Girl, they're all nuts," Bev said. "You just gotta find the flavor you like best."

"I guess I'll keep sampling for the time being," Angela shrugged. "What about you?"

Bev shook her head. "I work in a nut house. God knows, I don't need any more at home. I have to keep some small thread of sanity."

Angela politely laughed, and they finished their drinks. A little buzz and a little more small talk seemed to melt away more of the tension.

Finally, Bev asked, "Are you feeling thoroughly mentored and coached as an employee?"

"Yes," Angela affirmed with a lie, eager to put an end to this awkward evening.

"Here, here," Bev added officiously. "I then nominate The Nook as our formal conference locale. Do I hear a seconding?"

"Aye," Angela agreed with bravado on the outside and doubts in her gut. "I will second the motion."

"Motion carries," Bev stated. "Now off with you, and enjoy your weekend."

PART II

Breaking Points

Chapter 9

Kevin
(Late October)

Kevin left the frayed couch and his afterschool dose of anime cartoons and went into the kitchen of his family's trailer. "Mom, I think it's time for my meds."

"Not tonight," Raelyn snapped. "We're trying to save money, so I sold half of them."

Her voice croaked from her parched throat. She was only 35, but she looked 55. She was dangerously thin, and her skin was leathery. Her front teeth were missing. Her dark eyes were sunken, and her brown hair was a mess. She considered hygiene optional. Her johns had long since given up on standards.

"Mom," the boy impatiently explained. "You heard the doctor say I needed to take them all the time."

"Shut yer fuckin' hole," she spit. "Go back and watch yer stupid, fuckin' cartoons."

She slapped his face. He went back to the couch, brooding.

Raelyn reached into her filthy jean jacket and pulled out a tiny Ziplock baggie. "Marcie," she addressed her pregnant 18-year-old daughter. "Look what I scored with the little shit's dope."

Marcie's dull eyes lit up when she spied the two small rocks now in the palm of her mother's gnarled, trembling hand.

Raelyn's hands twitched more with each passing second. Her earlier meth fix was wearing off. Her head was splitting open, and only another hit could cure it.

Marcie took a little glass pipe from the front pocket of her stolen Hoodie.

Kevin heard a lighter and knew without looking what was transpiring.

Raelyn felt immediate relief, with her first hit. She relaxed for one whole second before her nerve endings tingled with lightning. She felt invincible.

Kevin also knew she soon would be tapping into her hatred and rage. He tried to minimize his presence as much as humanly possible to ride out the next several hours.

"Hey, Kevin," shouted his 15-year-old brother Reggie from their bedroom door beyond the kitchen. "If you help me find my football, I'll help you train to beat Charlie."

Kevin jumped at the idea of getting out of the house. "Sure!"

As Kevin trotted through the kitchen, his sister gave him a full body check with her growing belly.

"Ow, that hurt," Kevin grunted.

"Well, you shouldn't get in my way, you little fucker," Marcie venomously replied.

Raelyn laughed at her daughter's cruelty, but Marcie was pissed because she hadn't triggered a miscarriage. Too lazy to get an abortion, she was counting on the drugs and physical mistreatment to expel the little kicking tumor growing in her uterus. Getting so large cut into her profits and, subsequently, her ability to feed her addiction.

Kevin continued on into the bedroom. The football was right on top of his bed. "Stupid," he called Reggie. "It's right on the bed."

"Go get it, and I'll play with you."

Kevin sighed and trudged into the room.

Reggie slammed the door shut. Kevin's eyes widened, and fear bolted through his system. *Not again!*

Before he could turn to fight, his brother was on his back—knocking him to the bed and forcing his pants down.

Kevin squealed in terror, screamed for help. He kicked, rocked and bit—anything he could do to escape. The whole trailer shook with the struggle.

"Fuckin' knock it off in there before I kill you both," raged Raelyn, indifferent to the rape but infuriated by the noise and commotion.

Reggie leaned on Kevin to subdue him and hotly whispered, "You fuckin' heard her. She'll fuckin' kill you if you keep makin' so much goddamn noise; so shut the fuck up."

The loss of control, bodily invasion and the pain were too much for the 11-year-old boy. He sobbed loudly as he clenched the football tight to his chest.

"Fuckin' crybaby," his brother grunted.

Chapter 10

Eating Her Words
(The Next Day)

Angela and Ronnie greeted the school bus as they did every morning to shepherd their students to the classroom.

Unlike most mornings, as the old, heavy-set bus driver opened the doors he shouted, "Out! Out! Gidoutta my bus, we're here!"

Freddy growled and scampered off—wild-eyed, claws bared. "Bitchells," he yelled back at the bus and tried to run away. Angela quickly grabbed him and tried to sooth him.

Lionel sullenly dragged his backpack down the stairs. "Fucker," he darkly muttered about (not at) the driver.

"Ronnie, did you hear that?" the driver spat. "Make sure that young man is punished."

Ronnie imposed a heavy fine of $5, but Lionel only looked at her and glowered. "I don't care."

Edward ran out of the bus. He was scared and hugged Ronnie's waist for protection. She gently pried him off and tried to get him and Lionel to form a line.

Angela saw she was needed but was checked from doing much by Sammy's flight risk. She held his hand, and tried to usher the other kids off the bus—allowing Ronnie to maintain order in the growing line.

Ted exited the bus shrieking and swinging his arms wildly, as if he were a monkey. Angela punished him by verbally taking away some of his classroom money.

Charlie and Kevin laughed viciously on their way down the bus stairs. Angela understood the way the two operated and docked Charlie $10 for setting Ted up to act like a monkey and docked Kevin $5 for encouraging Charlie and Ted.

Franz wasn't spacey for a change, but he was highly agitated. He glared at everyone while burying his head into his smelly, stained coat.

Jefferson and Lashaun were practically angels, earning lots of extra money, while looking very upset by the chaos going on around them.

"Where's Violet?" Angela asked the angry and put upon bus driver.

"Oh, she's back there," he fumed.

119

Still holding Sammy's hand, Angela climbed into the bus, and it looked empty. A phantom voice came from the back calling to her. "I'm not leaving."

"Violet, you're at school now." Angela calmly explained. "It's time to learn about cool new things. Maybe Mrs. Regina will teach you more about bugs. Come off the bus with me, and let's find out."

"You can't make me."

"By God, child," bellowed the bus driver, as he turned around in his green vinyl seat. "I can make you get off this bus."

Violet was silent but in full oppositional-defiance mode. Angela put her free hand on the bus driver's forearm to settle him. "It's okay. I've got it."

The behavior specialist called down to the invisible voice. "What's the problem, Violet? Why don't you want to get off the bus?"

Angela already knew the answer. Violet was inappropriately seeking negative attention and trying to hold up the morning routine. The trick Angela had learned was to find a clever way to coax her off the bus without a physical restraint and removal.

"The boys were bad to me," Violet answered. "And the driver is mean."

The driver shouted back, "Well if you weren't so busy getting in those boys' faces an' irritatin' 'em, they'd leave you alone."

Angela tried to remain slyly unconfrontational. "Violet, if you think the bus driver is mean, why do you want to stay with him on the bus?"

Violet was silent, trying to figure out a logical answer.

After a short pause, Angela encouraged, "Come with me, and you won't have to see this bus driver any more today."

"No!" Violet wasn't about to fall for another of Angela's tricks. Violet wanted disruption and negative attention, and she was determined to get it.

Angela sighed and softly apologized to the driver. "I'm sorry. This is gonna take a few more minutes."

"It would really make my day if I got to drag her ass outta here," the frustrated driver offered.

"No. Thank you, but we'll take care of it."

Outside, the other students were getting more out of control and Ronnie implored Angela to speed things up.

"Why don't you take them to class and send Carla back to help with Violet." Angela requested.

Ronnie consented and began the long march following a line

painted on the pavement that led them inside and down the hall.

Angela led Sammy out of the bus, knelt down and bribed him. "Sammy. If you follow them to class quietly, I'll push you extra super hard on the swings at recess. Okay?"

Sammy nodded. He was still Freddy, and she thought he might still try to run away. Yet, she also couldn't keep him here, especially if Violet was going to have a violent escalation. Angela also knew she couldn't leave Violet alone with the driver who was ready to beat her. While the behavioral specialist was fairly certain the driver wouldn't beat the girl, she knew Violet would do whatever it took to push the driver over the edge.

One last pinky swear with Sammy and she cut him loose. When Sammy began to follow the line, he never took his eyes off Angela for more than a second. Angela knew that if she stepped back on the bus too soon, Sammy would bolt. She watched him with a smile and wave as he made his way inside the double doors. She waited a few extra seconds after the doors closed behind him before re-entering the bus.

Apologizing again to the bus driver, Angela made her way to the back of the vehicle in search of Violet. Finding the gangly girl lying on the second to last row's bench, Angela sat on her knees, facing backward from the third to last bench.

She gave Violet a conspiratorial smile. "I don't suppose you'd do me a huge favor and just walk with me to class, would you?"

"No."

"I didn't think so," she sighed. "All right. It's your choice. You can choose to get off the bus and walk to class, or you can choose to be taken off the bus and go to timeout."

Violet said nothing

Angela waited for back up. She was surprised when Mrs. Regina climbed into the bus.

The teacher was all business this morning. "Violet, do you really want to spend the morning in timeout?"

The girl's silence was her answer. Her monstrous lip pouted, and her eyes scowled.

"Okay, Angela. You get on the seat behind her, and we'll try to get her out of here somehow."

"What can I do?" the driver asked.

"Stay out of the way," Mrs. Regina discouraged, but amended her initial request. "But try to pry loose any limbs that snag onto the seats."

As everyone moved into position, Violet dropped to the floor. She hooked her legs around the central support bar that connected her bench to the floor of the bus. Her left hand grabbed the left bench leg, and her right arm wrapped over the bench seat, slipping her hand between the cushions—clutching the bottom cushion as best she could.

Mrs. Regina had the right hand free in seconds, but the left was difficult to free one-handed.

There was little Angela could do from her initial position, so she had to lie on the filthy dust-and-gum-covered rubber floor and crawl under the heavily bubble-gummed bench to free Violet's legs. In the past six weeks, the rookie had given up worrying about the filth and germs encountered on floors, in timeout and on the often times grimy children.

Violet's legs were so strong; Angela didn't have the positioning to pry them loose. It wasn't until Violet started kicking Angela's legs that the behavior specialist managed to grab them and keep them from rehooking onto the bar.

Once the 10-year-old was free, the two women only had the tiger by the tail. Pinned under the bench, Angela had no way to help carry Violet. Eventually the women decided to push/drag Violet into the bus' aisle. Once the child was clear of the bench legs, Angela let go of the girl's feet to climb out from below the bench.

Mrs. Regina had Violet standing in an upper-body MANDT restraint, but after the girl's feet were freed, Violet used the floor and the teacher as a springboard. She jumped, almost knocking Mrs. Regina over backward. Her upper body still restrained, Violet kicked her legs outward and upward. She managed to lock them on the back of the bench—conking Angela on the head as the woman attempted to stand.

"Jesus!" Angela cursed. "That really hurt."

For the first time that day, Angela was truly angry. She regained her footing and checked her head to see if she was bleeding.

"Little help," grunted Mrs. Regina, whose back was breaking under the weight of the girl she was holding aloft.

Angela quickly regained her senses and jerked Violet's legs up and off the bench back. Violet screamed in protest but was uninjured.

"Sorry," Angela grunted, out of breath. "But if you didn't choose to cling to that dah...darn seat, you wouldn't get hurt."

Angela could see that Mrs. Regina's strength was waning, and, instinctively, the two women tried to make a move toward the front of the bus before their strength gave out.

Violet had other plans. With Angela standing between Violet's legs, holding the girl tightly by the knees, Violet used her powerful thighs to propel herself forward and back using her head as a battering ram into Mrs. Regina's sternum. She succeeded in knocking the wind out of Mrs. Regina but was accidently dropped head first to the floor, as the teacher could no longer hold on to the writhing girl.

Mrs. Regina was mortified that she dropped the child and went to her knees, wheezing, to check on Violet. The girl didn't seem to feel an ounce of pain, and she latched onto the nearest bench leg. Angela still clung tightly to the child's legs.

Seeing that Violet was okay, Mrs. Regina took a breather and leaned against a nearby bench while still sitting on the floor.

Angela and Violet firmly held their positions, but they also took a silent moment to rest and reassess the situation.

The driver was awestruck at the fierce struggle in his bus. "Are you ladies okay?"

Breathing hard, both silently nodded.

"I sure hope they pay you well because there's no way in Hell I'd ever want your jobs. Are you sure there isn't something I can do to help."

"Not really," Mrs. Regina said. She doubted he had signed a waiver or had the proper restraint training, not that MANDT ever advised carrying a patient. Regardless of the strictest rules, she had a class to run, students who needed her and no one to babysit Violet in a bus all day. This was the only way to get the job done, she figured, though she felt awful about dropping Violet. She apologized to Violet and checked the girl's head. No blood, only a little bump.

"My head hurts," Violet finally said, more as a matter of fact than a complaint.

"Mine does, too," Angela complained, shooting a fiery gaze into Violet's eyes.

"I'm sorry. I didn't mean to hurt you, Angela," the girl relented.

"Thank you. I didn't mean to hurt your legs on the bench, if I did." Angela replied tersely.

"Oh good," Mrs. Regina exclaimed with renewed enthusiasm, trying to take advantage of the reconciliatory mood. "How about we all walk out of here and back to class together?"

"That sounds like a good idea," Angela said, mustering encouragement from deep within.

"NO!" Violet braced herself for the next round of prying.

Mrs. Regina calmly took a deep breath and looked Angela in the eye. "Once I'm holding Violet by the wrists, I want you to hold her by the ankles. Then we'll carry her out of here the safest way I can think of."

"Okay." Angela readied herself for action.

After several minutes spent struggling, Mrs. Regina had Violet by the wrists. Angela moved her grip to the girl's ankles. Counting to three, they hoisted the gangly girl several inches off the ground and shuffled their way toward the exit. Violet screamed, twisted, punched and kicked as best she could, but she had virtually no leverage to maneuver with, regardless of her raging strength. Awkward as it was to carry her, the two women had a far easier time removing her from the bus than they had on their first attempt.

The bus driver slammed the door to the bus shut just as soon as Angela cleared it. He sped off, and the women caught their breath without putting Violet down.

The 10-year-old kept screaming at the top of her lungs. Mrs. Regina and Angela knew that Violet couldn't possibly be in that much—if any—pain and were unmoved by the noise. However, as they regrouped their senses, they became painfully aware that half the student body and most of the teachers were watching them through the big picture windows.

"Oh, Lord," Mrs. Regina muttered to Angela. "This isn't good."

Angela grimaced, and Mrs. Regina smiled as broadly as she could and faced the windows, shouting, "It's okay. Somebody's just having a bad day. Nobody's hurt. It's okay!"

Angela joined in. "It's okay; just go back to your work."

The children in the windows didn't move, but their teachers tried to redirect them. The daytreatment class went wild, shouting out at Violet, taunting and threatening. They weren't trying to help their classroom staff, they just delighted in watching someone else suffer—glad it wasn't them out there being carried around like an animal carcass headed for the big tribal roast. Ronnie and Carla did all they could to settle them, but it was useless. They also knew they couldn't go help their co-workers outside because they couldn't keep a handle on all that was happening inside, especially without Bev at school, yet.

"Who are you yelling at," Violet asked, her curiosity piqued enough to stop struggling.

Mrs. Regina replied, "The whole school is watching you make a fool of yourself out here, Violet."

The child became overwhelmingly self-conscious in a heartbeat.

"Even the other classes?"

"Everybody," Angela explained.

"Okay, okay, okay," Violet pleaded. "I'll behave. Put me down. I'll behave."

"Can we trust you to put your feet down?" Mrs. Regina asked with grave sincerity.

"You can trust me; I'll behave."

The teacher nodded to Angela, who gently placed Violet on the ground—stretched to the full length of her body, to avoid any attempts to kick her in the head again.

"Very good," Mrs. Regina said when Violet didn't flail about on the ground. "Will you walk into class now?"

"Uh-huh," the girl agreed. As she watched the crowded windows staring back at her, her hands sweat profusely.

"Okay, then. Stand up," Mrs. Regina gently commanded.

Violet stood.

"Good. Now Angela, why don't you take Violet by one hand, and I'll hold her other. Then we can all walk inside together."
Angela took one of the hands Mrs. Regina still held high over Violet's head, and they started to walk toward the door.

As all the school children, except for those in daytreatment, went back to work, Violet silently let her feet fall out from under her.

Her handlers dragged her for one surprised second and then moaned in frustrated disappointment.

"C'mon, Violet. Stand up and walk to class like a big girl," Mrs. Regina tried to encourage without success. "Do you really want to be carried inside with all those kids watching from the doorways?"

Violet grumbled, but she got back on her feet.

A few steps later, Violet erupted in cheerful chatter, as if the past half hour of screaming and fighting had never happened. The two women ignored her obsessive discussion about bugs. And so Violet went limp as a matter of principle.

Sick of the situation, the teacher and behavior specialist quickly reassumed their positions at the girl's wrists and ankles and carried her back into room 36 amid howling protest from Violet.

When the trio arrived, both timeout booths were occupied. Carla held the latch shut on one booth with Sammy violently thrashing about inside, but she quickly sent Kevin to the arts-and-crafts table to finish his open-door timeout.

Placing Violet face down on the floor mat of timeout barely gave

Angela and Mrs. Regina enough time to escape and slam the door shut. Once trapped, Violet renewed a rage that made Sammy's bouncing off the walls of the other booth look tame.

Ronnie was alone in the growing pandemonium of the classroom, so Mrs. Regina didn't get a moment's rest—racing next door to help. Angela remained to perform guard duty with Carla.

"What has gotten into these kids today?" Angela asked incredulously, catching her breath.

"It's more like, 'What didn't get into these kids today?' " Carla returned.

"What do you mean?"

"Well," Carla explained, nodding to Kevin who was sitting at the table in the center of the room to finish his timeout. "He said he didn't take his pills this morning. I'd venture to say that three quarters of our kids missed their meds."

"Everybody slips up now and then, but everybody at once?" Angela questioned. "Did they plan this?"

"Nope," Carla matter-of-factly said. "Usually once or twice a semester the stars just align against us."

Violet continued throwing her body against the timeout door. Angela was continuously amazed by the girl's energy and stamina.

As the noise in the classroom subsided, Carla asked Kevin, "Are you ready to go back to class?"

"Yeah," he sluggishly sighed.

"Okay, you can go," Carla authorized.

"Where's Bev?" Angela asked, suddenly aware of her boss' absence.

"I was kinda hoping you knew. She never called in while you were outside."

"Huh." Angela didn't remember Bev telling her about any meetings. "I'll give her a call if I ever get Violet to calm down."

"That phone's gonna see a lot of action today. After Bev, someone's gonna have to call all of these parents and get them to bring in some damn meds. Even better. Get 'em to take their kids home. This is too wild, even for us."

"Won't the school nurse bring in her morning round of pills?"

"She only brings in pills for two or three kids in the morning," Carla explained. "Violet, Sammy, Kevin, Charlie and Ted all need their mothers to bring in a dose."

"Don't call my mother!" Violet shouted, scrambling to the back of

126

the booth and sitting down. "Look at me. I'm being hav." (pronounced: heyv)

Angela looked in the window. "Yes, you are behaving very nicely, but you know I have to tell your mom about what happened on the bus. You also need your medicine."

"No, no. I promise I'll be good."

"Violet, you should have made that choice a long time ago, but I'll be sure to tell her that you're making good choices now."

"No, no, nooooo." Violet tantrumed like a 2-year-old on the timeout floor. She pounded her fists and feet. When that didn't work, Violet assumed a hyper-sexualized spread eagle/missionary position on the floor. Angela gagged with revulsion, as she averted her eyes from the apparent sexual advance made by the still-clothed 10-year-old girl.

"What's wrong?" Carla asked.

"I think Violet's trying to bribe me with sex to keep me from calling her mother."

"Yeah," Carla dispassionately acknowledged with a hushed voice. "She does that. For the past year or so, that seems to be her final line of defense to get people to do things her way. I don't care what they say about some of the boys in this program, she's the biggest sexual predator of the class. It's disgusting."

"It's so sad," replied Angela, equally hushed. "You know what that means don't you?"

"Of course. We've suspected her uncle for some time, but naturally we can't have her removed from the home. Technically, only she and her mother share that house. And we have no physical evidence or confessions to legally stop her uncle from seeing her."

Angela shook her head and quietly complained. "She's already so psychologically desensitized to sex that she uses it as a commodity...*at age 10!*"

"Man, it took me five years of marriage before I learned that was the only way to get my husband to do anything," Carla dryly quipped. It wasn't that Carla didn't empathize with Violet, but in this line of work, if you didn't develop a thick skin and a profoundly dark sense of humor, you just wouldn't be able to cope with the constant barrage of suffering.

In spite of herself, Angela smiled.

Carla turned her attention to Sammy, who was now sitting quietly against the back wall of timeout. "Are you ready to go back to class?"

"Yes," he grunted.

"Good. Go on back, then."

Sammy hustled back to class with determined steps. He barely acknowledged Angela. He wasn't upset with her. It was simply her proximity to the timeout booths. He wasn't in the mood to tarry. Otherwise, they had grown quite close since their first recess at the swings. Sammy was often speaking complete sentences, holding appropriate conversations for his age. There were always lapses of spitting and bitchells, but they were subsiding.

A new ruckus was starting next door, so Carla rejoined the class to help.

Violet's tantrum was finally winding down. With one ear on the chaos next door, Angela decided to forego the promised all morning punishment for Violet and offered her the usual deal. "As soon as you sit quietly against the back wall for five minutes, I'll let you out."

Violet gave her patented face scrunch with full lip extension, took a minute to think the deal over and eventually followed Angela's directions. Angela marked her watch.

Now an hour into the school day, Bev scurried into the room out of breath. "I'm sorry; I've got some meetings to go to. I'll be back later."

"Wait!" Angela called to Bev, who was already heading back out the door. "We need you. No one's on their meds. We've been in crisis all morning."

"I'm sorry, gotta go."

"I don't remember any meetings," Angela protested. "Do I need to be there, too?"

"No. See ya." Bev closed the door behind her.

Bev's random behavior threw Angela for a loop. It wasn't like Bev, regardless of how neurotic she got, she never left the program behind in an emergency.

There wasn't time for Angela to think about it. Ronnie burst into the room toting a flailing Lionel.

"Let me at that son of a bitch!" he demanded.

Carla led a calmer Ted into the room.

Angela peered in at Violet and then checked her watch. "Oh, gee. Look at the time, Violet. Your five minutes are up. Go back to class."

Violet was reluctant to leave. She understood she was now in a position of power and decided to milk it for extra attention—by delaying the start of Ted's timeout. As soon as she reached the booth's door, Angela gently pushed Violet out of the way and promptly closed the door for Carla, entrapping Ted.

Violet scrunched her way back to class.

"What got into those two?" Angela inquired.

Ronnie started, "I restrained Lionel just as he was about to slug Ted."

Carla finished, "And Ted hit Lionel after Lionel was safely restrained."

"He started it!" Lionel vehemently shouted from his booth.

"No, I didn't!" returned Ted.

"Both of you be quiet and sit against the back walls!" Carla yelled.

"Do you want me to rewind the security tape to see what really happened?" Angela asked.

Ronnie deterred her. "Not now. It's Mrs. Regina's only defense in there. We can check it out later."

"Christ," Carla muttered. "There isn't enough aspirin on the planet to get through today."

"I've got some valium in my purse, if you want it," Ronnie offered.

"Nah, I've already got some similar stuff in mine. Maybe after school," Carla said. She laughed darkly. "Hell, if we make it today, I might just take a whole handful of your valium."

Ronnie chuckled, but Angela only laughed nervously to go with the flow. The pill swapping was a legitimate offer, which made her uncomfortable. The very real thought of two drugged out aides in addition to the classroom chaos today made Angela nervous—as did illegal prescription trading.

"How about you, Angela," Ronnie offered. "God knows you've earned one."

"Nah. I'm just ducky—havin' a blast," she sarcastically shrugged, hoping not to show how freaked out she was by Ronnie's kind but illegal offer. "Can I take over a door for either of you?"

"No," Carla declined. "You better call as many parents as you can before someone else escalates."

"You got it," she said, happy to have diverted the conversation. She hated to sound so square when it came to drug use. She didn't honestly care what other people did on their own time. Prescription drugs, pot, cocaine, whatever, as long as you didn't hurt anyone else by doing it. For her, drugs were an issue of control. She didn't do illegal drugs for the same reasons she didn't take legal psychological ones. She hated the idea that she'd have her mental clarity fogged or thrown off kilter. She hated the prospect of losing control.

Her relationships with her client's parents were equally complex.

She had met all the ones that still had any dealings with their kids and didn't like most of them. To her way of thinking, there was little to like: They abused their kids.

Yet, with the exception of Lulu, these parents didn't know what Angela thought and were impressed by the way she seemed to handle them fairly, was popular with the kids, and helped improve their children's behavior. And on her part, Angela had to concede that some parents were much easier to work with than others. Some of the parents even felt remorse for their actions—Lashaun's mom, in particular. She had overcome so much to truly put her life back on track. Angela respected that but always remained wary of her. Angela also understood that all of the parents themselves were abuse victims who needed help as much as their children did. Be that as it may, she refused to accept that as an excuse for continuing the cycle of violence. If her own mother had broken that cycle, so could they.

Cradling the phone to her ear, Angela punched the digits to connect with Violet's mom, Pauline. Pauline always struck Angela as being one of the coldest parents in the program. The woman could work with brutal, premeditated intent against anyone she saw fit—frequently Violet. If any of the parents were a threat to the staff, both physically and litigiously, it would be Pauline. A victim of sex abuse herself, Pauline was remarkably street smart and book smart. She seethed with anger, and she would tap that anger for outbursts or slow-burning revenge. The staff unanimously agreed she was the one most likely to sue them for anything—just because. And they all knew that any given weekday something potentially law-suit worthy occurred. As the phone line rang, Angela reminded herself to be both straightforward and diplomatic.

"Hi, Pauline? This is Angela from Violet's daytreatment program."

"What's wrong?" Violet's mother grimly asked.

"I don't think Violet has had her meds, and we need you to bring them in."

"I gave them to her myself this morning."

"Maybe she spit them out."

"What has she done?" Pauline knew full well what her daughter was capable of doing, yet she sometimes doubted the competence of the program staff. She wanted to make sure she really had to leave work and threaten her always tenuous relationship with her superiors.

Angela told her *every* detail about the bus and timeout.

Pauline sighed with disgust about the daughter with whom she was saddled. "I'll be there in 15 minutes." She slammed the phone down.

The behavior specialist worked down the list of emergency contacts taped on the wall next to the phone. Most of the parents were pissed they had to leave work. None sounded concerned their child was in trouble.

Unemployed Lulu just didn't want to be bothered and made a dozen excuses for not coming. Angela remained a cordial as possible to prevent anyone from accusing her of picking on "a poor, defenseless mentally disabled single mother." Angela knew Lulu was linked to at least six different agencies that could get her to school in fewer than 20 minutes. Angela patiently talked Lulu through how she could ride the bus to bring Sammy his much needed medications. Lulu intentionally stalled and pushed Angela's buttons, but Angela refused to cave in and remained upbeat. When Lulu saw she had no way out of the situation, she slammed the phone in Angela's ear.

By the time Angela was done calling parents, Ronnie, Carla, Ted and Lionel had gone back next door.

Pauline was the first parent to arrive. Pauline wasn't your average daytreatment mom. She was 26 and looked like a super model. Thin and toned, she had an aquiline nose, luscious lips, big breasts, no hips, good makeup and professionally styled and dyed hair. She wore a white ruffled blouse and a tight, black leather mini skirt. She had a track record of seducing her employers, getting fired when they were done with her.

Violet, the proud and defiant, was cowed before her mother. The young girl's shoulders hunched, and her eyes watched the floor. The only defiance left in the child was a slight pout of her lower lip.

Angela went to get Violet a glass of water to take her medicine. In the hall, on her way back, she could hear Pauline giving Violet the chewing out of a lifetime.

"I can't believe you spit out your meds! What a stupid thing to do. Do you have any idea how busy I am at work? If I get fired because of this, it's your fault! Is it so hard to get off a bus?! Christ. Why did I get stuck with..." Pauline paused when she saw Angela in the doorway.

"Here's your water, Violet," Angela said.

Violet said nothing but took the glass.

"Open," commanded Pauline.

Violet complied and her mom put a pill in her mouth. Violet took a drink.

"Swallow it," demanded her mother. "Don't make me hold your

mouth and nose shut."

Violet took several more gulps.

"Open. Lift your tongue." Pauline stuck her fingers in Violet's mouth and checked the girl's gums for a hidden pill. "Okay. If I ever have to come back because you spit out your meds, your punishment will be worse than anything you can possibly imagine. You're in for it enough when you get home tonight."

The threat sent chills down Angela's spine. "That's not necessary, Pauline. I already punished her with nearly an hour of timeout. She's been behaving much better since then."

Pauline gave her a smile that conveyed, *That's nice, College Girl, but you've got no idea what you're doing.*

Yet Violet's mother swiftly changed gears and offered an earnest apology. "I'm sorry Violet has been such a hassle. I appreciate you keeping me up to date on her behavior. Now I've gotta get back to work before they fire me."

Pauline was out the door without another word to Violet.

The next to arrive was the district's beleaguered nurse, making her morning rounds, bringing Lionel, Edward and Lashaun their assorted medications. She also brought medications for other students in the school during her morning and afternoon runs. Budget cuts had reduced her to being a pharmaceutical drug mule. Whereas in the old days each public school had a registered nurse, these days each district had a roving nurse or two. In Average Little City that meant one nurse covered three elementary schools and two middle schools and another covered an elementary school, a middle school and two high schools. And as it was illegal for a nonregistered nurse to administer a student's daily medicine, the district nurses had no choice but to run the gauntlet of medicating four or five schools twice a day. If one of the nurses got off schedule, she could send the entire district's body chemistry out of whack. If a student got sick or hurt at school, there was little the school could do aside from either calling the child's parents or 9-1-1.

Although Lionel had been on his med sched, the electricity of the day led him in and out of trouble. Edward had been having a decent day except for his fear of what his classmates might do to him. Lashaun was having a really difficult day keeping it together. It wasn't so much pharmacological as it was pressure. Charlie had been riding him all day. Lashaun really wanted to fight back, but he knew if he could hold it together without any misbehaving, he could mainstream with a normal 5th grade class next week—and never have to deal with daytreatment again.

Charlie understood this pressure and wanted to break Lashaun. A year older than Lashaun, Charlie hated the idea of being beaten to being mainstreamed and being stuck in the room filled with "losers." He couldn't be more jealous of Lashaun. Fueled by a lack of meds, he was willing to bring Lashaun down at all costs today.

After the school nurse made her exit, Kevin threw a chair while being restrained. "Stupid monkey!" he shouted, angling to get a shot at Ted. "Let me at him!"

It took both Ronnie and Mrs. Regina to restrain the raging boy and remove him from the classroom. As Angela opened the door to timeout, a strange, dry shout came from the doorway.

"Kevin!"

The boy and the three women stopped dead in their tracks to face the filthy, gaunt, toothless apparition of a woman in the doorway.

"It's good to see you, Raelyn," warmly greeted Mrs. Regina, as she regained her composure.

Kevin went slack in everyone's arms. "Hi, Mom."

"Here's your damn meds," she declared, thrusting forward a fistful of pills for her son to take.

Angela took off to get a glass of water. Kevin sheepishly took the meds.

"If I miss my Goddamn business meeting because of you..." Raelyn trailed off. She already was trembling a little from her need of another fix.

Angela returned with some water and couldn't fathom what type of meeting this woman would attend looking like a drowned rat shriveled by the sun on the bank of a river. Even after Ronnie explained that Raelyn was a crack and meth whore, Angela couldn't comprehend what kind of a man would be so desperate for sex that he'd turn to Raelyn and actually pay her for it.

Kevin took his pills under his mother's burning gaze. She walked out of the room without another word.

Kevin took the break in the battle as a chance to return to class and hammer Ted a few times. Again it took all of Ronnie and Mrs. Regina's strength to wrangle him into timeout. Angela manned the door while the other two women caught their breath at the arts-and-crafts table. Kevin only made a few half-hearted attempts to beat down the door. Unlike Violet or Sammy, he stopped when it started to hurt.

"Make sure he stays in there for at least 20 minutes," Mrs. Regina

133

instructed Angela. "That's at least how long it'll take for his meds to kick in."

"Did you hear Mrs. Regina?" Angela asked the boy through the wooden door. When she peeked through the timeout window, she was shocked by what she witnessed. "Oh my God. He's peeing on the wall."

Ronnie and Mrs. Regina got up and looked. Sure enough, Kevin stood profile to them, pants around his ankles, wagging his penis like a little watering hose—spraying one wall quite thoroughly.

Angela began to unlatch the door to get him out, but Mrs. Regina stopped her. "Wait till he's empty, Dear. No sense getting doused."

"Ew. Good call. Thanks."

After Kevin shook the last yellow drops free, he checked the window. He was startled to see the three women staring at him in disgust. Suddenly embarrassed, he covered his genitals with his left hand and pulled up his pants with his right.

Angela now opened the door, and Mrs. Regina asked Kevin, "What was that all about?"

Kevin grinned impishly. "I don't know."

He was docile during the booth transfer, but he began to laugh maniacally after he was trapped in the dry booth. "Stupid Monkeys!"

Ronnie called the janitor to steam clean the soiled booth. The staff needed it back in service as quickly as possible. It didn't matter if it was wet, as long as it was sterilized.

Ronnie went back to the class to help Carla.

Angela guarded the latch on Kevin's booth, giving Mrs. Regina more time to recuperate from the stress and chaos of the morning. "You said it would take 20 minutes before his meds kick in?"

The teacher nodded.

Not facing the booth, Angela called out to Kevin, "Are you sitting against the back wall?"

When he didn't answer, she peered in through the window. Now truly disturbed by what she saw, Angela could only stammer for a second. "Uh, uh, uh, Mrs. Regina?"

"What is it?"

At a loss for words, Angela just shook her head and pointed. Mrs. Regina came back over to look.

Kevin was lying on the floor, his feet perpendicular to the door. His pants were at his ankles again, and his naked butt bobbed in the air as he humped the coarse canvas floor mat.

134

"Kevin! You stop that this instant!" Mrs. Regina shouted.

The 11-year-old boy emitted an agonizing scream followed by monkey shrieks.

The teacher turned to Angela, "Where on earth is Bev?"

"I don't know. She stuck her head in the class for three seconds, said she had a meeting and wouldn't be back until later. I told her we're in crisis, but she said she had to go."

Carla and Ronnie called for help before Mrs. Regina could respond to that news. She ran next door, and a few seconds later Lionel and Carla entered the room.

Angela warned Carla about the urine-drenched timeout booth, forcing the aid to perform a full restraint in a chair.

Watching the open daytreatment room door for the janitor, Angela witnessed Kevin's mother whisk past the room. Raelyn was carrying the school's entire lost-and-found box worth of jackets, boots and gloves. The meth addict moved so silently and deftly, Angela almost didn't trust her own eyes. The day was turning toward the surreal. Too busy guarding the addict's masturbating son, as another aid struggled with an escalated child, Angela chose to ignore Raelyn—pretending as if she saw nothing.

There was nothing she could do at that moment anyway. So, Angela reached out for a kiddy chair to sit on, resting with her shoulder situated in such a way that she could keep the latch in place while making the most of a moment's quasi-rest.

Within a few minutes, Roland, the school's janitor, strode into the room—his neck wrapped with wires and hoses, his forearms bulging as he carried the steam cleaner, which was preloaded with a mild soap-and-bleach solution.

"Hey," he jovially greeted. "You guys must be having quite a day; we can hear ya all the way at the other end of the hall."

"Sorry," Angela apologized. "It's a nightmarish zoo."

"Well, I'll get this booth operational for you in no time."

"Thank you very much," Angela said with the purest appreciation—grateful she didn't have to clean up other people's bodily waste for a living.

Roland had encountered that a lot over the years and smiled. "Hey, no prob. It could be a lot worse."

"How?" Angela muttered.

"I could be stuck with your job," Roland said with a friendly wink.

Angela laughed for the first time all day. "Well, don't go counting your lucky stars just yet. It might be worse for you in a minute, depending on what the young man in this booth is doing."

"Nah. These booths clean up pretty easy."

With the flick of a switch, the room was flooded with the thunder of the mighty steam cleaner. Carla and Angela found it oddly soothing. It drown out all other sound. Lionel was transfixed by big machinery in action. He ceased struggling and sat calmly in the chair in which Carla was holding him.

When the cleaning was done, Angela opened Kevin's door. There was no trace of semen anywhere. Kevin's humping had been an impotent act of rage and frustration. Now his pants were back up, and the boy was sitting with his back to the wall. He held his head between his knees and sobbed uncontrollably.

"Kevin, Kevin. What's wrong?" Angela sympathetically inquired.

She couldn't understand him through his sobbing and repeated herself.

Through his sniffling and heaving, Kevin croaked, "I only wanted to play football with my brother."

Unfamiliar with what happened the night before, Angela tried to console him. "I'm sure you can play with him after school."

Kevin only sobbed.

While Angela talked with Kevin, Ted ambled into the room. He was there without permission and fishing for more information about Kevin's escalation.

Did Kevin really pee in timeout? Did I, Ted, really cause Kevin to blow a gasket? The rush of power he felt was immense.

"Can I have some paper and scissors to make you a card?" Ted asked Angela, with his faux baby lisp.

"No. Please go back to class. It's inappropriate for you to be in here right now," Angela commanded in response.

Ted continued to walk around the room with false blithe innocence. As Carla and Angela were preoccupied with their students, Roland spoke up while gathering the last of his equipment. "Young man, I believe your teacher told you to go back next door."

Ted looked at the man and shrugged. The 9-year-old had found the long, sharp teacher's scissors on Bev's desk. "Just a little card, real quick." He peeked over Angela's shoulders from across the room to spy on Kevin.

Angela stood to redirect Ted. "No. I'm busy with Kevin, and you need to be next door."

136

Leaving the room, Roland interrupted. "Call me if you need anything else."

"Okay," Angela said, turning to wave good-bye. "Thanks, again, for your help."

"LOOK OUT!" Carla screamed.

A flashing silver blade, held tightly in Ted's fist, came lunging at Angela's belly. She barely shuffled backward in time to avoid the first thrust of an unexpected attack. Ted's calm, emotionless eyes were locked on her's. He charged her again. Fear and adrenaline poured through her veins so quickly, the world began to move at an agonizingly slow pace. As the boy's stabbing swing passed her a second time, Angela, instinctively, grabbed for his wrist. Her synapses were firing so quickly, it felt impossible to move fast enough to stay alive, unharmed. But in reality, she moved with unparalleled speed and agility. She managed to clasp on to the hand with the scissors, but his free hand immediately went for the potentially lethal weapon.

Two thoughts raced through her mind, *I've got to catch that second hand; I'll die if I don't.* Her movements were almost entirely subconscious. Knowing there was no way to catch that second hand in time, Angela spun the boy around fast and hard with the hand she did have. As he regained his bearings she managed to grab his free hand.

Even now, she had little control of the situation. She had both of Ted's wrists, but she couldn't let go or properly restrain him without plunging what was essentially an 8-inch dagger in her own chest.

"Somebody grab the scissors!" she cried out, but even her mouth and words seemed to move in slow motion with the adrenaline surging through every edifice of her body.

Her cry for help broke the stunned inaction of the adults in the room, but it was Lionel who came first to Angela's rescue. Latching on to the scissors with both hands, Lionel fiercely struggled to break Ted's grasp.

"No, no! Lionel, let go! You'll get hurt!" Angela frantically warned.

Pushing Lionel aside, Roland stepped in and yanked the scissors from Ted's hand, nearly dislocating several of the boy's fingers.

Once the scissors were free and safe, Angela dragged Ted to timeout and hurled him inside it. There was nothing professional or ethical about her actions, but she was still half afraid he had some backup shiv to stick her. The boy was unhurt but soggy in the padded cell when Carla slammed the door shut on him.

Angela couldn't stop checking her torso for holes and blood.

"You okay?" Carla asked.

Shaking, and still checking herself over, Angela slowly realized that she was, in fact, okay. "Yeah, I think so."

She then looked at Roland with profound gratitude. "Thank you."

"Don't mention it," he shrugged with his usual nonchalance. "What do you want me to do with these?"

He dangled the scissors in mid-air.

"As long as I never see them again, I don't care. They have no business being in a class like this."

"Consider them disappeared." He put them in his back pocket and gathered his cleaning equipment to leave. "Later."

"'Bye, and thanks again." Angela said before turning to face Lionel. She squatted like a catcher to be eye level with him. "And you, my brave little knight in shining armor...I thank you for your courage to help me. But what you did was very dangerous, and I don't ever want you to do that again. Always let the grownups do the dangerous stuff. I don't ever want you to get hurt."

Lionel beamed with pride as only a child-hero can. He explained himself with absolute innocence and sincerity. "I didn't want you to die, Angela."

Assuming she already would be fired for throwing Ted into timeout, she didn't hesitate to draw Lionel in for a long, loving— absolutely nonsexual—bear hug. He returned it with equal fervor. Then she held the scruffy looking little boy out by his shoulders, lowered her head and looked him straight in the eye. "Now I want you to promise that you'll never do anything dangerous like that again."

"I promise," he lied. At that moment, Lionel would have stepped in front of a moving train if it meant saving Angela.

"Okay. Now go back to class, get Mrs. Regina for me and promise you won't get in trouble for the rest of the day."

"Okay," he said and scampered back.

He was true to his word except Mrs. Regina was already in the room. Knife fights had a way of attracting her attention. She had seen everything from the point where Roland took the scissors. She now guarded the timeout door, sending Carla back to the classroom.

"You okay?" the teacher asked.

Angela ran her hand through her raven hair. The realization that she was just inches from spending the rest of the day at the hospital's I.C.U. passed through her again like an earthquake's aftershock. She bit her lip and replied, "Yeah, I think so. That was a close one though."

"It sounds like it, but from what I saw, you did just fine."

No, I didn't, Angela thought. *I just threw a kid into timeout, and then hugged another from the front, not the side.* "Thanks," was all she said, completely unconvinced. "Little victories, I guess. Right?"

"I mean it," Mrs. Regina said. "You kept your head, neutralized the situation and no one got hurt."

"Now what do I do?" Angela asked, confused and still a little shaken.

"You call the police, have Ted cited and removed, and then you go take a well-earned break."

"Cited for what? Removed to where?"

"How about attempted murder, and we'll let the police choose where. It doesn't matter to me because he's not coming back into my class today."

Angela's mind was in a bit of a haze. "Okay. How do I call the police?"

Mrs. Regina smiled; she'd been there herself more than once. "Most people dial 9-1-1. Are you sure you're okay?"

"I'm sorry, Mrs. Regina," Angela apologized. "It's just a lot to process all at once."

The behavior specialist pulled herself together and made the call.

The kids in the classroom overheard that the police were on their way. That news mixed with the fresh supply of chemicals in their bloodstream made them behave like cherubs. Sammy was the only unmedicated kid left, and he was ecstatic. The police were his favorite people; he loved them. They kept kids safe; they had guns; they had sirens; and they usually let him sit in the front seat when he was picked up for running away. The boy never allowed himself to dream much, but when he did, he saw himself wearing a starched blue uniform when he grew up.

Sammy was sorely disappointed when his mother was the next person to walk through the classroom door. Unbathed and pitiably dressed, her hair a greasy brown helmet, she arrived with her Average Mental Health Center social worker. Lulu affected no emotion as she stood in front of the class. The students looked on her as a curiosity, some understanding a little bit more about Sammy at the sight of her. Sammy cautiously approached her.

"Here," is all she said as she extended a fist with a pill clasped in it.

He let the pill fall from her grubby hand into his and swallowed it with a cup of water one of the aids got him. Wordlessly, he trudged back to his seat.

Lulu and her caseworker entered the daytreatment room shortly after Angela had gotten off the phone with the police.

The behavior specialist and Mrs. Regina warmly welcomed the two visitors.

Lulu didn't say hi. She whispered to her caseworker, who closed the pass-through door.

"Uh, Angela," the caseworker nervously addressed her colleague from the mental health center. "Uh, Lulu wanted me to tell you she didn't appreciate the way you treated her on the phone this morning."

After the morning she had, this chastisement was almost more than she could take. Yet, she remained calm and kept her game face. "I'm afraid I don't understand."

Lulu whispered again.

"Um. She says she didn't like your tone. She also wanted me to emphasis how hard it is for her to get here."

Mrs. Regina rolled her eyes and checked on Ted through the timeout window.

Angela poured on the sweetness, directly addressing the caseworker. "I don't know why she thinks I had a tone. I even helped her with directions for the bus system."

Clearly, the caseworker had already heard an earful from Lulu who whispered again.

"Uh. She says that you are the one who's responsible for Sammy during the school day, and you can't always interrupt her busy schedule and make her find a way to school when she doesn't have a car."

Remaining pleasant and chipper, Angela locked eyes through the yellow, oil-coated Coke bottle lenses. "Certainly, as you know, being a good mom is hard work, but it's also a 24-hour responsibility. From making sure your son takes his medicine every day, to sacrificing when he's having a hard day—going out of control—at school, being a good mom is the burden you have to bear."

Before Angela got into too much trouble, Mrs. Regina added, "You also have to remember, Lulu, that we aren't allowed to store or administer medicine in the classroom. Only a parent or nurse can do that."

Lulu broke eye contact with Angela and gave her caseworker a look that conveyed, *See how they gang up on me and pick on me, a poor disabled single mother.* Lulu then turned and left the room, her caseworker apologizing in tow.

Certain the two had left the building, Mrs. Regina muttered to Angela, "What a piece of work."

The behavior specialist shook her head in disgust and returned to Kevin who had remained in time out despite the door having been unlatched. The boy had stopped crying during the scuffle between Angela and Ted. He had been angry with Angela and everyone else, but he didn't want anyone to get hurt. Now he was sitting quietly with his back against the wall.

"How are you feeling?" Angela inquired.

"Okay," he said softly. "I'm sorry I peed in timeout."

"I accept your apology, but the janitor is the one you should really apologize to. Will you tell him you're sorry?"

He nodded yes.

"Good. We'll go visit him in a little bit. In the meantime, I wanted to tell you that you made some very good choices by not leaving timeout when I wasn't watching the door."

He shrugged his shoulders.

"I don't suppose you'd like to tell me why you were so upset a little while ago? I remember that you wanted to play football with your brother, but I know that's not enough to make you cry. What happened?"

"Nothing," he sighed softly. The meds helped him regain control of his repression, and he was determined not to be a *cry baby* any more. He tried not thinking about what had happened. It was over and done.

"Are you sure? You can always tell me or anyone else here, if you want."

He gently shook his head, refusing to make eye contact.

"Well, then," Angela said at a loss for any other way to connect, "Do you think you're ready to go back to class?"

"Yes,"

"Okay. You have my permission to go back."

Kevin left. Angela faced Mrs. Regina and whispered so Ted wouldn't hear through the door. "Am I going to be fired?"

"Whatever for?" asked the astonished veteran.

"For starters, I threw Ted into timeout. Then I gave Lionel a normal front hug. Couldn't I be thrown in jail for both physical and sexual abuse?"

The tough-as-nails teacher warmed to Angela and tried to allay her fears. "Honey, I saw both events. First off, there was nothing sexual about that hug. These kids need a little normal, appropriate adult-to-kid love from time to time. To protect ourselves and the kids, the side hugs work best as a policy. But there are extenuating circumstances when it's just the right thing to do.

"As for throwing Ted...given the urgency and threat to your safety...I don't think anyone will ever say a word about it. A dozen cops and lawyers are gonna look at that tape, and all they're gonna see is him trying to kill you. It's safe to say many of them would have done worse than throw him into timeout. At worst a defense attorney will complain, but if you ever get more than a reprimand, I'll be stunned. I doubt you'll ever hear a word about it, unless you start throwing kids every time you put them in timeout."

"Are you sure?"

"Well, of course you'll get in trouble for throwing them every time you take them to timeout."

Angela smiled as the teacher aped her usual style of humor. "Thanks."

"Don't mention it," Mrs. Regina assured her. "Why don't you go to the therapy room and get Ted's files to help the police when they arrive."

It didn't take long for a police officer to arrive. He knocked on the open door to the daytreatment room and looked apprehensive about being in an elementary school for an attempted murder charge against a kid.

He looked at Mrs. Regina at the timeout booth and asked, "Angela Marengo?"

"Right behind you," Angela said, scooting past the tall, handsome officer while she carried two heavy case files held to her bosom.

He stuck out his hand to shake.

"Hold on a sec," the behavior specialist said on her way to the room's main table, where she dropped the case files with a resounding thud. "C'mon in."

She shook his hand, and Mrs. Regina passed control of Ted's booth over to Angela, excusing herself to return to class.

"I'm pretty new to this process," Angela began, "Where do we start?"

"Is the suspect in the box?" the policeman inquired.

"Yes, but we call it a timeout booth."

"You can let him out, and we'll talk about what happened and go from there."

"Okay," Angela said with a cautionary voice. "Be ready to catch him in case he decides to run."

The cop agreed but looked as if she had to be kidding.

"Ted," Angela addressed the boy, as she opened the door. "This is officer…"

"Jose Estrada," he said.

"Hi," said the boy, his eyes wide and innocent.

"Why don't we all sit together at the table," Angela suggested.

She showed Ted the way with a sweeping arm movement. At the table, she positioned herself between Ted and the door. The policeman sat opposite them.

"Angela, why don't you tell me what happened first," Officer Estrada said, opening his steel-box clipboard and removing a note pad and disposable pen.

The behavioral specialist explained the entire event with as many details as she could remember. The young officer cringed as she described how close the scissors came to her belly.

"Is this true, Ted?" he asked.

Looking as innocent as ever, Ted spoke with his affected baby lisp. "Oh no. I would never want to hurt Angela. She's my bestest friend."

The boy stood up and put his right arm around Angela's shoulders and rested his head on her left shoulder.

"You did not ask permission for a side hug," Angela coldly reprimanded. "That is very inappropriate touching and lying."

Officer Estrada thought Ted was a pretty cute kid. He also thought Angela's way of talking to the kid was just plain weird. "Um, Ms. Marengo, were there any witnesses? Maybe that lady who was in here earlier?"

"Not Mrs. Regina, but her aid Carla and the school janitor saw what happened." Angela said. "Better still, we taped the incident with our security cameras. Come have a look. Perhaps, Ted, it'll help jog your memory."

Ted's eyes burned with hatred, but he knew there was nothing he could do with the policeman present.

Angela led the way to the VCR and set up the tape. Trapped between the two adults and forced to watch, he had no choice but to admit what he did. Officer Estrada marveled at the images of the little boy lunging at Angela with the scissors and clear intent to hurt her. He was more amazed at how convincingly the 9-year-old lied to him.

They didn't have the sound on, so the policeman asked Angela,

"What did you say to him just before he came at you?"

"I told him he couldn't make me a card and that he needed to go back to class."

"Wow," he said, shaking his head and backing up to give room for everyone to head back to the table.

Ted saw the opening and made a run for freedom.

Angela practically knocked Jose over as she ran the boy down. Held back by only his shirttails, Ted wheeled around with a knotted fist. Angela caught it and used the boy's momentum to spin him into a perfect MANDT restraint.

Officer Estrada was astonished by the young woman's reflexes and efficiency of motion. "With those moves, you'd be pretty good cop."

"Thanks," she spit, as she hustled the struggling child into the wet timeout booth. "Give me a hand, and close this booth door when I say so."

"Sure."

"Now!"

The cop slammed the door shut, and Angela pulled up the latch.

"As I asked earlier, what do we do now?" She pulled a strand of hair away from her eyes.

Jose was transfixed for a brief second by the combination of her beauty and all that she was clearly capable of handling. He had to pull himself back together. "Right. Umm. Well, the juvenile court system is a little different than regular courts, but we'll charge him with the equivalent of aggravated assault with a deadly weapon, simple assault for what just happened and something called being ungovernable."

Ted began ramming his head into the padded door. "Bitch!"

"We can cite him for that, too," the policeman said.

Angela smiled and sighed, "Nah. You'd be here all day writing hundreds of tickets for the swearing."

"This will take long enough," he said, heading back to his steel box on the table. He began filling out forms in triplicate. Angela directed him to the files to answer any technical or identity questions.

Ted eventually wore himself out, trying to escape timeout and sat against the back wall.

When the officer finished, he began to head for the door. "I guess that just about does it."

"Wait a sec. Aren't you going to take Ted?"

"We don't usually arrest kids and take them to jail," he sheepishly replied.

"I'm sorry," Angela said, "But he can't stay here. Not today. Not after all this."

Perplexed at what to do next, Jose asked, "Can I use your phone to call my sergeant and see what we can do?"

"Sure."

The policeman jabbed at the big numbers on the phone's face and got a direct connection. "Hi, Sarg, it's Jose...Yeah, the kid was frickin' psycho, I saw it on a security tape...Well, I've got a little problem. I've cited the kid, but now they want him removed...the boy's nine...too young for juvie hall?...Okay, I can call his parents. We'll go from there. Thanks."

Jose hung up and asked, "Can you give me Ted's parents' numbers, again?"

"I thought you wrote it on the ticket," Angela said, tethered to the timeout latch.

"Opps, I forgot," he said, opening his steel box.

"Why can't juvie take him?"

"Apparently, due to budget cuts, they are only licensed to take kids 12 to 18."

"That's insane," Angela declared, even more frustrated by the ever present, increasingly stifling budget cuts.

Officer Estrada called Ted's dad at work.

"Mr. Greelak. This is Officer Jose Estrada of the Average Little City Police Department. You're son Ted has just been cited for attacking one of his teachers with a very sharp pair of scissors...No...She's got fast reflexes, and your boy missed...but he tried to kill her...No. Now we need you to come and remove him from school for the rest of the day...No, sir...We can't take him to Juvenile Hall...I realize you have to work, but this is a very serious issue, and you need to come get him...Can his mother get him?...Oh. Does he have any other relatives nearby?...Then, I'm afraid you'll have to take a sick day or something...Sir! It is your problem...Sir?...Sir?"

Jose turned to Angela and explained with exasperation, "I can't believe he hung up on me AND he won't pick up his own son."

"What are you going to do now?" Angela asked.

"I guess I'll take him downtown, and we'll sort it out there," the policeman shrugged. "Go ahead, open the door."

Officer Estrada took his handcuffs from his utility belt and read Ted, who was now very docile, his rights.

They left the room quietly, but there was something very unnatural to Angela about witnessing a 9-year-old led out of a room in handcuffs. The first-grade lunch crowd found it particularly unsettling as they marched toward the cafeteria. They had met Officer Friendly for the first time last week, and Officer Friendly never said anything about arresting their young peers.

Mrs. Regina wisely decided to make her students eat their lunch in the classroom. Only Lashaun was allowed to go with Ronnie, Carla and Angela to help bring back the hot lunches.

After the double whammy of getting their meds and learning about Ted's arrest, they behaved very well. Everyone was released for recess.

Angela stayed behind to get caught up on the dozens of forms she needed to fill out for the morning's restraints, time outs, Violet's tantrum and Ted's assault.

The phone on Bev's desk rang, and Angela answered.

"Hello, Angela. This is Donna at headquarters, may I speak with Bev?"

"She's not here right now."

"Where's she at, I just heard from the police about some incident at your program."

"She's been at meetings all morning. I assumed they were with you guys."

"No. I haven't seen her in several weeks," Donna said. "I heard someone was attacked with scissors."

"That was me."

"Are you okay?"

"I'm fine. It was a close one, though."

"Why didn't you call me?!"

"It didn't seem that important. It's been pretty chaotic here, but we had the situation under control. No one was hurt in the end, and there was too much going on afterward."

"Any time a student attempts to kill you, it's a big deal, whether they succeed or not! Especially if you have the child arrested!" Donna scolded. She knew Angela was still pretty new to the bureaucracy, but still, who the hell doesn't know to check in with their superiors in situations such as this one. "Tell me everything that happened."

Angela did, and Donna made sure the behavior specialist knew all the reports she needed to fill out and how. Donna also made Angela swear to make Bev call her whenever she returned.

Donna was worried more than before she had called the elementary daytreatment program. She was supposed to know about all of Bev's meetings, but she didn't know about these. Angela wasn't supposed to be left alone, especially on a crisis day. If it was a crisis day, those kids needed somebody—either Bev or someone from the center.

What got Donna worried to begin with was that Bev hadn't answered her e-mail or phone messages in two weeks. Bev's paperwork was drastically behind, and her behavior was increasingly erratic. Something was wrong, and it threatened to bring down the program…maybe the mental health center.

While Angela had dutifully filled out all of the proper billing paperwork, Bev wasn't supplementing it with the proper forms and reports. And no matter how good Angela was, the mental health center couldn't bill for her services. Bev's services were bankrolling the show, and the insurance companies had stopped paying claims without the proper supporting paperwork.

Average Mental Health Center was dangerously close to running its budget into the red. The state and insurance companies already made sure AMHC ran close enough to that margin without an AWOL therapist screwing up the system. In short, Donna and Richard were starting to sweat bullets over Bev.

As the lunch recess neared its end, Angela was putting the finishing touches on her reports.

Bev sashayed into the room, looking way too fresh and energized. "I'm gonna go grab a bite to eat and come right back," she announced to Angela, who was only just looking up from her papers.

"Are you kidding?" the behavior specialist asked in disbelief. "You can't go now. These kids are desperate for some time with you. Almost everyone has been in crisis *all morning*, and lunch is about to end. Even Donna needs you to call in."

"It's okay," Bev coolly reassured. "They can talk all they want as soon as I get some food. I'm famished; I've been in meetings all morning."

Angela's filthy hands had been trembling from hunger, fear, adrenaline and exhaustion for the past hour and a half. Now, what little energy she had left made them tremble in anger. She focused on staying calm by speaking through clenched teeth. "Must be rough. I'm also starving, but I've been kicked, pounded and stabbed at all morning. I watched Kevin piss and masturbate in timeout. I sent a kid to jail. I've been spit on and screamed at. My only break so far has been spent furiously filling out more than a dozen pages of reports. I need you to

147

stay and help me. These kids need you now."

Bev engaged her therapist voice. "I understand how you feel. Believe me, I've been there. But I can't help anyone on an empty stomach. I'll be back before they return from lunch."

The bell rang. Bev wiggled her eyebrows like Groucho Marx and left before Angela could get another word in edgewise.

The behavior specialist threw her pen on her desk, got up, closed the doors to room 36, entered the dry timeout booth, slammed the door behind her and hollered until her lungs emptied. Her throat sore, she left the booth, grabbed her sack lunch and took a real break.

Using several handfuls of soap, Angela twice washed her arms up to her elbows in the small confines of the teachers' lounge bathroom sink. After so many restraints, with so many dirty children, she felt more than a little grody.

In what had become a bit of a running joke between them, Angela caught Rachel O'Malley picking through her lunch bag.

"I see, young grasshopper, you have yet to show any respect for your elders by bringing them any chocolate," Rachel clucked.

Angela wearily smiled and changed the subject. "Monsters one and all."

"Kids getting to ya today?" Rachel asked, sitting on the couch.

"Kids, adults—everybody."

Rachel shrugged her shoulders. "It's probably a full moon or somethin'."

"Oh, I saw a full moon alright. It was bobbing up and down in timeout as a kid was humping the floor. (Rachel's upper lip curled in disgust as Angela kept talking.) That's not even the worst of it. Another kid came within inches of plunging a pair of teachers' scissors into my stomach."

"Dear, God," Rachel exclaimed. "Are you okay?"

"By sheer luck and fast reflexes, yes. But that's only half the misery," Angela continued venting. "Most of the parents didn't medicate their kids this morning. Dealing with them is horrendous."

"Who? The parents or the kids?"

"Take your pick. Worst of all, my boss, the therapist, refuses to stay and help. She has some meeting no one knows about or she has to go eat lunch or whatever. She refuses to stick around, even though I've told her how badly we need her."

Angela plopped down on the couch next to her friend in exhausted frustration.

"Don't get me wrong, Ang. I know your job is necessary, but you couldn't pay me enough to tolerate anything like that," Rachel commiserated.

Quick, heavy footfalls approached from the office. Mr. Franklin appeared; his face was pink with restrained anger. "I just learned from one of the first-grade teachers that one of your students was arrested in the hallway by the police just before lunch. Is this true?"

"Yes, except the boy was arrested in class, not the hall."

Rachel silently watched for Mr. Franklin to explode.

"Why wasn't I informed?!"

Angela's brain raced in search of an appropriate answer: *It didn't really concern you. There was nothing you could have done; I was a little busy at the moment.* None seemed appropriate to soothing his nerves, so she stole a page from her student's playbook. "I don't know."

"You don't know?! What was he charged with?"

"Assault with a deadly weapon, simple assault and ungovernable."

"Assault with a deadly weapon?!" roared Mr. Franklin. "What did he do?"

"He attacked me with a pair of long, sharp scissors. I caught him just in time. There's nothing to worry about. Everything is taken care of," the behavior specialist calmly explained.

The principal gaped at Angela, who, to his way of thinking, obviously didn't get the gravity of the situation. "Angela, a principal needs to know every major event that happens in his school. In a time where kids are mowing down school yards with assault weapons, when a student tries to stab a teacher to death in class—I NEED to know."

Angela lowered her voice and convincingly lied with her apology. "I'm sorry; I'll be sure to tell you the next time anything major happens."

Mr. Franklin thanked her and went back to his office. There really was little else he could do. As Angela wasn't his employee, he had little power over her. And as his school was the only one in the district up to the standards of the state to host such a class as her's, it would take a lot more than this to get rid of the program. The two weren't normally combative, but Mr. Franklin hated the lack of control he had over the daytreatment program.

Angela knew this and her lie wasn't an act of malice but of congenial political gamesmanship. She knew damn well he didn't want to know all that really went on in her program. Even when he learned about minor chaos that was normal for severely emotionally disturbed children, like the swearing or the spitting that the staff no longer thought twice about, he would over-react. He'd cut access to as many mainstream benefits as he could for all the students, regardless of the ones who behaved well during the given benefit. The staff agreed that keeping him out of the loop was the wisest policy, so long as any tragedies were averted. Sure they'd throw a few softballs at him along with the progress reports to make him feel like he was a part of the action, and this way he felt well informed and ready to answer any questions from his superiors. But in reality, he wouldn't last 15 minutes in their combined classroom on a good day...at least without doing everything in his power to shut it all down.

Angela made the mental note, *Call him the next time the police are called in.*

"You're just having a sucky day all over," Rachel consoled.

Angela worked to control her frustration and volume. "Would it be so hard for the day to give a full 10 minutes without someone misbehaving or yelling at me?"

"Yeah, probably," Rachel playfully mocked. "By the way, did I tell you how awful your hair looks today? And that T-shirt. Please."

Angela gave her a sidelong grimace. "Bite me."

By the time Angela finished her lunch, Bev still hadn't returned. Donna called again, but all the behavior specialist could tell her was that Bev was out to lunch. Both women silently wondered how out-to-lunch Bev was.

Fortunately for the daytreatment program, the food and the meds had settled the children. It was quiet enough for Angela to wrap up her loose ends from the morning.

The only outburst of the afternoon came from Sammy when his workload became too stressful. After a handful of bitchells and a 10-minute timeout, he was good to go.

With only 45 minutes to go in the school day, Bev finally strolled in. "Hiya, Kiddo. Did ya miss me?"

If looks could kill, Angela's would have eviscerated the therapist mid-stride through the door. "Where have you been?!"

"Lunch, I told you."

"That was hours ago."

"Was it?" Bev tried to disarm her with a laugh. "You know how I am with time."

"I told you we are in crisis. Not only do I—your teammate and friend—need you, more important; the kids really, really need you. We've still got enough time for one therapy session, plus Donna has been trying very hard to reach you all day."

Bev readjusted herself to project a more professional attitude. "Who should I start with?"

"Well, since Ted is in jail, I'd recommend Kevin—not that you'd be wrong to choose Violet."

"What's this? Why didn't you tell me Ted was in jail? What happened?"

"I tried, but you wouldn't listen to me and left me for your precious meetings and extended lunch. Now why don't you work with Kevin while there's still time, and I'll explain the rest to you later."

"How dare you take that tone with me?! I'm still your boss, I'll have you know."

Angela was silent, her eyes unblinking daggers dueling with Bev's icy gaze. Angela didn't give a damn if she had overstepped her bounds with Bev, who was the one person she refused to let trample on her after the miserable day she'd put in without this woman's needed support.

"We'll finish this later," Bev coldly threatened, backing down to treat Kevin.

Her session with Kevin was a total bust. Too much time had passed since he was ripe for therapy and talking. Now his meds had full traction, and he could regain control of his repression.

The session ended just before school let out. When the driver, who was still angry about the kids' behavior in the morning, whisked those same kids home, Ronnie, Carla, Mrs. Regina and Angela truly relaxed for the first time all day. Their muscles stopped bracing for impact, and their eyes stopped dancing with hypervigilance. They slouched around a circular classroom table for their afternoon meeting. Several exhausted sighs were heaved.

"We survived," declared Mrs. Regina. "Thank God I'm another day closer to retirement."

Bev entered the room last. "Tough day, huh?" she merrily inquired.

Four pairs of eyes scornfully focused on her.

"Honestly, I had some very important meetings to attend today," Bev said. It was true, in a sense. Her car was barely chugging along, and she had made the appointment to get it fixed weeks ago. Then she got a courtesy ride to the mall while she waited. She figured she had earned a mental health day as much as anyone. Given her fragile mental state, maybe she would have had trouble coping with the class. When she ran into an old friend at lunch, she decided to continue her active avoidance of a stressful day. She didn't dare breathe a word of this to anyone at the table. She felt guilty when Angela told her about Ted, but there was little anyone could do about that now. The women at the table didn't seem at all convinced by her meeting story, so Bev nervously offered, "Hey, I'm here now. At least I can help clean up the aftermath."

Despite their temporary misgivings about Bev, the survivors of the day took turns venting about the details of their day.

"Ya see, Angela," Bev playfully gloated, "I told you, you'd change your mind about giving kids meds."

That was almost too much for Angela, and she glared at the therapist.

"C'mon, admit it. Meds are good," Bev joshed.

"Fine," she spit, before eating the words from her interview. "Meds are useful, now leave me alone."

"Ease up on the girl, Bev," Ronnie said in Angela's defense. "She really got stuck with the worst of it. Ted could have killed her."

All of the survivors were amazed at how oblivious Bev was to their really trying and stressful day.

Bev was growing equally irritated that no one was appreciating her attempts to loosen them up a little. She also didn't need any more guilt, teetering as close as she was to a nervous breakdown.

The meeting adjourned with little being truly accomplished. The classroom staff left early, leaving Bev and Angela alone.

Bev was frosty again. "You know, I can appreciate you having a really hard day. And from the sounds of it, you handled it very well. But as your boss, I will not stand for your disrespectful attitude. Those meetings I had to attend, they were very important."

"You keep saying that, but what were they for?" Angela asked.

"I can't tell you."

"Why not?"

"I just can't."

Angela tried to keep her head from spinning 720 degrees and exploding. "Listen. All I know is that we were in the middle of a half-dozen crises at once and you seemed to completely ignore my pleas for help. The children were particularly vulnerable and in need of your help. And you appeared to have let us all down for these mysterious meetings and a two-hour lunch. Why shouldn't I be upset?"

The phone began ringing, but Bev didn't answer it, scolding Angela instead, "This type of insubordination is unacceptable. Don't forget your six-month review is coming up. If you lose this job, it won't look good to the graduate schools you apply to."

"Are you threatening me? I've quit better jobs than this—jobs where no one tries to kill you! Feel free to start looking for my replacement. It'll take you longer than my six-month review to find her," Angela fought back, before gruffly answering the phone. "Yeah, she's here."

Angela handed the phone to Bev. It was Donna. Bev dismissed Angela for the night, knowing the chewing out she was about to get from Donna and not wanting her insubordinate subordinate to hear it.

Chapter 11

Sammy

(Early November, Sunday night)

Sammy peacefully played with some Matchbox cars under the cheap closed Venetian blinds in the front room of the public housing apartment he shared with his mother. He quietly talked to himself, imagining that he was driving his favorite police car, while his crime fighting buddy Angela drove the blue car. Even in imaginary form, to be allowed to drive the blue car was an honor few would achieve, as it was the only car in his collection that had doors that opened and closed.

On the other side of the room, Lulu was watching her 12th straight television show of the afternoon. She turned up the volume to drown out Sammy's soft, contented babbling. As the loudness didn't seem to diminish Sammy's enjoyment of his cars, Lulu wasn't satisfied.

"Shut the fuck up," Lulu yelled. "I'm trying to watch my programs, you worthless little shit!"

Sammy stopped talking to himself, but he kept playing. Lulu felt he showed neither the proper disappointment nor fear.

"Don't make me come over there and take away your stupid cars," Lulu threatened, before loudly muttering, "God, I wish I never had that little fucker."

Sammy feared the loss of his cars and pulled them in close.

This was the reaction Lulu was seeking. She smiled menacingly.

Lulu lifted her fat, unwashed self from her ratty recliner. She wore only sweat pants and a bra. She kicked or crushed his other cars, as she approached.

"Gimme those cars you dumb little boy," she grunted, breaking a sweat in the short walk across the room.

Sammy clenched his police car in one hand and the blue car in the other.

"No?" Lulu asked incredulously, arms akimbo. "Give 'em to me now!"

She batted him across the temples several times with open hands. She ripped the cars from his hands, as he screamed in pain. She opened the door and threw each car out into the dark courtyard below.

Sammy jumped up and tried to run out the door after his cars. He knew the other kids in the complex would steal them if they found them before he did.

Before he could escape, Lulu slammed the door shut. He began to twist the door knob, but she turned the deadbolt too quickly. As Sammy pounded on the door, Lulu picked him up, turned him around and bashed him against the door. She pinned him to the door by the shoulders, three-feet off the floor.

He didn't dare move.

She pressed her forehead against his. "I guess you'll fuckin' listen to me the next time, Retard. You worthless nothing. You're so retarded, nobody can possibly love you now or ever. How could they; you're so worthless."

She bashed him against the wall, again. "Do you know anyone who loves you? I sure don't, you stupid little bastard."

Sammy nodded.

"You know you're stupid, or you know someone who loves you?" She got in his face again.

Sammy meekly whispered, "Angela."

"That filthy, disgusting bitch hole doesn't love you," Lulu roared with a fury to rival any tempest. "I'm your mother. I'm the only one who will ever love you—you stupid, dumb, ugly piece of shit."

"No," sobbed Sammy.

"That dirty little Spic slut is only nice to you because they pay her to be nice to you. They pay her to say shit like 'You're special,' and 'You're good.' She doesn't believe it. She even told me she hates you. She wishes you'd die, so she won't have to be nice to you anymore."

"No," Sammy whimpered.

"Yes," Lulu raged. "And I think I'll help her, you dumb little bastard."

Lulu grabbed the thin, rayon chord from the blinds, and pinned Sammy to herself, his back against her front. She jerked the cord around his throat and hotly whispered in his ear, "Angela doesn't love you. She'd save you if she did, but I don't see her here. Angela hates you because you're a worthless little shit."

Sammy tried to pry the chord from his neck, but he couldn't get his fingers under it. He tried to run, but only got a step before his mother jerked him back into her swollen, sweaty breasts and belly.

"Angela hates you; Angela hates you; Angela hates you," Lulu chanted in hushed tones, as the little boy grew weaker and weaker, slipping into blackness.

His mother didn't release the chords around his throat for a solid minute after he lost consciousness. When she casually let the chord go, he fell to the floor in a heap. Without a second thought about her son, Lulu went back to her recliner to watch some more television. She didn't check, nor did she care, to see if Sammy was still alive.

It was well after midnight when Sammy came to. The apartment was pitch black. He hated the dark. Freddy lived in the dark. His mom attacked more easily in the dark.

He heard her snoring in the recliner.

Fully awake, Sammy knew two things. First, and foremost, he had to get out of the apartment. Second, he had to find his cars before the other kids found them. He owned few things and couldn't stand to lose the things he loved most.

Quietly, he found the door and left—ever so slowly and soundlessly closing the door behind him. Outside it was cold. The moon was full and gave him some light with which to search.

Sammy spent the next several hours combing the courtyard before he found both cars. He was frequently interrupted by stumbling drunks or opiate addicts on their way home. To avoid them, he hid in some prickly bushes. He tried not to think about what Lulu said about Angela, but deep down he was certain his mother was right. How could anyone possibly love him? *I am worthless and retarded*, he agreed inside his head.

By the time he sneaked back into the apartment, his teeth were chattering, and he was in danger of developing hypothermia. But to avoid raising his mother's ire, he put his cars in his pants pockets and lay on the floor where he collapsed. He didn't sleep easily and was up with the sun to make sure he got to school on time.

Chapter 12

Snapping Like a Twig
(Later That Morning)

After Bev and Angela skirmished on the infamous Day of No Meds, Bev closed out the week on her best behavior. The therapist chalked up record hours with private sessions with the kids and began putting a dent in the paperwork Donna so desperately needed to have filled out. Bev even took Angela out for wine and apologized.

Yet, in the two weeks following that one, Angela hadn't seen Bev for a full day at work. Oodles of meetings, late arrivals, long lunches and early departures. Even when Bev was at work, she was a scattered, at times almost incoherent, mess.

None of the staff knew exactly what to do, even though it was clear Bev was having a nervous breakdown. Even Angela, who had already dealt with her own mother's breakdown, naively held out hope that Bev would pull it together. She didn't tell anyone at headquarters about Bev, but she also never lied to cover for Bev. She simply told the truth: She stepped out; she's at lunch; she told me she had a meeting to go to; she hasn't come in yet, etc.

In fact, Angela felt she was accomplishing more without Bev's help. Angela never attempted therapy with the kids, but they were really opening up to her. She mastered the token economy and could usually get the kids to do whatever she wanted. Lashaun mainstreamed. Although Angela truly had little to do with that, it was a big victory for the program. The staff, kids and even some parents had really come to trust Angela.

Of course, Angela still hated DCW, but she was accepting that as a part of life.

Even Ted was doing better. After trying to stab Angela, he spent the night in the men's lockup downtown. No one else would take him. Because of that, a judge temporarily removed him from his father's custody and placed him in a group home that specialized in severely emotionally disturbed boys. Ted was still sociopathic, but the peace and stability of the group home made him easier to contend with at school.

Things were generally going well for the program, but because of

Bev's erratic behavior, everyone knew it was just a matter of time before something would really go wrong. Not knowing what was going to happen or how was what made it nerve wracking for the staff.

Sammy was a mess coming off the bus. He was Sammy and Freddy both, grunting and gasping as his head swiveled in search of danger in every direction. This was normal for Sammy three months ago, not now. Even more out of place was how clean he was. Scrubbed, shampooed, and dressed in a warm, sophisticated turtleneck and spot-free trousers. He didn't look nearly this good on picture day. The staffs' Spidie sense started tingling. What was wrong?

Angela escorted Sammy to his place in line to gauge his proximity to escalation. "My, my, my. Who is this handsome young gentleman?"

He ignored her completely.

"The nerdiest spaz on the planet," cracked Charlie, making Franz and Kevin giggle.

"That's a minus dollar, Charlie," Angela scolded, before offering him advice. "You know, if you dressed this nicely, the girls would be throwing themselves at you."

Charlie laughed. "No, they'd be beating me up."

Kevin and Franz laughed harder.

"Minus dollar for each of you," Angela subtracted. That silenced the older boys, so Angela turned back to Sammy. "May I hold your hand on the way to class?"

She held out her hand, but Sammy thrust his hands into his pockets. He clenched the prized cars he had successfully transferred to these pants without Lulu seeing.

Normally, Sammy preferred holding Angela's hand. She was the surrogate mother he always wanted and being with her made him feel safe. Today, he remembered all of the awful things Lulu said about Angela as she strangled him. *She hates me. She only likes me because they pay her to like me.*

Despite all that his mother said, Angela seemed as nice and trustworthy as ever. Sammy was very confused. He couldn't get his mother's voice out of his head.

To Angela's surprise, Sammy marched defiantly into school without even speaking to her. She wondered what was wrong, but she was confident she'd find out something soon. Something or someone would trip his trigger.

Bev still hadn't arrived, so it was up to Angela to lead group. She

160

was at ease with the task now, even if her group sessions were exceedingly "lame" in the eyes of the kids and un"therapeutic" in the eyes of the state and insurers. Regardless of Bev's presence, the classroom staff desperately needed that half hour to teach age-appropriate lessons to the age group left behind.

On this grey November morning, big-kids' group went well. Little-kids' group went well up to a point…the point where Sammy got so bored that he took his Matchbox cars from his pockets and began to play on his rug.

The sight of toys and play hit the other kids like the craving of a sobering alcoholic in need of a fresh infusion of booze.

"Nice cars."

"Can I see one?"

"I promise I'll give it right back."

"I'll be your best friend, if I can play with one."

Angela asked Sammy to put them back in his pockets. She tried to bribe the other kids into ignoring him, but they kept pestering him.

Sammy ignored them well until Lionel reached out and touched the police car. Sammy clenched the cars in his fists and socked Lionel in the lip with one. The punch split Lionel's lip.

"LIONEL, I'LLGIVEYOU50BUCKSIFYOUDON'THITHIMANDQUIETLY-GONEXTDOORFORHELP!" Angela shouted with rapid-fire clarity, springing into action trying to restrain Sammy before Lionel killed him.

"Fifty?" Lionel eyed her sharply, fist cocked. He desperately wanted to steam roll the kid he considered the biggest freak in the program. His little tongue curled out to lick his swollen, bleeding lip. "Fifty?"

"Fifty," she reaffirmed, now holding Sammy in a proper MANDT restraint. "It would prove to me how mature and responsible you are growing up to be, making good choices and earning a ton of money for store."

Lionel weighed the risks and benefits for another second. Sammy struggled fiercely in Angela's arms, but Lionel slowly lowered his fist and went next door without another word. Angela congratulated him and loudly awarded the biggest cash deal of the class' token economy. Sammy spit at Lionel and missed. He readjusted his aim for Ted and Edward.

"Five dollars to both of you for ignoring Sammy's spitting and for you to go back to class, right now."

The boys cashed in on the easy money.

Sammy only fought harder to escape.

"It's okay, Sammy." Angela soothed, unaware she had him trapped too much like last night's near-death experience for him to settle down. "Calm down; it's okay. It's just you and me. You're safe."

Angela was reluctant to put Sammy in timeout because of the way it terrified him, yet his struggling only continued to intensify.

"Hate me. Hate me. Hate me," he grunted and rasped, his voice damaged by the cords around his neck.

Reverting to his babyish verbal patterns, Angela translated Sammy speak without the use of personal pronouns.

"I don't hate you. I like you very much," she tried to reassure him.

Sammy began to cry, as he wiggled and jerked to get free. "Paid to say. Hate me."

"I don't hate you. No one pays me to say I like you," Angela tried to reassure, putting together the pieces that seemed to point to Lulu messing with Sammy's mind somehow. "Sammy. You are one of my favoritest little boys in the whole wide world. Who else gives me such 'pitty' rocks and plays with me every day on the swings?"

Unlike the first time she talked him down from suicide, this time Angela spoke from her heart. She had come to love him like a member of her own family. It was no secret that he was her favorite, although she went out of her way to treat every child in the program equally.

Sammy was still horrified by the restraint performed by the woman his mother said wanted him dead. When Angela whispered low into his ear to sooth him with all the reasons and ways she liked him, it triggered a posttraumatic flashback to Lulu choking him. Putting him in timeout would spark a different but equally horrific flashback, and Angela knew she was at a loss for effective action to neutralize the situation.

Sammy cried and spit at her. "Hate me. Hate me."

"I don't hate you. (Dodge goober) I like you. (Dodge goober) I love the pictures you draw for me. (Dodge goober) I like holding your hand and walking down the hall. (Dodge goober) I love talking with you. (Dodge goober)"

As Sammy craned his neck to get a better shot, Angela noticed something below the collar of his turtleneck.

Angela's voice transformed from behavior specialist to concerned mother. "What's this? Stop a second; I want to see something."

Sammy heard and could feel a total change in Angela by her voice and grip. He was still for a second.

Angela released her formal restraint and held him lightly by the shoulders. "If I let you go, will you promise not to run away?"

He nodded.

Angela turned him around and got on her knees. He shirked back, as she slowly reached for his collar.

"It's okay. I promise I won't hurt you. I just want to see something for a second."

She gently pulled down the turtleneck collar and saw two deep-pink lines wrapping from his esophagus back past each jugular vein. Each thin line dug in at least 1/8th of an inch.

The sight alarmed Angela, but she had come a long way in improving her therapist's poker face. "What happened to your neck?" she casually asked.

Sammy stiffened. She'd seen. She knew. Now he felt he was in real trouble. If he told her what happened, he knew she'd report it, and he'd be in more trouble than ever if Lulu got in trouble. Maybe next time he wouldn't wake up. Of course, she'd call "them" anyway, but at least he could tell Lulu he didn't say a word. She might go easier on him.

"It's okay, Sammy. I promise nothing bad will happen. I'll protect you," Angela was gravely sincere. This was all she needed to get Sammy permanently removed from his home. All he had to do was say that his mom strangled him. If he could tell her, uncoached, what happened and then repeat it for DCW without Angela in view, his mother could be locked away for the rest of his childhood.

Just three words, Sammy: "Mom did it." That's all it takes to end the abuse. Please, God, please make him say it, Angela silently prayed.

The 6-year-old looked deeply into Angela's brown eyes. It was instantly clear to him that Lulu was wrong and that Angela did love him. Angela was his friend. He knew she meant what she promised about protecting him. He knew she could not. *If I see Mom, again, she'll kill me,* he thought. *I must keep Angela from calling.*

"Please, Sammy," Angela requested, "Tell me what happened to your neck."

The 6-year-old spit in her face. He felt terrible about doing it, but it was the only thing he could think to do to keep her from the phone. He transformed into Freddy, to escape his guilt.

Wordlessly, Angela wiped her face, stood and gently shepherded the re-escalated boy into timeout. She bolted the door; he raged. *There is more than one way to skin a cat,* she said to herself. *I'll make DCW come out and look at this. There's no way they can deny those strangle marks. He'll never have to go into that apartment again.*

In the meantime, Angela wanted to quickly de-escalate Sammy, so Mrs. Regina could see the marks on his throat. She decided to break the teacher's cardinal rule about opening the door and talking with the student. "If you sit against the back wall, I'll open the door."

The idea appealed to Sammy. It beat having the door bolted shut. He sat cautiously against the back wall.

Angela opened the door a crack. She sat on a small chair, blocking his escape route. Sammy remained calm.

"Why did you spit on me?" Angela asked.

Sammy sheepishly shrugged.

"Although my feelings are hurt because you spit in my face, I want you to know I still like you and want to be your friend."

Sammy meekly chirped. "Sorry."

"What?" Angela decided to make him work for it.

"I sorry I spit."

"You need to start speaking like a big kid, again, Sammy. I'm sorry I spit in your face, Angela," she instructed him to repeat.

He did.

"Thank you. May I have a side hug?"

The little boy walked over and hugged her shoulder.

"Okay, kiddo. Are you ready to go back to class?"

Sammy nodded.

"Okay. I want you to sit in this chair for just a minute," Angela said, as she rose.

Sammy followed her instructions, and the behavior specialist summoned Mrs. Regina at the pass-through door.

Angela whispered, "I think Lulu tried to strangle Sammy to death last night. I want you to see his neck. He's calm and ready for class, so don't make a big deal of it. I'll call DCW after he's settled back in class."

Angela turned to Sammy and beckoned. "Why don't you come over here and show Mrs. Regina your neck."

Sammy ambled over and indignantly pulled down his collar.

Mrs. Regina didn't flinch and allowed Sammy back in her room. She asked Angela, "Did he say it was his mother who did that?"

"No, but who else could have? He has no other family and isn't allowed out of the apartment."

"Good luck convincing DCW," the veteran teacher said and

164

returned to her class.

Angela went to her desk and was about to pick up the phone when Sammy peeked into the room.

"Hi, Sammy. Can I help you?"

He shyly approached her desk. He reached into his pockets and pulled out two Matchbox cars.

"Do you want to play?" Angela inquired.

The boy shook his head no and rolled the police car on the smooth surface of her desk.

"Do you want to give me a present?"

Again he shook his head.

"You have to talk to me, Sammy. I don't know what you want."

"You keep."

"Do you want me to keep them safe in my desk?"

He opened his mouth and nodded.

Angela rolled a little blue car with one finger. "I'll keep them right here in this top, right-hand drawer. You can play with them any time you get permission from next door. Okay?"

"Friends," Sammy said.

"Friends," Angela replied. "Now, I think they probably are missing you in class."

Sammy smiled and walked to class with Angela. This time she gently closed the door behind him and made her phone call to Cora, Sammy's new caseworker who replaced Twyla.

A different woman answered Cora's direct line. "Hi, I'm Blanche, Sammy's new case worker." Blanche sounded a little embarrassed by that fact.

"Hi, I'm Angela Marengo from Sammy's daytreatment program at Average Elementary," the behavior specialist introduced herself. "Wow! I only talked with Cora once—hardly enough to frighten her away so quickly."

Blanche laughed. "Who leaked that you have a bit of a reputation around here?"

"Let's just call it my feminine intuition," Angela dryly replied. "I'm really not that bad. I'm just trying the best I know how to save some kids' lives."

"Well, no one can fault you for that."

Angela let a small, ironic laugh slip. "Ohhhh, I think you'll change your mind in a couple hours."

"Uh-oh. What's wrong?"

Angela already liked this new caseworker's attitude and decided to play nice. "I'd really appreciate it if you could come here as soon as you can to see Sammy. He has some really nasty lookin' rope or string marks of some kind dug pretty deeply into his neck. I think someone choked him pretty badly last night."

"Oh my God!" Blanche exclaimed. "Who did it?"

"I'm certain it was his mom, but you really need to see for yourself. The marks are so deep and red. Really painful looking."

"I'll be there as soon as I can."

"Thanks," said Angela, amazed that she might see some action from DCW after just one phone call.

Donna called as Angela filled out her requisite paperwork for Sammy's escalation and her call into DCW.

"Hi, Donna. Bev's still not in," Angela answered before she was asked. "I'll have her call you as soon as she gets here."

"That won't be necessary, she's here." Donna sounded perturbed.

"Oh," Angela reacted, genuinely surprised. "She didn't tell me anything about a meeting."

There was a hint of a threat in Donna's voice as she commanded, "You must come to headquarters after school gets out."

"Okay. I'll see you then," Angela agreed, her voice serenely innocent. Donna hung up, and the behavior specialist knew the jig was up.

Whatever was to go down at the HQ wasn't going to be pleasant, but Angela was remarkably unconcerned. She was inundated with work to keep her busy until then, and in her heart of hearts, she knew she had done nothing wrong as Bev melted down.

A knock at the door broke her train of thought. Angela opened it and greeted a blonde woman her age. "Blanche?"

"Yep. You're Angela?"

"No fangs or claws, even," Angela smiled. "Disappointed?"

"A little," Blanche shrugged and shook her counterpart's hand.

"I'll get Sammy for you," Angela said. "Have you met him, yet?"

"No," the social worker replied. "I've only read his file."

"Oh," Angela halted, before getting the little boy. "Be sure to give him lots of space. He's very shy and scared of new people. If he gets wild eyed or starts talking about Freddy, call for help, immediately. That's the sign he'll escalate. Trust me, you won't want to handle that alone."

"Thanks for the heads up," Blanche said. "Before you get him, can you tell me a little more about 'Freddy.' There are a number of vague references to Freddy in our files, but no one really knows what it means."

Angela explained how Sammy used the Hollywood monster as a multifaceted emotional defense mechanism.

Blanche absorbed the explanation and asked, "Do you mind if I talk with Sammy in here? Maybe it'll make him more comfortable."

"That's fine with me, I'm sure they can find something for me to do next door."

"Uh, would you mind sticking around, in case he spazzes out? I've heard horror stories."

Angela leveled with the case worker. "Listen. I don't mind, but I don't want to be in the way, be accused of coaching Sammy or in any other way negating your findings. This kid has probably suffered the worst abuse of any kid in this program, and I refuse to risk standing in the way of his safety."

"I promise, you won't be in the way," Blanche assured. "I want you to know that I also want to save as many abused kids as I can, too."

Blanche's blue eyes intensely probed Angela's face for any evidence of trust. Angela warily yielded some. "Okay. I'll get Sammy."

She returned with the apprehensive child in a matter of seconds. "Sammy," Angela enthusiastically addressed him. "I'd like you to meet Blanche. She's your new DCW case worker."

Blanche extended her hand and smiled. "Hi. It's good to meet you, Sammy."

Sammy stood expressionlessly before Blanche.

"It's okay, Sammy. Shake her hand," Angela encouraged. "Would you like to show Blanche your cars and play?"

Sammy shook his head no.

"Would you like to color," Angela probed.

The 6-year-old cautiously scrutinized Blanche and apprehensively walked over to the main table in the room. He sat as far from the stranger as he thought he could, but she insisted on sitting directly across from him.

Angela brought over a bucket of crayons and some paper. As she left to return to her desk, Blanche asked Sammy, "Would you like Angela to color with us?"

Sammy nodded yes, to Angela's dismay. She didn't want to be considered a coaching interloper under any circumstance, and she knew that DCW's director might view her close presence suspiciously. She quietly sat next to Sammy and began drawing Fur-nando.

Sammy scribbled, and Blanche drew a dog.

As they colored, Blanche asked, "Do you know why I'm here, Sammy?"

He played dumb and shook his head no.

"Well, I heard there was something on your neck I should see."

He shook his head no, and Angela remained silent.

Blanche playfully pouted. "Pretty please?"

Sammy heaved an exasperated sigh and pulled down his turtleneck.

Blanche flinched. The ligature marks looked like fresh scar tissue, as if Sammy was recovering from having his throat slit. She leaned in for a better look.

"Does it hurt?"

"No," Sammy lied.

"How did you get that?" Blanche inquired.

Sammy shook his head and let his collar ride back up.

"What does that head move mean?" Blanche asked.

Sammy's eyes widened. A twisted smile grew across his face.

Angela nonchalantly put down her crayon and prepared for Freddy.

"How did you get those marks?" Blanche pressed.

"Bun-ny rab-bit," Sammy said in a darkly silly voice.

"How could a bunny rabbit do that?"

"Claws," explained Freddy with his hands in the air to demonstrate with his bladed fingers.

"Okay," Angela said, though it pained her to interrupt. "Visiting time is over. Sammy, you have two choices: classroom or timeout?"

Without looking at Angela, Freddy threw crayons at Blanche. Angela sighed, restrained him and shepherded him to timeout. Sammy head butted the door when she raised the latch into place.

"Please tell me you'll remove him from that apartment," Angela pleaded with Blanche in a whisper.

"You know I can't," Blanche whispered back.

"You saw his neck. His own mother strangled him. You can't in good conscience send him back to that hell hole."

"Angela, he never said it was his mother. It was a bunny, according to his demented little mind."

"Come on. You studied psychology. You know he's exhibiting classic PTSD symptoms. You know that his mother caused it."

"No, Angela. Unless he confesses she did it, she confesses she did it or a witness is willing to testify they saw it first hand, any one could have done it," Blanche replied, her voice growing more and more snippy.

"You've read his file. The only people he deals with are at school or his mother. She never lets him leave the house—even to play with other kids. There has got to be something you can do."

"Well, I will go and talk with Lulu. Maybe she can tell me what happened."

"Don't, please," Angela begged. "She'll only hurt him worse tonight, if she finds out another call has been made against her. She might kill him. That's textbook pathology for her and every other abuser on the planet. Don't tell her."

Blanche got up to leave. "You know. They were right about you, back at the office. You've got to end your obsessive persecution of that poor, defenseless disabled woman. I've never even met her, and I feel sorry for her."

Blanche left, and Angela's vision blurred with white-hot anger. *Another fucking blind caseworker*, she wanted to scream. *Why is it I'm one of the only people who can see what is happening? Why is it all of the people who need to see this are refusing to accept that I know what I'm talking about? What the hell else does it take to connect the right people to the clear and obvious facts?!*

There was a reason Angela connected so well with Cassandra when she read Homer's, "The Illiad."

Sammy stopped pounding and sat against the back wall.

Angela opened the door. "I'm sorry, Sammy." She paused, knowing Sammy knew what she was talking about. "Will you let me push you way, super high on the swings at recess?"

Sammy nodded, but Angela could see in his face that he knew he was doomed.

The school day ended, and Angela was filled with growing remorse. Her colleagues in the classroom agreed that Sammy was a marked "man." They went out of their way to go easy on him for the rest of the day, and Angela and the classroom staff subconsciously took their leave of him as he boarded the bus, counting on the inevitable later that night. Even Carla, who genuinely didn't like Sammy after all his spitting and bruising, felt terrible about sending him home.

Ronnie and Mrs. Regina tried to console Angela by reminding her it was her legal duty to call DCW about Sammy, but she countered that just because it was the law for good Germans to report Jews to Hitler, didn't make it the right thing to do. While they countered that the comparison might have been a little excessive, that's how it felt to Angela.

Angela's day was about to go from bad to worse. She still had her meeting at headquarters. Whatever was about to happen, it was guaranteed to be unpleasant.

The drive over was short but tense.

She braced herself in the parking lot, trying to self-rehearse her plans, arguments and defenses. *Alright. We know why they're unhappy, and we know what's going on. Be polite and respectful, but don't take any shit. They have no clue how much you know or how well you can read people. They think you're the stupid rookie; play the role a little with some humility, and you'll go far. Don't apologize for anything you didn't do. Stay strong, but play it cool. Don't tense up. Get loose. Let's go do this.*

Angela entered the facility with grace and confidence. She smiled and greeted the women working at the front desk. They all smiled back except for Donna.

"Follow me," she said flatly.

Donna was all business. There was no small talk, as she led Angela down the hall to Richard's office.

Bev emerged from a hallway door. "Hey, Ang! How's it goin'?"

She was as manic as ever.

"Hi, Bev," Angela replied, but Donna beckoned her on before allowing the women to talk. Donna leveled an intimidating gaze at Bev, which forced the therapist back into the office.

Richard had his usual hang-dog expression and greeted Angela at his office door. Donna closed it behind them. Richard offered Angela a seat in the center of the room. Donna took the one closest to the door.

Inwardly, Angela laughed. They had her trapped in the office the way she'd trap a student who was a flight risk.

"I suppose you know why you're here," Richard opened, stern but not menacing.

Angela felt she was still rookie enough to play a little innocent, without giving herself away. She wanted to find out all they knew first so she could act accordingly. "I can make a few educated guesses, but I don't know the exact reason."

"We're letting Bev go. As you well know, she hasn't been at the program nearly as much as she should. And although you've managed to stay on top of all your paperwork, she hasn't. And frankly, if she hasn't, yours is inconsequential because without Bev we can't bill for any of it. Subsequently, your program has gone bankrupt and is bleeding the rest of the mental health center dry.

"At this point," he continued, "we would normally scrap the elementary school program, and you would be out of a job. Unfortunately for the city, and lucky for you, we run the city's only elementary-based daytreatment program. Because of the city's, county's and state's legal obligations, it would be illegal for us to shut down. And we're lucky those governments are helping us work out a deal with the insurance provider to keep us from going under and agreeing not to sue us for negligence."

Angela nodded and listened respectfully. She had no idea how bad things really were on the business side. With the new understanding that she was a part of the legal problem, her palms began to sweat. She knew she was in far more trouble than she previously calculated.

Richard's woebegone face turned to paternal reprimand—not the quick flash of anger that leads to a swift swat on the behind but the icy I'm-sending-you-to-your-room-to-think-about-how-bad-you've-been-and-how-much-you've-let-me-down look.

Donna silently watched the behavior specialist with an unnerving burning heat.

Richard continued, "We have every reason and justification to fire you, too. You should have told us about Bev as soon as you knew something was wrong. Your loyalty is to the company, not your superior. This situation could have gone far worse very easily. When those kids are in crisis, a real, professionally-trained therapist should have been there. If something truly awful happened and someone got hurt, we could be sued out of business—and I don't just mean your program. I mean the whole gosh-darn operation. You've displayed a reckless disregard for the chain of command, and you've exposed us to phenomenal liability issues."

There was a long, heavy silence before Angela spoke.

"I'm very sorry, and I meant no disrespect to you or the center. I certainly had no intention of exposing the center to so many legal problems," Angela sincerely apologized. "Bev had her good days and her bad days. Her good days were amazing, and I always felt comfortable handling the rest. As stupid as it sounds, I never thought that I was putting the Center in any sort of legal trouble. I never lied to you or played therapist to the kids. I do think I understand these kids very well, and I do think I've made a lot of progress with them within the boundaries of my job."

That was the point on which Richard would relent. The young woman hadn't missed a day of work and was the most promising rookie he'd seen in years. She certainly wasn't the best behavior specialist in the company, but when it came to working with the kids, she was very talented.

Richard and Donna exchanged glances and intentionally drew out the silence to build more tension.

"Angela, under any other circumstances, I would fire you without a second thought," Richard explained. "However, I've spoken with your classroom staff, school administrators and even the parents of your program's children. With the exception of Lulu, they all speak well of you and agree you work very well with the kids.

"If we are to have any success transitioning in a new therapist, we'll need your help with the children. Of course, if you ever do what you did, again, you will be fired immediately."

Angela let out a small sigh of relief. "Thank you. I promise I'll call immediately if I see any problems with the new therapist."

"Good. In the meantime, you are to call me any time there is a crisis at the school. I'm a licensed therapist, and I can fill in whenever there's an emergency."

Angela promised.

(Thursday)

The past two days were rough ones at the daytreatment program. Sammy hadn't been heard or seen from, and Bev's sudden departure without proper closure was difficult for the kids to handle. She didn't say good-bye because she wasn't allowed.

Angela and the classroom staff repeatedly tried to explain the situation to the children without telling them that Bev was fired or that Bev had serious mental health issues like they did. They tried to explain Bev wasn't coming back...that Bev was okay...that Bev really liked them a lot and the children did nothing to chase her away.

Regardless, all of the children took it personally; the older kids took it hardest. Bev had worked with Charlie and Franz since they were in first grade. Franz escalated several times because of the news about Bev. For his emotions to override his pharmaceutical fog, they had to be extremely strong.

Angela called in Richard to help Franz with an emergency session. Even though Franz was de-escalated by the time the big boss arrived, it made a good impression on Richard that Angela was following orders and trying to earn back his trust.

The classroom staff had been expecting Bev's termination but was sad to lose her after all this time. Mrs. Regina had worked with her for five years and felt they worked a good program together. She hated the idea of breaking in a new therapist so close to retirement.

On the flip side, the staff was happy Angela was staying. She worked hard and knew what she was supposed to do.

Not overshadowed by all of this was Sammy. He hadn't returned to school since the cord marks were found around his neck. Lulu wasn't answering her phone. Angela called DCW repeatedly asking for Blanche or other caseworkers to check on Sammy. DCW never got back to her. A sense of foreboding settled over the women of daytreatment's souls.

After Thursday's group sessions, Angela decided to cut through all of the red tape at DCW.

"Good morning," she cheerily greeted the DCW receptionist. "May I please speak with Virginia Van Hess?...Sure, I'll hold."

She didn't give her name and was as chipper as could be. She didn't want to raise any warning flags to sideline her call. Her plan worked, and her call was put through. She remained ultra cordial.

"Good morning, Ms. Van Hess. My name is Angela Marengo; I'm

the children's behavior specialist at Average Elementary School. I believe we met at an I.E.P. with Sammy and Lulu."

Virginia gave a polite, but ironic, chuckle. "Yeah, I know who you are."

Noting how far her reputation preceded her, Angela remained unperturbed. She needed information and wasn't about to get under their director's skin. "I didn't call to pester or be a pain…"

Virginia cut her off. "Don't apologize. You do your job well. That just happens to irritate us some times. How can I help you?"

"On Monday, I reported that Sammy had strangulation marks around his throat. It looked like someone wrapped garrote wire around his neck. We haven't seen him at school since. I've called his apartment numerous times. I've called Blanche several times. She told me she'd go check on him and get back to me, but I haven't heard from her. I'm getting worried Sammy might be lying dead in his bathtub or something."

"Oh my goodness, no. He's fine," Virginia said. "I'm sorry you didn't know. Blanche told me yesterday that she was going to get back to you. I guess she didn't."

"That's quite a relief," Angela sighed. "But why isn't he in school? And why didn't Lulu call to tell us or even answer her phone?"

Virginia paused a bit before tackling this one. "Umm. She has caller I.D. and screens her calls very closely. Also…, umm…she says you are very intimidating to her."

"Intimidating?" Angela asked incredulously. "Why on earth would she think that?"

"She thinks you are out to get her. She thinks you have a thing against disabled parents—especially disabled single parents."

Mentally disabled, my eye, Angela thought before seriously explaining, "I can assure you I have no prejudices against any disabled people or single parents. There are many wonderful, loving parents who are single and mentally or physically disabled.

"Unfortunately, as I'm sure you know, those aren't the people either of us deals with every day. The students I deal with have been raped, beaten, starved or severely neglected by their parents," Angela was fighting the urge to get on her soap box, but she also knew this might be her only chance to present a logical case to someone who could make a difference in Sammy's situation. "In the short time I've worked here, Sammy has come in many times without being fed since the previous day's school lunch, he's run away from home a half a dozen times, he's come in black and blue, he's been suicidal and he's most recently come in with deep cord or shoelace wounds around his neck. I've reported each incident, as you know.

"I have nothing against disabled parents, but there is something definitely wrong in Sammy's home life. I've been told that Sammy is virtually never allowed to leave the apartment or see other people. That leaves only one person with whom he has any contact outside of school, and that leads me to think Lulu is behind these incidents.

"I studied cycles of violence at college, and those studies always said the cycles get progressively worse until the victim is either killed or finds a permanent way out of that relationship. The violence against Sammy is getting extremely severe..."

Angela let her unfinished sentence dangle in the open, knowing that Virginia would know where she was taking this whole conversation.

"You've signed a confidentiality statement, right?" Virginia inquired.

"Several."

"Then I can tell you in the strictest of confidence what we've been doing behind the scenes here?" Virginia confided without expecting answer. "My staff and I are sympathetic to Lulu. She's had a miserable life made even more so by her disabilities and single motherhood. She needs all of the love and help we can give her. (Angela's blood pressure spiked, but she didn't interrupt.) However, I have come to realize that she has some parenting issues, and those issues are starting to make me worry.

"No one has legally proven to me that she has ever hurt Sammy, so he can't be removed. It's the law that says I must do everything possible to prevent the state from taking custody of the child. Yet, it is also the law that says I must do everything possible to keep every child safe from abuse."

Angela tried to sympathize. "Kinda damned if you do; damned if you don't, huh?"

"Not really," Virginia explained. "I don't think Lulu's hurting her son intentionally. She wouldn't fight so hard to keep him if she didn't love him. However, she was reared in an extremely abusive household, too. I don't think she knows better."

Angela didn't say a word as Virginia kept disclosing her point of view. Nonetheless, Angela's mind was racing, as she couldn't disagree more. While it was obvious to her that Lulu had been badly abused, it seemed equally obvious that her relationship with Sammy had nothing to do with love. Angela was certain that to Lulu, Sammy was the manifestation of every male that had ever hurt her. Lulu needed Sammy to have power and extract revenge. She kept him so she could vent her rage. She kept him so that at least one man would suffer for the pain inflicted upon her by other men.

With one ear open as her mind raced, Angela was still listening to Virginia speak, "In an effort to protect her and Sammy both, I'm working out a deal with Lulu. In it, Lulu would have to take free parenting classes downtown. She can take as long as she needs to complete this extensive program. In the meantime, and forever after, the incident reports about Sammy must decrease. If they do, she may keep him with no fear of loss. However, if severe incidents continue happening or if she drops out of the class, the state will have absolutely no choice but to remove him. This might take some time. It's a long-term solution, so I don't want you asking for Lulu's head every time Sammy gets a paper cut. BUT, I do want you to keep us informed and reporting incidents."

Angela's heart swelled to the bursting point with euphoria and hope. If these were the rules of engagement, she was certain it was a battle she could win. If Angela's analysis of Lulu was right, she knew Lulu would keep hurting Sammy no matter what classes were involved. All Angela would have to do is be patient, and all Sammy would have to do is stay alive. Neither would be easy, but neither was impossible with the knowledge that a safer, brighter future lie ahead. It wasn't what Angela wanted immediately, but it would lead to her goal.

The behavior specialist kept her voice calm and diplomatic, "That sounds fair and reasonable. When will you propose it to Lulu?"

"I'm setting up a meeting with her next week."

"Excellent. When is Sammy coming back to school?"

"Well, she really doesn't want him back in your program."

"That's no surprise, but I'm afraid we're the only game in town."

"I know, and we've explained that to her. She said she'd like to see Sammy mainstreamed."

"I would love to see Sammy mainstreamed," Angela agreed. "But you and I both know he's nowhere near ready for that. Even on his best days, he still has a minor escalation or two."

"Yeah," Virginia acknowledged. "I know. I think we can get him back in class by tomorrow."

"Sounds great!" Angela encouraged. "I've really enjoyed our conversation. Please don't hesitate to call if I can help you in any way with our shared kids."

"Thanks. You do the same."

The women hung up, and Angela performed a happy dance by the phone.

"Little victories, little victories, little victories," she sang under her breath. She couldn't wait to pass on the good news to the classroom staff.

Later that day, Richard called. "How's everything going today?"

"Great," Angela declared. She told him all about Sammy and DCW.

"Very good," he complimented. "I've got some good news for you, too."

"Cool. What is it?"

"Due to a small stroke of serendipity, I've found your program a new therapist."

"Wow. That was fast. Who is it? When can I interview them?"

"I stole him from a local group home," Richard explained. "It turns out they pay even less than we do for a master's level therapist. You can meet him when he starts Monday. I'm certain you're gonna like him. See you then."

He hung up.

Angela was more than a little miffed. *Who is he? Why didn't I get to interview him? Christ. I'm gonna be the one stuck with him. I could do a good job weeding out the loonies and people incompatible with our kids.*

"Arrrr," she growled like a pirate.

She took a deep breath and reminded herself, *Okay, it's not technically my program to run. I can't complain too much, as I'm still not in H.Q.'s good graces.*

That afternoon's after-school meeting was filled with excitement. Mrs. Regina, Ronnie and Carla grilled Angela for all of the details about DCW's deal with Lulu and the little Angela knew about the new shrink. They were skeptical about the mystery surrounding the new therapist but anxious for success with Sammy.

The classroom chatter was interrupted by the phone ringing.

Angela was closest and jovially answered in Spanish, "Hola."

"Angela, I'm so glad it's you," panted Bev in a desperate hush. "I really, really need to talk to you."

177

There was an urgency in Bev's voice that scared Angela.

"Uhh. We're in a meeting, Bev. I can't right now."

"No, no. Later, later."

"I've got plans. I can't."

"Awww, c'mon," Bev implored, sailing on a manic high. "I thought we were buddies, pals, amigos. How are things? How are you? How are the kids? I need you. I need to talk to you."

"I've gotta get back to the meeting, Bev. I don't think this is appropriate. Talk to you later."

"No, no, no, no, no, no—no. Don't hang up."

Angela sighed.

Bev continued, "How about we get a glass of wine? Yeah, let's get some wine? You like wine. My treat. Seven O'clock at the usual place."

Ronnie called out to Angela. "C'mon let's get this meeting over with so we can go home."

"Okay," she replied to Ronnie, and then to Bev, "Okay, fine whatever. I gotta go."

"Wait, wait! I need a ride."

"What?! What happened to your car?"

Bev stalled then lied. "Uhhh, I don't have it. It's in the shop. Yeah."

"I don't know…"

Bev interrupted. "I'll be at my house at 7. See ya then."

She hung up.

Angela hung up with the dial tone buzzing in her ear.

"What was that all about," Carla asked.

The behavior specialist slowly walked back to the table with a puzzled look on her face. "I don't know. That has got to be one of the weirdest calls I've gotten in ages."

"Was that Beverly?" Mrs. Regina inquired.

"Uh-huh," Angela grunted. She described the conversation and Bev's dark intensity.

"I don't like it," Ronnie said. "I wouldn't go, if I were you."

"Ronnie's right," Mrs. Regina agreed. "Something doesn't sound right about that whole call."

"Chick is off her rocker," Carla assessed.

Angela shook her head. She regretted saying yes and felt trapped.

"Well, if you go, be extra careful," Ronnie cautioned.

Angela agreed, and they wrapped up the meeting on a down note.

At her apartment, Angela fed Fur-nando and tried to eat dinner. She was too creeped out to eat much. The prospect of meeting Bev after that phone call was just too eerie.

In her final analysis of that call, Angela decided Bev was most likely suicidal. The urgency, desperation, manipulation. It just felt very connected to suicide for Angela. What scared her most was what Bev had envisioned of Angela's role for the evening. Did Bev want her to find the body? Did Bev want a witness to blowing her brains out? Out of fear and a twisted sense of camaraderie, did Bev want to kill Angela first and then commit suicide? Whatever her plan was, Angela didn't want any part in it.

At 6 o'clock, Angela called Bev to cancel. No answer—and Bev's message box was full. Damn. 6:30 same thing. 6:45 same thing.

Freaked out and determined not to get involved, Angela packed an overnight bag and raced over to her best friend's apartment to spend the night. She needed an alibi for 7 p.m., in case something happened. She also needed a safe place for the night in case Bev decided to track her down at her apartment. She also really needed someone she could trust to talk to.

Grateful for her friend's emergency hospitality, Angela still slept little that night.

She questioned her sanity for getting into this situation. She was barely making enough money to support herself. She was far from any family protection. She was exposed on every possible level to life-ruining people and situations: a deranged ex-boss, spit and blood-borne diseases, sexual predators in her class or their parents, lawsuits from any parent or kid that wanted to make up a story about her inappropriately touching or molesting a kid…the list was endless. Did a career in psychology mean that much to her? Would these strange threats to her existence or career lessen with a master's degree or doctorate? It was time to get serious about applying to graduate schools. Would her precarious position with the mental health center submarine her chances? Could she even get a recommendation at this point? How would a master's degree or doctorate help her help others?

Life seemed to just follow one simple track when she was a child: do well in school, go to college, go to graduate school, get a career, get married, live happily ever after. A sound foundation to live by for sure, but now things were getting confusing. Far more seemed to be at stake, and she questioned both the practicality and black-and-white clarity of goals that she previously took for granted.

Mostly, she was really shaken by Bev's behavior. She didn't want to get killed by this nut job. She didn't want to be implicated somehow in Bev's suicide...if Bev was planning on suicide.

Angela got up early and was at work 45 minutes ahead of schedule to make sure the school was safe for the kids. She could imagine how the kids would react to discovering their former therapist in a bloody heap on the floor.

Fortunately, no trace of Bev was to found when Angela arrived.

She called Richard as soon as she was sure the rooms were safe. She told him every single detail and dark suspicion. He thanked her for calling and promised to look into it.

He called back before the kids went to lunch.

"Angela, do you have a minute?"

"Yes."

"Donna and I went to Bev's house after you called. She didn't answer her door, so we looked in the windows. Her house was a mess, but we couldn't tell if anything was wrong. We tried the door again. She still didn't answer, so we tried turning the knob. The door opened, and we went inside. We looked all over and couldn't find her.

"We called the police and emergency services.

"I finally found her at Average Little City Hospital. They would only confirm she had been admitted. As I have a few connections there, I was able to pull a few strings and get a few details. It turns out she spent the night in the I.C.U. She is in stable condition but can't see any visitors. One friend told me she's being transferred to Ward 6 and must stay there until next week."

"What's Ward 6?" Angela asked.

"That's the short-term mental health ward. It's where adults go before doctors decide whether someone needs to go to the state mental hospital or be released back into the community."

"Oh my God. I feel so sorry for Bev."

"Don't take it to heart," Richard told her. "It looks like your assessment that Bev was suicidal was correct, but there was nothing you could have done. You did the right thing by staying safe and calling me."

"Thank you for finding out what happened and telling me. I wish there was something I could do—without getting involved."

"There isn't anything you can do," Richard assured her. "Are you going to be okay?"

"Yeah, I'll be fine. It's just a little unsettling, but I'll be okay."

"Feel free to call me any time if you need to talk," Richard offered.

"Thanks. I'll be sure to do that."

They hung up, but Angela didn't have time to dwell on what happened. Lunch awaited, and the kids were already lining up. Some days the constant motion in the program was the biggest boon to survival.

Chapter 13

Franz
(Sunday Afternoon)

"Greta," rumbled Heinrich, Franz' father, as the portly man emerged from his bedroom where he'd been watching skin flicks. "Franz, where's your goddamn sister?"

The boy looked up from where he was playing on the furnitureless, filth-strewn living room floor. "Jeez, Dad!" the disgusted boy exclaimed after seeing his father's erection standing tall beneath the man's sweat pants.

"I said, 'Where's your goddamn sister?'"

Franz looked at the mud-stained carpeting. "I don't know. She's probably at the mall with her friends or something."

The man dug through the mess on the floor and came up with an almost empty box of tissues. "Goddamn twat. She's never fuckin' around when I need her."

Heinrich went back to his room and slammed the door.

Not wanting to listen to his father masturbate, Franz went to his own room.

Weekends were an exceptionally weird time for Franz. His mother insisted he go off his meds so he could live a "normal" childhood on the weekends. It was the only time he got to explore himself. During the week he was so heavily sedated, he moved through life in a gelatinous fog. He was lucky if he could follow a conversation during the week, but on the weekends he could think clearly.

The weekends forced him to cope with his anger, frustration and sense of worthlessness. He screamed and cried a lot, even when his father wasn't beating him or his mother wasn't psychologically tormenting him. He cried at anything, at nothing. Off the meds he could feel the stirrings of adolescence.

Off the meds, there was a lot in life to juggle.

Yet, he loved the way he thought more clearly. He liked solving problems by thinking—even though he hated the trauma he thought about. Too much thinking led to outbursts and escalations, but he also found amazing ways to escape reality by using his imagination.

Recently, he had begun writing stories in a notebook stashed under the stuff littered about his room. They were crude and unrealistic stories, but they provided such wonderful relief.

And so, as Heinrich furiously fantasized about his daughter down the hall, Franz reached for his notebook and pencil to fantasize about anything else.

Chapter 14

Fresh Meat
(Monday)

Angela was busy preparing the room before the new therapist and old students arrived when an apparition from her junior year of college silently appeared in her doorway.

"Hiro? Hiro Yamamoto?" Angela asked, a little confused. "What are you doing here?"

The Japanese-American man flashed a toothy grin. "Meet the new boss."

Angela hopped, ran over to her old friend and gave him a hug.

"I told you you'd like him," Richard said, stepping into the room.

Angela held her friend with outstretched arms by his shoulders. "You look good. What's it been, a year and a half? I take it you passed your state clinicals with flying colors? How's the missus?"

"Yes, yes and Melissa's expecting."

"Wow! That's great. Congratulations," Angela sputtered, turning to Richard and asking, "Why didn't you tell me Hiro was going to be the new therapist? I worried all weekend you might have hired some deranged lunatic."

Hiro interrupted and pointed at himself, "Excuse me. He did hire some deranged lunatic."

"I like to keep you on your toes," Richard explained. "Why don't you give us a quick tour and introduce Hiro to the classroom staff before the students get here."

Angela gave them a quick rundown about the dual token economies, timeout and various classroom procedures. The introductions were cut short by the arriving buses and Richard left with a few brief words of encouragement, an invitation to visit him at the office after school and a veiled reminder to Angela to make sure she remember where her loyalties lie.

As he closed the door behind himself, Richard renewed his worries about hiring Hiro. The therapist's credentials were top rate, but his past friendship with Angela concerned him. Old friends don't always make great boss/employee relationships...and Angela had clearly shown with

185

Bev that she lived by her own rules of loyalties where the company was concerned. Yet he was up against it for a replacement therapist, and he knew they were both talented people—what else could he do but roll the dice?

Back in the daytreatment room, Angela opened the teachers' closet. "Let me take your coat."

"Thanks," Hiro said. "What's today's game plan?"

Angela led Hiro to his new desk. "Traditionally, we start group shortly after school starts—big kids then little kids. Each lasts half an hour. That's followed by recess, which I usually help Ronnie and Carla with. The next hour and a half is reserved for paperwork and putting out fires. It would be an ideal time for you to run therapy sessions. Then the kids have lunch, and again I help Ronnie and Carla. Then I get my own lunch. The rest of the day is putting out fires and filling out paperwork for me, therapy sessions for you. It's also in the afternoon that the kids get gym class or library time. Now that you're here, I'm hoping we can do a lot more therapeutic stuff. But that's all up to you."

"Great," Hiro said. "I figure we'll take it easy at first. Let's let the kids get comfortable with me and go from there. After a couple days, I'll probably figure out some changes to help the program to better fit my style as a therapist, but I don't want to stress out the kids or the staff."

"Oh, good," Angela relaxed. "I'm sure they warned you at headquarters—these kids don't deal well with change. They tend to *escalate*."

Hiro sat on the edge of his desk and spoke in hushed tones as he could hear the kids slamming their lockers in the hall and entering the classroom next door. "That's to be expected, but, listen, I have to get something off my chest first."

"Sure."

"I want you to know I almost didn't take this job once I learned I'd be your boss. It has nothing to do with you except that we used to be friends outside of the professional environment, when you helped with my master's thesis project."

"It's not like I didn't get college credit for helping," Angela tried to ease his concerns.

"I know, but I really wasn't your boss in the same way. Your last supervisor was nuts enough, and I don't want to develop a weird dynamic with you," Hiro paused. "You had great insight and instincts for psychology in school. Richard and Donna both say that hasn't

186

changed. You also have experience with these kids that I'll count on during the transition. … I guess what I'm trying to say is that although I'm your boss, I'll treat you as an equal. And I'd like us to work together more as a team."

"I'll admit I was a little apprehensive when I first saw you standing in the door," Angela confessed, "but this sounds like a more than generous proposition."

Hiro stuck out his hand, and Angela shook it.

There was a gentle knocking on the pass-through door. Kevin peeked inside. "Are you ready for group?"

"Give us just a second," Angela replied. He closed the door, and Angela turned to Hiro. "How do you want to run this?"

"Why don't you run group today, until I get the hang of it?"

"No problem. Today will be easy with introductions." Angela handed Hiro a clipboard with a bead sheet for Hiro to translate the rewards. Then she gave Hiro the "visitor's" carpet and got her own before inviting the big kids to join them.

Kevin, Franz, Jefferson, Charlie and Violet slowly entered the room, taking their time to check out the new Bev. They scrutinized his round smiling face, his spiky blue-black hair, his blue jeans and his black sweatshirt festooned with anime characters. The sweatshirt earned him brownie points. The children got their rugs and quickly returned to the circle to scrutinize the man some more.

No one said a word. The big-kids' group still felt abandoned and betrayed by Bev. Her sudden loss was still painful, and this new therapist's appearance was suspicious. Was he another traitor, an imposter, trustworthy?

Violet shrugged her shoulders and huffed, "He's sure not Bev."

"Was that an appropriate comment?" Angela asked. Violet's only response was her classic pout.

We don't need to start this off with a big scene, Angela restrained herself and spoke to the entire group. "I'd like to introduce you to the new daytreatment therapist, Hiro Yamamoto. He has a master's degree from Average State University, right here in town, annnnnd, the really cool thing is that he and I actually used to study together when we were students."

A hand shot up.

"Yes, Jefferson?" Angela called.

"Did you guys grow up together?"

"No," Angela replied. "We just went to State together."

Charlie's hand shot up and he cracked wise. "If you're a hero, where's your cape, and what are your super powers?"

Franz and Kevin laughed.

"Capes are very out of fashion," Hiro said, rolling with the punches, and riffing off the kids' movie "The Incredibles." "And my name is spelled H-I-R-O. It's Japanese, not hero like in comic books."

More hands shot up.

"Wait a second," Angela said. "Why don't we let Hiro tell us a little about himself? Then you can ask more questions. If you listen quietly, you'll each earn a bead for listening. But first I'm taking away a bead from Charlie for being rude with inappropriate comments."

Kevin and Franz had long since learned not to laugh at Charlie's being reprimanded and remained silent. Angela had become quick at taking their beads for inappropriate behavior. She let them slide for laughing at Charlie's initial joke.

Hiro began his self-introduction: "You already know I went to school with Angela...let's see. I'm married. I don't have any kids yet, but my wife and I are expecting one in late June. I have a golden retriever named Rhett and a black-and-white cat named Oz. I love to read, and I love to go skiing on the weekends."

Angela quickly awarded the listening beads and offered the prized 25-cent turquoise bead to all who shared something about themselves with Hiro. Hiro got just about the same answers Angela got on her first day. Only this time Violet didn't obsess about bugs. As the bugs were dead for the winter, she obsessed about snowflakes.

Fortunately for the new therapist, Angela was more adept at curtailing Violet's rambling ways and moved the group ahead of schedule.

"Wow. That went a little faster than I expected," Angela said. "We still have about 10 minutes left of group. Does anyone have any more questions for Hiro?"

The mood in the room had shifted away from curiosity, and five pairs of eyes stared vacantly at Angela.

"How about you, Hiro? Do you have any questions for the group?"

Five pairs of eyes desperately avoided contact with the new therapist.

"Can we play a game for the next 10 minutes?" he asked.

Now five pairs of eyes looked expectantly, pleadingly at Angela.

"I don't see why not. What did you have in mind?"

"I see Sorry on the shelves behind our desks. If a couple people don't mind teaming up, we can play."

There were four "Yeas" and one pouting Violet in opposition.

"Okay," the behavioral specialist agreed. "But, I want everyone to promise me that no matter where we're at in the game in 10 minutes, everyone will go back to class quietly."

The boys nodded; Violet sulked.

Hiro asked, "Violet, will you be on my team?"

The girl brightened and sat next to the new therapist, while Angela retrieved the game.

"Angela, will you be on my team?" Charlie leered.

"Sorry, Charlie," Angela rejected. "I'm gonna sit this one out and award beads for good sportsmanship. Why don't you and Franz team up?"

"Okay," the horny youth sighed.

The group had the game set up in no time, and Angela was quick to reward and punish the children's mix of behaviors. It helped keep the game moving smoothly with little chicanery.

Naturally, the kids didn't want to quit when their time was up, but Angela's exaggerated bead inflation kept them from escalating.

Rumors about playing games from the big kids brought excellent behavior to the little kids' group. Sammy was the only one in his own time zone and reluctant to participate in the discussion. He and Edward each remained wary of the new therapist and stayed close by Angela's side. Angela just hoped Hiro's honeymoon lasted longer than her own.

The introductions went well. These boys had more questions about Rhett and Oz, and they didn't make fun of the therapist's name. The little kids' group also introduced themselves well, except for Sammy who was sliding back into his Freddy mode.

Hiro could see the extra attention bothered Sammy, and he deftly avoided an escalation by quickly bringing up the subject of a game of Sorry. Lionel, Edward and Ted thought it was a brilliant idea and worked quickly to help set up the board.

Not yet comfortable with the new therapist, no one wanted to partner up with Hiro. Instead, Lionel and Edward formed a team.

The game went well for the first two rounds, but tensions soon developed between Lionel and Edward as to who would turn a card and who would move the pieces. Ted kept cheating, and Sammy didn't understand how to play. Angela moved quickly with the beads, but there was only so much with which she could break through to these kids by token economy. Freddy made a full blown appearance by the third round.

"You take Sammy, I'll take care of everybody else," Angela said to Hiro, jumping to her feet. The children were a little surprised the behavior specialist didn't intervene with Sammy. She was the Sammy expert. Yet Angela wanted to test Hiro. She knew he was brilliant in an academic setting, but she needed to know where his skills were at in the real world. Did his time at the group homes break him into the nitty-gritty side of the job?

"Five beads to everyone who ignores Sammy," Angela informed the rest of group. "Lionel, I'll give you five extra beads for putting away the game as fast as humanly possible. Ted, I'll give you five beads for putting away all of the carpets. Edward, I'll give you five beads for being the first to get into line."

The boys were up and cooperating at record speed. Angela dished out the beads and ushered them next door. When her task was accomplished, she held back and watched Hiro with Sammy.

"It's okay, Sammy," Hiro soothed. "There's no Freddy here."

Sammy gave him a wild-eyed grin and scissored his fingers.

"It's okay, Sammy. It's just you and me."

"Bitchell!"

"That's not a very appropriate use of your words, Sammy. I'm going to subtract a bead until you apologize."

"Bitchell!"

Hiro subtracted a bead but realized the token economy didn't influence Sammy one iota. "Okay, Sammy, you can choose to calm down and go back to class or go to time out."

"Bitchell! Freddy's gonna get you. Bitchell!"

Angela tried not to smile as Sammy spewed bitchells. Although Hiro clearly knew nothing about handling Sammy, he was clearly working through a series of appropriate responses in dealing with Sammy. He remained calm and outwardly unfazed by Sammy's growing escalation. Clearly, Hiro had picked up a lot from his year at the group homes.

"Okay. It's time for timeout," Hiro said, approaching on his hands and knees.

"Bitchell!" Sammy shouted, spitting on Hiro's anime sweatshirt.

Hiro didn't hesitate and kept moving forward to either herd Sammy into timeout or restrain him.

"Bitchell!" This time he spit in Hiro's face and scampered under the big arts-and-crafts table.

Hiro followed, pausing only to wipe off his forehead. Sammy crawled out from under the table, as Hiro picked up some steam and caught him.

Sammy flailed as Hiro put him in a proper MANDT restraint. Sammy showered Hiro in spit and yowled, "Freddy's gonna get me. Freddy's gonna kill me."

Angela ran and manned the timeout door in time to trap Sammy in the booth, as Hiro escaped.

The new therapist sighed heavily once the task was complete.

"Do you want me to watch over the door while you clean up?" Angela asked.

"No thanks," Hiro cheerily replied. "I'll get cleaned up when he's back in class."

"That might take a while," Angela cautioned, as Sammy screamed in terror and feverishly tried to beat down the walls of timeout.

"That's okay," Hiro explained, taking control of the latch. "I put him in there; I'll stay with him until he's ready, so he knows he can trust me."

"Well, you certainly passed the Sammy Spit Test," Angela congratulated. "I must admit, I feel a little bad. Normally, I help a lot more. I just wanted to see how you'd handle that type of pressure. I promise I'll be more helpful in the future."

"You were plenty helpful," he said. "You got the classroom cleaned and the kids out in one fell swoop. Besides, I didn't want you to think I was some kind of wuss. I've faced down my fair share of spit in the past year. Plus, Sammy and the rest of the class can now know I'll be safe when they escalate."

"Well, ya dun good," Angela complimented.

Sammy was oblivious to their discussion. He was still busy trying to tear down the walls.

As they stood there, Angela explained about her long history working with Sammy and all of the accomplishments she and program had made. She also explained about the politics of DCW and Lulu. As thorough as she was, she missed one point Hiro was very intent on learning.

"What's a bitchell?"

Sammy caught that word and started shouting it repeatedly.

Angela laughed and whispered, "Damned if I know, but I get the distinct impression that it isn't good."

Hiro smiled. "Duh."

Richard sat Angela and Hiro on the couch in his office. "I know I'm not telling you anything new by reiterating that your program is in a financially dire situation that has put the entire company in jeopardy. As a nonprofit, we usually flirt with very little income, but this is worse, and we have little time to transition you in, Hiro.

"In order to tread water, we need you to perform 6 one-on-one, half-hour therapy sessions a day. If we're going to recoup any losses, you need to do at least 8 sessions a day. That's four hours of therapy a day, plus one hour of group therapy. Given the transition times, that won't even give you an hour for lunch.

"Don't perform any hourlong sessions, unless it is ab-so-lute-ly necessary; the insurance companies don't pay for anymore than half-an-hour."

"But, sir," Hiro interrupted. "Psychology isn't factory work. You can't expect every child to magically heal in convenient half-hour blocks. Sometimes you'll be on a roll, really helping a child through some tough issues, and they won't be ready to stop at the half-hour buzzer. They might need 45 minutes or an hour. That's the best part about the flexibility of being able to work with these kids daily at school."

Hiro continued, "What about kids in crisis who need therapy all day? Or kids who are okay or don't want to talk and 15 minutes is all they need? Treating someone strictly by the clock and not their needs is ridiculous."

Richard shrugged. "I'm sorry, but these are the rules of the game with the state's privatized insurers and contracting system. If it doesn't fit into their formula, they won't pay us.

"Now, you can bill for 15-minute sessions, but we won't get paid as much. You can also bill for family therapy sessions where you talk with the parents. But you can only talk about the child, otherwise we can't bill for it."

Hiro rolled his eyes. "What if the parent's issues are what's causing the problem? If the parent's issues don't get resolved, the child will have a far more difficult time coping."

Richard had heard all of this before. He agreed with Hiro, but there wasn't anything he could do about it. All he could do was be patient. "There are other agencies for those other problems. We are under contract to only treat the children. We don't get paid for anything else."

Hiro pushed back. "I thought it was our duty to help these children and their families to the best of our abilities. How on earth can a remote system of state and private bureaucracies know what's best for our clients, without actually knowing them or establishing realistic guidelines for treatment?"

Angela tried not to look bemused as she watched Hiro tilt at windmills. She completely felt his sense of righteous indignation. However, these past few months in the trenches taught her to see some of the futility of this argument. She was learning to pick her battles, and she knew that there was nothing Richard could do this time.

The program director did his best to respond to Hiro's arguments. "We are supposed to provide the very best treatment possible. However, we cannot provide any services without any money. And the only way to pay our bills is to maximize the billing process. The children won't get any help, unless we do things the way the state and insurance companies tell us."

"Okay," Hiro conceded with a sigh.

"I'm sorry," Richard said and meant it. "That's not even the worst of it. At the start of every school year, each program is allotted $1,500 in discretionary money for token economy goods, supplies, emergency clothing for the kids, etcetera. Bev spent your program's money by the second week of school.

"On what?" Angela asked, as she considered the program's meager inventory.

"Apparently on whatever you have in class," Richard explained. "The receipts checked out okay. Purchases at crafts stores, toy stores and stuff like that. I've know Bev long enough to be pretty certain that she didn't steal it—even if she's got other problems."

"What are we supposed to do until next school year?" Hiro inquired.

"Well," Richard said. "I asked the other programs to kick in what they could afford to help. They managed to sacrifice about $150. It isn't much, but it might help in a pinch, if you're frugal. Otherwise, you're entirely on your own."

Hiro shrugged off the new obstacle. "You promised this wouldn't be an easy job. We're pretty resourceful; we'll manage. Please thank the groups that gave up some money for us, though."

"Will do."

Hiro pressed forward. "What else did you want to discuss?"

"There is one more piece of bad news," Richard said. "Again, in order to stay afloat, your program needs at least 10 students. It was

193

designed to have up to 12 students, and we need you to have 12 students in order to make up for this semester's short falls."

"Richard," Angela calmly stated. "The program is barely manageable with our nine students. Those kids are gonna test the living daylights out of Hiro through New Year's. Three new kids will test all of us to the limit. Plus, a sudden change in the classroom dynamic will create general pandemonium amid the ranks of the students."

"Without Sallie and with Lashaun mainstreamed, you have no choice. I want you and the classroom staff to have that program filled by the start of next semester."

This bothered Angela much more than the money. She was used to having no money, but she also only barely knew how to deal with the chaos of nine emotionally disturbed children. *How could the program possibly handle three more over-amped E.D. kids? What if we got two new Sammys?* It exhausted her just thinking about it.

"How on earth do we even go about getting three more little cherubs?" Angela inquired.

"That's pretty easy," Richard proclaimed, ignoring her sarcasm. "Believe it or not, everyone wants into your program. We get requests all of the time from teachers, social workers and parents. If we can't do it from our waiting list, then it just takes a little recruiting—first from your school's most troubled kids, then the rest of the district's elementary schools. You'll have it filled in no time."

"What about Mrs. Regina?" Angela countered. "She's retiring this year. How are we going to convince her to make her own life more difficult?"

"That's even easier," Richard said. "I've got connections with Mr. Franklin, and I know he can be very persuasive."

Angela felt particularly uncomfortable with her boss putting the screws to Mrs. Regina. The woman had been teaching for 13 years longer than Angela had been alive.

"Anything else?" Hiro asked, moving the discussion forward.

"That's all the bad news," Richard promised. "Now I want to go over all of our paperwork procedures and figure out new ways to maximize our billing."

They spent an hour going over tons of forms: student attendance, group billing, group notes, private therapy billing, private therapy notes, family therapy notes and billing, phone call billing and notes, etc, etc, etc.

Angela's duties forced her to take on a greater brunt of the paperwork because Hiro needed to be freed up to take on more therapy sessions with the kids. Angela correctly assumed that the paperwork was going to get more mind-numbingly boring and time consuming. Everyone knew it would be so much easier and more cost-efficient if the state provided direct funding, without the need for middle-man insurance bureaucracies to pad for "administrative fees" and executive salaries. Yet, that's not how patronage works, and politicians continued privatizing the state's social structures to benefit their corporate backers in the insurance industry…and a lot of other industries.

Chapter 15

Viva la Revolucion!

"I'm so glad you all could get here half an hour early today," Hiro opened his informal meeting with Angela and the classroom staff. "As you can imagine, I've come up with some changes that I would like to make to the program, but I'd like to run them past you first and get your opinions."

The staff was as resistant to change as the students. They felt comfortable with their system, which they believed worked well. Mrs. Regina, Ronnie and Carla promised Angela they'd at least hear Hiro out before politely denying his changes. With their arms folded across their chests, they silently nodded, acknowledging Hiro's greeting and letting him continue his speech.

"First, with your permission, Mrs. Regina, I'd like to stop using a separate bead economy and just switch over to your play-dollar economy. This way we're all on the same page, and it'll be less confusing for us and the kids. Is that okay?"

"I don't have any problem with that," Mrs. Regina conceded, having expected a much more disruptive request than that one. "It sounds like a good idea."

"Yeah," Ronnie added. "We could print up more fake money for you today, if you want."

"That'd be great. Thanks," Hiro said.

Angela only had an inkling about what was to come next, and she was decidedly on the fence. She knew her work affiliation made her side with Hiro, but it was the other three women she worked with who had gotten her through the past few months. She didn't want to be caught in the middle if Hiro's ideas didn't go over well, and she knew it might be up to her to sell those ideas to the two aides during recess or lunch.

Hiro was well aware that some of his new ideas wouldn't go over at all with the classroom staff set on old theories in psychology that didn't work nearly as well as some newer concepts he wanted to employ. He decided to loosen up the staff with a series of easy changes first and work on convincing them on the bigger changes.

"Next, I'd like to blend our stores and hold store every day," Hiro explained. "I think, especially for the little kids, that the store concept is a little too vague for them if they can only shop once a week. For someone like Edward, losing dollars for Friday on Monday is a little like asking him to understand the concept of a 401k account. He has yet to fully comprehend how his actions in the present affect his future."

"I agree in principle that it's a good idea to do this," Mrs. Regina grudgingly relented, a little. "But, that's the end of the day, and during that last half hour I read to the children. It helps soothe them and prepare them to calmly ride the bus home."

"That is important, and I promise not to disturb that as much as possible. Angela and I will be very strict, only taking one student at a time, holding on to their purchase until they line up for the bus. This would prevent them from playing with their new stuff and disrupting your reading time."

Mrs. Regina thought about it for a minute. "Okay, but only if you promise to revert back to the old way if it doesn't work."

"You got it. I promise," Hiro affirmed. "I also want to start developing more family involvement. The more appropriate parent-child therapy and interaction we can foster might reduce the amount of abuse our children suffer—especially with harsh but loving parents such as Lionel's. Certainly, none of you would be required to attend these after-school events, but I want you to know that you're always invited."

Everyone nodded that it was a good idea, without committing to actually attending.

Next he tackled bigger issues, trying to soften opposition as he went. "I'm also making some fundamental changes in my own room—changes that I'm not expecting you to make in your room, if you don't like them—but changes that will definitely happen for any events that transpire in my room."

There was a heavy pause, as Hiro tried to read the three women of the classroom staff. Visibly, only Carla grimaced.

"Another thing I want to encourage in the children is talking about their feelings. I want to get them to lash out less, hurting fewer people or destroying less in class. This new development will include mandatory apologies. The children must take responsibility for their actions and apologize for any injuries: physical or emotional. What I ask of you is to make sure no child is released from timeout without apologizing to whomever it is necessary to apologize to. That includes us adults."

Ronnie supported the idea whole heartedly. "That would be really nice for a change, especially the next time someone bites me or hawks a luggie in my face."

"Yeah," Carla growled, uncertain how they could possibly enforce such a policy.

"That sounds perfectly reasonable," Mrs. Regina agreed.

Angela agreed, too, but had been kicking herself since Hiro first mentioned this to her last night. *Use your words. How many times did my professors try to grind that phrase into my head?* She felt bad having gone half the year without hammering those three little words into the children's heads.

Hiro was getting nervous. He was pleased at the ease with which he won these concessions, but he knew this last one was going to stir up a hornets' nest. He took a deep breath. "And finally, I want to phase out closed door timeouts. The kids are mortified by those booths, and, frankly, so am I. Listen to how they scream and struggle to claw their way out.

"Instead of assigning extended time periods, during which they aren't allowed to speak, I think we can make each timeout a simple therapeutic intervention that any of us can perform. I think it'll calm the children more quickly, preparing them to return to class and learn in half the time it usually takes."

The classroom staff was aghast.

"Hold on," said Mrs. Regina. "Are you saying we shouldn't punish the children for breaking the rules or close the doors on them when they're escalated?"

"No," Hiro said, preparing to elaborate. "I'm not saying we won't close the door. Jesus, when Sammy goes ape shit, it's the safest for everyone to have that door closed. But when the child has de-escalated enough to sit quietly against the back wall, I'm saying we should open the door. At least a little, and look in. We'll ask them why they are in timeout. This will help them take ownership of their actions. We'll ask them what they're feeling and what they need to do to act more appropriately to be allowed back into class. Then we will make them apologize before they are allowed out of the booth."

"That's ludicrous," Mrs. Regina said. "When these children misbehave, they need to be punished. If these kids grow up and commit crimes in the real world, they are going to jail. They are not going to have a mushy heart-to-heart and go about their business."

199

Hiro tried to placate Mrs. Regina. "You have a very good point. However, this isn't quite the real world; it's a therapeutic-education program. My job is to provide the therapeutic component, and I think this will be a good crisis intervention strategy that'll be beneficial to both of our components. I'm not saying that the kids will be released while they're still escalated, unapologetic or otherwise unready to return to class. This will just cut down on the time they spend in timeout and increase the time they spend in a good learning environment."

"In all of my 30-some-odd years of working and running this type of program, I can assure you that mollycoddling the students this way will only lead to trouble. They'll get into trouble just to hang around and talk to you or Angela to avoid their work. They need punishment as a negative reinforcement."

"No," Hiro countered. "The children won't just be hangin' out and shootin' the breeze. Either they stick to the therapeutic dialog, or they will be ignored. If simply ignoring them or redirecting them to the appropriate conversation at hand doesn't work, the door will be closed. The goal is for them to take responsibility for their actions, discover what is causing them to act that way, think about what they're doing and apologize for making poor choices that hurt other people or themselves. I will, we all will, need to be strict about making sure the kids stick to this program."

The staff could see the school buses through the room's large windows. The meeting had to come to a close, even if they weren't ready for it to.

Mrs. Regina gave an exasperated sigh. "This is your room, so, I guess we'll have to do this your way. But hear me now, while your motives are noble, this timeout thing will fail miserably."

The teacher huffed out of the room to get the kids. Carla followed, rolling her eyes in disgust.

"We'll see how it goes," Ronnie said with a shrug before leaving on a more conciliatory note. She figured it could go either way. She just wanted a plan that would work well.

Alone, Angela and Hiro talked.

Angela stuck out her lower lip and shrugged. "That went…sorta okay."

"Yeah, it went great except Mrs. Regina thinks I'm a soft-headed moron."

"You'll have plenty of opportunities to prove your theory about working timeout. Not to worry."

The commotion next door indicated the big kids' group was ready. Angela got them, and Hiro led group. He explained the new timeout policy. The kids rolled their eyes at the touchy-feely lameness of it that would make them apologize. No one, however, felt like acting out to be the first to experience the new policy.

The little kids found the open-door timeout policy more appealing.

Ted was quick to see if he could hold the therapist and behavior specialist to the new policy. In a foul mood, he decided to pick on Lionel.

As Lionel was finishing his turn describing his night, Ted told him he was stupid.

Lionel jumped to his feet, ran across the circle in which the group was seated and grabbed Ted by the shirt.

"Use your words," Hiro practically shouted at Lionel.

Holding Ted with his left, Lionel cocked his right.

"Ten bucks if you ignore his set up and don't hit him," Angela said, relying on the distraction of big green. She began counting out bills from the wad in her hand.

His right still cocked, Lionel's eyes widened. "Really?"

"Yup."

Lionel let go of Ted.

"Pussy," Ted muttered.

Lionel hit the seated boy in the forehead so hard the boy was knocked flat on his back.

Hiro restrained Lionel, who struggled all the way to timeout.

"I'm taking $10 for falling for Ted's set up, Lionel," Angela said. Then she looked at Ted who was upright and rubbing his head. "I'm taking $5 from you for each time you set up Lionel. That's 10 bucks."

"What?!" Ted yowled in protest.

"Do you want to go to timeout, too?" Angela sternly asked.

"No," Ted spat, glaring at her.

Hiro closed the door on the agitated 7-year-old. Lionel began pounding on the padded door.

"As soon as you sit quietly against the back wall, I'll open the door," Hiro stated.

Lionel looked at him incredulously. He pounded the door once more for good measure, walked to the back of the booth, faced Hiro with a piercing gaze of vehemence, crossed his arms and sat down.

The therapist opened the door about a foot and faced Lionel while sitting on a small class chair. "Are you ready to talk?"

"No," he spit. "Open the door all the way."

"This is as far as I'm going to open it until I'm sure you won't try to escape."

Lionel fumed wordlessly.

The kids in group were impressed that the door was open at all. Angela rewarded the rest of group for watching quietly and behaving.

Hiro gave Lionel about a minute to cool and asked, "Why are you in timeout?"

He looked at him as if he were the world's dumbest person. "Why do you think I'm in timeout? You put me here."

Hiro calmly responded to the child's sarcasm. "I guess I'll wait another minute for you to calm down enough to speak to me appropriately."

Another 30 seconds passed before Lionel answered. "Because I hit Ted because he called me a pussy."

"Yes, because you hit Ted," Hiro clarified. "Someone calling you a bad name is not reason enough to hit them. What should you have done?"

Lionel's eyes narrowed. *I did exactly what I should have done*, he thought.

"What do Angela and I always tell you to do when someone is setting you up?" Hiro prompted.

Lionel heaved a heavy sigh. "Ignore 'em."

"And?" Hiro pressed.

"And?" Lionel quizzically repeated.

"And earn lots of money for ignoring his set ups."

Lionel smiled brightly with avarice.

"Are you ready to come out, apologize to Ted and rejoin group?" Hiro inquired.

"Why should I apologize to him; he started it."

"Well, he must apologize to you, too."

"Okay," Lionel relented.

Lionel was de-escalated and out of timeout in 7 minutes. It had to be a record for the daytreatment program, but Angela and the rest of the group were guarded with their enthusiasm, unsure if Lionel would snap, again.

"Ted, are you ready to apologize to Lionel?" Hiro asked, holding Lionel's hand—just in case.

"Why do I have to apologize? He hit me."

"You set him up by insulting him."

Ted looked defiantly into Hiro's eyes. Hiro had no intention of bending on this one. Ted didn't feel like bending, either, and didn't say a word.

"You have a choice, Ted. You can apologize or go to timeout."

There was a lot of tension in the room, and Lionel enjoyed the moment, as he had inadvertently put Ted on the hot seat. By playing by the rules, he was making Ted's life miserable.

"Lionel," Hiro said. "Use your words, and tell Ted how he made you feel when he said those mean things to you."

The black-haired boy scrunched up his round little face, very uncertain about the wisdom of such a move.

"It's okay," Hiro encouraged. "Everyone is safe right now."

Lionel cocked his head to the right and raised his shoulder, as if to say he'd give it the old college try. "Ted, when you called me stupid and a pussy, it really hurt my feelings and made me mad."

"Very good," Hiro congratulated, and rewarded Lionel with $5. "Now, what do you have to say Ted?"

Ted was seething with anger that Hiro was putting so much pressure on him when he felt only Lionel deserved any punishment.

"I'll give you to the count of three, Ted," Hiro threatened. "One, twooooo, ..."

"Okay, I'll apologize," Ted harrumphed. *This isn't worth going to timeout for,* Ted calculated silently in his head. "Lionel, I'm sorry I called you stupid and a pussy."

"Very good, Ted," Hiro complimented. "You just earned $5, too."

Hiro turned to Lionel and asked, "Do you accept his apology?"

"Yes."

"Don't tell me, tell Ted."

"I accept your apology, Ted."

"Here's a dollar for you, Lionel," Hiro said warmly. "Do you have something to say to Ted?"

"Ted, I'm sorry I punched you."

"Excellent. Now you earn another $5," Hiro congratulated, before turning to Ted and asking, "Do you accept his apology?"

"No," Ted peevishly declared.

Fresh anger flashed in Lionel's eyes. Hiro was quick to intervene. "He doesn't have to accept your apology, Lionel. But if you think he's setting you up, what should you do?"

"Ignore him," he growled through clenched teeth.

"You are a very smart young man. Here's another dollar," Hiro rewarded. Lionel smiled and took the dollar. "Now go back to your seat in group."

Angela awarded another dollar to the other students in group who behaved well while watching the entire incident.

The remainder of group carried on without a hitch, and the children transitioned smoothly back to class.

"That went well," Angela said in an effort to bolster Hiro's morale. "Nothing to worry about."

Hiro's outlook was still a little grim because of that morning's meeting. "We haven't proved it to the classroom staff. They didn't see it."

"We could show them the tape after school."

"Nah. That might look like sour grapes. They've got to experience it firsthand."

"Day's still young," Angela darkly encouraged. "Those kids still have at least two or three more good escalations in them. In the meantime, I'm going to recess and talk up the new strategy with Ronnie and Carla."

Winter did little to change the recess dynamic. If anything, it made it more fun for the kids. Coats kept everyone warm and added a layer of protection against violent classmates. The snow had the same effect, softening the impact with the ground allowing glamorous diving catches in football.

Sammy still couldn't get enough of the swings.

The adults, on the other hand, weren't quite as enthralled. When they weren't breaking up fights, they huddled like penguins for warmth while keeping an eye on their young.

Angela joined the huddle after spending a few minutes getting Sammy going on the swings and passing a Nerf football to Charlie and Kevin a few times.

"God, Angela," Carla protested. "What's with your new boss and this stupid new timeout idea? Does he have any idea what type of fallout we'll have to deal with?"

"Beats me," the behavior specialist replied, intentionally letting Carla blow off some steam. "I couldn't believe it when he told me after work yesterday."

"Couldn't you talk him out of it?" Carla pressed.

"Not really," Angela sounded dejected. "I'm in enough trouble with the higher-ups. I didn't want to push it."

"I don't know," Ronnie chipped her two cents into the conversation. "A lot of what he said made sense. I think it'd be fun to actually do something to help these kids on the psychological level. It didn't sound too hard."

Carla stuck her thick, gloved finger down her throat. "I'm just not into all that sensitivity crap."

"I'm with Ronnie when it comes to having fun with psychology," Angela said, making her move. "And as admittedly hare-brained as it sounds, I saw Hiro in action during little kids' group."

"What happened?" Carla asked, huddling closer to Angela and Ronnie.

"Well, Ted set up Lionel, and Lionel belted him and knocked him over. Hiro restrained Lionel and put him in timeout. He closed the door until Lionel sat against the back wall and started answering all of his questions. Next thing you know the boys were apologizing to each other.

"And the part that really blew me away...Hiro had Lionel out of timeout in seven minutes."

"C'mon. You're shittin' me," Carla said in disbelief.

"I swear to God," Angela reassured. "Not only was Lionel calm, he apologized and everything."

"Seven minutes?" Ronnie shook her head. "No one's ever come out in just seven minutes."

"It's the truth," Angela repeated. "It sure beats standing at the window for twenty minutes watching them sit still. I hate to admit it, but I'm kinda curious to try it."

Carla remained skeptical but grudgingly conceded. "I guess it wouldn't hurt to try, but I'll only believe it when I see it."

"Fair enough," Angela agreed.

An escalating conversation between Edward and Lionel was making its way to the peripheral of the women's hearing.

"Fucker."

"Bitch."

"Fucker."

"Bitch."

"Fucker!"

"Bitch!"

The three women rushed to the scene but were beaten there by another teacher, who was already berating the boys.

Edward was so scared by the yelling teacher he had never met, he was about to pee his pants.

Lionel wasn't about to take any guff from some outside interloper—after all, he and Edward weren't physically fighting. It was more of a scholarly debate for those two.

Lionel waited for the teacher to take a breath before enunciating his response to her diatribe against swearing at school. "Ffffffff…"

Angela ran up to him and clamped her hand over his mouth. "I'm sorry," she interrupted Lionel, her eyes pleading with the teacher not to report them to Mr. Franklin, again. She then sternly addressed Lionel and Edward. "Boys, you're in a heap of trouble. I cannot believe the horrible words I just heard coming out of your little mouths. Where did you ever hear such words?"

The boys faced her, their faces twisted in confusion. They knew she heard them say those words at least two-dozen times a day.

Carla and Ronnie intervened with the teacher—temporarily distracting her.

Angela winked at Lionel and Edward. Lionel grinned back at her, and Edward gained firmer control of his bladder. "If you don't apologize to this teacher, you will lose recess for the rest of the week."

Reassured by Angela's wink that some sort of fix was in, the two played along—putting on their best hang-dog expressions and speaking in unison. "I'm sorry."

"That was a nice apology," Angela said with matronly assurance. "But now we have to go inside."

"What?!" asked Lionel, angry and confused. His mind raced, but his lips stayed silent. *We fuckin' apologized already. It's not like we don't swear all the time.*

Angela took them by the hands and marched them inside, saying just loud enough for the offended pedagogue to hear, "That type of language is not tolerated on the playground."

It was a smooth move on her part, and Carla and Ronnie coaxed the recess-duty teacher into dismissing the event.

Once inside, coats and hats put away, Angela closed the door and sat the two potty mouths at the table. She sat across from them and leveled with them. "Listen guys, I don't care if you swear all day long. It doesn't mean anything to me. Words are just words. Buhhhht, words like the ones you were using offend the other teachers at this school an awful lot. They don't use them, and they don't let anyone else use them."

"I know they are bad words," Lionel said. "But so what? It's not like I was talking to her. She had no right to butt in on us."

"That doesn't matter to the other grownups at this school. If they hear those words, they get really, really mad. Mr. Franklin wants to take away our recess time so the other kids in this school won't hear those words."

"He can't do that," Edward cried defensively.

"He can; it's true," Angela assured him.

Now the boys were scared. Recess was sacred.

"I want you guys to promise me not to swear in front of the other people in this school until after Christmas break. Do you think you can do that?"

The boys fervently swore not to swear.

Angela doubted they could make it the rest of the day without swearing, but she knew they'd hold out for as long as they could if recess was on the line. To help them out, Angela put a plan into action that she had been thinking about for the past couple of nights.

As she began to explain it, Hiro returned to the room with his microwaved early lunch and sat at his desk. Seeing that Angela had the situation well in hand, he left them to their own devices, eavesdropping while eating and completing paperwork.

Adjusting her position in the chair, Angela hushed her voice loud enough for Hiro to listen but low enough to draw the boys in closer. "Because you guys promised to not swear in front of the other teachers, I want to help you keep that promise. If you think you absolutely have to swear, do it in Spanish so the other teachers won't know what you're saying and you won't get in trouble. Does that sound fair?"

"Yahhhh," Lionel exhaled in awe at the prospect of cussing out people in a foreign language. He and Edward nodded vigorously, and their eyes blazed as if they had just discovered el Dorado.

"Okay. I'll teach you one word a day, if you promise to behave. Do you promise?"

They promised.

"What word will keep you out of the most trouble?"

Lionel blurted, "Fucker."

Angela became very solemn. "Feliz Navidad. You can shout it if you're really angry. Feliz Navidad! Or if you really want to burn somebody, say it as nicely and sweetly as you can. Feliz Navidad."

Hiro almost snorted macaroni out his nose, suppressing his laughter at Angela teaching the kids to replace fucker with Merry Christmas in Spanish.

Angela pressed on. "Repeat after me: Fay-leez"

"Fay-leez," the duo repeated in unison.

"Nah-vee-dahd," she enunciated, and they repeated.

"Very good, mi muchachos," Angela praised.

"Hey!" Lionel shouted accusatorily. "What did you just call us?!"

"Muchachos. It means friends."

Lionel eyed her suspiciously.

"Go ahead, why don't you guys practice saying Feliz Navidad for the rest of recess?"

This suggestion eased Lionel's suspicions greatly, and he and Edward traipsed about the room chanting "Feliz Navidad."

It wasn't long after recess ended that Hiro could prove to the classroom staff that his new timeout theory worked.

Kevin came crashing through the daytreatment pass-through door on his way to timeout with Carla hot on his heels. Cussing up a blue streak, Kevin stopped walking and refused to enter the timeout booth. Carla gently muscled him over the threshold and slammed the door behind him, securing the door as he pounded on it with his fists.

"Cripes," the teacher's aide huffed. "That kid gets set off so easily sometimes."

Hiro dropped his pen on his unfinished reports and brought two chairs over to Carla.

"What's this for?" Carla asked, eyeing Hiro suspiciously.

"I'm gonna help you through this new procedure," Hiro explained. Carla rolled her eyes, as he reassured, "I promise this will work out great. Now, first tell Kevin that if he sits quietly against the back wall you'll open the door."

Hiro set down Carla's chair and placed his own chair behind her to be totally out of Kevin's line of sight.

Carla looked in the timeout window and explained the deal to Kevin. He distrustfully glared at her. She continued, "Go on. You heard what I said."

Kevin reluctantly retreated and slumped his rump to the floor.

"Okay," Hiro whispered to Carla. "Open the door a little. Compliment him for making a good decision, then ask him why he's in timeout."

Carla cautiously opened the door about a foot and peeked inside the booth. Kevin was still against the back wall glowering at her.

"Good job sitting against the back wall. Smart decision," Carla said, as if she were reading from a script for the first time. "Now, why are you in here?"

" 'Cause you pushed me in here, Bitch," Kevin resentfully answered.

Carla slammed the door shut and latched it. Turning to Hiro, Carla stated, "I'm not gonna put up with that from him."

Kevin rammed the secured door with all of his might.

Hiro explained, "I'm not asking you to. Just be patient, and we'll start over again. He'll apologize before we're done."

Carla sighed and spoke through the booth door. "As soon as you sit against the back wall and talk appropriate to me, I'll open the door."

It took another minute, but Kevin eventually sat back down. "I'm ready," he called out.

Carla checked the window first, then opened the door, again. "Now, can you tell me why you're in here?"

" 'Cause you made me mad."

Carla looked back at Hiro for her next move. Hiro mouthed the word: how.

"How did I make you mad?" Carla probed.

"You made me do spelling," Kevin grunted.

"We always do spelling after recess."

"Yeah, but I wanted to finish my math, so I wouldn't have any homework."

Carla turned again to Hiro, who inquired with a whisper, "Is there any way to do that before spelling?"

"No," the aide replied. "He's got like 20 problems left. That'll take all day."

"Any chance he can do it before school gets out?" Hiro whispered.

"Maybe around story time."

"Okay, tell him."

"Kevin," Carla started. "You know we gotta do spelling after recess with everyone else, but maybe we could work on your math together before story time."

"Okay," the boy said in a reconciliatory tone.

Carla turned and whispered again, "Now what?"

"Ask him what he should do the next time he feels like escalating in that situation, again."

"Good," Carla said to Kevin. "So what should you do next time you're gonna blow up in class?"

"I don't know," he said, uncertain.

Carla turned to Hiro, "What should he do?"

"Tell him to express his feelings."

Carla explained to Kevin, "Tell me the next time you're gonna blow a gasket, and see if we can't do somethin' to help you first."

"Okay."

"Thanks," Carla said to Kevin, then to Hiro, "Cool, now what?"

"Let him know that if he's ready to do his spelling assignment in class he must apologize to you first."

Carla did this, Kevin offered a weak apology. "I'm sorry."

"For what?" Carla pushed.

"For calling you a bitch and goin' to time out."

"Thank you," Carla said and smiled. She fully opened the door to timeout. Cocking her head toward the classroom door, she said, "Let's git outta here."

Kevin eagerly followed her suggestion.

Carla checked the wall clock. *More like 10 minutes, not seven,* Carla thought. *But that's still a lot better than standin' here for half an hour.*

"Thanks, Hiro," she said, giving an upward nod of her head before closing the pass-through door behind her.

By the time lunch rolled around, the threat of no recess had spread from Lionel and Edward to the entire class. Mr. Franklin, as the primary authority figure who would take away their recess, was officially the enemy of the day. Annnd Feliz Navidad was the word of the day.

Oh, the joy of calling someone a fucker with them too dumb to know the difference, the kids collectively thought.

With a new enemy and an enlarged vocabulary, the students made life for the staff pretty easy for the remainder of the morning. The buzz of Spanish didn't bother the staff, especially since they knew what it really meant.

Angela helped lead a nearly perfectly behaved line of students to lunch.

Halfway down the hall, they encountered Mr. Franklin performing a snap inspection of all the classes heading to the cafeteria. Angela, Ronnie and Carla were anxious, knowing their students' disposition toward the principal today.

"Good morning, class," he said and smiled as he looked the line over.

The students were silent and earned his praise. As he was letting the line pass, Lionel, in his most angelic voice replied, "Feliz Navidad, Mr. Franklin."

The other students giggled and followed suit.

The principal was dumbfounded by the seemingly sudden change in the students' attitudes. He wondered if Angela had really transformed them from feral to polite, sweet bilingual children.

Mr. Franklin stuttered to affectionately reply. "Merry Christmas, kids."

The children giggled and collectively thought, *Ha! We sure fooled that dumb old fucker.*

Ronnie hustled them down the hall before pandemonium ensued.

Mr. Franklin pulled Angela aside. "Since you've come here, these kids have really made some remarkable strides."

"Thank you," she blushed. "But it's really been a team effort."

"Well, please tell everyone they're doing a great job, too. And now you've teaching the kids Spanish? That's amazing."

"Not really," Angela demurred, with no intention of telling Mr. Franklin the kids thought they just called him a fucker to his face. "It's just one phrase."

"Well, it's a good start. Keep up the good work," the principal complimented with a pat on her shoulder, before examining the next line coming down the hall.

Chapter 16

Charlie
(T'was the Last Week of School Before Christmas)

Katrina was perpetually sick of her three kids, and today was no exception. While they made great leverage to dangle over their three biological fathers whenever she needed money, she had no other interest or use for her children.

She had no more physical use for their fathers, either. She was happily divorced and collecting child support and alimony. She'd had a rough past with men and rarely wanted them around. But, she also learned how to make the good, but not too smart, ones pay for the misdeeds of the bad ones. The dim honest ones made great meal tickets.

Unfortunately for her today, the kids were the problem. Nellie was her oldest at 15. Charlie was next at 12. Rita brought up the rear at 10. While Rita still could win points with Katrina for being cute, Nellie and Charlie were royal nuisances with raging hormones. And the last thing she wanted was the older two scaring off her new boyfriend tonight.

Katrina met her new man during the past weekend at a bar. He was a nice enough character with a bad case of the Christmas blues. Single, not conventionally handsome and a little socially awkward, he was easy pickings, as the other women in town—both good and bad—seemed to miss the fact that he was loyal, compassionate and employed with a high-paying job in computer programming.

His quaint sense of prehistoric chivalry thwarted her efforts to seduce him by playing drunk and horny and willingly compromised. So she moved to plan B, and was pretty certain that she could get him with a candle-lit, home-cooked meal. She was well aware that she no longer needed to get pregnant to work this game, but she knew the sooner she got him between her thighs, the sooner she could work the powerful potion of sex and guilt to milk his bank account.

If she was really lucky, he'd even be exceptionally attentive while in the sack.

To find out, she had to lose the rug rats. She gave the brats $50 and told them to go to the bowling alley at the end of the street. "And don't come back until they close."

It didn't matter that the alley closed at midnight on a school night.

Upset, but powerless to argue without getting a whupping, the three children donned their shabby winter gear and began trudging down the street.

As they walked, Nellie pulled out her cell phone and began texting six of her friends to come join them.

The bowling alley was a blue-collar relic. It once sustained league play five nights a week and Sunday afternoons, with Saturday reserved for early tournaments and cosmic disco fun at night. With the exporting of the town's factory work to the sweatshops of China and India, the alley fell into disrepair—a seedy hangout for shadowy characters and underemployed but die-hard bowlers.

It wasn't a place for children to be without an adult, but the manager knew them well. As the kids never caused much trouble, he agreed to Nellie's request to stick them on an end lane when she paid for their shoes and limitless games until closing.

Orville, Nellie's boyfriend, arrived first. Then came couples Adel and Chester, followed by Melanie and Theo. Nellie's chronically single, acerbic friend Tawny showed last. Although Tawny didn't fit into the group dynamic very well, Nellie kept her around because they had been friends who survived rough childhoods together. They were always there for each other when the chips were down.

Now that all of her friends had arrived, Nellie addressed Charlie and Rita. "Get lost."

She handed her little sister the last remaining $20, and the girl ran off for the arcade room.

"I said beat it, jerk," she shouted at Charlie. "Go take care of Rita."

"She can take care of herself," Charlie fired back. "I'm not some fuckin' baby any more. I wanna hang out with you."

Nellie was about to punch him when Orville intervened.

"Lil' bro wants to hang with the big kids," the boyfriend and ring leader taunted. "I say we make him prove he's man enough first."

There was ominous agreement and sinister laughter.

Charlie was nobody's fool and willing to play their game. He mustered all of his moxie to look cool in front of the other kids. "I'm man enough for whatever you can dish out."

And the crowd teased, "Ewwwwwwwww," to accept his challenge.

"Well, if you are really a man, you'll have hair on your nuts," Orville proclaimed. "Let's see it, Mr. Man."

Shit, Charlie thought. *Outgunned by biology.* As much as he enjoyed jerking off whenever he got the chance, there was no trace of pubic hair. Nonetheless, he couldn't figure out why another guy would want to see his nads, and he debated whether to call Orville's bluff.

"Too chicken, or just a hairless baby," Orville taunted. That was enough to push Charlie over the top.

"I'll show you hairless baby," Charlie said, climbing up on his chair to offer a clear view for all to see.

The teenage boys squealed with the adolescent laughter of disbelief.

Charlie thrust out his groin and slowly began to unzip his fly.

The girls, unashamed, jockeyed for a closer look—all the girls save one.

"Christ!" exclaimed Nellie in disgust. "I don't want to see my brother's fuzzy little balls."

Thank God, Charlie thought, as he climbed down from his chair.

Chester pulled a zip-lock bag from the cargo pocket of his baggy pants. "A real man can handle some of this shit."

There was hushed agreement from all of the teens, who began to form a circle around the table to better hide from any prying adult eyes what Chester was offering.

Charlie relaxed. "I've smoked marijuana before, that's nuthin'," he blustered.

"Shhhh!" The six teens hushed, in fear of being caught.

Gutsy kid, Orville thought, as he leaned into take Charlie under his wing. "Listen, you might have partied a little with Mary Jane—smoked some weed. But no one calls this shit marijuana outside of your fuckin' D.A.R.E. class. Got it?"

Charlie gave him a wide grin and a little nod. Charlie was certain he could pass this test because his own mother had shared her stash with him and Nellie several times. She did it mostly to calm them down and keep their hormones and rebellion from driving her batshit.

Under the rapt gaze of his peers, Chester managed to roll several phatties to pass around the table.

Theo menacingly grabbed Charlie by his T-shirt. "You tell your mom about this, and you're a dead man."

Charlie tried to peel off Theo's meathooks. "Don't worry, man. You think I want you *and* her to kill me?"

"Chill out, Theo," Orville lackadaisically commanded. "Charlie's my homie. He's cool."

Theo let him go with a little intimidating shove. "Jus' playin', Dawg."

Theo took a drag off the joint and passed it to Charlie. Well practiced at home, the tween took a hit off the roach like a pro. The teens congratulated him, accepting him into their clique.

"What kind of pussy did you think I was?" Charlie posed, with the cool of a born rebel.

His moment of glory quickly passed when the girls started demanding some attention from their boyfriends. Taking two tables of booths, the teens split off—one couple per bench. Kissing quickly turned passionate, and the petting got heavy.

Repelled by watching his sister make out, Charlie focused on Adel and Melanie as they made out with their boyfriends. He never kissed a girl before, and he certainly never touched a girl sexually before. Watching the veritable orgy turned him on and filled him with wonder.

His gaze eventually landed on Tawny, who was watching him from her lonely bench seat.

"Great," she sighed sarcastically. "I get pee-wee the boy-man."

She spoke up and caught Charlie's attention by asking, "What do you know about pussy anyway?"

She had him there, and he turned pale. He barely knew what one looked like, let alone the rudimentary basics of what to do with one. He couldn't bluff; she would know he was a phony. He was motionless, but desperately wanted to see, feel and experience a woman's vulva in action. Hell, just getting to see or touch a breast was more than he anticipated for years to come.

Tawny sighed scornfully. "Well, c'mon over here."

Fear, lust, dread, excitement, guilt, adrenaline. Charlie could barely compel himself to move forward.

Tawny was far more confused by the situation than Charlie would ever know. She just had a better poker face. Below the surface in her deeper psychology roiled conflicting emotions and physical yearnings.

Up until that moment, Tawny's experiences with sex were mostly horrifying. It started with her birth. Before she could lift her head, her father had abandoned her and her mother. Her mother had many miserable, often rough, sexual relationships. Tawny's maternal uncle took to molesting Tawny when she was 7. Since then, Tawny hated any creature with a penis for good reasons. Then came puberty. She still hated males of all ages, but her biology stirred an inexplicable sexual curiosity...but not like with her uncle. It was so frustrating and confusing.

Watching her friends kiss and touch swelled her desire, envy and disgust. As she watched Charlie, she could see that he was practically a little kid claiming to be a man. To her he seemed like someone with whom it would be safe to experiment. He was so naïve and easily overpowered—physically and mentally. Lust and curiosity tingled through every nerve ending from head to toe. Her need to explore temporarily overrode the hatred and fear, as she decided to take advantage of the tween.

Although she didn't have much of a clue herself, she brazenly asked, "You know anything about kissing, Little Man?"

Before Charlie could answer, Tawny locked lips.

Charlie couldn't believe his luck. Kissing was way cooler than he imagined! He could hardly catch his breath.

He almost erupted when she put his right hand on her left breast.

Suddenly, Tawny pulled away. "What the fuck are you doing?! You're not testing a goddamn cantaloupe at the fucking grocery store for rot."

Charlie's emotions went from elation to shame. The hurt showed in his face.

Tawny leaned in and whispered, "Rub it gently." She kissed him more.

After a minute, she slid her hand down the front of his pants. Just being touched like that by a girl sent Charlie's hormone ravaged body into a pulsating bliss of euphoria. He was in love, in lust, a man at last and for one nano of a second in a state of unimaginable ecstasy.

The next 99 nanos of that second were the worst of his life.

"Jesus!" Tawny shouted. Her natural curiosity vanished the instant Charlie flooded her hand with wave after wave of nightmarish memories about her uncle. "You're supposed to warn me before that happens."

Everyone, even Nellie, was looking at Charlie.

He felt abject horror and absolute humiliation.

"God, what a sick little pervert," Tawny scolded. She wiped her hand on the outside front of Charlie's crotch and pushed him off the bench. She stepped over him and spoke to her gawking friends. "I couldn't find a single pube."

Fits of laughter aimed entirely at Charlie erupted from the boys and girls. Tawny made for the women's room.

Charlie ran after her and managed to block her entrance. His eyes

217

flooded with tears. "Wait. What's going on? Why'd you do that? I thought you liked me? Aren't you my girlfriend now?"

She shot him a look of pure venom. "Whatever. Get out of my way, loser." She body checked him with her shoulder and forcefully entered the women's room.

Heartbroken, unable to face his sister's friends and needing to clean up, Charlie entered the men's room.

Chapter 17

One Dickens of a Holiday
(The Next Day)

Contrary to the song lyric, it wasn't the hap-happiest season of all for the children of Average Elementary's daytreatment program. Abuse and insecurity at home soared as the 25th approached.

Lionel, already the caretaker at home, was inundated. His mom spent most of her time crying for no reason he could discern. His dad was too stoned to be of any use. If anyone was to get fed or bathed, Lionel had to take the initiative—even more than usual. He loved and protected his family and was proud he could do so much for them, but there also was a nagging voice in the back of his head telling him how out of control the situation was.

Why is Mom always crying? Why doesn't Dad do something? How can we make her happy, again? What happens with Sephie when I'm at school? Who takes care of her and Mom?

Speaking up at school would only lead to more problems. Lionel knew the system too well. If he mentioned anything at school, someone would call DCW. If DCW got called, his family could be split up. He feared he might never see them again, and he would be a failure as a responsible big boy. That's how he saw the situation, so he suffered in silence.

On the roughest days, Lionel pretended to be sick so he could stay home and care for everyone.

The daytreatment adults knew something was very wrong in Lionel's life. There was something very wrong in the lives of all the children in the program, which the holiday only exacerbated.

In an effort to make school a safer, happier environment, the grownups loaded up on Christmas cheer. There were lots of arts and crafts: cutting out snowflakes to decorate the room, cotton-ball snowmen, tissue-paper wreaths, etc. The biggest reward for the students came at the end of the day when they were given fruit and vegetable snacks while being allowed to watch DVDs of Christmas specials or movies.

The kids loved the TV time, but the adults saw that TV time didn't always work the way they hoped. Depending on the show, one or two kids would react negatively. Each show brought up different issues.

The Charlie Brown Christmas special was the one that got Lionel. He identified with Chuck. Like Chuck, Lionel was having a hard time getting in the spirit. All he really wanted to do was please everyone, get a little credit for it and live in peace. Even the sad little Christmas tree Chuck takes a shine to served as a metaphor for Lionel and his own pathetic, unloved family. But unlike the TV show, Lionel knew there was no one pulling for him…no one he could turn to who would save the day—at least not the way he wanted. Lionel didn't see a happy ending in his reality. He wasn't suicidal; he just accepted the only life he'd known. He just wished life was better so he could live it like the "normal" kids at recess do.

Lionel had seen Charlie Brown several times before it was shown in class. So when the adults put it on, Lionel got up and went to the back of the class, where the adults were keeping a watchful eye on the students. To Carla's surprise, he silently climbed into her lap without permission. As a rule, Carla kept her distance from the kids with a tough-love attitude. She wasn't the snuggly type. Yet her hard-hearted ways reminded Lionel of his mom. Unable to find any love at home, Lionel reached out for a surrogate, and Carla was his ideal for a temporary mother.

As Carla sat there on the plastic classroom chair, Lionel straddled her pelvis, wrapping his arms around her neck and nestling his head against her chest and throat. It wasn't sexual; Lionel just wanted to be held and loved in a somewhat normal parent-child capacity.

Too strong to cry, Lionel gently sobbed fat tears, soaking through Carla's old hooded sweatshirt.

It was enough to break even Carla's heart, so she wrapped her left arm around his bottom, gently stroking his boney back with her right hand. She gently rocked him and whispered that everything would be okay.

Lionel eventually fell asleep, and Carla held him close until the day's shows ended.

Technically, everything Carla did was against the rules. But if ever there was a perfect time to make exceptions, this was it. In the past week, the staff had been making a lot of necessary exceptions.

Lionel-like moments weren't the only reactions to the movies, where the stories always end with kids, whose parents love them, getting the presents they want. Not one of the daytreatment kids knew that reality. At least half were certain they wouldn't get anything. Not even Santa could be relied upon because he knew how bad and undeserving they were. That's what the kids thought. To ensure such self-fulfilling prophecies, the children misbehaved worse than ever. The boys became exceptionally aggressive and mean.

Violet became more introspective during or after a holiday movie. She'd pepper the daytreatment workers with a million irritating, obsessive questions as she usually did, but when she knew they were about to shut her out, she'd hit them with the question that was truly bothering her.

"Why don't I get Christmas presents?" "Parents don't really give up their own presents so their kids can have presents, do they?"

The question that really pierced Ronnie's heart: "Why doesn't my mom love me?"

Ronnie was stunned. She didn't know what to say, especially because she knew Violet was correct that her mother didn't love her. Ronnie simply pulled Violet in for a side hug and told her not to be silly. Of course her mother loved her, even if she didn't show it.

They both knew it was a lie, but Violet hugged her back. Sometimes just a little human contact made all of the difference in the world.

Hiro had scored his first little victory by getting Franz on a more healthful dose of medications. Franz was finally out of his fog and thinking clearly every day for the first time in years.

Angela and Hiro had also made great strides with Sammy's therapy. They thought they had seen the last of Freddy by December 1st, but he returned for more appearances the closer it got to Christmas. Even Sammy's clipped, psychotic baby talk returned from the grave.

Sammy once again escalated at least three times a day—spitting a torrent of saliva. The little boy once got so out of control Mrs. Regina called the police. They put a spit hood on him and cited him for being ungovernable, but the ticket meant nothing to him and the hood only increased his sense of danger, making him worse until the police gave up and left.

However, it wasn't a lack of presents that wound Sammy's clock. Angela could see a lot of bruises, despite his extra layers of clothes. She reported them all. The thumb-size bruise on Sammy's throat worried her most. She spoke with Sammy's newest caseworker and Virginia about it. No one came out to look at it! "Hands tied." "Too busy." "He'll be okay."

221

Angela's deal with Virginia appeared to have collapsed.

Angela was outraged. She gave Virginia an earful and got one in return. It was a bloody dog fight, which nobody won. It wasn't that Virginia didn't want to help, but if Average Elementary Daytreatment had a lot of abuse-related trouble, DCW had an entire county's worth. There just wasn't enough time or staff to do what was promised in regard to Sammy and Lulu.

Determined as ever to help save Sammy, Angela kept making calls to DCW. The whole staff was convinced Sammy would be killed before the holidays ended. Angela thanked God every day Sammy came to class.

On another front, Angela's Spanish lessons had been a wild success—at first. The boys all were shouting and screaming "Feliz Navidad!", "Te Amo" (I love you), "Besa me" (Kiss me), and "Eres tan bonita" (You're so pretty) every chance they got.

Unfortunately, when one student's mother translated Feliz Navidad for her son after he yelled it at her with great invective, the jig was up. The students felt profoundly betrayed by the one grown up they thought they could trust. Angela was in the dog house and felt awful about it.

Yet Angela's stock climbed with Richard and Hiro. With the program out of cash, Angela started a fundraising campaign, raising money from local businesses. Several grocery stores donated about $25 a piece worth of healthful classroom snacks. A mom-and-pop toy store donated a few items for the classroom's store. And then came the shocker. Big Box Store offered the program a gift card worth $40 every month for one complete year. While Angela generally hated Big Box Store for its poor labor practices, foreign sweatshop-made merchandise and negative impact on local small businesses, she had to hand it to them for saving her program and allowing her and Hiro to make sure their kids had enough gloves, hats, school supplies and daytreatment store "merchandise."

And while the students might have still been mad at her, Angela was the hit of the Average Elementary teacher's party, held at Rachel's house, with her parody of "Winter Wonderland," which she renamed "Daytreatment Wonderland."

Children scream;
They won't listen.
Bite and swear,
What's a missin'?

Hack and spit just for fun,
Or they tantrum and run,
Welcome to Daytreatment Wonderland.

Far Away,
In the boonies.
Here to stay,
Stuck with loonies.
I'd bitch and I'd moan,
But I'm all alone,
Workin' in Daytreatment Wonderland.

In the courts we have administrators.
They pretend our problems aren't abound.
We ask can you help us with facilitators,
But no they say there's none to be found.

Later on,
On the playground.
Blood and teeth
For our lost-and-found.
I'll face unafraid,
My work, stock and trade
Workin' in Daytreatment Wonderland

In timeout,
When they're poohin'
Go find out
What else they're doin',
Occupational chore
That's never a bore,
Workin' in Daytreatment Wonderland.

When the big kids ran into the psych room for group, Angela and Hiro knew they were in for a rough session. Franz, Kevin and Charlie were particularly wired.

On a lower dose of meds, Franz had really come alive. He was attuned to class and group. He was discovering his most repressed emotion: anger. It was healthy for him to be angry, but it was harder on the staff as he learned to cope with his emotions stemming from the

223

abuse in his home.

Today, he was very excited, grinning as if he had a great secret about someone else he was busting to tell. Kevin was feeding off that energy and fidgety.

Charlie's eyes were bloodshot; he looked exhausted. He managed to remain alert and seemed to be holding court with his minions: Franz and Kevin. He radiated a sense of command and the authority of cool.

Violet and Jefferson were clearly out of the loop and calm.

"Alright, guys. What's up?" Hiro flatly inquired.

"Nothin'," Franz coyly explained, looking at Charlie and giggling.

Kevin looked at Charlie then Franz and Charlie, again. He chortled.

"Charlie?" Angela asked. "Care to tell us what these guys think is so funny?"

"No," he said, stoned and flirtatious. He stared at Angela's breasts and wondered if they felt like Tawny's.

Angela sighed and crossed her arms in front of her chest and tried to shift the attention away from the boys and spoke to Violet. "Can you tell us what you did last night?"

"I think the boys are being very immature," Violet answered. She hated being left out of the loop when a juicy story was circulating.

"I'm subtracting a dollar for…"

"HA. HA," Charlie mocked. "That's funny, you calling anyone immature, Violet."

"…I'm taking a dollar from you, too, Charlie," Angela declared. "Violet, you can earn your dollar back by apologizing to Charlie, Franz and Kevin for calling them immature."

A power struggle soaked up the next five minutes. Violet refused to apologize first. She didn't give in until Angela and Hiro each had her by a bicep and were about to drag her into timeout.

"Okay, Charlie," Hiro explained. "Now you need to apologize to Violet."

"Uh-uh, uh-uh, uh-uh," he responded, shaking his head and grinning like a toddler. He was positively goofy. "Hey, guess who I'm being. I'm Sammy. Uh-uh, uh-uh, uh-uh."

"That's another dollar lost," Angela said. "If you don't apologize to Violet, you can go to timeout until you can apologize to her."

"Sorry," he grunted. "Now where's my dollar."

"You don't get one until you apologize like you mean it."

Charlie's next apology improved, but not enough for a dollar. Franz and Kevin giggled, losing a dollar apiece.

Hiro switched the subject to defuse the power struggle and rewarded Jefferson for his perfect behavior.

"What did you do last night, Jefferson?" Hiro asked.

His night was mundane, but it earned him more money for talking and avoiding set ups.

"Franz, what interesting things do you know?" Hiro kept the ball rolling.

Franz was oddly coy again and looked at Charlie. "I didn't do anything *interesting* last night."

The three boys giggled.

"And you, Kevin?" Hiro continued.

"I didn't do nothin'."

Hiro sighed.

"Alright Charlie, what did you do last night?" Hiro asked, as if he didn't actually want to know.

His tone sparked a compulsion in Charlie to respond. Charlie's bloodshot eyes widened, and he giggled. "I had a date…"

He trailed off for dramatic effect.

"You had a date?" Angela asked with a touch of incredulous disbelief.

"…with Mary Jane," Charlie finished his sentence before giving out with an inexperienced low-stuttering stoner laugh.

"Are you stoned?" Angela calmly asked.

"Huh-huh-huh," Charlie sheepishly laughed.

Man, was he ever baked. After Tawny humiliated him, Charlie hoped to find some refuge in the men's room. Braced for the taunting of his life, Charlie washed the semen off his pants as quickly as he could. He soaked his crotch thoroughly, which only made it look like he pissed himself. At least, he thought, no one would be able to tell what really happened. When Orville, Chester and Theo entered the restroom, they were laughing at Charlie pretty hard. But after the initial laughter subsided, they embraced the boy as one of their own, whooping it up.

"Way to go! I wish I could get a decent hand job."

"Hey, who cares if your nuts are hairless. You still squirted her good."

"Don't let that skank upset ya; she's a bitch."

"You the man!"

In a gesture of reconciliation and congratulations, the older boys broke out the baggie of pot. The pubescent hero of the hour was given more than enough weed to stupefy his feelings of guilt, anger and confusion.

Charlie was still higher than the International Space Station in group. He reveled in the cool points it earned him with Franz and Kevin, but he also was getting really irritable with his apparent inability to come down.

Hiro and Angela didn't know about the sex, only the pot, and no matter how much the two probed, Charlie was determined not to mention anything about the sex to them.

Hiro explained the dangers of drug use and kept digging for more information about how Charlie got the drugs. It didn't take long to figure out that a lot more than smoking pot transpired at the bowling alley, but neither Hiro nor Angela had a clue.

"What else happened?" Hiro bluntly asked.

"That's it," Charlie defensively answered. He was getting more and more annoyed with the mental health professional. Kevin and Franz nervously laughed. They knew the whole story.

"C'mon, Charlie," Hiro cajouled. "I'm not stupid. Something happened. What was it?"

"Nothing happened! It's none of your damned business!" Charlie yelled.

"There's no need to shout. And, yes, it is my business," Hiro said and softened. "It's okay. You can tell me, and I won't get you in trouble."

"SHUT UP!" Charlie jumped to his feet. His awful memories about his first sexual encounter flooded his head like an inescapable tsunami. "LEAVE ME ALONE!"

Everyone was taken aback, not expecting Charlie to snap. Charlie hadn't escalated in years. He was a set-up artist and a master of getting the other boys to do his bidding, but he hadn't physically gotten violent in some time.

Angela was on her feet in a heartbeat. "It's okay, Charlie. There's no need to make a fuss."

"I SAID, 'LEAVE ME ALONE, BITCH.'"

"Alright," said Angela nonchalantly. "Time for a timeout to cool off."

The behavior specialist invited him to walk into timeout with a sweep of her hand toward the booths. He pushed her hand away.

"Now," she calmly insisted. Angela turned the boy's shoulders to point him toward timeout. It was a routine maneuver—her traditional warning preceding a restraint.

Charlie jabbed his elbow hard into Angela's breadbasket. It knocked the wind out of her for a second. When she recovered, she put him in a full restraint. She had never restrained Charlie before and realized how much more difficult it was with him being only a little shorter than her. He bucked and jerked to free himself, and Angela could barely hold on. Hiro had to help her get Charlie into timeout.

Charlie punched and kicked the padding of the booth once before tears welled in his eyes.

Hiro took over the door, hoping to get the whole story from the tween.

Angela returned to the group and tried to get the story from Franz and Kevin. Charlie threatened them from the timeout window, and it kept the boys silent.

Hiro saw that nothing therapeutic was going to be accomplished with the group still in session, so he dismissed it early. After the kids had gone back next door, Hiro instructed Angela to call Charlie's mother. "If he's this stoned, I don't want him in school."

"No problem."

Charlie never actually cried, and now his tears were gone and he defiantly stared at Hiro through the timeout window. The boy refused to sit against the back wall or talk about his night.

After trying both her home and office number, Angela couldn't reach Katrina.

"What should we do now?" Angela asked Hiro.

"I seem to remember seeing his father's name and number in his file. Ring him up."

"I didn't know Charlie had a dad we could reach."

"He's probably a *deadbeat*," Hiro silently mouthed the last word. "But what have we got to lose. I won't have a stoned kid in school, and I won't have his parents kept in the dark about drug abuse."

Angela rooted around through Charlie's file to find his dad's work number. There were hardly ever any references in the file to the man at all, even though what few references there were seemed to be good—considering the program's bad track record with fathers.

Charlie's father worked in a warehouse, and it took a few minutes for a receptionist to find him and get him to a phone. Angela spoke when she heard him pick up the connection. "Uh, hi. Is this Ray Carazo?"

"Yeah, whatch you want?" the man said, speaking with a bit of an

East Coast blue collar accent.

"My name's Angela Marengo, and I work with Charlie at his school, and we need you to come pick him up."

"Can't his muddah do it? She's got custody. I'm pretty busy here at work."

"We can't get a hold of her and need someone to come get him."

"Sumpin' wrong? My boy okay?"

"Yes and no," Angela explained. "Charlie's fine. He's not hurt, but he's pretty wasted on marijuana. We can't have him here like this today."

"What?!" spat Ray, not expecting an answer. "Jesus. The boy's 12, where the Hell did he get some pot, and why the Hell would he be smoking it? He's frickin' 12 for chrissake."

"Sir, I don't know why he smoked it, but I do know he got an awful lot of it from some teenagers at the bowling alley last night."

"Where was his muddah?"

"I don't know. From what I heard, it didn't sound like she was there."

"Christ," the man sighed and paused for a few seconds before speaking again. "I gotta talk to my foreman."

Angela didn't know whether she was supposed to wait or hang up and let him call her back. As there was no noise indicating the other line disconnected, she waited.

Several minutes passed before Charlie's dad returned. "I'll be there in 10, 15 minutes."

"Thank you, Mr. Carazo," Angela said.

Although he refused to sit against the back wall of timeout, Charlie was practically angelic waiting for his father. He chatted up a storm about any subject other than the previous night. Hiro refused to open the door until Charlie started co-operating with his instructions.

Ten minutes later, a stocky man wearing a tan Carhartt coat and stained blue jeans appeared in the daytreatment door. Despite his many layers of clothes, he was obviously strong as an ox. He had the face of a man who had fought for everything his entire life. There appeared to be nothing in a back alley that could take him. He was intimidating to say the least.

"That my boy in that box?" Ray pointed and hesitantly stepped into the room.

Hiro and Angela had been talking with Charlie and were startled by the confrontational question by the hulking figure.

"Yes," Angela answered. Disguising her initial fear, she briskly approached Charlie's dad with her hand extended. "Mr. Carazo, I'm Angela, the woman you spoke with on the phone. This is Hiro Yamamoto, our program's therapist."

Ray shook her hand but didn't take his piercing, yet bewildered, gaze off the timeout booth. "Why is my boy in a box?"

"Sir," Hiro explained, "We prefer to call it a timeout booth. Your son escalated pretty severely."

"He what?" Ray asked, taking his eyes off the wooden cell for the first time.

"He went berserk," Angela translated. "He even hit me in the ribs as hard as he could with his elbow."

Ray looked Angela in the eye. When she didn't blink, he looked her down then up. It wasn't sexual. He was sizing the slender Hispanic woman up like a fighter. She looked toned, but small enough for his son to actually hurt. Ray's hard gaze met her eyes again and moved to her boss'. "Can you hear me, Charlie?"

"Yeah," replied the now submissive 12-year-old.

"Are they tellin' me the truth? Did you go berserk? Did you hit this lady?"

"Yeah," the boy meekly answered.

Ray approached the timeout door, which Hiro opened for him. Ray's frame filled the width of the portal. "Was she tryin' to hurt you?"

"No," the boy said.

"I am really disappointed in you, then. I told you nevah, evah hit a girl."

Charlie opened his mouth to speak, but Ray cut him off. "I don't want to hear it. Nevah hit a girl. If I evah hear about you hittin' a girl again, so help me..."

"Sir," Hiro and Angela tried to intervene.

Ray spun around so quickly, the two instinctively flinched backward out of reach. But instead of lashing out at the daytreatment workers, the man became profoundly humble. He removed his longshoreman's stocking cap from his shaved head and wrung it in his hands, as he addressed Angela. "I'm very sorry about my boy's behavior. He don't normally act out like this. I don't know what came over him."

Ray's apology was genuinely sincere. He didn't sound like he was faking it like all of the other parents who had been through this routine before.

Angela accepted his apology, and Charlie started to cry. He left timeout and put his arms around his father's middle and sobbed into the big man's coarse coat.

Ray was befuddled. He put his left arm around his son's shoulders, but he didn't know what to do with his right. "Say, what's goin' on here?" he asked Hiro and Angela. "What typeofa class is this, anyway?"

"Do you have a few minutes, Mr. Carazo?"

"Yeah, I got all afternoon now. And just call me Ray."

"Why don't you have a seat and let's talk," Hiro invited.

Angela brought two chairs in front of her's and Hiro's desks for Ray and Charlie.

Hiro explained Charlie's diagnosis, the class and treatment. He showed him Charlie's case file. Katrina and Charlie had kept him entirely in the dark about all of this, and Ray slowly leafed through the case file, absorbing all of this new information.

Hiro didn't discuss his theories about Katrina in front of Charlie, but he didn't need to. Ray was already putting together the pieces of the puzzle he'd been struggling with for years. He had always known Katrina was no good for him, but he figured a mother would be better at raising kids than a father. It was dawning on him that that old-fashioned notion wasn't always true.

Ray asked a lot of questions about psychology and his son, and Hiro answered.

An hour passed before Ray asked his last and biggest question of the day. Turning to his exhausted, bleary-eyed son and speaking with a voice so deep and soft he asked, "Why didn't you evah tell me any of dis?"

Charlie had wanted to so many times, but he never knew how. He never thought it would be okay. His father was his idol. He was always so tough, strong, macho and cool. Ray was everything Charlie wanted to be, except for a star quarterback. To Charlie's way of thinking, admitting to being the way he was, was basically admitting he was a total sissy, whom his father would probably disown entirely. How do you explain all of this to someone you're only allowed to see for a couple hours every month? *How do I explain it now?* Charlie wondered.

The 12-year-old wouldn't make eye contact and practically whispered, "I don't know."

For one brief second Ray looked wounded. Then he braced himself with new resolve.

"Thank you for callin' me an' tellin' me dis stuff," he said to the treatment team. "I'm gonna take care of dis, you'll see. I wanna talk again soon."

"No problem," Hiro replied. "I'm glad we can help."

Ray got up and signaled to Charlie that it was time to go. He turned back to Angela and Hiro. "Don't hesitate to call me. I'll come git 'im if dere's evah a problem. If I don't, my, uh, girlfriend, Simone, can come git 'im. We been livin' togethah for several years now. You can trust 'er. But, please, always let me know what's goin' on."

Hiro assured him that he would.

As the father and son made their way to the door, Ray smiled. "Yeah. All dis kid evah tells me is how great his arm is at football."

Ray put a fatherly meathook on his son's shoulder. Charlie beamed.

"That kid doesn't have an arm..." Angela broke the revelry, her face emotionless.

Charlie's face fell. She'd seen him every day at recess and lunch launching all kinds of pin-point passes. *How can she lie about my arm?* The boy wondered, hurt.

"...that kid's got a cannon," she grinned, and gave Charlie a wink.

Charlie's heart started beating again.

Ray mussed Charlie's hair. "That's my boy."

Angela and Hiro looked at each other expectantly until they heard the outside door click shut.

When they knew no one was listening, Hiro asked, "What do you make of that?"

"I don't know," Angela replied. "My gut tells me that Ray really likes Charlie. He wasn't faking anything, but I don't know how he could have been so clueless about Charlie's mental health issues?"

"Yeah, that's really weird. I just assumed he was a deadbeat who didn't care. Maybe he really was just blind to it and never probed Katrina or Charlie for deeper information about his son's life."

"Well, it's good to have him helping now," Angela said.

"I wouldn't get too excited, yet," Hiro warned. "Ray might bail on Charlie when he realizes how much trouble raising Charlie really is. He hasn't been the most responsible parent to date."

Richard dropped by for an unexpected visit that afternoon. Angela told him about her success with the donations, while they waited for Hiro to finish a therapy session with Edward, who was having a difficult time with "The Muppets Christmas Carol."

When Hiro was done, he ushered Richard and Angela into the little therapy room.

"Good to see you, again, Richard. How can we help you today?" Hiro cheerily greeted.

Their boss chuckled. "I actually came here to ask you the same question. How are you settling in?"

"We're doin' pretty well. Did Angela tell you about her big score with the donations—especially from Big Box Store."

"Yes, I'm quite impressed."

"Thank you," Angela accepted the compliment with a nod.

"How are you handling the holiday chaos?" Richard asked Hiro.

"Minute by minute."

"Yeah, I'm afraid that's how it goes," Richard conceded. "Look on the bright side, it'll be over in a couple days when Christmas break starts."

"We'll hang in there. They'll just be a rough few days."

"Well, to prove I'm not all doom and gloom," Richard opened a new topic, "I also came here to compliment you. Hiro, you are doing an amazing job tracking and billing the therapeutic time spent with the children. You're billing at a pace I've never seen before. The insurance company isn't going to like this, but you're documenting *everything*, right?"

"I wouldn't bill a dime that wasn't documented."

"Good."

Angela inquired, "Why won't the insurance company be happy? We're doing everything exactly the way they've asked. We're playing by their rules."

"It isn't a problem, yet," Richard explained. "But at the rate this program is going, it would appear that you've beaten them at their own game and are actually making them pay us more than they actually wanted or expected to pay."

"If they didn't expect to pay us this much, why did they set up the rules this way?" Angela continued.

"You've complained what a chore it is to fill out all of that paperwork. They count on making the process so difficult that they don't have to dish out all of the money the state gave them. And if they don't have to redistribute it, they can either keep it or at least make money off the interest they make by holding on to it longer."

Angela sighed in disgust at the insurers and her own naivety. *You'd think I'd have figured this out by now,* she thought.

"Don't let it bother you," Richard encouraged. "They haven't changed anything, yet."

Angela shrugged her shoulders, and Richard addressed Hiro about his final reason for visiting. "Although you're doing a great job billing for our current kids, I also came here for an update on your progress in finding new students for the program."

"I just haven't had time yet, Richard," Hiro said. "I've just started, and I'm still getting to know the current students, their parents, the classroom dynamic and a million other things. Throw in the holiday hullaballoo and the fact that the semester has less than a week to go, I think it would be an extremely bad time to take on new kids."

"Did I not make explicitly clear how crucial it is for us to fill this program to capacity?"

"You did, but I've also raised our billing rate substantially. I haven't been wasting any time, and I do need time to adjust to this job," Hiro defensively countered.

Sparks began to fly as the conversation got a little more heated. Angela did her best to stay out of the way.

As the head cheese, Richard ended the discussion. "I don't care. We need this program full by the end of January, and I want at least one new student in here before the new semester begins."

Ba humbug, Hiro thought.

Chapter 18

Intake
(Early January)

Hiro and Angela did their best to mask their anger at Richard for calling them in during the winter break to interview a prospective student/client for the program. The three mental health professionals were now sitting on one side of the arts-and-crafts table, and Carole, Reginald and their 8-year-old daughter, Cassi, sat opposite them.

Cassi was delighted she could use the entire classroom bucket of crayons to color while the adults talked. She thanked Angela profusely for bringing her all of the crayons and paper. Her mother also was thankful.

"I'm just so glad you took the time to see us during the holiday break," Carole said, her eyebrows knit in deep gratitude and concern. "We need someone to help us with little Cassi."

Hiro and Angela looked at the polite little blonde girl contentedly coloring on the far end of the table.

"What seems to be the problem?" Hiro inquired.

Carole clasped her husband's hand in her's. "I'm afraid she is another one of the millions of tragic American children afflicted with A-D-D."

Carole enunciated A-D-D clearly, with great emphasis, to prove she was quite savvy about attention deficit disorder.

"Why do you suspect that?" Hiro probed.

"Well, she's just full of so much energy," Carole answered. "She's brilliant, always exploring and active. It's difficult sometimes to make her settle down."

Reginald shamefully added, "I'm afraid it's my fault. I probably would have been diagnosed with ADD as a child. I was always so rambunctious and athletic. I loved to play sports all of the time."

Carole put a supportive arm around her husband's shoulders, sympathetic to his faulty genetics. Embraced so, it was difficult for the mental health workers to discern where one matching Ralph Lauren outfit ended and another began. Cassi carefully picked out her favorite crayons and started drawing a new picture of her mom and dad playing with her and all of her Christmas presents. Angela wanted to roll her eyes at the overly concerned parents.

Hiro kept asking questions. "Does Cassi get in trouble at school a lot?"

"Oh," sighed Carole, "All of the time. Sometimes her teacher even sends home notes."

"It's dreadful," Reginald confirmed.

Angela handed Cassi a crayon and asked, "What type of trouble do you get in at school?"

Before the girl could open her mouth, her mother encouraged her to speak. "It's okay, Baby, tell these nice people everything you get in trouble for."

"Thank you for the galaxy blue crayon, Miss Angela," the precocious child said before answering. "Sometimes I get in trouble for whispering to my friends after recess. Sometimes, the teacher has to yell at me after the bell rings to leave the playground."

"Anything else?" Angela asked.

The little girl let out a small sigh of shame. "Sometimes I don't want to do my reading work, but my teacher makes me."

"Thank you for using your words and sharing," Angela praised.

While the parents were distracted by Angela's and Cassi's conversation, Hiro shot Richard a dirty look. There was no way this child was an appropriate fit for this program. She was a perfectly normal second grader. Richard looked back sternly, silently warning Hiro to keep his mouth shut.

Realizing he couldn't outright tell the parents that they shouldn't enroll Cassi in his program, Hiro hit them with reverse psychology. He told the loving, yet overly fretful, parents about the program in graphic detail. Hiro described the restraints and timeout. He described Sammy's psychotic explosions and Ted's homicidal tendencies. He described the horrifying abuse these kids suffered at home. He warned them about the foul language and violence in the classroom. Hiro painted the perfect picture of elementary school hell on Earth.

"Wow," said Reginald with a low murmur when Hiro finished.

"Yeah," said his wife. "If you can't cure our little girl, no one can. This program will be perfect for her."

Hiro looked pleadingly at Richard to reject Cassi.

"I'm sure Hiro and Angela can help Cassi," Richard said, closing the deal. "Are you sure you don't want your insurance agency to cover this cost?"

"Oh, no," Reginald said. "We don't want little Cassi labeled by the insurance industry at a young age. We are more than capable of covering the costs. $100 a day and $70 a therapy session sounds more than reasonable and much less expensive than sending our baby to an institution for months at a time."

Angela involuntarily choked. She knew the state's insurance company paid a quarter of that price.

Richard wanted to kick Angela under the table. The rates were genuine, but unfortunately the insurance companies refused to pay that price, and something was better than nothing.

Reginald pulled out his checkbook.

Richard interrupted his action. "That won't be necessary. We will send you a monthly bill. Will Cassi be ready for class when school resumes next week?"

"Absolutely," Carole assured them. She turned to her daughter and asked, "What do you think? Would you like to make this your new school next semester?"

"Yes, Mommy. I think I'll like it a lot," the girl smiled brightly at Angela.

Angela smiled back but felt sick to her stomach for taking part in this meeting.

"I can assure you, Carole," Hiro said. "We'll make sure Cassi will be ready for her regular school by the end of this semester."

"Thank you, Hiro, but don't rush on our account. We only want the best results, and if that takes time, that's okay," Carole encouraged.

The adults all stood and shook hands, and the family departed.

"See, piece of cake," Richard said, after everyone was certain the family was out of the building. "I told you it would be easy to refill this program. They had been on the waiting list for a while."

"Richard, what we just did was abhorrent," Hiro bluntly stated. "That little girl is no more emotionally disturbed than any other 8-year-old in this school."

"Her parents say she has ADD," Richard countered. "Observe her for a while and make your diagnosis then. Redirect her when she gets a little hyper and call her cured by the end of the semester. Her parents will be grateful and can move on to some other misperceived problem. This case is an easy one that won't stress the class dynamic. Let's not look a gift horse in the mouth."

"Where the hell did you study ethics?" Hiro asked incredulously.

Richard became uncharacteristically aggressive. "How dare you question my ethics? If those people are willing to pay the full rate, they can keep this program afloat, which means nine kids with real problems can keep coming to school and get at least some of the treatment they desperately need. Those parents have been shopping for the diagnosis they want and won't stop until they hear what they want. Better that child come here with some safety than head off to a more dangerous program or some institution."

Hiro could see the validity of Richard's argument but still vehemently disagreed. Before he could fight back, Richard cut him off. "I will not discuss it any further."

Richard took his coat and left, slamming the classroom door behind him.

"Jesus," Hiro spat under his breath. He faced Angela. "C'mon, let's get out of here. You wanna get some coffee."

The two mental health professionals found a quiet table at a local coffee shop and settled in with their specialty brews.

"Angela, have you given much thought to your future?"

"What do you mean?"

"In mental health. Where do you see yourself in a year or five?"

"I don't know," the confused behavior specialist replied. "I always figured I'd do this for a while, save up some money and get my master's or doctorate. I've been so busy, I really hadn't put much thought into it."

"Do you have any back up plan incase anything should happen?"

"What are you getting at, Hiro? Do you know something I should be worried about?"

"Not specifically," Hiro cupped his hands around his coffee for warmth. "There's just lots of little things. We're walking on pretty thin ice with this job."

"Isn't that the nature of this line of work?" Angela shrugged.

"It shouldn't be," Hiro explained. "I haven't worked here very long, and I'm already making enemies of my employers. You aren't on the best of terms with them, either, after your last boss. We both work hard and are dedicated to helping these kids—we just haven't done a lot to ingratiate ourselves with the hierarchy. I also was reading online that the state's lawmakers were planning on cutting social services by another 25% to make room for more tax cuts this upcoming session."

"What? Where can they possibly cut any tighter? No service has enough money to do a good enough job as it is," Angela blustered.

"It's a perfect trap," Hiro said. "We already can't possibly do a thorough job with the money they give us. Then because we can't do a thorough job on that money, they say we're just being wasteful and inefficient, so they can cut our budgets further."

Angela growled through her teeth in disgust. "You know by that same logic, it is amazing they don't slash the police budget. We've pumped hundreds of millions into their department for a century, and we still have crime. Obviously, they're just too lazy and wasteful."

Angela shook her head at the stupidity of such an argument.

Hiro brought the conversation back to the track on which he started. "It's not totally impossible to see us losing our jobs in the next three to six months."

"Do you have a plan?" Angela inquired.

"Do you promise not to tell anyone?"

"Of course."

"A couple of my friends in the biz and I are thinking about starting our own small mental health clinic. It would just be me and two other therapists sharing an office. We would offer affordable therapy to the poor at prices they could afford—with or without insurance. Even getting rock-bottom rates, I could double what I make at the center, maybe triple it."

"Really?"

"Yeah," Hiro said. "Plus I wouldn't have to put up with as much of the bureaucratic bullshit and worthless company policy restraints that Richard imposes.

"Don't get me wrong; there'd be a lot of hard work and no guarantee of success, but I think the other therapists and I can make it work. Plus we could help so many people who might not normally seek out treatment."

Angela probed, "Richard really burned you up, didn't he?"

"Don't tell me that taking on this case doesn't upset you."

"Oh, it does," Angela told him. "But it doesn't get to me half as much as DCW ignoring our reports and sending kids back to sadistic parents."

"Yeah, that bothers me, too, but at least I feel better knowing that I've done all I legally can."

The two were quiet for a moment, lost in their thoughts.

Angela was the first to break the silence. "Your little clinic wouldn't happen to need a behavior specialist, would it?"

Hiro smiled. "I'd hire you in a heartbeat, if it did. We haven't formally started anything yet. And if we do, none of us would probably draw a paycheck for several months. Even *if* we did hire someone, it would be a receptionist who could handle wrangling payments out of the insurance companies."

"I'd rather shoot myself than do that," Angela earnestly declared.

"I figured as much," Hiro said. "You really would be a great therapist, though. Have you thought about where you want to go to grad school?"

"Not really. I'd have to pay for it myself, so I'd probably go back to State. It would be cheaper, and they have a good cognitive-behavioral modification program. I'm sure I could get in and enjoy it."

"I'm not one to play the race card," Hiro stated. "But I'm sure that with your excellent grades, a year of field experience and being a Hispanic woman, you could probably get a ton of scholarships to attend wherever you wanted. What do you really want to do in psychology?"

"That's actually what really bothers me," she confided. "I'm not sure."

"You're great with the kids, and you have incredible insight into human behavior and emotions."

"Thanks," she said, "But what do I do with that? Obviously, it would be a critical part of being a good therapist. But how far can I really go with that? What I really want to do is help the children get out of those awful homes and into a safe setting. I want to heal them, too."

"You can do that with a master's or doctorate and get paid a lot better than you are now," Hiro explained, hoping to shore up her doubts with some incentives.

"Of course," Angela agreed. "The trouble will still be the same that we have now. An advanced degree won't change the laws. Won't make insurance companies suck less. Won't make lawmakers listen or care. I have all of these ideas and all of this energy, but I don't know where to put it to do the most good. To be the most effective. I'm really frustrated."

"That's true, but I know you'll have far more options with more initials after your name," Hiro encouraged.

"Certainly," Angela conceded. "I honestly haven't given actual graduate programs much thought, yet."

"I'm certainly not trying to scare you out of working for the Center, but you might want to start thinking about it more seriously. The grad school application deadlines are usually up by the end of February."

"Thanks. Maybe I will start looking into it."

Chapter 19

A Suicide Squeeze
(Mid-January)

Angela was late getting to school, and she didn't care. She was excited to see Luke, her best friend in college and former debate-team partner who was back in town that night from law school. Angela planned on getting through the workday on autopilot and having a lot of fun catching up with him.

The students beat Angela to school, and Hiro was already supervising Lionel in timeout.

The kids had survived a miserable two-week vacation. There was far too much for them to cope with at once. The first week and a half back was uncharacteristically worse than the two weeks preceding Christmas.

Sammy greeted Angela at the door of the daytreatment room with Carla by his side.

Carla did the talking. "He's been asking for you since he stepped off the bus. He wants to give you something."

"Hi, Sammy," Angela said warmly. "How's my favorite swing-set friend?"

"Hi," the boy grunted.

"Did you have something you wanted to tell me?"

Sammy looked over his shoulder suspiciously at Carla. "I want to talk to you," he groused secretively through clenched teeth.

"I'm right here," Angela coaxed.

"Not with her," he whispered loud enough that Carla heard him.

"C'mon, Sammy," Carla said. "We gotta get back to class so the big kids' group can start."

Sammy looked pleadingly at Angela.

"Give me a few minutes to get settled," the behavior specialist replied. "I'll see what I can work out."

"Promise?"

"Promise."

"Here," Sammy grunted and handed Angela a folded piece of

notebook paper. He then walked back next door with determined little steps.

Carla held back for a minute, and Angela asked, "What was that all about?"

"Beats me. These kids are squirrely as hell today. Must be a full moon or somethin'."

Angela strolled over to her desk and put her lunch bag down. She twirled Sammy's folded paper through her fingers like a silver dollar and smiled. Sammy wrote or drew her a dozen messages a day.

Ronnie and Kevin burst through the partition door. Angela stuffed the paper in her back hip pocket and raced to help Ronnie restrain Kevin's flailing arms and legs. It took them a minute, but they managed to get him safely into timeout.

Angela manned the latch, as Ronnie caught her breath. "Ronnie, I'll take this one and let you get back to class if you want."

"I'm not sure I want. Good golly, that was a tough one."

"I sure won't tell on you if you want to hang out for a few minutes."

The two made small talk over Kevin's tantrum—his second of the morning.

After a minute, there was a crash next door, and Ronnie ran over to help. Angela began talking Kevin down. Hiro moved Lionel to the arts-and-crafts table for an impromptu session, freeing the booth for Mrs. Regina, as she hauled Franz in for a timeout.

Sammy peeked into the daytreatment room and caught Angela's attention. "Talk?"

"Not yet, Sammy, I'm still with Kevin in timeout. Soon."

"Read note?"

"I'm sorry, Buddy, I haven't had a chance. It's in my back pocket, I promise. I'll read it as soon as I can. Go back to class now, okay?"

Sammy huffed in frustration and went back to his seat. Angela thought his behavior was cute and was impressed by how well he had been handling the turmoil in class. She wanted to help him, but talking Kevin down was the priority. Sammy had made so much improvement.

Angela kept talking with Kevin, until she noticed Sammy peering in, again.

"Sammy, I promise, just another couple minutes."

The boy's eyes widened and rolled. Angela wondered if she saw Freddy or frustration flash across his face before he turned around.

Lionel returned to class, and Kevin was just coming out of timeout when Angela, Hiro and Mrs. Regina heard a tussle in the room next door. A familiar psychotic giggle meant Sammy's patience with Angela had run out.

Ronnie led him from behind into the daytreatment room.

"Bitchell!" He started spitting. "Bitchell! Kill me! Bitchell!"

Nobody escaped at least one luggie, before he was bouncing off the walls in timeout.

"What set him off?" Hiro asked.

"Nothin' I know," Ronnie said, excusing herself to clean up.

"I know he wanted to see me about something," Angela said, holding the latch.

"Kill me!"

"I'd say he has your attention now," Mrs. Regina darkly quipped.

"I want to die!"

"Sammy," Angela called to him through the door. "I'm not going to kill you. If you sit against the back wall, I'll open the door and we can talk."

"Kill me!" he shouted, ramming the padded door in a futile attempt to escape. "Give me knife! I want to die."

"I'm not going to kill you; I like you," Angela reiterated, growing concerned about his suicidal outbursts. "I don't even have a knife."

"Kill me! Knife! Give me knife!" Slam. Slam.

"I don't want you to die, Sammy. I like you. I'd never give you a knife to hurt yourself."

Hiro and Mrs. Regina observed Angela and Sammy in action, ready to help.

"Kill me!" Sammy writhed against the walls, tormented by his psychological demons, and unable to escape his skin or die. "Knife! BACK-PACK!"

"You don't have a knife in your backpack," Angela didn't believe him.

"Yes. Giveittome!"

"No. You can't hurt yourself. Now please sit against the back wall, so I can open the door and talk with you."

"Kill me!"

Mrs. Regina called out to Carla next door. "Get Sammy's backpack, and tell me if there's anything in it."

"Kill me!"

"No, Sammy. I like you too much and would never hurt you."

"No you don't. Kill me!"

"Of course I like you," Angela said with playful sincerity, trying to defuse his rage. "You're my buddy. Please sit against the back wall. I want to open the door and hang out."

Carla arrived. "Where do you suppose he got this?"

Sammy saw the gleaming, serrated cake-icing knife through the timeout window. "Knife! Knife!" he excitedly shouted. "Give me knife! I kill me!"

"No, Sammy." Angela repeated. "You can't kill yourself. Think of how much I'd miss you. Who would I push on the swings at recess? I like you. I'd miss you too much if you were gone."

The knife scared Angela. It wasn't particularly dangerous. Its tip was rounded, and the serrated edge would take a lot of painful sawing to reach an artery. What got her adrenaline pumping was the fact Sammy thought he could do serious damage with it. It meant he was planning to kill himself and wanted to follow through on it. He wasn't just making noise and venting frustration to cope.

"Kill me!"

"No," Angela curtly said. "And I'm not going to talk to you any more until you sit quietly against the back wall.

Sammy raged for several more minutes. Angela took the opportunity to take a better look at the knife before Hiro locked it in his desk. Then she took Sammy's note from her hip pocket:

Dear Angela, Kill me. I want to die. Kill me. I hav nif. I want to kill myself. Help me. Love, Sammy

He illustrated the letter with a picture of his knife and a blocky picture of himself, arms spread, appealing to Angela to either kill him or help him not kill himself. She regretted not reading his note earlier and dropping everything to talk with him. Yet, as he gave her so many silly notes or drawings every day, she just didn't expect anything so severe.

The behavior specialist passed the suicide note to Hiro. He sighed and shook his head.

Angela spoke to Sammy through the door. "I read your note, Sammy. I want to help you. I'm sorry I didn't read it earlier."

Sammy slumped against the back wall. His eyes welled with tears. "Kill me," he whimpered and sat down.

Angela opened the door all the way and positioned her chair in the center of the entrance. "I won't kill you," she said softly. "You really are one of my favorite little boys in the whole wide world."

"No, I'm not," he cried. "They pay you."

Lulu had gotten to him, again.

"We've been over this before, Sammy," Angela gently explained. "They pay me to do a job. Nobody pays me to like anyone. Nobody pays for my friendship. I choose to like you and be your friend because you are a nice, wonderful, smart little boy."

Sammy argued over his sobs, and Hiro asked, "Who lied to you about Angela not liking you?"

Sammy paused and looked at Hiro with bleary eyes. He figured that telling him the truth could get him killed, so he remained silent.

New tears welled up. "I bad. I stupid."

"You are NOT bad or stupid," Angela countered. "Do bad people color beautiful pictures for their friends? Do bad people give their friends shiny, pretty rocks at recess? Do stupid people read their friends books, like you do with me? No. You are a very smart and good person."

"Bad. Stupid. Can't be policeman. Too stupid." Sammy cried, revealing the heart of the problem with which Angela and Hiro were dealing.

During her latest episode, Lulu laid into Sammy's sole dream of becoming a police officer—driving a cool car with lights and a siren, wearing a badge, carrying a gun and catching all of the bad guys. It was the only thing he wanted out of adulthood, and Lulu couldn't stand to even let him hope for it. She ground into him over and over how he was too stupid to be a cop, too bad to be a cop, too incompetent to be a cop. And as was always the case, she wore him down to a state of abject hopelessness. Now, he reasoned, if he was too worthless to be a policeman when he grew up, there seemed little point to continuing on with life. His whole short little life already was too overwhelmingly depressing and without any worthwhile future.

Angela reacted quickly to his statement. "What?! Who told you such nonsense? You will be a great policeman. You're such a smart and helpful young man, already. I bet you'll set records catching so many bad guys."

Sammy, Angela and Hiro went around and around about his police worthiness until Sammy began to believe them and believe in himself, again.

Without a word or permission, Sammy slowly stood and clumsily approached Angela. She had never seen such troubled insecurity in eyes so young. His dried tears left trails down his cheeks.

"What?" Angela softly asked.

Sammy wrapped his arms around her neck and began crying again.

Angela should have scolded him for hugging her without permission, but this was yet another of many extenuating circumstances since Christmas, and she hugged him back and whispered over his sobs. "It's going to be okay, Sammy. Everything is going to work out this time, I promise."

She gently stroked his trembling back, and after a minute asked, "Are you ready to come out of timeout?"

He stepped back and nodded. She asked him to apologize for spitting on her and the other adults, and he did.

"Thank you," she accepted his apology. "How about we color for a little bit before going back to class?"

He nodded again.

They colored for a little while, and when Sammy was ready, he went back to class.

Angela closed the dividing door behind him. She turned to Hiro and gravely asked, "This is it, isn't it?"

Hiro's head solemnly bobbed down then back up.

Angela smiled like an athlete on the verge of victory, knowing that so long as she didn't trip, she'd take the trophy. "Are you sure this will be enough to get him out of that house?"

"He's suicidal," Hiro affirmed. "He has a written plan. He brought a weapon to school. He has insufficient supervision at home. With his extensively documented track record, no one will successfully argue otherwise."

"So what do we do?"

"We get Sammy committed to Average State Children's Mental Health Hospital. It'll be a 30-day stay, and his doctor will have to see how awful his home life is and have Lulu's custody revoked. Sammy will then spend as long as it takes to regain his full mental health at the hospital and eventually enter a permanent foster home back in the community, go to school, continue getting therapy and live happily ever after.

"All we need is the local hospital's psychiatrist to sign off on it, and they will with this much evidence. We'll keep DCW in the loop, but even they can't stop it, although I doubt they'd disagree with sending Sammy to the mental hospital after this."

"Sounds great," Angela said.

"Yeah, all we have to do now is report this suicide attempt to

DCW, our headquarters, his social worker and Lulu. You call DCW and his social worker, and I'll call H.Q. and Lulu. Let's have everyone meet here in half an hour, and we'll figure out the process from there."

The mental health workers sprang into action, making calls and filling out reports in preparation for sending Sammy to the emergency room psychiatrist.

Within 15 minutes people started arriving for the big meeting about Sammy's future. Lulu didn't have time to rally her full cadre of enablers and was left with only Sammy's Average Mental Health Center social worker, Emma, and Sammy's latest DCW case worker, Barb.

Lulu arrived with Emma. Although Lulu dressed in clean Winnie the Pooh gear, she clearly hadn't bathed in days. Her hair was more matted than ever. Her glasses were foggier with facial oils than ever before. She smelled bad. Clearly, her inner demons were in the full swing of their torment. It wasn't surprising that she vented them on Sammy.

Lulu silently listened to Angela explain the morning's events. The young woman passed around Sammy's suicide note and the knife while Hiro explained that he thought Sammy had no other safe option than to go to the state mental hospital.

The two social workers were appalled by the suicide note and agreed that he needed to go to the mental hospital for emergency treatment.

Angela could barely contain her glee. She had never worked so hard to maintain a professional demeanor.

Lulu copped a pleading "not-my-baby" expression, but it was all part of her act—not true emotion. It didn't faze Angela or Hiro for a second, but it tugged on the social workers heartstrings.

"I'm sorry," said Barb. "This is for Sammy's own good. You don't want him to hurt himself when you're not looking, do you?"

"You're taking my baby away from me?" Lulu asked as pathetically as she could.

"No, Lulu," Emma explained. "It's just for 30 days. Then the doctors will decide the next step. He'll probably be home in no time."

"I don't want him to go," Lulu declared, no longer pleading or pathetic. "He's my child, I'll do with him what I want."

"It's the law," Barb said.

Back to pathetic, Lulu explained, "They locked me up once. Not my baby."

"It's not like that," Hiro countered. "These days mental hospitals are much better. They'll take good care of Sammy."

"You can visit him any time you like," Emma cheerily reported. "I'll clear time in my schedule once a week so I can take you to see him."

Lulu conceded a temporary defeat. She knew she could wear Emma down and get her not to send Sammy away, but she knew she couldn't do it with Angela and Hiro present. She'd have to wait for the right moment.

"It's settled then," Barb said. "I'll call ahead to the hospital, so the psychiatrist will be waiting for him."

Emma added, "I'll drive Sammy to the hospital."

Lulu saw her opening and took it. "I'm going, too. I want to be there to say good-bye—make baby feel better at the hospital."

Angela saw through Lulu's ploy and looked pleadingly at Hiro who suggested, "Angela, why don't you go, too. You were the primary witness to the whole event and can explain it best to the psychiatrist."

"Yeah, I'd love to help," Angela said. The battle lines were drawn, and Angela knew with Lulu present this wouldn't be an easy in-and-out procedure. She casually retrieved her lunch from her desk and got her coat, as Emma rounded up Sammy and Barb fired up her cell phone.

Barb went back to DCW, after making her call, and Emma, Lulu, Sammy and Angela piled into Emma's old sedan. Emma and Lulu were silent in the front seat. Angela repeated what Hiro explained to Sammy about the state and local hospitals. Sammy was excited to see all of the doctors and nurses. He doubted he'd get sent to the state hospital, but he desperately hoped it would happen.

Barb's phone calls paved the way for a quick admission into the emergency room, and the four were asked to wait in a large, private examining room filled with a bed, life-saving machines and several simple grey-plastic chairs on steel legs.

Expecting the doctor any minute, Sammy sat on the paper covered examining table and the three adults sat quietly on the chairs. An awkward silent tension grew as the minutes dragged on. Angela set her sack lunch under her chair and pulled some Matchbox cars out of her coat pockets for Sammy. The boy delighted at the site of toys.

Time kept passing slowly for the adults. Emma and Angela made strained small talk, and Emma got up to find the psychiatrist after 15 minutes had passed.

Lulu, sitting opposite Angela, initiated a staring contest with her rival. The behavior specialist's mouth twisted upward with a smirking grin at the silent challenge. Without blinking, Angela carried on a merry one-sided conversation with Lulu who broke eye contact when Emma returned empty handed.

"No luck?" Angela asked.

"Several doctors and nurses paged him, but nobody seems to be able to get a hold of him."

"That's odd," Angela replied. "It's not like he doesn't know we're here. Barb called him before we even left the school."

"I'll try again and see what I can turn up," Emma said and left.

Boredom overtook Sammy, who started pushing buttons and messing with stuff Angela felt probably needed to be left sterile.

As Angela wasn't Sammy's mother, she didn't feel it was her place to discipline the boy with Lulu present. Yet, as Sammy meddled more, Lulu refused to even look at the boy.

"Lulu, he's your son," Angela said. "You have to stop him before he breaks something."

"Sammy," she mumbled without looking at him.

The child looked at her and continued exploring the room's equipment.

"It's gonna take more than that," Angela sighed, growing concerned Sammy might damage something or hurt himself.

"Sammy," Lulu mumbled to the floor. "Don't do that."

"Christ," Angela muttered. She stood up and walked to Sammy who was now jumping up and down on a collapsible gurney. "C'mon, Buddy. Let's go find Emma."

She picked up Sammy and placed him on the floor. He took her hand, and they headed out the door. "We'll be back in a few," Angela called back to Lulu.

Angela was surprised to find Emma wasn't at the ER nurses' station. She and Sammy checked the admissions desk without success. Angela grew a little worried when she returned to the examination room. Emma wasn't there, either. Back at the nurses' station, Angela struck up a conversation with the nurses. She explained why she and Sammy were there and asked if the psychiatrist was on his way to see them.

Two nurses exchanged nervous glances. The lead nurse apprehensively opened, "Uh. I thought someone told you. He's out of town today. I think he's at some meeting. He won't be back until at least 4."

"Can you call and tell him this is an emergency?" Angela asked.

"I suppose we can try to reach his cell, but it will take him at least an hour and a half to get here."

"That's better than 4, and my friend here needs to get to the state mental hospital as fast as someone can sign off on it."

"We'll try."

The other nurse made the call, but Angela overheard her leave a message.

The behavior specialist grimaced. *Why isn't it ever easy?*

"May I use your phone for a second to call my boss at the mental health center?"

"Sure thing, Hon." The nurse turned the phone around, so Angela could more easily dial it.

"Hi, Hiro. I've got some bad news, the psychiatrist is going to be out until four, and I can't find Emma…Yeah, we're still at the hospital…No, there's nothing you can do here. I just won't be back for a while…Thanks, but I'll be all right. I brought my lunch for a reason…I will. You take care."

Angela turned the phone back to the nurse. "Thanks."

Emma returned to the nurses' station. "Hi."

"Where were you?"

"I had some calls to make. We can't get a psychiatrist to see Sammy until at least four, so I was trying to see what else we could do."

"Yeah, I already knew about the shrink. What else can we do?"

"My boss said a regular ER doctor could fill out the paperwork."

"Great, let's get one," Angela said. She turned expectantly to the head nurse.

The woman was again apprehensive. "We only have one doc in the ER today, and he's pretty busy. It might be a half an hour or so."

"That's okay," Angela affirmed. "It's still better than four o'clock."

Sammy and the two women shuffled back to their exam room. The wait dragged on and Angela and Sammy took to pacing an empty corridor near the room. They could only count the tiles and the steps it took to traverse the hall so many times before it started driving both of them crazy. They returned to their exam room.

Eventually a doctor in his late 30s arrived in scrubs.

Angela and Emma explained the situation in great detail. Angela showed him the suicide note, and he cringed a little while reading the depressing missive.

"It sounds like Sammy meets all of the right requirements to be sent to the children's mental hospital, but I'm not sure I can sign off on it," the doctor said. "Normally, the psychiatrist has to do this."

"He'll be out until four," Angela pleaded, aware of how painfully long their wait will be.

"Let me make a few calls," the doctor said and left.

Angela followed him out into the hall, cornering him in front of the nurses' station.

"Listen, I don't mean to be a pest," Angela tried to reassure the man. "But I can't stress enough how important it is to get this boy into the state hospital by this afternoon.

"I know his mother looks pathetic and innocent, and that she looks safe enough to send Sammy back home with, but she's not. She's evil."

Angela summarized the two attempted murders, the starvation, neglect and psychological trauma and the troubles with DCW. She didn't become melodramatic, but she made it crystal clear how this one signature could save this little boy's life. The doctor and nurses understood the score, they'd seen it many times before and were sympathetic.

"Okay," the doctor agreed. "I really will do everything I can to help as quickly as I can. I just can't make any promises about speed. That's out of my control."

Angela waited and eavesdropped as he made his calls. It quickly became obvious that the hospital administration had no clue whether the doctor could sign off. Their orders were to wait for the psychiatrist to return. Another call was put into the shrink. Another message.

"I'm sorry," the doctor apologized to Angela.

"That's okay," Angela glumly responded. "It's not your fault. Can we at least get all of the paper work ready for the psychiatrist when he gets back?"

"Sure."

"Thanks." Angela turned to the nurses. "Sammy's a great kid for the most part, but he's getting bored beyond belief. Do you mind if he and I explore around here a little, if we promise to stay out of the way."

"I suppose. Just don't go in any rooms that are occupied or say 'Personnel Only.' "

"Thanks."

Angela went back to the exam room and told everyone the news about the wait. Then she took Sammy to cruise the halls.

It took about 30 seconds to realize that an ER was the worst place to wander with a boy who had recently turned 7 years old. They passed a room where a woman was giving birth in plain sight because there wasn't enough time to get her to a proper delivery room. She turned Sammy away from the woman's screams to be confronted by a flat-lining heart attack victim being wheeled in from the ambulance bay on a mobile gurney with a short nurse in scrubs straddling his waist performing CPR.

There were plenty of other sights to absorb, as Angela briskly walked Sammy to the doors leading out of the ER and into the admissions area.

Sammy was confused by what was going on and asked tons of questions. "Why was that lady screaming? Why didn't the doctors make her better? Why was that other lady hitting that old guy's chest? Where did that blood on the floor come from? Who were those people crying?"

Angela answered all of his questions as best she could, but they didn't stop his brain from racing. They paced new hallways, until he was out of questions. As tedious as it was, at least they were burning down the clock.

Their explorations led them to the hospital's small gift shop, but staying there took more effort than it was worth, as Sammy kept trying to pocket all of the knickknacks.

In the regular waiting room, Angela hoped to distract Sammy with television or magazines. Daytime programming didn't cooperate. Sammy had no interest in soaps or talk shows. Likewise, the reading material was way too adult or geared toward 3-year-olds.

Throughout their meanderings, they'd touch base with Lulu and Emma every 15 minutes, hoping in vain that the psychiatrist had returned. With nothing to do in the exam room, Sammy and Angela would quickly resume their perambulations through the hospital.

Eventually, they stumbled upon the hospital's small chapel. Sammy insisted they investigate its every corner. Angela held him back for a minute to peer inside to see if they'd disrupt any service, prayer or grieving person. The last thing she wanted to do was have Sammy escalate and see Freddy Kruger hanging out in the stained glass with the 12 apostles.

The coast was clear, not a soul lingered in the chapel.

"Okay, Sammy. Be very quiet and don't touch anything," Angela commanded with a low whisper, as she opened the door for him.

"Okay," he whispered back.

Sammy gingerly entered and was followed by Angela. He looked around the clean, quiet room with a little awe and reverence. Angela couldn't quite discern what the interior decorators of the chapel were aiming to achieve. It was a hybrid church, funeral home and 1920s' movie theater. The cheap, thick, padded carpeting was vintage funeral home, as were the large, tasteful bouquets of flowers. Yet, the large, ebony facades backlit by pink and mint neon lights on beige walls were vintage art deco. On a raised floor behind the altar, a ¾-size porcelain Jesus lie dead in Mary's arms, a gaping spear wound in his ribs. Behind them was a backlit stained-glass window with a cross in its center.

Sammy cautiously wandered around the room, gazing raptly at all of the imagery.

Angela poured herself into an ebony pew. Her feet, legs and lower back were killing her after all of the aimless walking around the hospital. It felt so good to sit down. It was 3 o'clock, and they still had at least an hour to go. She hoped Sammy would be content to hang out here for a while.

Hunger also was taking its toll. Neither she nor Sammy had eaten yet. She would have shared her lunch with Sammy, but realized it had been left alone with Lulu for several hours. Angela reasoned that if any parent were to tamper with her food, it would be Lulu, and who knew what she had access to in an emergency room. Although Angela tried to convince herself that she was just being paranoid, she still tossed out the lunch. Having little cash on her, she bought two mini bags of chips and two sodas. Now, the more her stomach growled the more she couldn't wait to eat a big dinner with Luke.

For the time being, she was just grateful for a little peace and quiet and a place to rest.

Taking a seat next to Angela, Sammy asked about the statute of Jesus. "Is he dead?"

"Yes."

"Couldn't the doctors save him?"

The question caught Angela a little off guard. Her parents had rejected their Catholic upbringing before her birth, and although Angela didn't believe in organized religion, she took for granted that everyone of every age knew the basic story about Jesus.

Sammy's question highlighted a paradox that even she hadn't previously considered. *Isn't it odd that people derive comfort from an image of someone being tortured and brutally murdered? What exactly*

253

does that say about most of Western society?

"No, Sammy. Doctors couldn't save him," she said softly.

"Is he God?"

"Some people think so."

"God hates me," the boy meekly and fearfully said, without spite or malice.

"God doesn't hate you," Angela gently insisted.

"God hates me," Sammy insisted, not in an escalated frenzy but in an uncharacteristically philosophical tone.

"God loves children," Angela said.

"Not if they're bad."

"You're wrong, Sammy. Who told you that?"

The boy didn't answer, and he didn't need to. The behavior specialist knew.

They were silent for a few minutes, and Angela was glad he didn't keep disagreeing about God. The kid could make a pretty solid argument that God did, in fact, hate him. It would have taken Angela's best debate skills to convince him otherwise.

"Can the doctors save me?"

"I think so," Angela said, putting her arm around his shoulders.

"What they do?" Sammy said, slipping a bit back into baby speak. "Pokey?"

"No pokies," Angela stated with a smile. "These doctors only like to talk like Hiro and me. You'll even get to ride in an ambulance to get to this special hospital. What do you think about that?"

Sammy brightened. "Lights?"

"It's an ambulance. They have to."

He beamed. "How long?"

"I suspect you'll get a nice long ride, maybe an hour or two."

His little body was filled with joy, and he wondered if it would be as cool as the police cars in which he had ridden.

Angela continued describing his trip for him. "You'll get to go to a big building where you get to color, play and talk to people all day. They feed you lots of yummy food three times a day. It should be lots of fun. I wish I could go."

"Swings?"

"I don't know, but I imagine they should have some."

"Way super high?"

"Maybe."

It sounded like heaven to Sammy.

Angela didn't envy the ambulance crew the lengthy road trip ahead of them. She wondered if the novelty of the ride would end before the spit and bitchells returned.

A few more minutes passed, and boredom began to creep back into Sammy's soul.

"C'mon, Sammy. Let's go check on your mom and see if the psychiatrist has arrived."

It was still too early, but that didn't mean they couldn't hope.

As they approached their examination room, Angela could see that the door was closed. Through Venetian blinds to the room's window, she saw Lulu and Emma crying together. Lulu had gotten to the social worker. Hoping to head off trouble, she steered Sammy back the other direction.

The door opened behind them.

"Angela," Emma's voice cracked in an attempt to rapidly recompose herself.

One thought flew through Angela's mind. *Sammy is definitely not going to be subjected to this.*

The behavior specialist turned to face Emma. "Yeah."

"Can I talk to you for a minute?"

"Hold on," Angela replied. "Let me get Sammy situated."

"That's okay. His mom wants to see him."

"Not yet," Angela coldly blocked the request. "In a minute."

Angela took Sammy to the nurses' station. "Would you please watch my friend for just a minute?"

The lead nurse smiled and agreed to keep an eye on him. The staff was sympathetic to her and Sammy's steadfast wait for the psychiatrist. They wished they could do more, but what else was there to do? The nurse took a plastic model of a skeleton she used to show other kids what bone they had broken and gave it to Sammy to play with. To Angela's surprise, Sammy wasn't horrified.

The behavior specialist joined Emma just in front of the exam room door so Lulu could hear everything they said. "What's up? Doc almost here?"

"No," the social worker whispered. "It seems like forever. Why don't we just forget about this whole thing and go home? Sammy seems calm, and Lulu is just a basket case about losing her baby. You should hear her; she's heartbroken."

Angela was livid, but she didn't show it. She didn't want to risk losing the upper hand. Instead she stepped into Emma's space and locked eyes. She spoke sternly and loud enough for Lulu to hear but not Sammy who was about 50 feet away. "Just a few short hours ago, this boy wanted to kill himself. He asked me to kill him. His heart's desire is to die.

"You're a trained psychological professional, and you know damn well that calming down and pacing the floors of a hospital won't make that feeling go away forever. This isn't about Lulu's needs; this is about what's best for Sammy. Sammy needs more help than the three of us can give him.

"Besides, it's the LAW. Sammy had the desire, the note, the plan and a knife he thought would be sufficient to kill himself. He must get mandatory emergency psychiatric treatment.

"Are you willing to break the law? What would happen if he did kill himself? Do you want to be one of those social workers you sometimes see in the national news spotlight because she ignored the mandates of her job and has her career and life ruined by the death of an innocent child?"

Lulu broke into tears again. Emma followed suit and offered one last appeal on Lulu's behalf: "No, but…"

Angela cut her off. "No buts. If you and Lulu want to go home, that's fine with me. I'm more than happy to wait all night with Sammy."

The social worker backed down permanently. Angela shot Lulu a cold, piercing stare filled with disdain.

"My baby," Lulu unconvincingly simpered.

"Maybe you should say your good-byes now," Angela suggested through the ice in her throat. She fetched Sammy, who was contentedly playing with Mr. Bones.

Although he didn't want to give up the toy, he didn't want to incur his mother's wrath.

Lulu made a last ditch effort to keep Sammy by putting on an affectionate show for Emma. Lulu drew the boy in for hugs and kisses, and he struggled with all of his might to escape—fearing the worst from Lulu's nearly lethal touch. Oblivious to Sammy's struggles, Emma cried and looked pleadingly at Angela who returned a dispassionate gaze. Angela knew she held all the cards and would not be budged.

After an acceptable minute, she held out her hand to Sammy. He gladly took it, and they left the room to continue their rounds.

Time crawled, and the psychiatrist didn't return until 5:45 p.m.

Angela was afraid she'd miss her dinner with Luke when the shrink finally showed.

She braced herself for one more battle—one more pitch to convince someone Sammy was suicidal. Yet, when the big moment came, all she did was show him the evidence and briefly sum up the event. He signed the paperwork in fewer than five minutes after he arrived. The hospital had all of the papers ready and an ambulance waiting. The psychiatrist barely even looked at Sammy.

Angela found it to be very anti-climatic after all of her fighting on Sammy's behalf. She said farewell to her little friend and gave him a big hug. Lulu opted to ride in the ambulance with Sammy to the children's mental hospital, but now that the papers were signed, there was nothing she could to do about Sammy for 30 days. He was safe.

Angela thanked all the nurses for their help on her way out of the emergency room. As she walked out of the waiting room, a huge, irrepressibly goofy grin spread across her face. Her steps grew quick and light, and as soon as she was outside the hospital's sliding double doors she cut loose with a loud victory yip.

Angela never felt so good in her whole life, as she walked to the downtown restaurant where she was to meet her old friend. Euphoria pumped through her veins, chasing away the sheer exhaustion caused by the tedium of the day. She couldn't wait to tell Luke about saving Sammy's life. It was too bad confidentiality statements prevented her from disclosing all of the gory details.

When she opened the restaurant's door, the smell of cooking food overwhelmed her starved body. She almost didn't notice her friend waiting in the lobby.

"Luke!" He stood, and she gave him a hug.

"Angela. Good to see ya. You look great."

"Ha! You're still a convincing liar. Thanks, but I couldn't be more frazzled. My clothes are covered in spit from this morning, and I've just had the best and worst day of my professional life. I can't look near as good as you do."

"And you still open up by hitting with everything you've got. Never a dull conversation around you. So what happened?"

"I'll tell you all about it, but let's eat first. I'm famished."

They were seated and ordered quickly. Angela inhaled her salad and steak. As she ate, she grilled him about his law school experiences. She finished well before him, and told him as much as she was allowed about her day and her job in general. She told him about the bureaucrats, insurance companies, politicians and anybody else she thought stood in the way of giving these children the proper treatment they deserve.

Luke began to think law school wasn't nearly as difficult as it seemed an hour before talking with Angela about her job.

"I don't know, Luke," Angela said, gnawing on a breadstick. "I love working with these kids, but I despise just about every other aspect of this job. If all of these agencies helped as they theoretically should, this job would be great. As it is, I'm growing more dissatisfied every day."

"What would you do if you quit?" her friend asked.

"I don't know. I hadn't thought about it until Hiro mentioned he was considering his options. I certainly wouldn't abandon the kids mid-year, but I just feel I could be doing so much more than I am. Maybe I'll apply to grad school."

"And study what?" he asked, before taking a pull off his beer.

"Psychology, I guess."

"Wouldn't you still have the same problems when you got out? It's not like we're gonna get universal health care any time soon. It's not like the state agencies are going to get improved funding, either."

"You're right. I really don't know what I'm gonna do," Angela sipped her cocktail and slowly shook her head.

Luke smiled at her. To him, the answer to her problem seemed obvious. "You really want to make a difference?"

"Yeah."

"Become a lawyer."

"What?" she asked incredulously. "C'mon, you're kidding me."

"No, I'm serious," he said. "Think about it. You could work for yourself or the state and specialize in prosecuting child abusers. Maybe you could become a district attorney one day or become a politician who rewrites the laws and makes sure they're funded so they work."

"Really?" she asked, still unconvinced.

"Think about it, Ang. You'd be great," Luke encouraged. "I can guarantee you've got better debate skills than most professional lawyers. All you need is the right education and some experience to match it. You're a good academic. You're a relentlessly determined woman when you set your mind to something. You'd be phenomenal."

Angela looked at him skeptically.

"Really," he persisted. "At least think about it."

"I will," she said, but the seed of another idea had already begun to germinate in her mind. "Doesn't case law get boring? I love arguing, but endlessly studying old cases and the myriad nuances of legal proceedings sounds so dry."

"Well, yeah," Luke agreed. "The real action though is arguing before a jury and trying to win them."

"That would be fun," Angela agreed. "I just think I have a greater gift for psychology. I really love learning about people, how they function and how to help them with their problems."

"You'd be helping people as a lawyer," Luke said.

"Undoubtedly, but a lot of people can argue and research. A surprisingly large number of mental health professionals have difficulty connecting the science of their field to real-life situations. And then there's the power that psychiatrist had at the hospital. He didn't even talk to Sammy for 5 minutes and could sign off on sending the boy away from his abusive mother and get him the help at the mental hospital he needs."

"Yeah, Ang," Luke explained, "but that's 8 years of medical school and 6 years of earning a second doctorate for psychology. 14 years! You'll be 36 before you graduate. What happens if you want to get married and start a family? Aren't you going to be sick of living in virtual poverty for the next 14 years while earning that degree. Oh my God, and the debt. I'm going 80 grand into debt for law school. I can't imagine you could become a psychiatrist for less than 300 grand. That's a house and two luxury cars."

"Jesus," Angela gaped at the astronomical costs. "That's a lot of money."

"No," Luke said. "That's a lot of debt. Figure in the interest, too. Even if your starting salary is $200,000 a year, mix in a mortgage, car and the essentials plus that debt. How long will it take to pay off."

"Holy shit," Angela was awed but not deterred. "They have these degrees called a PsyD. It is a doctorate in psychology, but you also get enough medical training to prescribe a limited number of psychological medications. Those only take about 6 years to earn. You still make great money, but you also get the power to make real decisions that can save lives…. That can end abuse."

"That sounds a lot better than 14 years," Luke affirmed. "I still say you'd make a helluva good lawyer. I wouldn't want to take you on in court."

"Of course you would," she teased. "It'd be the most fun either of us had at work. I'd kick your ass, but it wouldn't be as easy as taking on those other lawyers."

"I seem to recall beating somebody who was pretty full of herself during the final at the state college championship our junior year," Luke reminded.

"Yeah, that was the woman who knocked you out at the first round the following year, wasn't it?"

The two rehashed good times, but the realities of what Angela could accomplish with a doctorate began to bloom in her consciousness. In the days that followed she began looking up careers in psychology that could make the most impact at the highest and lowest levels.

Chapter 20

The Morning After

The morning after Sammy's committal, Angela was still riding high from finally getting her little friend safe. Screw little victories; this was a humdinger.

She swaggered into work dressed as nicely as she dared. She wore some light make up and did up her hair. She felt great.

The conquering heroine was greeted with high fives from Hiro and the classroom staff.

She called State Children's Mental Hospital after her co-workers settled down. She spoke directly with Sammy's new doctor and explained every aspect of her interaction with Sammy. She gave the woman graphic details about how best to interact with his various psychological states; his documented abuse and the way Lulu operates. Hiro discussed his diagnosis with the state doctor. Both daytreatment workers vowed to do anything they could to help the state doctor and her staff.

The doctor was overwhelmed by the daytreatment team's efforts so far. The majority of the cases she saw were dropped in her lap and forgotten until she sent the patient back from whence they came.

However, not everyone appreciated Angela's victory. Her students were afraid of her. Most of them suffered varying degrees of Stockholm Syndrome—a condition generally attributed to hostages who come to side with or sympathize with their captors. Her patients knew they had bad parents and hard lives, but the prospect of being plucked from the relative safety of the known and forced to go far away for a long time with strangers was unbearable.

Group provided its usual menagerie of reactions. Hiro broke the news to the big kids first.

"Good!" Franz expelled with vehemence followed by nervous laughter.

"Why do you think that?" Hiro asked.

"'Cause," Franz said. "I was sick of that little monkey."

Kevin laughed. "Yeah, little monkey."

"I'm taking a dollar from both of you," Hiro calmly adjudicated.

"Sammy's still our classmate, and there is no reason to be disrespectful to him."

Franz and Kevin turned to Charlie, expecting him to lead the charge in mocking Sammy some more. Their ring leader remained silent.

Charlie had mellowed considerably, as he spent more time living with his father. He was at an odd juncture in his life. Despite the new found safety and stability at home, his confidence was shaken because he now felt he had something to fear…losing his father's love and support. After a young life of relative abandonment and neglect, the boy couldn't comprehend his father's unconditional love.

"Good job ignoring that set up, Charlie," Angela said, awarding him a dollar for not contributing to his friends' mischief.

The spotlight off her for too long, Violet whined, "I ignored those stupid boys' set ups, don't I get a dollar?"

"Violet, you lose a dollar for…"

Franz interrupted Hiro. "You're stupid, Violet."

"Yeah," added Kevin.

"Hiro, Hiro. They called me stupid. Did you hear? Did you hear?" Violet breathlessly pouted, pointing at Franz and Kevin.

"STOP!" commanded the therapist. "All three of you lose 5 bucks, and the next person to mock Sammy or set up anyone else is going straight to timeout.

"Now, Jefferson and Charlie," Hiro continued. "You each earn $5 for ignoring all of those set ups."

Facing the three offenders, Hiro offered, "Each of you can earn $2 back, if you apologize appropriately to one another."

Grudgingly the children apologized.

"Good," Angela complimented. "Does anyone have any questions about Sammy or where he is?"

Jefferson raised his hand. "How long will he be gone?"

"About 30 days," Hiro explained. "He might stay longer if the doctors think he needs more treatment."

"Are you sending anyone else there?" Charlie asked Angela.

The young woman was taken aback, as she came to understand the students feared she was going to send them all away. "Well, no, not unless they need that kind of special help from some doctors. I didn't really 'send' Sammy there. Sammy threatened to hurt himself very badly, and it is the law that makes us make sure he gets the best help we can get him."

"Hmmm," Charlie contemplatively grunted.

Hiro wrapped up the talking part of group and assigned the children to make cards for Sammy. While the cards might have lacked any heartfelt sentiments, he hoped they would help Sammy feel remembered and loved—and teach the group a lesson in kindness.

In little kids' group, Lionel, Edward, and Cassi were the most affected by the news and more openly emotional, wearing their fear on their sleeves.

"Why did you get rid of Sammy?" Edward asked. "Was he bad?"

Angela smiled warmly and tried to ease his worries. "I didn't get rid of Sammy. You all know he's my buddy. He had to go to a special doctor. He'll be back before you know it."

"Was he hurt?" Cassi asked.

"Not like an owie," Angela explained to the innocent little girl who proved more and more with each passing day that she didn't belong in the program. "He hurt inside his mind and wanted to hurt himself with big owies."

"Why would he want to hurt himself?" she persisted, confused.

Before Angela could answer, Lionel protested, "You're not going to send me away."

He was scared because he remembered the time Angela made him promise not to use sharp things without grown-ups present. He knew she knew he also wanted to hurt himself sometimes.

"I have no desire to send you anywhere, Lionel," Angela said.

"I'm not leaving my mom or Sephie," he boldly stated.

Cassi gasped. "Angela can take us away from our mommies?"

"Wait, wait a second," Hiro intervened. "Everybody calm down. Angela can't take anyone away from their moms. She doesn't want to. Like I said earlier, there are special rules for what happened to Sammy. Sammy wanted to hurt himself very badly, and we wanted to help him be super safe where special doctors can take extra special care of him."

Hiro's head was almost spinning because he had to find a way to connect with all of these children about concepts that were so layered and complex many adults had difficulties understanding them. Taking an extra second, he figured out a solution, boiling the children's problem with the Sammy episode down to its lowest common denominator.

"Sammy's mom knows where he is," Hiro explained. "She rode with him in the ambulance to the hospital."

"Oh," Cassi said brightly. "That's okay."

Edward agreed, but Lionel knew the system better than that and remained wary. He figured there had to be a catch.

Ted, on the other hand, didn't care about any of it. Sammy was merely a nuisance to him. And as far as parents were concerned, Ted believed everyone was better off without them.

Angela was glad to get the help from Hiro. She never expected to be vilified by the children for rescuing Sammy.

"Who wants to help me make a get well card for Sammy," she asked.

The children offered unanimous support with crayons, glue and construction paper, and Angela began rebuilding some of the damage to her reputation with the kids.

(30 Days Later)

Dr. Miranda Menlo ran a hand through her shoulder-length, grey-flecked black hair and sighed. It wasn't the kids at the state hospital that were changing the color of her hair; it was moments like these.

"Will you bring me Sammy's file, Nurse Wofford?" she asked from her office desk.

She looked at her reflection on her computer screen. Nah, it wasn't the kids, they were fun and kept her feeling young at 40. It was these one or two cases a year that she felt powerless to resolve that drained her.

The thick case file arrived, and she pored over it one last time. Clearly there was a history of abuse and neglect. Clearly there was little direct evidence to prove it in a court of law.

In 30 short days Sammy blossomed from a terrified little boy, frightened by imaginary bogeymen, to a cheerful, curious student at the hospital school. The child seemed to thrive and could easily benefit from a stay lasting a year or two. But his inadequate insurance and state laws designed to minimize the amount spent on such patients meant difficult decisions were due.

The boy's school daytreatment workers were a blessing with their advice and dedication to his case. It was Sammy who was working against himself.

To guarantee a longer stay and permanent removal from his mother's custody, all the boy had to do was discuss some of Lulu's abuse. Yet his past was the only thing he wouldn't discuss. Dr. Menlo discovered he'd talk her leg off about any subject other than home or Lulu. His daytreatment therapist said the boy wouldn't talk about anything, and just getting him talking was phenomenal progress, but the therapists agreed it wouldn't be enough to "really" help him.

Whenever Dr. Menlo discussed Lulu, Sammy would become very tense and apprehensive—a clear indicator something was very wrong.

Lulu's weekly visits were the only time Dr. Menlo saw Sammy tremble with fear.

Nurse Wofford returned with a cup of coffee for the doctor and sat in the comfortable, but inexpensive, swivel chair across from her desk. "What are you going to do, Miranda?"

The doctor leaned back and fidgeted with a pen between her fingers. "There's not much I can do. He won't talk."

"He will if we give him more time," the veteran nurse reassured. "They always do."

"Vivian, you know the 30-day papers need to be signed today," the doctor explained. "We must send him back tomorrow. We've got nothing to legally hold him for."

"Throwing in the towel? That hardly sounds like you."

"It's not that," Dr. Menlo confessed. "This mother is smart, and for whatever twisted reason, she wants to keep Sammy. Any idiot can see she's abusing Sammy, but on paper there's only circumstantial evidence. On paper she looks great. She attends better parenting classes. She travels more than 100 miles every week with her social worker to visit Sammy."

"Yeah, but she doesn't do anything with him," the nurse politely argued. "The two of them practically ignore each other for a full hour and sit on opposite sides of the visitation room."

"That doesn't matter," Miranda countered. "The state simply sees that she went out of her way to visit him and that she didn't hit or threaten him during that time. A lawyer with half a brain can explain away awkward visits with some B.S. about them being intimidated by the unfamiliar surroundings or whatnot. To the court, the situation looks healthy or at least attempting to be healthy."

Nurse Wofford folded her arms in silent protest against state regulations that only impeded intervention on behalf of a severely abused child. She knew it wasn't Dr. Menlo's fault, and she did her best to keep from going on a rant.

Dr. Menlo continued explaining herself. "Under normal circumstances, you know I can get most parents or guardians of kids like Sammy to voluntarily commit him to the hospital or even give up their custody rights. The vast majority of those parents don't want to be bothered with those kids to begin with. Lulu's different. I've tried to talk her into it, but she has her own depraved agenda. Outside of lying and risking my entire career, there's little left I can do."

"What's today's plan?" Nurse Wofford asked.

"I'll do all that's left that I'm allowed to try." Dr. Menlo said. "I'll give Sammy one last session. If he remains silent about his abuse, I'll try to buy him a little more time through foster care. I can only authorize a month of community transition, but it should be a month without being strangled, beaten or starved."

"If that's the best we can do, that's the best we can do," the nurse sighed. "I'll go get him for you."

A few minutes later, while she was reviewing some files online, Dr. Menlo spied a little boy peering in from around the door jamb.

"Who goes there?" Miranda playfully bellowed.

"Sammy," said the smiling, enthusiastic child stepping into full view.

"If it isn't my favorite peeper. Come on in."

Sammy traipsed into the room, hopped into the swivel chair across from Menlo and took a spin.

"Ah-ah, what are the rules?" Dr. Menlo gently reprimanded.

Sammy stopped and droned, "No spinning unless I ask first."

"Thank you."

"Can I spin?"

"What's the magic word?"

"Can I spin, please?"

"May I," the good doctor corrected. "May I please spin?"

Sammy looked up in exasperation. "May I please spin?"

"Yes, but only once, we've got a big session ahead," Dr. Menlo said, getting up to close the door to her office.

Sammy looked over his shoulder as Dr. Menlo passed by and sneaked in an extra spin.

"Ahem," Dr. Menlo cleared her throat with playful authority. "How many spins was that? You know I have eyes in the back of my head."

Sammy nervously giggled, before hopping back out of the chair and heading for the play-therapy area. Without fail, he went to the toy shelf and selected a play police badge and hat. Then he grabbed the bucket of toy soldiers, which he brought over to a play table.

Sammy never really pretended to play policeman while wearing the costume. He just felt better wearing it.

Dr. Menlo and Sammy talked as the boy set up a battlefield of good guys and bad guys. Despite the soldiers' long-range weaponry

266

complete with machine guns, mortars and assault rifles, the combat was always close quarters, and it was difficult to differentiate between the sides. The soldiers' allegiances switched on Sammy's whim.

"How's your day going, Sammy?"

"Good."

"Why?"

"Just is," Sammy said, chipper and focused on his action figures.

"Did you play on the swings?"

"Yeah."

"Did you go way super high?"

"Not as high as Angela pushes, but pretty high."

"What are you learning in school?"

"Stuff."

"Reading any good books?"

"Goosebumps," Sammy said, his brown eyes lighting up with the delight of being horrified in a safe way.

"Tell me about it. Why do you like it?"

"Ghost."

"Is it a good ghost or a bad one?"

"Spooky."

Regardless of his social progress, Dr. Menlo suspected Sammy was still only decoding books without much comprehension. If there was a ghost on the cover, Sammy figured the ghost made an appearance on every page. The thing that got Dr. Menlo about Sammy was how the boy who clearly lived in a demon-haunted world could never read or watch enough scary books or movies. They usually showed up in his nightmares, but he couldn't get enough of them while the sun shone.

"I know we've been talking about it all week, Sammy, but today is going to be our last session—at least for a little while."

Sammy's play with the soldiers became a slow fumbling. He grew silent.

"Your mom will be here tomorrow to take you home."

Sammy sucked in a short panicked gasp and clenched a plastic soldier in each fist.

"What's wrong Sammy?"

The joy Miranda had seen in his eyes moments earlier drained. They became black and hollow with dread.

"Did I say something wrong?" the doctor probed. "You look scared. It's okay. Tell me what you're thinking."

Sammy took the police badge off his shirt and held it in his cupped hands. He stared at it for a moment, tracing its edges with his finger.

"You can keep playing with that Sammy. Our session isn't over for some time."

Sammy reluctantly ambled to the toy shelf and took one last look at his badge. He tucked it securely behind a stack of puzzles with which no one played. He put his hat back, too. Then he lifelessly returned to the table and sat down.

"Please tell me what's wrong, Sammy. If you tell me what you're scared of, I might be able to let you stay here longer. I can help you."

"No you can't," Sammy softly replied.

Dr. Menlo pulled her seat next to Sammy's and spoke with the utmost confidence and optimism. "Of course, I can. I can do almost anything."

Sammy remained silent.

"You don't believe me do you?" Dr. Menlo questioned him. "Watch this. I can even pull my thumb off without losing a drop of blood."

Miranda performed one of the oldest magic tricks in the book, and Sammy still wouldn't look at her.

"Did ya see that?"

He nodded. Normally, that would be enough to impress him, but it didn't distract him from the impending misery he knew life back home with Lulu would be.

"See, I can do almost anything. If you tell me what's wrong or tell me how I can help, your problem, it's as good as fixed."

The 7-year-old heaved a heartbroken sigh of despair and resumed play with his soldiers.

No one survived the battle, good or bad.

Dr. Menlo shrugged her shoulders. "Well, if you won't talk, I will. Here's what you can expect when you go home. I'm going to arrange for you to spend a month in foster care with a very nice family. You'll go back to school with Hiro and Angela, if everything is okay. Then you finally go back to your mother. Does that make sense? Do you have any questions?"

Sammy shook his head no.

"You know, Sammy, I'm really going to miss you."

He nodded.

"I mean it," Dr. Menlo said. "You're a really special little boy. You are one of the smartest kids I know, and I think you're going to be a great cop one day."

Sammy smiled weakly but remained silent.

Dr. Menlo leaned down and cocked her head to try to make eye contact. "Are you going to miss me? Maybe a little?"

Sammy nodded, again.

"Are you sure there's nothing you want to tell me about?"

Tears welled in his eyes a little, but all he did was nod. He was still certain no one could help him.

(2 Days Later)

Disappointed by the state's decision to send Sammy back home, the daytreatment and classroom staffs prepared to make his return to school extra special. At least he'd be in foster care for the next month.

When the buses arrived and unloaded, all of the students were accounted for except Sammy. Concern grew within the treatment team. Past absences were never a good sign, and although Sammy was only supposed to drive home with his mom to his foster family, the team knew Lulu was capable of anything.

"The tardy bell hasn't rung," Mrs. Regina reminded everyone. "Keep your hopes up. We'll call after it rings."

A few tense minutes passed, and there was a small knock on the daytreatment room door. Angela opened it and exclaimed, "Sammyyyyy!"

She gave him a quick side hug and mussed his spiky brown hair. "Oh my God. You've only been gone a month, and you've grown so big. I missed you. C'mon on in."

Hiro and the staff gave high fives to Sammy, who was rendered even more sheepish and shy by all of the extra attention. Embarrassed as he was, he still couldn't repress a closed-lip grin.

A tall Nordic woman entered the room unnoticed. "Wow. Sammy sure is a popular young man," she said.

"He's such a great kid," Angela said before gently challenging. "Who are you?"

The blonde stuck out her hand. "Calista Montgomery. I'm Sammy's foster mom."

Angela shook her hand and introduced herself and the daytreatment team.

"I brought Sammy in because we aren't on the bus route, yet, and I wanted to see where he went to school. I hope you don't mind."

"I'm glad you did," Hiro said, shaking her hand. "Do you have a few minutes? I'd like to talk with you about Sammy if you have the time."

The classroom staff closed the partition door, and Hiro and Angela sat with Calista at the arts-and-crafts table for a friendly interview.

"It's so good to see Sammy, again," Angela said. "I don't suppose you heard anything about his stay at the hospital?"

"Not much," the foster mom explained. "They told me about his diagnosis and all about his medications. That was about it."

"How has he been for you so far?" Hiro inquired.

"Pretty good. He's very quiet and shy—not very physical. Preston, my husband, tried to play catch with Sammy with a football, but Sammy had no interest."

Hiro and Angela exchanged glances at quiet and not physical.

"Give him time," Hiro explained. "He hasn't been around many men, and I don't think he has ever played catch in his life."

"What? He seems like such a popular boy here. I'd figure he'd be playing football or soccer all of the time."

"What exactly did they tell you about Sammy?" Angela asked.

"Oh the usual: suspected abuse, a little wild. Pretty normal stuff for foster parents, but if the past 36 hours have been any indicator, we've had a lot wilder."

"How long have you and Preston been foster parents?" Hiro questioned.

"Oh, a couple years. We've probably hosted a half dozen kids or so."

"May I ask why you decided to get into it?" Hiro continued.

"It's really not a secret. Preston and I want to have children of our own, but we can't. Being devout Christians, we decided to share our love and help others in need."

Upon hearing "devout Christians," Angela worried about how Sammy would react to their beliefs given how he believed God hated him.

Trying to play it cool, Angela stayed away from the subject with her questioning. "I'd like to make an observation, but I don't want to offend you."

"Fire away."

"Well, you strike me as being a rather polished and clean-cut type, and I was wondering ..."

"...How I handle the kids when they get out of control?" Calista interrupted.

"Yep."

"Preston and I are fully MANDT, CPR and first aid certified. We've defeated 3 cases of lice and helped one kid with a fairly heinous bowel disorder. We haven't quit yet."

Her answer was so graphically direct, Angela began to warm up to her.

"If that's the case, I suspect you can handle the truth about Sammy, without us scaring you," Hiro speculated.

"What's there to know?"

Hiro and Angela gave Calista the complete 15-minute history about Sammy without pulling any punches. They told her all about the warning signs to watch for and how to handle him. They also warned her about Lulu.

It was a lot for Calista to absorb. Sammy was to be the most challenging child she and her husband had taken in. As intimidating as the next month seemed, Calista kept her fear in check and looked forward to really helping this little boy.

"There's one more thing I'm worried about," Angela said. "I know it is poor manners to bring up the topics of religion or politics in polite society, but I have a concern regarding Sammy and Christianity."

"Why's that?" Calista asked. "His mother marked it on the form as something she preferred for him."

"I don't doubt that at all," Angela furthered. "It's not even traditional Christianity that I worry about. Sammy's only exposure to religion has been Lulu-based, not biblically-based.

"His mother appears to have spent the better part of Sammy's life telling him how God and Jesus hate him and want him dead."

"Oh, dear," Calista uttered.

Hiro warned, "It wouldn't be unreasonable to expect that a discussion about religion or a church outing might escalate his behavior."

"That's horrendous," Calista exclaimed. "I've always found such comfort in my beliefs. Who on earth would tell a child that Jesus hates him?"

"His mom's crazy," Angela reminded her. "You might not see it right away. Others might tell you differently. But regardless, she's a nut case."

"So I shouldn't take him to church?" Calista asked.

"That's not what we meant to imply," Hiro apologized. "You have to keep living your life the way you normally would and involve Sammy. He's a bright boy; he'll figure things out. Just be ready in case some aspect of the experience freaks him out. It might trigger some PTSD-related issues."

"So what should I do?"

Hiro and Angela offered their best advice to de-escalate Sammy, without getting the congregation's Sunday best doused with spit.

"I appreciate all of your help," Calista said, standing to leave. "I'd like to stick around a little longer, but I have some errands to run."

"No problem," Hiro said, as he rose. "Give us a call any time you have any questions or problems. We'll be here to help in any way we can."

"Absolutely," Angela concurred, handing Calista a slip of paper with phone numbers for the school and classroom. She added with a smile, "Welcome to the fold."

Their impromptu conference had put the classroom staff off of their schedule by half an hour. The big kids group was eager to line up, and the session went well. The old students were apprehensive about Sammy's return to the classroom dynamic, wondering if he'd continue to freak out on them like the old days.

Recess followed, and Angela and Sammy had a delightful swing-set reunion. Many of the other kids joined in the fun, and Angela was busy running up and down the line of swings pushing everyone way super high.

After recess, Angela lined up the little kids for a belated group session. She gave Sammy the honorary first position in line for his return to class. Lionel got jealous and tried to set Sammy up to lose his place in line, but Sammy ignored the set up and earned dollars while Lionel lost some.

In the clamor for the group rugs, Sammy stepped aside and let Lionel go first. Even getting his rug last, Sammy didn't dawdle getting to the circle, as he once did. Lionel made a show of sitting as close to Angela as allowed, but Sammy shrugged and sat on her other side.

It became clear to the psychological professionals that Lionel was upset and up to something, but they hadn't yet put their fingers on it.

As Sammy avoided each of his set ups, Lionel's chest grew tight with anger. He wanted to make Sammy wig out. It used to be so easy to do. It used to be so easy to control him.

Although Lionel couldn't verbalize it or possibly even consciously rationalize it at his age, he wanted Sammy to fail today. Lionel wanted to prove to Angela and Hiro that sending Sammy to the state hospital was the wrong thing to do. He wanted to prove to them it didn't work.

To prove to them they should never send anyone there—especially him. He still thought leaving his mother and sister was the worst thing imaginable.

Sammy, though still frightened and shy, had learned how to better control his fears and ignore set ups. He was growing more confident that he could be perfectly safe as Sammy, and not Freddy, at school.

Lionel hadn't forgotten Freddy, and he hatched a new plan. His eyes narrowed and a menacing smirk crawled across his lips.

"I see Freddy over there, Sammy."

"Lionel, I'm taking away a dollar," Hiro said. "Sammy you get a dollar for ignoring him."

"His claws are really sharp."

"Li-on-el, what's gotten into you? That's another lost dollar," Angela scolded. "Sammy you get another dollar."

"He looks really angry," Lionel prodded.

"I don't see him," Sammy said, a hint of anxiety in his voice.

"That's because he's not here," Angela soothed, before turning to Lionel. "Alright, this is going too far. Timeout."

"What?! I didn't do anything," Lionel protested.

"You're setting up Sammy and trying to scare him. Now go to timeout," Angela commanded.

"No."

"You have until the count of three to earn a dollar for going into timeout on your own or losing a dollar if I have to restrain you and take you there."

Lionel folded his arms in the MANDT position, bracing for the restraint.

Angela counted to three. She labored to get to her feet in an effort to give Lionel an extra second to change his mind and walk in under his own power. He didn't budge, and Angela restrained and hustled him into timeout.

Lionel shouted through the door on deaf ears. Hiro awarded big bucks to the entire group for ignoring Lionel. Angela maintained a watch over the timeout door, standing in front of the window and denying Lionel his audience.

Sammy's demeanor amazed everyone. No outbursts. No baby talk. No Freddy. He was still frightened and on edge, but he kept it together.

As Angela began talking Lionel down in timeout, Hiro kept group moving. "Sammy, would you like to tell us about where you went?"

He shrugged.

"What did you do? Did you get to play at all?" Hiro pushed. Hiro knew that the odds were in favor of several of these kids making a trip to the state hospital, and he hoped Sammy's frank discussion about it would help ease their fears.

"Yeah."

"Did they have a nice playground?" Hiro inquired, staying in safe territory for Sammy.

"Yeah."

"Nicer than ours?"

"Yeah, I guess."

"What did it have?" Edward asked.

"A twirly slide that spins down and a big metal thing."

"Like a jungle gym?" Cassi inquired.

"I dunno. I climbed on it and ran around."

"That sounds like a jungle gym," the prim girl politely explained.

"What else did you like?" Hiro asked, as Sammy began to come out of his shell.

"Swings."

"Did you go way super high?" Angela asked from the booth.

"Yeah," Sammy emphatically decreed.

"Did any one push you as high as I do?"

"No," the boy said with a sheepish smile.

"HA!" Angela said with playful bravado. "That's because I'm the best."

"What else did you do?" Hiro redirected the conversation. "Did you have school there?"

"Uh-huh."

"Was it harder?"

"No."

"What was different?" Hiro continued.

"You sleep there."

"Was it scary?" Edward asked, sucking in his breath, anticipating the worst.

"No." Sammy said. In fact, it was the safest he had ever felt.

"Was there someone there like me—someone to talk to?" Hiro probed.

"Yeah."

"What was he like?"

"He was a girl, but she was nice."

"What did you think about the whole place?"

"It was good. I liked it," Sammy understated as usual. He loved it and wished he could live there.

While Sammy's summary of the state children's mental hospital was brief, it had the effect Hiro desired.

As Lionel sat out the remainder of his timeout on the padded floor of the booth, he listened to Sammy. Going to the state hospital and being separated from his family was his greatest fear. And here Sammy was telling them all about his stay, and it sounded okay.

If a wimp like Sammy can take it, anybody can, Lionel thought.

The rest of the week went well for Sammy. He didn't escalate or spit on anybody. He did get frustrated once at Hiro while leaving the daytreatment room and muttered a token "bitchell" under his breath.

The therapist and Angela overheard it and almost laughed. They almost missed his raging bitchells in the past five weeks and decided to finally get a definition from Sammy.

"What did you say?" Hiro asked.

Sammy stopped and huffed. No one was supposed to have heard him.

"It's okay, Sammy," Hiro said. "Come over here and tell me what you said."

The boy shuffled toward him. "I'll get in trouble."

"No," Hiro promised. "Just tell me what you said."

"Bitchell," Sammy said through clenched teeth, certain that he'd get in trouble any way.

"What was that?" Angela asked.

"Bitchell," Sammy blushed.

"I don't get it," Hiro said. "What's a bitchell?"

Sammy rolled his eyes, confused and convinced he was dealing with an imbecile. "It's not bitchell, it's bitchell."

He changed the sound of the second bitchell, but it still sounded like bitchell because he said it so fast.

"Slow down, Sammy, and say it again," Angela encouraged.

Embarrassed beyond all measure, Sammy tried again. "Bitch. Hole."

"Oh!" the daytreatment team said in unison.

"Can I go now?" Sammy asked.

"Sure, and thank you," Hiro said.

Sammy left, and Hiro turned to Angela. "What the hell's a bitch hole?"

Angela laughed. "I've never heard it before in my life. It's probably some crude slang for vagina."

"I was wondering. It could be that. Maybe it's the mouth. Like if you're bitching up a storm and someone tells you to shut up. Shut your bitch hole. Kinda like shut your pie hole."

"Should we ask him back in to find out?" Angela inquired facetiously.

"Nah, I think we put him through enough already. He would have snapped if we had grilled him like that a month ago."

Chapter 21

Angela
(Mid-March)

"Hello, Daytreatment, Angela speaking," the behavior specialist answered the phone, 10 minutes before school started.

"Angela Marengo?" asked a feminine voice in its late middle ages.

"Yes, can I help you?"

"My name is Judith Steinhaus, and I'm the dean of the School of Psychology at Average State University. Did I catch you at a bad time, or do you have a minute?"

"Oh my goodness, uh, yes, no, uh, I don't mean to be rude, but I only have a minute. My students will be arriving soon," said Angela, befuddled with excitement. After giving Luke and Hiro's suggestions serious consideration, she felt certain she could accomplish much more for the children with a doctorate, fight with greater authority and have a much more lucrative career. She made a hastily prepared, last-minute application to the school to slip it in before the deadline. She assumed she'd be rejected outright with a form letter. Although she believed she gave them a good interview, she hadn't even taken the Graduate Records Exam, yet. She mostly wanted the experience so she could better prepare for the process the next time around.

"That's okay," the dean assured. "This won't take long. I just wanted to be the first to congratulate you on being accepted into this fall's entering class for the doctoral program."

Angela was breathless.

"Are you still there, Ms. Marengo?"

"Uh, uh, yeah. I can't believe it. I mean, thank you."

The woman on the other end of the line laughed. "Your debate references said you were never at a loss for words. (Another gentle laugh) You'll be receiving you official acceptance in the mail within the next several days, along with instructions and information about registering and preparing for instruction."

"Wow. Thank you very much," Angela said, coming back to her senses and trying to rein in her adrenaline rush. "I thought I applied too late. I haven't even taken the GRE. I don't even know how I'm going to pay for this."

"Your acceptance papers will get into all of this in more detail," Judith explained. "You did apply too late, and your acceptance is conditional. You must score well on the GRE being administered this summer. However, given that you were a straight-A student in college, I have every reason to believe that you'll do well.

"The reason the admissions board and I agreed to accept you was because we believe you are a very promising prospect. Unlike many of the students who apply, you have some very specific goals you want to achieve. Plus, you have the real world experience in the system you want to tackle. You know the pitched battle you're getting into and you are intimately familiar with the difficulties and expectations of the work. You aren't afraid of it; you want to help people even more because of it. I like that moxie in a student. Add in your excellent academics, and I think you should do very well in our program.

"As for the money, if you score well on the GRE, you'll find we have several scholarship and work-study opportunities that should suit most of your needs. You'll see what we've decided to award you in the coming papers. I wouldn't worry, if I were you."

Stunned by her good fortune, "Thank you," was all Angela could think of to say.

"You'll stop thanking me this fall when I put the screws to you," the dean said, savoring the joy of telling someone they've been accepted. "In the meantime, have a good day."

"You, too," was all Angela got in before the line clicked dead.

Angela hung up the phone, did a spin and let out a victory whoop. "Guess who's goin' to graduate school?"

"Hey! Hey! Congratulations!" Hiro said, getting up from some paperwork he was filling out and giving Angela a hug. "I knew you'd get in."

Ronnie poked her head into the room. "What's this I'm hearing? You got in?"

"Yep."

"That's great! Let me come over there and give you a big ol' hug!"

The yellow buses started passing their windows.

"Okay, okay. Nobody say anything to the kids. I don't want them freaking out and thinking I'm leaving mid-semester. I'll let them know closer to the end of the school year."

Chapter 22

Kevin, again
(April)

Kevin and his brother, Reggie, were sitting on the grimy, tattered couch of their meth-ravaged trailer home. Nothing particularly good was on TV, but the fighting and yelling on TV was better than fighting and yelling at each other.

A sharp rapping on the flimsy door jolted each boy from a near comatose state of television viewing. Neither answered. There was no need. The only people who knocked like that were strung out johns or short-changed drug dealers. Their mom was out, and neither boy wanted to get involved with the menace at the door.

The knocking resumed, harder and louder. The brothers refused to break their gaze, fearful that doing so would mean they'd have to answer the door.

The knocking shook the trailer.

"Would one of you shits answer the goddamn door!" roared Marcie, their older sister, from a back room. "I'm too fuckin' busy."

Reggie punched Kevin in the shoulder.

"Jeez, I'll get the fuckin' door," Kevin said. "Ya didn't have to fuckin' hit me."

The 11-year-old cautiously opened the door, expecting to be attacked by a raging maniac. He was petrified to discover six uniformed cops aiming pistols at his head.

The man knocking on the door was wearing a bullet-proof vest over a white shirt and tie. He recoiled a little when the child opened the door to such squalor. "Uh, hi. I'm Detective Rich Middleton with the ALCPD. I have a warrant to search this trailer. Is there anyone else here with you?"

"No."

"Is your dad or babysitter here?"

"Marcie!" he hollered to his sister. "The police want you."

"What?!" she hollered back, coming out of her room. Thinking her brother was trying to trick her, she was startled to see that the police really were at the door.

"Ma'am, I have a court-ordered warrant to search these premises," the detective said, handing her the signed documents.

"What's wrong?" she asked.

"We just arrested one Raelyn Smith this afternoon on meth possession charges. If you please stand aside, we'll make this as quick as possible."

Reggie sprang from the couch and ran to the back of the trailer. Two uniformed cops knocked Marcie and Kevin aside to chase after him.

A brief tussle rocked the trailer and ended with the recitation of Miranda rights from a back room out of view. Kevin next saw his brother in hand cuffs, a bright red mark on his cheek, as he passed by.

Kevin trembled. He hated his brother, but it was scary seeing him beaten and dragged out of their home in chains by the police who had just arrested his mother.

"Hey, Sarge," one of the policemen addressed Middleton. "He was trying to flush this down the toilet."

The uniformed officer held up a sandwich bag a quarter full of marijuana.

The detective looked sternly at Kevin. "Son, are there more drugs in this place?"

Kevin wanted to shrink into a speck of dust. *Probably,* he thought. But he knew if he ratted in front of his sister, she'd make sure he suffered later. Yet, if he lied to the police, he worried he'd spend the rest of his life in jail.

Kevin looked up at Middleton, wide-eyed, and shrugged.

"Alright guys, tear this place apart," the detective commanded.

The police soon found a small stash in his sister's room and cuffed her, too. There was a lot of paraphernalia and drug residue found throughout the trailer.

In a matter of minutes, the only life Kevin knew—miserable as it might have been—was entirely stripped away.

Kevin was in shock. *Where will I stay? Where will I eat? Who will take care of me? What will I do? Am I going to jail? What are they going to do with me?*

As the investigation wrapped up, Middleton lumbered toward Kevin.

"Don't arrest me," the boy pleaded. "I'm not a junkie."

"I'm not going to arrest you; you're just a kid. You got any place to stay?"

"No." Kevin trembled.

"Don't worry about it." Middleton patted him on the upper arm and called out. "Someone get social services over here. We got a kid who needs to go to the group home until all of this gets sorted out."

Chapter 23

Ray
(May)

Angela shifted her weight as she sat on an uncomfortable wooden bench at Average City court. She bit her tongue listening to Charlie's mom testify at the custody hearing brought on by Charlie's father.

Katrina's lies painted her as the modern Claire Huxtable, not a full-time man-eater and part-time hop head endangering her kids with drugs and neglect. She was a smart liar, peppering her testimony with enough personal flaws to not unnecessarily set off the judge's inner polygraph machine.

"I love my kids, your honor. They always come first with me, especially my little man, Charles. He's my big helper. And while it's true I don't always have enough money to feed them proper, they always come first."

She's smooth, Angela thought. *That woman's got a job and three child-support checks coming in. No one's going hungry. That and Charlie's not the big helper type. He'd let her dangle. He wants her to.*

Angela took notes she hoped might help Ray's lawyer, Dale.

The whole trial fascinated Angela who remembered Luke's suggestion that she go to law school. The organized arguing got her heart pumping. There was obvious strategy in the way the two seemingly low-rent lawyers were building their cases. Despite the fact she knew nothing about the law or the legal system, Angela felt confident she already could beat both lawyers with superior strategy and her debate skills.

As focused as she was on the custody hearing, Angela couldn't help but think about the machinations that brought her there.

Ray brought his lawyer to school to talk with Angela and Hiro about his custody case. They had a long discussion to help the lawyer get his ducks in a row. Angela eagerly volunteered to represent the treatment team. Hiro was glad to stay behind at school. He could bill for his time working with the kids, and Angela couldn't.

As a formality, Dale warned Angela that she'd have to be subpoenaed—even though she agreed to testify. Armed with this knowledge, she still thought it was a little scary having a sheriff's deputy show up at her apartment to officially serve her with papers.

Once Katrina finished her testimony, the judge called a 15-minute recess. Angela gave Dale her notes detailing Katrina's lies. She also pointed out how he forgot to cross-examine Katrina about using marijuana. Most of the information came too late, but Ray thanked her with sincerity.

Ray couldn't have looked more out of place. An intimidating tower of muscle and attitude outside of court, inside its officious hallways and chambers he cowed before a world of academic intelligence and sophistication he didn't understand. His tough-guy fashion statement of country-western sports coat over a brand new black T-shirt, tucked into new dark-blue Levis and a pair of polished brown leather work boots was working against him. The intimidating, blue-collar cool outfit might have impressed his fellow warehouse workers, but it made him look like a bully with a chip on his shoulder—not a caring father—to the judge.

His ex-wife looked more appropriately matronly with pressed slacks, a nice blouse and an attractive brooch borrowed from her lawyer.

Ray looked rattled by the hearing that seemed to be slipping out of his favor. The behavioral specialist stepped toward him in the hall and put a reassuring hand on his sizeable bicep sheathed in tweed. "Nothin' to worry about, Ray," she whispered. "We're gonna kick ass when we get our shot. You'll have Charlie back in no time."

Ray smiled wanly.

Angela went to the water fountain, got a drink and returned to the courtroom. Ray and Dale stayed a few moments longer for more coaching and planning.

Angela reflected further about the way the trial had been going. Most of it was procedure with which she wasn't familiar. It wasn't nearly as dramatic as it was on TV. It was more straightforward.

When Dale called Angela to the witness stand, her palms began to sweat. With all of the attention on her, Angela became very self-conscious. She was afraid of a withering cross examination of misinterpreted testimony that would inadvertently lead to a 10-year prison sentence for perjury.

She watched far too much "Law & Order."

It took some effort to get a good clear view of the judge from the stand, Angela discovered. Her view of Ray, Dale, Katrina and her lawyer was unimpaired. The court's gallery was empty except for the people arriving for the trial following this one.

Dale began asking questions: "Please tell the court your occupation and how you are connected to this case."

"I'm a behavioral specialist with the Average City Mental Health Center at its elementary school daytreatment program where I work with Ray and Katrina's son, Charlie."

The court recorder caught Angela's attention by furiously typing a transcript on the odd little machine with seemingly too few keys.

"How long have you known Charlie?"

Distracted by the typing, Angela almost failed to answer.

"Oh, uh, since near the start of the school year."

Oh, crap, Angela thought. *Did that woman just type that remarkably stupid sounding 'Oh, uh' I just said?*

Angela explained the boy's diagnosis while still watching the court recorder. She spoke in quick bursts and deliberate slowdowns. The court recorder kept pace beautifully. It was fascinating to watch this woman work and wait on Angela's every word.

Snap out of it, Angela said to herself. *You're not here to watch someone type what you dictate. Focus so you can help Charlie without sounding like an idiot.*

Angela looked anywhere but at the court recorder in an effort not to absorb herself in the other woman's motions.

"Why does Charlie have this diagnosis?"

The question was far too open for conjecture, so Angela asked him to rephrase it.

"What causes Charlie to have these problems?"

"I don't know, sir. I suspect it has something to do with his upbringing, but I can't say so with absolute certainty."

"Have you seen any evidence of family sexual or physical abuse?"

"No, sir."

Katrina's lawyer smiled. Angela worried Dale was inadvertently leading her into a trap that would favor Katrina maintaining custody of Charlie, as nothing would appear to be a problem to the judge.

Dale tried a new tack.

"Have you noticed a change in Charlie since he started living with his father?"

"Yes, sir."

"Describe that change."

"The biggest change is that Charlie seems more relaxed. His

285

symptoms have lessened, and he's less apt to bully the other children. He's also opening up more during his sessions with our program's therapist."

"Doesn't this strike you as strange, especially since Ray has been mostly out of Charlie's life until now?"

"Yes and no."

"Please explain."

"Until a couple months ago, we didn't know Ray existed. I assumed he skipped out on Katrina and Charlie shortly after the boy was born. Neither Charlie nor Katrina mentioned him.

"The only reason we met him was that during an emergency I found his number buried in Charlie's file. Katrina wasn't answering her phone at home or at work, and we needed to have Charlie removed from school because he was stoned out of his mind

"Ray came…

Dale interrupted, "Did you say Charlie, a 12-year-old boy, was stoned at school?"

"Yes."

"How did you know he was stoned?"

"Charlie told us during our morning group therapy session. He said he had been smoking a lot of marijuana the night before. His bloodshot eyes and inability to focus seemed to confirm it."

Katrina's lawyer shot Charlie's mom a stunned look. Katrina responded with an "oops-I-forgot-to-tell-you" shrug. Then her eyes narrowed, as she shot Angela a menacing glare.

Dale continued. "Who gave him the drugs?"

"Some teenage friends of his older sister."

"His sister was doing drugs, too?"

"Yes. Charlie said she was."

"Where was Katrina?"

"I don't know. All Charlie said was that she sent him, along with his older and younger sisters, to the bowling alley down the street until closing time around midnight. He met the teens there."

"How did Ray react when he picked up Charlie at school?"

"At first he was mad, but he became more confused as we explained what was happening. It genuinely appeared that no one had ever told him his son was in therapy, let alone in a daytreatment program. He also was shocked that his son had access to and used drugs."

"What did he do to Charlie?"

"Despite his anger, I was surprised at how firm but tender Ray could be. Ray's kindofa scary lookin' guy with all those muscles, but he never raised his voice or appeared as though he would strike Charlie. He was stern, but he also gave the boy a hug when he saw how upset Charlie was."

Angela felt she was in the zone now. She was thinking clearly and saying exactly what she wanted, and Dale was picking up on the cues she was leaving for him. Although she might have embellished a little, she was telling the whole truth. She felt good punching holes in Katrina's case. The drug stories were Ray's best chance at winning custody.

Dale backtracked a little. "Your earlier statement made it sound as if Charlie had used drugs before. Would you please clarify?"

"Charlie has admitted drug abuse several times in the past in Katrina's house. Each time it was with marijuana. The program staff and I have often speculated that he got it from Katrina, herself, but that has never been confirmed."

"Objection, your honor!" Katrina's lawyer stood. "Please have that last sentence struck from the record, as it is only idle speculation."

"Sustained. Please strike that last sentence from the court record," the judge instructed.

The objection rattled Angela, and she became a little nervous again. What she said was true, and it threw her not to have it on the record.

Dale continued. "One last question, Angela. To your knowledge, has Charlie had any contact with marijuana since he began living with Ray?"

"No."

That was it. Katrina's lawyer didn't dare cross-examine Angela for fear she might say more damaging things about her client. There was no theme music or commercial break; Angela was simply sent back to work at the school.

Angela's adrenaline roared through her veins. Her first courtroom experience seemed to be a smashing success.

Again, unlike TV, there was no quick court resolution at the end of the hour. Several weeks passed before Angela and Hiro learned the judge's final decision in favor of Ray.

Upon hearing the news, Angela turned to Hiro and smiled, one eye brow cocked. "Little victories."

"I'd say we've got a much bigger victory this time."

Chapter 24

High Noon Showdown
Early June

Observed by security cameras, Hiro and Angela entered the first of two sets of doors whose windows contained bullet-proof glass. The high security at DCW was an ugly reminder of the violence DCW workers faced from raging parents and teens.

A woman at the front desk, on the other side of the second—locked—bullet-proof door, confirmed over the intercom that the daytreatment workers were expected for Lulu's custody hearing. She buzzed them into the building.

The inside of the government building looked like a doctor's office. It had beige walls with landscape art. The carpeting was flat and grey. There were magazines and children's toys in the waiting area.

The only things that were different were the two heavy doors with key pad access systems leading to the inner offices and the bullet-proof glass cage that housed the receptionist.

Most banks were nowhere near as secure as DCW.

The two daytreatment workers were about to sit when Virginia emerged from behind one of the heavy doors and invited them to the facility's inner sanctum.

"Good afternoon. You're a little early," the head of DCW warmly welcomed, as if there had been no past battles between them.

"Wellll," Hiro pleasantly replied. "We got done with lunch a little early and figured we'd swing on by, just to make sure we didn't miss out on anything."

The truth was neither he nor Angela was hungry, although their stomachs were as hollow as a kettle drum. The fear, anxiety and grim determination that precedes a fight had seized them before they went to bed the night before. It kept them awake. It prevented them from eating without feeling nauseated.

Today was the day they had waited months for. Virginia would preside over an out-of-court hearing that would seal Sammy's fate for better or worse.

After Sammy had been released from foster care to Lulu, his

amazing behavioral progress vanished. Lulu broke every condition of his release and resumed her abuse. DCW was reluctantly forced to call this hearing. Lulu was outraged and rallied her cheerleaders, who spent the past week lobbying DCW and ALCMHC on Lulu's behalf.

Hiro and Angela knew the facts favored Sammy's removal, but that never seemed to matter with DCW in the past. They felt a greater urgency to succeed at this meeting because it was their last. Hiro would open his clinic in two weeks, after school let out for the summer. Angela started graduate school in the fall. Both were cynical enough to doubt their unknown replacements' ability to resist Lulu's *charm* or discover a psychotic Sammy's actual charm.

"Would either of you like a soda?" Virginia asked.

"Sure, thanks." Angela accepted with a nonchalant shrug, playing off the fact her hands were buried in her pockets to hide their trembling. She wasn't afraid, but her inner fire burned with anticipation of today's duel, and it was getting to her. She wanted it over. She'd be fine as soon as the meeting started.

Hiro took one, too, and they were seated at a large, oval table in an empty conference room.

"You guys sure have a lot of security. It surprised me when I got here," Angela said, making small talk with Virginia.

"It keeps unwelcome bricks out of our windows and Molotov cocktails from doing much damage," the director explained. "About 10 years ago an arsonist took out our last office."

"Jeez," Angela said. "That's awful."

Virginia gave her a knowing smile. "We have a knack for making people angry."

Angela chuckled, rolling with the punches. *This is going to be a miserable meeting*, she thought.

"If you'll excuse me, I'm going to catch up on some notes while we wait for the others," Virginia said.

"No problem. Thanks for the sodas," Hiro excused their host.

With the DCW director gone, Hiro and Angela set up camp at the conference table. They stacked Sammy's three thick file folders in front of them. They also arranged their notes and talking points for easy access; each worried about leaving out a critical argument to defend their patient.

Once they were prepared, the second hand on the room's wall clock moved as if it were on Quaaludes.

Lulu arrived a few minutes late. As usual, she arrived with her entourage en masse. Virginia led the parade into the conference room. Lulu took a seat across from Hiro and Angela at the center of the conference table. Dressed in a new Winnie the Pooh outfit, she looked as pathetic as ever.

Lulu had her full herd of enablers and defenders at her disposal. On her side, blind to the truth and seemingly without regard for Sammy was Barb, Sammy's DCW case worker; a social worker from Angela's own mental health center; a court-appointed guardian *ad litem*; a CASA rep; her pastor; a volunteer childcare worker from the university and several other sycophantic supporters whom neither Hiro nor Angela knew. Fittingly, they sat as close to Lulu and as far from the daytreatment team as possible.

Angela shot Hiro a look of disgust, and Hiro put a hand on her knee to caution her to stay calm.

Playing along, Angela gave Lulu a big, warm greeting. She knew Lulu would see through it, but she wasn't about to cede any ground to Lulu over the entourage. The newest followers had heard an earful about Angela, The Child Stealer, but Angela's gesture lowered their guard when she appeared human—contrary to Lulu's descriptions.

Calista Montgomery, Sammy's one-time foster mother, arrived next, to Angela's surprise. She traded warm salutations with Hiro and Angela, as she took a seat with them.

Virginia was the last to sit, taking her place at the head of the table, calling the meeting to order. She then asked everyone to introduce themselves and asked them to explain their relationship to the case. Angela scribbled a snide note mocking the entourage to Hiro:

"I'm Mrs. Jones, Lulu's old home-ec teacher. I'm Bob, and I ride on the bus with Lulu.

She says she's a good mom, and I believe her."

Hiro smiled and scratched out the missive, passing it back. In several instances, Angela's sarcasm wasn't too far off the mark.

"Hi, I'm Hanna with the Women's Welfare League. I just wanted to tell you all how courageous I think Lulu is for coming here today and for being such a terrific single mom raising such a troubled little boy."

Each of Lulu's backers gave similar heartfelt testimonials supporting the beleaguered, innocent woman. Angela's anger broiled within her, but she maintained a cheerful outward countenance.

Hiro just wanted to speed the introductions along, and kept it simple.

Angela's temperament and debate instincts to frame the day's argument refused to let her take Hiro's practical approach to her own introduction.

"Hi there. I'm Angela Marengo, a children's behavioral specialist with the Average Elementary School Daytreatment Program. I, too, am impressed with Lulu's abilities. However, I would like to remind everyone that we are here today not for her but for her son, Sammy, and his best interests."

Lulu scowled at Angela, as several of her supporters nodded in agreement.

Angela settled down inside. She had taken her first swing with some success. Now it was time to pace herself and stay on top of the arguments with hard-hitting counterpoints backed by the evidence in Sammy's files.

Virginia laid down the ground rules for the meeting. "This is a state review hearing into the custody of Sammy. As an official representing the state, I will decide whether enough evidence exists to take a case to a state judge who can order Sammy removed from Lulu's custody and sever that custody forever. There will be two possible outcomes of this hearing. In one, Sammy can be removed into foster care until a judge makes a final decision about the case. In the other outcome, Lulu will maintain custody, albeit with possible caveats. Does everyone understand?"

She paused and got no response. "Lulu, do you have any questions?"

She moaned a pathetic "no," then decided to dig in her heels. "Why are you picking on me? I go to all of the programs you suggest and do everything I'm told. This is all Angela's fault. She's the one who called this meeting. She's the one trying to take my baby boy."

On the inside, Angela was grinning. The duel was on, and her thrown gauntlet was returned with a sting to her cheek.

On the outside, Angela maintained a stoic, professional appearance. "I can assure you I did not call this meeting."

Virginia stepped in. "Lulu. You and Sammy have a long history with DCW. Angela had nothing to do with this meeting. It is one the state organized."

Hiro heard the subtext that Angela missed and was impressed. Virginia was the one who called the meeting, as she represents the state. He took this information as an encouraging sign.

While attempting to whisper this to Angela, Lulu began blubbering crocodile tears. "I don't know what to say…"

Her network of social workers took over, making bitter accusations against Angela. "You've always persecuted Lulu because of your right-wing Catholic, anti-single mother agenda," said Barb, Sammy's DCW case worker. "Don't think I don't know all about you."

Another started, "Your agenda against the disabled…"

Angela stared at them incredulously. *Right wing? Catholic? Have these people ever met me? I couldn't be further from in either case*, she thought before battling back.

"Yes. I do have an agenda," Angela firmly replied. "I have an agenda against child abusers. I thought it was an agenda we all shared."

She picked up and shook one of Sammy's three thick files. "In these pages, I have documented all the abuse I've seen committed against Sammy in the past nine months. Since I've known this sweet, disturbed little boy, he's been strangled twice—once with a rope or cord that left deep marks around his neck and another time with hands that left a big, thumb-size bruise over his esophagus. I talked him out of committing suicide…twice. He has come to school with countless bruises. Even now, he comes to school hungry, often not having eaten since his school lunch the day before. He's been neglected. He has run away from home at least a dozen times since he entered our program three years ago.

"This is not the normal behavior of a well-adjusted kid with a loving mother and a safe home life. This is not even the behavior of a mildly abused child.

"Every time we have taken Sammy out of Lulu's house for foster care or a stint at the state's children's mental hospital, he has thrived. He grows so rapidly, both emotionally and intellectually. When he goes back to Lulu, he loses much of that progress.

"He even runs and hides from her when she comes to visit him at school. I know many of you have seen that at the various meetings we hold."

Angela paused to let her words soak in and the pieces of the puzzle come together for many members of the entourage. One or two looked troubled when smacked with the truth. Virginia let Angela speak her piece because she wasn't irrationally ranting and because it would be a lot easier to deal with her, if she wasn't constantly interrupting and fighting to get all of this out between every other statement.

"There are many wonderful single parents out there," Angela continued. "They struggle with jobs, finances and emotional problems and still provide great homes for their kids—homes free of abuse. There are also many disabled people who work miracles to raise their children well. All of these parents hold my highest regard.

"However, we should not let our prejudices, for better or worse, overshadow the fact that Sammy is a severely abused little boy with complex issues. He needs help, special help, immediately. This isn't about what Lulu wants. This is about what Sammy desperately needs."

There was a long silence after Angela's rebuke against her assailants. No one argued against the points she made, and in the silence after her speech, Angela's heart raced. The blood pumping through her ears was deafening.

"There will be no more personal attacks against Angela or anyone else in this room," Virginia demanded, taking iron-fisted control of the meeting. "Any outbursts or uncalled-for speeches will get you removed from the meeting. Is that understood?"

Everyone nodded.

"Hiro," Virginia resumed. "To give us an official starting point, please tell us Sammy's current diagnosis."

The therapist did so without speculation or embellishment. He explained Sammy's Posttraumatic Stress Disorder, depression, suicidal ideation and coping mechanisms. Several people asked for specific details about his psychology, but no one asked how he got PTSD. Angela felt it was a lost opportunity to take a few hammering blows to Lulu, but she remained silent and respectful—not wanting to risk being thrown out and unavailable at a potentially crucial point in the hearing.

Virginia next turned to one of the most prominent of Lulu's minions—Sammy's DCW case worker, Barb, the woman who had just attacked Angela's character.

"Barb, as part of Lulu's deal to keep Sammy last December, Lulu was to enroll in several parenting classes and receive special assistance at home. Is this correct?"

"Yes," the woman agreed.

"And did Lulu enroll in these programs?"

"Yes, she did," Barb said, smirking at Angela.

"Did she attend these classes, to the best of your knowledge?"

"Yes." Another smirk. "I drove her to several."

"Did she complete the programs, as she had agreed in our contract?"

There was a pause, and the social worker spoke with a hint of defeat, "No."

"Why?"

"Umm, she didn't attend all of the classes and earn her certificates."

"Was there any specific reason she didn't attend? Was she somehow prevented from attending?"

"No."

"What were the dates of those classes?"

She told her.

Virginia turned to the therapist: "Did you notice any improvement in Sammy's behavior during this time?"

"The only progress I saw was while Sammy was still in foster care. I noticed and reported consistent abuse and behavioral problems during all of the time he stayed with Lulu."

Another minion protested. "You can't expect instant progress overnight because of one class, after Lulu has suffered a lifetime of abuse."

"Excuse me," Virginia politely interrupted. "I am looking for any evidence of progress in Sammy's and Lulu's behavior, which can only help Lulu's case. I'm also looking for evidence of compliance to the conditions Lulu agreed to in order to maintain custody of Sammy."

Virginia asked more questions of the entourage with mixed results. Sometimes Lulu did complete a class. Other times she didn't.

Angela was amazed at all of the free services Lulu got. Free housing, free transportation, free childcare, free groceries, free medical care, free money. She even had a free volunteer maid service twice a week. Angela wondered what Lulu did with all that free time, aside from mooching government assistance and watching TV. A die-hard liberal who believed in those free services, Angela still thought Lulu was grossly abusing the system.

The hearing dragged on for more than two hours. Angela never got another chance to speak.

When the meeting reconvened after a short break, Virginia was expected to announce her final decision. Angela and Hiro were nervous. They knew what they'd heard from Virginia in support of Lulu in the past, and neither wanted to hear it one last time before they could no longer fight for Sammy through the mental health center. Angela's hands sweat, and her heart fluttered. She and Hiro exchanged anxious glances when Virginia began to speak.

"Lulu, after careful consideration, I'm placing Sammy in foster care and asking the state to terminate your custody rights. It is apparent that Sammy is not getting the healthy, loving treatment he needs while living with you to grow into a well-adjusted young man and productive member of society. The abuse continues at the risk of his safety, well-being and *life*. I will write and send both you and the state my formal decision, and I recommend you get a lawyer if you wish to contest this action.

"Do you have any questions?"

"Why are you doing this to me? My little boy needs me. I've done everything you've asked of me," Lulu declared, coldly and flatly, without any trace of sadness.

"No, Lulu. You've done this to yourself," Virginia disagreed matter-of-factly. "You haven't followed through on your promises. And you've done everything possible to draw out Sammy's suffering."

"But I'm an abused victim."

"You've had the choice to end the cycle of violence and raise Sammy properly since the day he was born. You chose not to. I'm sorry for your past suffering, but that doesn't give you the right to inflict that same suffering on others."

Lulu's angry scowl was magnified through her large lenses. She cast an accusatory glare at her minions who couldn't prevent this outcome. A few offered condolences, but none rose to her defense after getting the full story about her and Sammy.

Angela and Hiro were in shock. It took a second for what just happened to soak in. They won. Sammy would be safe—safe for good. They wanted to whoop and holler, hug and high five. Given the need for propriety, they shook hands under the conference table.

"Little victories," Angela whispered to Hiro as the people began to disperse from the meeting.

"No," Hiro countered. "This is the big one, and you should always remember it as the day you saved a child's life."

"I didn't make the decision," Angela said. "*We* did this together. I couldn't have ever gotten this far without your help."

"No one else would have ever connected with that little boy like you did, and no one else would have fought so hard for him and brought this case this far. Don't downplay your role. *You* saved Sammy's life."

Tears welled up in Angela's eyes. She hugged Hiro. "Thank you. Thank you for all of your help and encouragement. Regardless of what you say, I won't forget what you've done to help me with Sammy."

Angela wiped her eyes and looked up. Calista was standing next to her and watching. "What?" Calista asked, as she smiled, stuck out her hand and gave Angela a good-natured hard time. "You doubted this outcome? God wouldn't let Sammy go back to her."

Angela sniffed and shook her hand. "I've seen His past handiwork and am still skeptical, but I'm so glad you will be the one looking after Sammy. He likes you, and you and Preston will be great for him."

"Thank you, but I know you'll always come first in his heart. He chatters about you constantly. He'll miss you next year."

"I'll miss him, too," Angela said. "I'm just so glad I could get him safe before leaving the program."

"He'll thank you for it one day, even if you aren't around to hear it," Calista assured.

"I know."

They shook hands again. As Angela watched Calista leave, Lulu gave her one last venomous glare before departing with one of her drivers. Angela stared her down with a smile until she was out of sight.

Once Lulu was gone, Angela helped Hiro pick up their files and papers. She helped him to his car with them, and then headed around the building to her own car.

She basked in the warm June sun, hopping for joy and strutting off her excitement. She had never felt so good in her entire life.

When she rounded the corner of the building, she was startled to run right into Virginia, who was smoking a cigarette.

"Oh, hi there. I'm so sorry, I didn't mean to almost knock you over," Angela said, stepping back off of Virginia's toes.

"Don't worry about it," Virginia said and took a drag. "Thanks for your help in there. You did well."

"I really didn't do anything after that first 10 minutes," Angela said, still wary of the woman she considered her professional nemesis.

The DCW director exhaled a long column of smoke. "You set up my agenda pretty well, acting as a witness and saving me from having to review all the gory details of the past while redirecting the focus of the meeting to Sammy."

As Virginia sucked down another soothing lungful of nicotine, Angela shared the compliments. "It was my pleasure, I can assure you. Thanks for taking my side on this one."

Virginia folded her arms under her breasts and flicked the ash from her cigarette. "Just so we're clear, I didn't take your side. I've been on Sammy's side all along. I'm almost always on the side of the kids.

"The problem, as you've well learned, is that the law usually sides with the parents, unless the kid comes out and describes what her or his parents did to them in graphic detail. Even then the state can go either way. Sammy wouldn't talk. That's why it has taken four years to finally get a case together to get him out of Lulu's house."

"It took four years to get an air-tight case against her?" Angela asked, rolling with Virginia's gentle rebuke.

"No. It's far from air tight, but it ought to be good enough to cast enough doubt on Lulu's fitness as a parent to guarantee she never gets near him again without state supervision."

"Good," Angela nodded with approval. She hoped the conversation would end so she could get away from Virginia and get on with riding the euphoria of her victory.

Virginia dropped the smoldering butt of her cigarette on the sidewalk and extinguished it with a pivot of her shoe. She lit another Kent. "So, I hear you're going to graduate school in the fall."

"Yep," she said tersely, watching her opportunity for a quick getaway disappear.

Virginia read her body language like a book and cracked a smile; she had some unfinished business of her own with Angela. "You're gonna be one helluva doctor."

"I don't know about that, but I'll try. Thanks, though."

"You know I'm not your enemy, right? I want the same thing you want."

Angela relaxed and sighed. "I know. I just hate all of the damned hurdles we have to jump along the way."

"Me, too. Trust me," Virginia declared in knowing frustration.

Angela smiled back.

"What do you hope to do when you graduate?" the director asked.

"I'm not sure about the specifics, yet. I plan to carry on the fight— so to speak—one way or another."

"Ya know, we need good psychologists we can turn to who understand what it takes to get these children out of abusive homes and into appropriate treatment," Virginia began planting the seed of an idea. "And God knows I could use a highly qualified doctor with a true passion and zeal for locking away child abusers. Someone I could trust in handing over a case to. The city, county and state need more doctors who specialize in child psychology and treating abuse."

"Do you really mean that?" Angela asked, truly honored by the compliment.

"I'm just sayin'," Virginia played coy. "It's something to think about."

Angela paused a moment to think.

"I could get used to working with the system, knowing I'd have someone inside I could trust," Angela ventured.

"Do you really mean that?" Virginia inquired.

"It's a long way between now and then...I'm just sayin'. It's a thought."

Epilogue
(The Next October)

The last school year came to a close in mid-June. Hiro, Angela and Mrs. Regina bid a tearful farewell to the students, bringing closure for the students and themselves as best they could. After 35 years of helping troubled youth, Mrs. Regina was honored by the school district and given a hero's sendoff.

Before he left, Hiro had his own big victory by getting Ted into an institution that specialized in working with kids with sociopathic tendencies.

Hiro opened his clinic with his psychologist friends at about the same time his wife gave birth to a healthy baby girl. As hectic as his summer was, he made time to join Angela in briefing the program's new therapist and behavioral specialist for the coming year. Their replacements seemed remarkably green to them, and the veterans gave them all of their hard-learned advice—most of which would go unheeded until they also learned the hard way. Nonetheless, Angela and Hiro were invited to visit the kids any time they liked.

Charlie mainstreamed and graduated to junior high, where he still got some therapeutic treatment every week. However, life with his father was a far cry better than he could have expected. That didn't mean they didn't have their problems, but it sure beat living with Katrina.

Kevin's family was sentenced to varying times in jail, and he grew to appreciate the group home in which he was staying. His mental health improved substantially with the stability and the talk time with the group home's therapist.

Angela studied hard, passed her GREs with flying colors and discovered she had a full-ride scholarship waiting for her.

She postponed her visit to the kids in the early fall because of the whirlwind of her own studies in graduate school and because she didn't want to set up the new daytreatment staff for the chaos her visit could cause.

But now that autumn had become crisp and invigorating, with the changing leaves and the morning frost, she decided it was time to check in on Sammy and the gang. She stopped by during first recess to meet briefly with the new therapist to gain her approval to see the kids.

"Peek-a-boo," Angela said, peering around the doorframe to the empty daytreatment room.

"Welcome," greeted the new therapist from her desk. "Come on in."

Angela entered and unzipped her jacket. "Are you sure today's a good day to swing by?"

"As good as any."

"How are the kids? How are you?"

"They're improving," explained the harried new therapist. "As you warned, it was a short honeymoon and a prolonged breaking in period. I think things are finally starting to settle down."

"Good. I'm glad to hear it. How's Sammy?"

"He's one of our best kids. He's difficult to set up, chatty and a very quick learner."

"We're talking about the same Sammy, right?" Angela inquired with disbelief. "No Freddy? No bitchells? No near rabid suicidal escalations with showers of spit?"

"Not really. We've had a few rough days, but nothing really that bad," the new therapist declared. "In fact, I wasn't certain you and Hiro were describing the same boy."

"His foster mom must really be working out well for him."

"She seems to be."

"That's great. Do you mind if I go outside and see them?"

"No. I'm certain the kids would love it."

Angela headed outside and quickly joined Ronnie and Carla. They were happy to see her and gave her hugs as they caught up.

"How goes the battle?" Angela asked.

"Christ," muttered Carla, rolling her eyes.

"You have no idea how hard it is to break in three new co-workers who get paid twice as much as we do and know half as much as we do," Ronnie said with a smile. "We'll take you back in a heartbeat. How's graduate school?"

"It's tough, but I'm really enjoying it. How are the kids?"

"They're still F.I.T.H," Carla said. "But in spite of their new teacher's best efforts, they're improving."

Angela began spotting her old students on the playground. Violet was at her usual place along the fence line looking for bugs to study.

Kevin, Lionel and Edward were playing football with the mainstream kids. Edward was still too small to be effective. Kevin and Lionel were tearing up the turf in the thick of the action. When Angela spotted Lionel, he was jumping up and snatching an interception from

302

the hands of a boy at least a grade older than him. Lionel only made it a few feet before being swarmed by the opposing team, yet his eyes radiated triumph, as his teammates gave him high fives.

Looking for more outside acknowledgement of his glory, Lionel saw Angela and ran to her.

"Angela! Angela! You're back! Did you see what I did?" He wrapped her in a monster side hug.

"You were amazing!" she hugged him back. "You might grow up to play pro football. How are you doing?"

"Pretty good. How's school?" he giggled. *Who ever heard of a grown up still in school?*

"I love it. I'm learning tons. How's school for you?"

"It's alright, but recess is great now that the other big kids let me play with them."

"Very cool."

The more he watched the game the more he was itching to get back into it. He also missed Angela and didn't want to leave her. Angela saw this and gave him the all clear. "I think you better get back out there. It looks like your team needs your help."

He looked at his team and back at her. "I think you're right. I better go help them out, but come back soon. I miss you."

"I miss you, too" she said and smiled. "Now go have fun and score me a touchdown."

As she looked around, to her surprise, Sammy wasn't on the swings but on the new jungle gym that had been put in over the summer. She made her way to the playground.

Sammy was wild-eyed and being chased by girls a few years older than him. Angela was about to intervene when she recognized they were playing some sort of a game and that the older girls were actually watching out for Sammy.

Angela called out to him from a distance, but he didn't seem to hear her. He didn't notice her until she was standing next to the jungle gym's bouncy bridge that he was running across. He stopped dead in his tracks.

"Hi, Sammy. Good to see you."

"Angela!" he smiled and huffed as he caught his breath from the chase.

"How are you?"

"Good," he said.

"Got some new friends, I see?"

He looked at the girls who were eyeing Angela suspiciously and blushed. "Uh-huh."

"Who's this Sammy? Your mom?" the ringleader of the girls asked, staying just far enough away from the stranger.

Sammy just blushed some more.

Angela smiled at her. "Nah. We're just old friends."

The girl warily backed away, her stranger-danger senses kicking in. *What type of grown up is old friends with a little kid?*

"So, Sammy? What's new? Go way super high on the swings lately? Read any scary books?"

He shrugged and watched the girls who called him to come play some more. He waited by Angela, who he was happy to see, but he wanted to go back to playing.

"Do you wanna go play some more?" Angela asked him.

"Yeah."

"Okay, go have some fun."

"See you later," he said as he ran off.

"You take care, Sammy," she called after him.

He laughed as he chased the older girls.

Angela was a little hurt that he no longer wanted to play with her, but she knew deep down that it was a good thing. He no longer needed her and was growing into a normal young man. That was her original goal, after all.

The realization of it caused a tear to roll down her cheek, as she walked backward across the playground, watching the kids play.

She smiled from the parking lot and gave an unreturned wave to the kids. She drove back to graduate school and whispered to herself: "Little victories."

www.ingramcontent.com/pod-product-compliance
Lightning Source LLC
Chambersburg PA
CBHW031551240626
47153CB00002B/466